WORKS BY S.M. PERLOW

Vampires and the Life of Erin Rose

Novels
Choosing a Master
Alone
Lion
Hope
War

Short Stories
Alice Stood Up

—

The Grand Crucible

Novels
Golden Dragons, Gilded Age

—

Other Works

Novels
Stealing the Holy Grail

Short Stories
The Girl Who Was Always Single

GOLDEN DRAGONS, GILDED AGE

THE GRAND CRUCIBLE

S.M. Perlow

Bealion Publishing

A Bealion Publishing Book

Editor: Laura Koons, Red Adept Editing Services
Cover design: Damonza.com
Print cover formatting: Streetlight Graphics
Maps: Streetlight Graphics
Formatting: Polgarus Studio

smperlow.com—updates, social media links, and more information about the story

ISBN: 978-0-9992858-9-3

1.0.4-p1

Taulus
Frodic Ocean
Conlin
Drimon
Dritus
Abilin
Terra
Red Forest
Nova
Taulus River
Lucia
King's Mountain
Canyon of Light
Ronnigun
Rone
Trillia
Alnara
Terrin
Prim
Hinlin
Lumilin
Lake Taulus
Oulos
Inar River
Edra
Fort Granenite
Evas
Little Forest
Niadia Ocean
Mindin Ocean
Gran
Inar River
Fort Rovan
Derundale
Lonely Stone Tavern
Great Desert
Blackburg
Red Desert
Fort Bones
Deroc
Solurn
N
Hedic Ocean
Gold dragons of Taulus
and where they dwell
Abilin
Galeron (Prim)
Gran
Gouyn (Blackburg)
Grafere (Solurn)
Lumilin
Galna (Trillia)
Gorvenal (Lucia)

1

Taulus

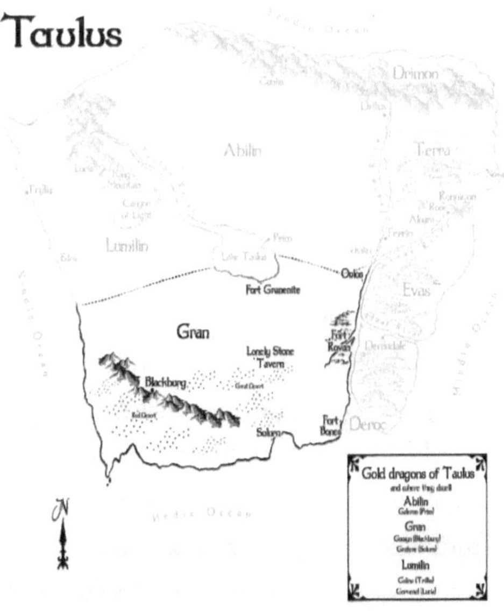

Not far south of Fort Granenite, in the north central plains of the kingdom of Gran, Randal made his way from the dirt path to a conspicuous boulder in the long, windswept grass. He knelt beside the smooth rock and smiled at the royal-blue, canary-yellow, and scarlet flowers for which he had made the trip.

"Hurry!" his friend Patrick called, holding the reins of

the young men's horses on the nearby path, shielding his eyes from the sun, and searching out into the plains.

Randal carefully picked a red flower. "Calm down." He placed it in his satchel then positioned a blue and yellow one beside it.

"We need to go," Patrick urged. "We shouldn't be doing this."

"He has a great deal of land." Randal picked a yellow flower and held it to the pale grass for comparison. "And he obviously doesn't know we're here." He placed the flower in his bag. "So we're fine."

"I shouldn't have come," Patrick said. "It's *your* stupid bet. And you only needed to pick one. Let's go."

Randal added three more flowers to his satchel and stood. "I do hope Gale likes these."

"*That's* why you agreed to this? She's out of your league."

"We'll see. And I'll win the bet anyway."

Patrick lurched forward, pulled by the suddenly spooked horses. He yanked the leather reins to settle the animals.

Randal squinted, searching the sky all around him. "There." He pointed at the approaching dragon. The farther Beore flew away from the bright sun, the truer the green of his dark wings appeared. The huge beast glided toward the boys.

Patrick mounted his horse. Randal pushed his satchel behind him, ran to his steed, and jumped into his saddle.

"Hya!" Patrick spurned his horse forward, with Randal close behind. Speeding down the path, his horse's hard-hitting hooves kicking up brown dirt, Patrick called back, "I told you!"

Randal gazed skyward. "He's taking his time," he yelled. "Looping down slowly."

Beore glided from behind Patrick and Randal and into their path. The old dragon gradually turned, continuing downward toward the boys.

"I told you!" Patrick repeated.

As Beore sailed high overhead, Randal ducked and stayed ducked until the broad-bodied, wide-winged, long-tailed, trailing shadow had passed completely.

"We're dead!" Patrick yelled.

"Hya!" Randal urged his ride faster, and the dust cloud beneath him intensified. He wondered, *was* Gale out of his league? *Patrick* was not the bravest, nor the cleverest, nor the handsomest. She was out of *his* league, for certain.

Beore growled, and the ground shook. He passed overhead again.

Patrick yelled, "What do we do?"

"Get to the fort! We'll be safe there."

"We won't make it!"

Beore completed another of his shrinking, looping, lowering circles above. Air from his flapping wings brushed Randal's cheeks.

"Just ride," Randal said.

"It's the flowers! Leave them!" Patrick called.

Beore roared.

"I won't!" Randal yelled to Patrick.

Beore spun and thrust his head forward, a column of fire spewing between his razor-sharp teeth and ending in a swirling ball of flame that warmed Randal's face.

Patrick veered right. "Leave them!"

Randal jerked his horse left, brought his satchel over his head, and threw it to the ground. Beore ended his fire and flapped his wings hard, darting at Patrick.

Patrick screamed.

With his paw, the landing dragon smacked Patrick and his horse, sending them tumbling into the grass.

Randal pulled on his reins, drawing his horse to a stop. She whined and reared, fighting Randal's control.

Beore growled from ahead on the path. He made no sound, but Randal heard his voice echoing in his head. *How dare you?* the dragon said. *How DARE YOU!* He screamed in Randal's mind, as the dragons had learned to ages before.

"I'm sorry!" Randal yelled, as frantic as the horse beneath him.

The dragon sprang forward. Randal spun as Beore's heavy talon flicked him into the grass.

Randal began, "I'm—"

Beore pushed Randal's face into the ground.

"I'm sorry," Randal said. Out of the corner of his eye, he could see the massive green lord of the land towering above him.

Those flowers bloom but once a year, for one short week, and you would steal them from me? Beore took Randal's right forearm between his talons. *You would steal MY FAVORITE flowers?* With a flick, Beore snapped the boy's bones.

Randal screamed into the dirt, his voice mingling in his ears with the sounds of horses galloping his way.

Or did you steal from me with your other arm? Beore snapped Randal's left.

Randal screamed again.

"Stop!" a woman yelled.

Beore turned and his voice tore through Randal's head once more. *Valencia…* Beore breathed a burst of fire that reached just short of the knight.

Beyond the green dragon towering above him, Randal saw the fort's commander leading six mounted knights of Gran—three men and two other women. Valencia, in chainmail, her long golden-blond hair pulled behind her, her sword and shield strapped to her steed, a steel-tipped spear in hand, urged, "Leave them! They are just children."

Beore scratched his chin before he spoke. *Fifteen? Fifteen-year-olds should know better.* He shoved Randal aside, flew fast at Valencia, and swiped at her from above. She ducked and dodged his claws.

Beore's next swipe connected with the other knights of Gran, who tumbled from their horses. *This is MY land!* he bellowed. *And every one of those flowers on it are MINE.*

"We know, Beore," Valencia called. Her knights scrambled to their feet and drew their weapons, but their commander lowered her spear. "It is our mistake."

Beore knocked a pair of knights back to the ground with his hind legs as he took flight. *It seems those in your little fort could do with a reminder.* He flapped his wings hard and headed toward Fort Granenite.

Valencia called to her knights, "Hayle, Bedra, get them to an emote to tend to their injuries." Valencia kicked her horse, let out a loud "Ya!" and, with the other five knights, started back in the same direction as the dragon, to the fort she was charged with defending.

————————

Beore bore down on Fort Granenite, the triangular stone structure situated at the shore of the great Lake Taulus that protected Gran's northern border with Abilin. The green dragon reveled in his size and strength. His scales had become incredibly hard over his long life, and the fire that spewed from his maw burned extremely hot—and had grown hotter each of his four hundred fifty years. But while that fire would turn men to ash and set wooden homes and shops ablaze, it would never be hot enough, even at close range, to melt granenite, the stone of which the people of Gran had built their fort, and which gave it its name.

Nevertheless, the blackened, once-white walls, bearing the marks of repeated repairs, evoked fond memories in Beore. His fire had discolored them, and his rage had damaged those stones.

He glimpsed the thieving people of Gran inside the walls of their fort. Knights shouted orders to other knights and to men, women, and children rushing around inside. Beore sailed overhead as they closed the massive wooden doors at the entrance and dropped a heavy metal gate outside them. Archers aimed for Beore. They shot, he swerved, and every arrow missed. Others shot at him from small slits in the walls, protected by the stone his fire could not overcome. Pairs of knights rushed to the two heavy, steel bolt launchers.

Beore's cry rang from the walls as he looped for another pass over the fort and called to everyone below, *Leave my flowers alone!* An arrow from a second volley grazed Beore's side. He ducked under a sharp rod shot from its huge iron launcher and raced to the weapon on the wall. He knocked the knights manning it into the fort, tumbling them off a barracks roof to the ground. Beore heard the shot from the other heavy launcher, flapped his wings, and rose above it. He darted to the launcher and smacked its operators out over the wall.

He picked a spot outside the gated entrance, jumped, and landed with a thud before streets of puny wooden buildings. He listened—no one inside the homes. He sniffed—no living scent.

Beore loosed a shrill scream skyward. He breathed a column of flame into a row of houses. A second breath of fire torched the homes opposite them and exploded the apothecary shop at the end of the street. Beore leapt and flapped his wings once, propelling himself back to the fort's gate. He belched fire, and the wooden door turned to ash. He inhaled deeply, leaned closer, and spewed a column of flame that heated and softened the iron gate. The stone around the metal, already blackened by years of Beore's assaults, remained solid as ever.

Beore leapt and perched atop the fort's wall. He let loose a burst of flame into the air, then prepared to dodge more arrows and metal rods from the knights. When no attack came, Beore said for all the minds of men and women to hear, *Do not pick my flowers. Any of them!*

Beore sucked air into his massive lungs and selected a section of gray wall. He leaned low, brought his snout close for maximum heat, opened his mouth, and shot a stream of fire at the granenite.

Fierce flame beat upon the stone. The old green poured it on. The stone darkened. Waves of heat and orange-black fire rolled out wide from his maw.

Beore stopped and closely inspected the blackened granenite. He tapped his sharp talon on the stone—hard as ever.

A small granenite window in the fort's outward-facing wall swung open. A young boy stuck his head out for a moment before adult arms pulled him inside. Beore leapt at the closing window.

The child managed another peek. He pointed skyward. "Gowyn!"

Beore spun and jumped aside, but the leaner, younger golden dragon moved too fast. Gowyn grabbed Beore and hurled him away from the fort, into the burning houses.

Enough, Beore, Gowyn called.

Beore righted himself on the ground. *They picked my flowers.*

You have more, Gowyn said.

You don't understand. Beore shrugged his broad shoulders. *But you couldn't, golden as you have always been.*

I understand, Gowyn said.

I permit them to travel on my land. They farm some of it. But those flowers… ask your father. Ask Galeron what those flowers mean to me.

I understand your arrangement with the people of Gran. Gowyn stepped toward Beore. *But leave them be now. You're in the right, but you've made your point.*

Beore surveyed the houses still standing before the fort, inhaled deeply, and said to the dragon prince, *Not yet.*

Gowyn leapt at Beore, but Beore dodged out of his reach. Fire shot from Beore's snout, torching more buildings to the left. Nearby homes caught fire as golden Gowyn drove his shoulder into Beore, sending the pair tumbling through burning wooden walls and roofs.

Beore shoved his three-hundred-year-old adversary off him and rose into the air. With quick flaps of his wings, Gowyn chased him.

Beore growled and flew higher into the sky, but Gowyn's lighter, sleeker frame rose faster.

Beore's mighty wings lifted him upward, but Gowyn closed the gap.

Beore rolled his big body… and darted down at Gowyn. Gowyn dodged and punched Beore's snout. Beore whipped his thick tail into the smooth scales of Gowyn's stomach. Gowyn drove his shoulder into Beore, knocking him backward.

Flapping wings kept the dragons aloft as they lunged at one another's necks. They grappled and bit, but neither landed a decisive blow. Gowyn punched under Beore's jaw, and avoided the tail whip that had caught him before.

The reptiles surged toward one another. Beore smacked his snout across Gowyn's. Gowyn responded with a square hit of his own. He shoved Beore away.

Enough, Gowyn said.

Beore spotted Valencia and her knights returning to the fort below, Randal and Patrick among them.

They'll rebuild their houses, Beore said. He stretched his bruised jaw, testing it. *The boy's arms will be healed. By tomorrow, I've no doubt.*

Lucky for you. Gowyn hovered out of the reach of Beore.

I hurt a single boy. Beore formed a small smile. *Perhaps his friend and those knights a little, as well. You care that much for them?*

Beore watched as townspeople rushed to the fires with water from the fort and the lake.

Gowyn said, *You know I do. I love them all.*

Beore nodded. *Well, I love my flowers.*

With that, Beore turned his back to Gowyn and flew away from Fort Granenite.

2

Taulus

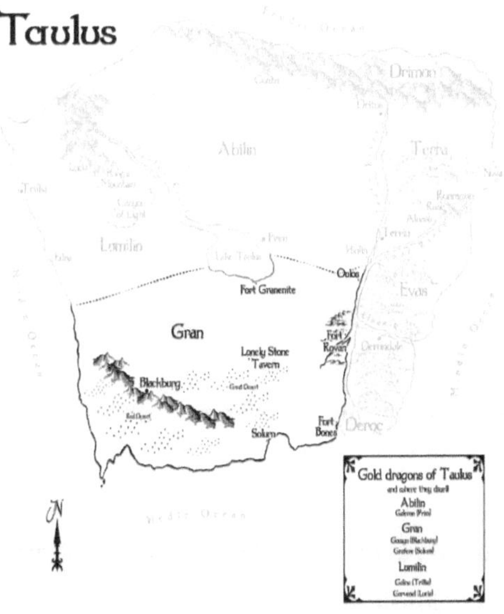

Taylan untied his black cloak and scrunched it beside him on the bench of his booth. He brought his gray shoulder bag over his head and set it next to the cloak. The tavern, doubtless filled with both locals and travelers like Taylan, was expectedly boisterous, unexpectedly jam-packed, and unquestionably not Taylan's preferred environment. But The Lonely Stone was the only place around for a hot meal at the late hour.

The tavern reeked of the stale beer soaked into the wooden tables, chairs, and floor, and the odor mixed with the aroma of that night's fresh pours and the dried-sweat stench of those drinking them. Hearty laughter two tables away annoyed Taylan. At the corner of the room, a stumbling man pulled a smiling, half-dressed waitress behind him and up the staircase. At the bar, three men raced to see who could finish their beer first then slam, slam, *slammed* their metal mugs down when they did.

Taylan shut his eyes and rubbed his temples. The vivid memory that had haunted him from sunrise to sunset—and on too many occasions before—replayed once more: Taylan ran from the pack of crazed, taunting boys into the woods. He raced between trees and stumbled to the ground. He spotted a moose. Why didn't *it* run? Why did the innocent animal stand there awaiting its doom?

Taylan drove his palms over the sides of his short black hair and against the subtle points of his ears.

"Here you go." The buxom waitress set Taylan's plate of chicken and bread on the table. "Nothing but water?"

Taylan opened his eyes. "No." He rolled the loose sleeves of his black tunic up his thin wrists.

The waitress placed her hand on his bony shoulder and gave him a warm smile. "You sure, honey? You look like you could use a drink."

Taylan slouched her hand away. "Water's fine."

She shrugged and left him to his meal.

Taylan bit into his chicken—tasty, juicy. He tried the bread—warm. A body occupied every seat he could see—or two bodies where a waitress sat on a customer's lap. The tavern was noisy. Wandering eyes gave Taylan disapproving looks, but they didn't last especially long or seem especially venomous.

The flavorful food had him thinking he might actually return to the place when traversing the Midlands again. Taylan would have to withstand those looks everywhere in Gran, and even if every night brought the same type of revelry, the tavern couldn't *always* be that crowded, or so damn loud.

A big broad-chested man took two steps into the building and surveyed the scene. A knight, Taylan guessed, despite the lack of armor and weapons. He wore brown pants and a plain shirt—decent but worn. He took a swig from a dirty bottle a quarter full with brown liquor.

"Hey, now," the bartender called to the knight over the pervasive hubbub.

The man wiped his mouth and stubbly cheek with his sleeve. "Eh?"

Former knight, Taylan decided.

"You can't bring that in here." The bartender pointed at the bottle in the man's hand.

The newcomer proceeded to a gap between groups of men at the long wooden bar and brought the bottle to his lips. He lowered it, watching a waitress passing behind him wearing a long skirt with a slit down the side.

She smiled confidently as she carried her tray of food past.

Her admirer drained his bottle and set it down. The

bartender snatched it and brought up a full bottle of whiskey and a glass from under the bar. When he finished pouring, the newcomer threw a coin from his belt pouch onto the bar, picked up the new glass, and pivoted.

He stumbled.

He steadied his glass high above his head and caught his balance without spilling a drop. He grinned… to no reaction from Taylan, or anyone else, as far as Taylan could tell.

The man made a disappointed face and looked around.

No empty stools at the bar, and Taylan didn't see any empty tables. Except for one, where a boy was getting up. And standing from the same table, a girl—pretty, and young to be in the tavern. The stumbling man made his way to the table they had just left.

Taylan washed down some chicken with his water, watching the pale boy and girl leave the tavern. The replacement at their table fit right in—drunk and ragged. The waitress with the slit skirt found her way to him and leaned close.

The boy walked back into the tavern, with the girl following, and headed Taylan's way. The boy was not as thin as the almost frail girl and stood a few inches taller—perhaps six feet, a good five inches more than Taylan. The girl whispered to the boy, who nodded. They approached the vacant wooden bench at Taylan's table.

"Can we join you?" the boy asked.

Taylan put down his nearly finished meat and wiped his hands and face on his cloth napkin. Small noses, brown hair—hers quite long. They looked alike, Taylan thought—

perhaps related. What did they want? What were they doing in the tavern at all? Had they come to mock Taylan for being half-elven, right to his face and to the pointy ears that gave him away at a glance?

"Please." Taylan motioned to the bench.

"Thank you." The boy stood aside so the girl could slide into the booth first. He sat once she had. "I'm Avery. This is my sister Avril."

"Taylan." He brought his hands together on the table. "Can I help you with something?"

"No," Avery said. "We're waiting for our father."

"No empty tables," Avril added.

"Ah." Taylan didn't mention that he had seen them leave a table, quite recently. "Well, I'll be gone soon, and this one can be all yours."

Avery and Avril both glanced behind themselves.

"Twins?" Taylan asked.

They turned to him.

"Yes," Avery said.

"Strange place for your father to meet you."

"He likes it here," Avril said.

"And they tolerate him," Avery added dryly.

Avril peeked behind her. Taylan wondered if she looked at the ragged whisky drinker in her old seat.

Avery tilted his head, Taylan assumed to get a better look at his half-elf ears.

The boy quickly righted his head. "What brings you to The Lonely Stone?"

"I'm headed to Fort Granenite," Taylan said.

"Why?" Avery asked.

Taylan tapped a finger on the table. "To meet a friend."

"Why?" the boy repeated.

Taylan formed a smile. "She sent for me."

Avery raised an eyebrow. "Have you been to the capital?"

"I have," Taylan said. "Have *you* been to Blackburg?"

Avery shook his head.

Taylan drank some water. "It's an impressive sight, the desert oasis. The two castles in the foothills of the broad mountain range. The mountains of—"

"Fire," Avery finished for him.

Taylan nodded.

"Have you been to Lumilin?" Avril asked.

"I have. It's every bit as beautiful as they say. Trillia especially. You should be sure to visit."

"All right." Avril looked behind her, just as her brother was.

Trillia, the capital of the youngest of the three kingdoms of men, brilliant white and encrusted in gemstones, glimmered in Taylan's mind.

And then it faded. Then the city rotted and became trees and forest and mud. The moose! Its pointed antlers sprouting from its long head... and then the animal lay lifeless. That damn dead moose! The jagged hole in its side... Taylan had lost the boys he'd run from that day, years ago, when they had taunted him for being unlike them, but he had not run from the moose, and sitting in The Lonely Stone Tavern, he could not escape the animal.

Taylan tried to ignore the memory and joined the twins

in looking at their old table. "Do you know that man?"

They shook their heads.

"Does he concern you?" Taylan asked.

"No," they said in unison.

Taylan scratched his chin, judged that they were lying, then decided against asking if the twins would be all right without him. He reached into his belt pouch for money. "Can I get either of you anything before I go?"

"No," Avery said.

"Thank you," Avril added.

Taylan set a short stack of coins on the table, pulled his bag over his shoulder, grabbed his cloak, and got up. He looked over the dingy, noisy tavern, then said to the pale twins, "Go see the great castles of Gran." Taylan tied his cloak. "You, me, the men and women here… we've known nothing but peacetime. Those castles and mountains have witnessed and withstood the momentous wars that won us this tranquil age." He checked that his shoulder bag hung where it should on his hip. "And do be sure to visit Trillia."

"All right," Avery said.

As Taylan stepped out the front door, satisfied with his encouraging words for the children despite how far from *tranquil* his own life had been, he noticed Avery and Avril had already switched to his side of the booth.

At the twins' original table, the ragged whisky drinker watched the waitress with the slit in her skirt approach.

She set down a glass. "'Gall,' you say?"

"No one calls me Gallchobhar," he said. "Not anymore."

She put her hands on her hips. "Abilin, Gran, or Lumilin? Where were you a knight?"

"Here. Gran." Gall sipped his whisky. "But not for a long while." He patted the bench with his palm.

The waitress raised an eyebrow then sat down. "I'm Madine." She gripped his large bicep. "Doesn't seem it's been *too* long."

Gall burped. "I'm a strong guy."

"Are you?"

Gall flexed his arm. "Never lost a fight."

Madine scooted closer and interlocked her arm with his. "No?"

Gall took a drink. "Not in a tavern, not in a battle. Never."

"Impressive. What do you do now, then?"

"Whatever's paying."

"And what's paying these days?"

"I'm headed to Blackburg," Gall said.

"To see the sights?"

"To catch a thief." Gall fumbled with his glass before getting a grip on it and sipping.

"What'd they steal?"

Gall glanced at her but kept quiet.

"Well, who'd they steal from?"

Gall pursed his lips.

She rested her palm on his thigh. "It'd be fun to know." Madine slid her hand up his leg.

"From an elf," Gall said, relenting. "They stole from an elf."

"Was that so hard? Thanks for telling me." Madine slid her hand higher. "Spending the night upstairs?"

"Maybe." Gall drank his drink dry. "Ahh."

Madine leaned close and took his glass from him. "I'll be right back." She kissed his cheek.

Gall stretched his arms above his head and watched Madine walk to the bar. He liked the way her hips moved. He put his elbow on the table and propped his chin in his palm. He liked her skirt, liked how it fit tight near the top and had a slit on the side. He liked how the slit reached a long way up.

Gall's elbow slipped off the table, and his head fell forward.

"Good sir." A well-dressed older—but fit—man, with a well-groomed black beard, blocked Gall's view.

Gall collected himself and leaned low to his right to see around the man. A few more drinks and then he'd like the idea of untying that skirt from Madine's narrow waist. He'd let it fall to the ground around her, then he'd—Gall's view became blocked by one of the two big, less-finely-attired men standing behind the bearded one.

"You are in my seat," the man who had arrived first said. A long knife hung at his hip. He pulled off a leather glove and laid it on Gall's table.

Gall leaned halfway to upright. "Huh?"

The man set down his other glove. "Thank you for keeping my seat warm." He glanced at the bar. "And Madine company."

Gall sat up straight. "I like this seat."

"Me too." The man grabbed Madine's arm on her way past with Gall's fresh drink. "And Madine's the best."

She failed at trying to rip her arm from his grasp, and the man pulled her close. Gall shoved the table out as he stood. Others in the tavern noticed, and quiet spread outward from the table. Madine again pulled away, and the man let go.

Madine moved close to Gall and said, "Not tonight, Ivon."

Ivon formed a sly smile. "We'll see. I will have the table though, for certain."

Gall took the whisky from Madine.

"He always sits here," she said.

Gall swigged his drink. He sat and pulled Madine down with him. He put his arm around her then looked at Ivon. "You're welcome to join us."

Ivon wrapped his fingers around his knife's handle. "I won't ask you again."

Madine rested her hand on Gall's arm. "He isn't worth it. I'll find you another table."

"I'd leave the table," Gall said. "Let him have it. But he's a *rat*." Gall made sure everyone heard the last word, then spoke quietly to Madine. "Won't leave *you* to him."

Her face warmed. "He is a rat. But he's harmless." She broke eye contact with Gall. "Sort of."

That settled it for Gall. He stood and asked Ivon, "In here or outside?"

Madine pulled Gall down to the seat. "You're drunk."

Ivon drew his knife. "Outside."

Gall shrugged at Madine. "I'm drunk a lot." He kissed

her soft lips then pushed the table farther away to make space to walk around it. Gall stood, steadied himself, and finished his drink.

Ivon took his gloves and turned to the door. His two men turned with him, and the interested crowd cleared a path, whispering and sizing up the unknown newcomer following Ivon.

When he was about halfway to the door, Ivon spun, slashing with his knife.

Gall jumped back, tripped, and crashed into the table behind him. The rat's two men hurried to their fallen foe. One kicked his side; the other punched below his eye. Gall got himself up enough to smack one man away. Gall absorbed another kick, then grabbed the leg and yanked its owner to the floor.

The tavern crowd backed away.

Gall got to his feet and avoided a stab from Ivon. A chair smashed over Gall's back and drove him to a knee. A fist across his face drove him lower. Ivon's boot kicked up into Gall's chin and sent him flying backward to the floor.

Madine rushed to Gall, put her hand on his chest, and shouted to his attackers, "Stop!"

"Get away!" Ivon ordered.

Gall wiped blood from his cheek. He winked at Madine. She slid her hand off him.

Gall pushed himself up. All at once, on the way to his feet, he grabbed a broken table leg and swung it low across the knee of one of Ivon's men.

The man screamed and crumpled to the ground, holding his damaged joint.

Gall swung the table leg, and Ivon retreated. His other man clocked Gall in the face, to little effect. Gall swung, broke the wood on his attacker's shoulder, and shoved him away.

The one with the wounded knee slashed his knife across Gall's arm. The crowd gasped, but he hadn't cut deep. Gall stabbed at Ivon with his short, sharp-ended table leg, but Ivon dodged. The three men circled each other.

Gall glanced behind him. "Your table's ruined."

Ivon slashed—Gall dodged.

Ivon stabbed—Gall avoided it.

"Let's just fight." Gall threw his table leg away. "No knives."

Ivon slashed once more, and as Gall evaded him, the man with the hurt knee smashed another chair over Gall's head.

Gall kicked the man's injured knee.

Its owner screamed and fell to the ground.

Ivon's other man punched Gall in the stomach. Gall's return blow to his gut sent the man to the floor.

"Gall!" Madine shouted.

He spun to see Ivon lunging at him with his knife held high. Gall shot his fist straight into Ivon's nose.

Ivon crumpled to the ground. Blood poured from his smashed nose. He lay still.

Heavy metal bashed into the back of Gall's skull. As he fell, he glimpsed the bartender holding an iron cooking pot lid, Ivon's face covered in blood, one of the men on the floor clutching his knee, and the other holding his stomach, gasping for air. Before darkness overcame Gall, he noticed a young boy and girl—too young for such a place—standing on the bench at their table across the tavern for a better view.

3

Taulus

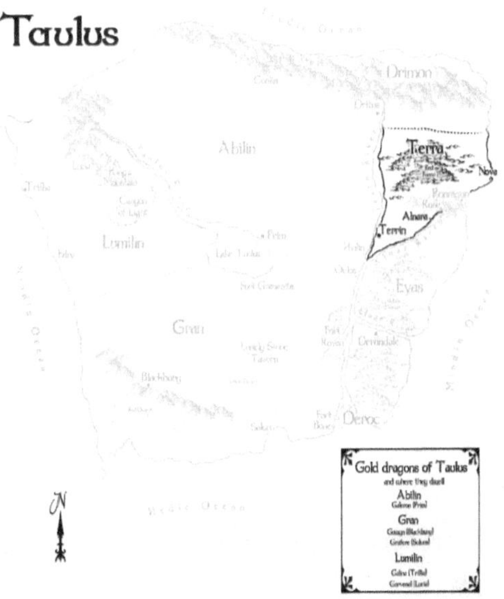

In the old forest, north of the Red Elves' capital city of Terrin, sturdy evergreen trees outnumbered those that lost their leaves annually. Red-grained bark wrapped around most, the color prominent in some and subtle in others. Ri, the lone human in the company of six traveling through the forest, sighed.

Her nearest elven companion glanced back at her.

Ri tightened the ponytail in her dark brown hair then stepped lightly and quietly on the cluttered forest floor, as the elves had taught her to years before. A long-sleeved green top and a green skirt, along with brown leggings, helped her blend into the surroundings. A warm, gentle breeze hit her cheek. She sighed more loudly.

Launfal looked at her.

"I'm bored," Ri said.

"I'm sorry."

Ri reached past the fine, dark-stained bow she carried slung across her back and pulled an arrow from her leather quiver. She twirled the red-feathered wooden shaft in her fingers.

"Why are you bored?" Launfal asked.

"How many scouting patrols have I gone on with you all? More than a hundred, I think."

"I thought you enjoyed them. I thought *home* bored you."

"Oh, Abilin's worse. Far worse." Ri put her arrow away. "Don't you ever get tired of scouting and patrolling?"

"It's important."

"But we never find anything. Nothing interesting."

Launfal nodded. "That is a good thing."

"Don't you ever want to fight?"

"No," Launfal said. "I've fought plenty."

"But I haven't. I'm not eight hundred years old. I've never tracked and shot at an actual enemy. All I've done is scout. I've never drawn my knife in real combat."

"You might enjoy such conflict, for a time," Launfal said.

"Your adrenaline pumping, your senses sharpened. It is an experience. But it's not as glamorous as you imagine."

Ri's hands went to her hips. "I know."

"Battles are hard. Friends may be wounded. Some may die."

"I know."

"Wars are harder," the elf said. "In a war, many of your friends, and perhaps family members, *will* die."

Ri let her hands fall. "I know."

Launfal stepped toward her. "Be thankful that our dark cousins and their evil dragons were defeated long before you were born. Be thankful for the peace we have."

"I am," Ri said quietly.

"We all are," Egan called from up ahead.

He, Addis, and Emlyn—the female elf in the group—made their way back to Ri and Launfal.

"But that doesn't mean I don't sometimes share your desire for the thrill of battle." Egan smiled.

Ri returned the expression.

Naelon, the second oldest and their leader, joined them to round out the team to the usual number of five elves. He pointed over his shoulder. "There's a doe out there that your jabbering has somehow failed to scare off. Who wants to race Ri for it?"

Ri glanced among her would-be competitors.

Egan began, "I wi—"

"I will," Launfal said. "I've no fondness for combat, but competition? I will enjoy teaching our little Ri a few things out here."

Ri crossed her arms. She wasn't little anymore. She *had* been, when she first begged the scouts to get her out of the music classes for which she had been sent to Terra so she could patrol with them instead. She still traveled from Abilin under the pretense of attending those classes with master elven musicians. Her parents, the king and queen, like everyone in Abilin except her youngest brother, didn't know where Ri snuck off to when she skipped out of those classes. They had no idea how much she loved being part of the company of elven scouts and, in the absence of real battles or conflict, how Ri relished competitions like the one before her. Those in Abilin had no knowledge of her very respectable win-loss record.

"Where's the deer?" Ri sniffed but failed to distinguish an animal's scent from the bark, leaves, dirt, and moss.

"She was to the south," Naelon said.

Launfal peered through the woods. "I see her."

Ri squinted in that direction. "No way."

"How do you know?" Launfal asked. "I'm not surprised that *you* cannot see anything."

"No." She leaned toward him. "But I *can* see your elven eyes just fine. And they say you are lying."

The other elves chuckled.

"Well," Launfal said, "I've no doubt I *will* see her first." He darted to the south.

Ri followed, veering left to increase the space between them. She stepped softly between the trees, through thin patches of long grass, and over the packed dirt of the forest floor. Launfal moved even more quietly.

But Ri kept quiet enough—she was confident of that. In her ten years with the elves, since just after her thirteenth birthday, she had successfully hunted lots of deer. Unencouragingly, she didn't have a great record when competing against Launfal. No one did.

He stopped—far to the right, just ahead. Ri stopped. Launfal knelt. He peered forward and tilted his head—perhaps to see around a tree trunk. Ri searched but didn't see the deer, so she watched her opponent.

He rose and ran on. She did the same and took a chance, speeding ahead, making more noise. Ri pumped her long legs, unsure if she could outrun Launfal.

She passed him and there, ahead—a fox, not their target. She raced on, until she couldn't hear the elf. She spun and found him behind her, facing to his right. He knelt and brought his bow off his back.

Ri searched the red woods past him and saw no deer.

Launfal carefully drew an arrow. Ri grabbed her bow and an arrow of her own. She *had* to find their target. She'd hit it, if she did. Probably before Launfal, if they readied to shoot at the same time. Ri didn't doubt her speed in that regard—or her aim.

Running toward Launfal, she nocked an arrow. He glanced at her then sprinted ahead, holding his weapon. She followed, and if he was running his hardest, her sprint was faster.

Ri closed the gap as she jumped down into a shallow stream, leaping from flat rock to flat rock. Beyond the stream, Ri weaved between muddy puddles and closed it farther. When she passed Launfal, he noticed but kept going.

A deer. Broadside to them.

Ri froze with her arrow loosely nocked on her bowstring.

The animal nibbled on tall grass beyond the tree line at the end of a clearing, far ahead.

Ri turned to watch Launfal. His focus locked on the animal, he knelt, nocked an arrow, and slowly drew it back. Ri yanked her bowstring back, aimed at Launfal's shoulder, shifted a smidge for the wind, and shot.

Whirling around to the deer and to a knee, Ri drew and nocked another arrow. She pulled it back and let it fly.

An arrow sailed too high over the deer. The doe tensed and lifted its head.

A second flew true and sank squarely into its shoulder.

"Corina!" Launfal shouted.

Ri saw that her first shot had lodged in the tree trunk where Launfal had been. "What?"

He scowled at her.

"Your vision," she called. "Your *elven sight*. You saw the arrow in time."

He breathed a long breath. "Good shots."

"Thanks," Ri said.

The rest of their company caught up.

Emlyn pointed at Launfal, who was pulling Ri's arrow from the tree. "What happened?"

Ri walked to her deer. "I'll tell you on the way back."

In Terrin, Ri sat on her bed and gazed out the window into the city's thick forest. A breeze rustled young leaves on an old branch of an ancient tree. A chubby squirrel scurried down its trunk.

Ri's hair hung to the middle of her back. She had traded her scouting uniform for a long, pale-green dress for the trip west, home to Prim, Abilin's capital. Her maroon belt matched the accents on the clothes worn by her elven friends, who she would in too few moments leave behind.

"Corina," her brother Gregory called from outside her door, "you ready?"

"Nearly," Ri said, slipping on her sandals. She was keenly aware that she had also traded her preferred name for the one her parents had given her. At least the elves kept her secret. And Corina was a fine name.

She loved her mother and father, and the bond between Abilin and the Red Elves had grown strong over the ages. But Ri's parents would never knowingly allow their only daughter to be out in the woods, *scouting* with the elves.

Ri descended a winding stone staircase through the trees from her room in the secluded palace. When she arrived in the clearing, Ervain, King of the Red Elves, was speaking to his son and Gregory. Farlan, a slender red dragon who had long been friendly with the elves, sat with them.

"A troll?" Ervain asked.

"Yes," Prince Erwyn said. "It returned south at our insistence, and under our watch."

"What happened?" Ri asked.

Ervain turned to her. "Scouts found a troll in our forest."

Ri pictured one of the ugly, hulking, gray-skinned creatures and frowned. Why couldn't *her* team have found it?

"But it is no matter." King Ervain smiled at Ri, hugged her, and whispered into her ear, "Good hunting today."

She leaned out of his embrace and let her face warm. "Thank you, Your Grace."

"Safe travels, Corina," Erwyn said.

She nodded to the prince. "Thank you."

Farlan leaned low, and Gregory climbed onto the fine saddle near her neck. Ri climbed on in front of her brother.

Launfal ran into the clearing, holding a wrapped rectangular package. "A gift for the princess."

Ri raised an eyebrow.

"For dinner tomorrow, perhaps." Launfal handed her the package. "Venison. Very fresh."

Ri smiled. "Thank you, Launfal."

He nodded and stepped backward.

Farlan leapt into the air, flapped her wings, and rose above the Red Forest. With the Green Mountains behind and the rushing waters of the mighty Tearn River before them, they headed west for Prim.

4

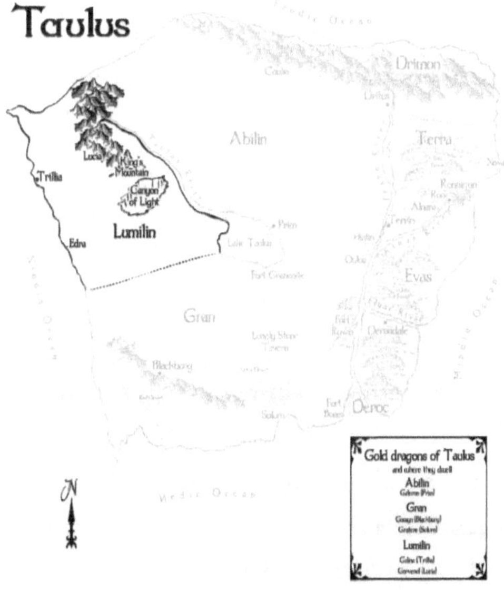

Gorvenal landed. Lila slid off the gold dragon's bare back, and her toes disappeared into lush, damp grass atop the Azure Cliffs, miles south of Trillia, the capital city of the kingdom of Lumilin. A loud ocean wave crashed into jagged rocks at the base of the blue rock wall on the western shore of Taulus. Gorvenal inhaled deeply.

"No." Lila's light blond hair blew all around her in the

salty ocean breeze. She held her loose white dress down over her thin thighs. "I like it this way." She didn't want him puffing his fire breath into the air to dry the cool dew on the grass.

Such a splendid morning, Gorvenal said directly in her mind.

As she made her way toward the cliff's edge, she ran her fingers across Gorvenal's hard, scaly body. He lowered his head to the grass, and when Lila sat against his long neck, the pair gazed out at the Nindin Ocean together.

"What would I do without you?" Lila asked.

You would do well, I have no doubt. You are the most beautiful young woman—the most beautiful thing I have ever set my sights upon, Lila. It is I who would suffer were we parted, for my eyes would be sadder, never brightened by a glimpse of you.

Loud waves crashed against the rocks in succession.

Lila leaned her head onto Gorvenal's neck. "Where would we all be without your kind protecting us?"

There was such a time, before gold dragons came to the aid of mankind. Before black dragons were created to man's great peril and my forebears eradicated those evil abominations. Before all that, and before the dwarves came to be, dragons could not communicate with man or elvenkind, and my ancestors sought to wipe those races away altogether. For hundreds of years after they suddenly appeared in a world already full of dragons who had never before needed to establish territories with any except other dragons, Taulus's new inhabitants had no allies, save each other. Gorvenal paused. *But you know this, Lila.*

"Tell me again." Lila closed her eyes. Her head rose and fell with each of the mighty dragon's breaths. Below, at the base of the cliff, waves hit rapidly, randomly, ceaselessly. "It is, indeed, a splendid morning, and to be with you, Gorvenal, on this morning… it is perfect. If you were to start that story, I know that you would finish it, and I also know that the tale would take longer than our time together today to tell. Before I fall asleep resting against you or curled beside you, I would know that there will be another morning like this one, because you would never refuse to finish the story."

I love you, Lila. And while I adore your words and that you make plots to keep my company, you needn't employ such strategy to get your next morning. You may have as many as you want, and I pray you want many. Of course I will tell you the great history of Taulus.

"I love you, Gorvenal." Lila's head rose and fell faster for a few moments on the scales of the golden dragon, son of Galina of Trillia.

Gorvenal had been told the story in very fine detail, by very old dragons, he had once explained to Lila. He aimed to relay to her a version with every bit of that detail in some places, and less in others, where he deemed appropriate.

He began, as always, *After the bountiful land of Taulus became filled with different grasses, various trees, and all manner of plants and animals—after he made the forest of the east run up to the foothills of the Endless Mountains of the north, and to the plains west of the River Tearn—after he tinted the desert beyond the broad mountains in the southwest red, and painted these cliffs their sky-blue color—once he had prepared all that to his liking, God placed four dragon eggs in the Canyon of Light, in the shadow of the King's Mountain.*

Lila scooted herself lower to more comfortably rest her head on Gorvenal's neck.

Most accept that all four eggs hatched at once.

Feinor, a big, powerful male red dragon, made his home in the desert beyond the Mountains of Fire, where the color of the clay and sand nearly matched his scales.

Railyn, a blue who could—and later would—equal Feinor's strength, found the lakes, rivers, and vast oceans most dear to her heart.

Grawlth, a wise, thoughtful green, spent many of his days on the plains but more in the expansive forests of Taulus.

Yalea, the tan dragon, my first ancestor, was the gentlest and the quietest of the four. She loved to lie and let the sun's rays warm her scales while the earth warmed around her. She took to the Great Desert of the south.

Lila pictured the four as babies, first learning to fly, and enjoyed imagining them older, flapping their mighty wings and gliding through the tranquil skies of their new world.

Then as now for all, save the golds and the blacks, dragons cherished the natural beauty of the world above all: majestic mountain peaks; thick, undisturbed forests; pristine water splashing into pristine pools at the end of long, sunlit falls— those lands the first dragons each claimed as their own. Among the four of them, there was plenty of territory for all.

Yalea and Feinor, the tan and the red, with their shared affinity for hot, dry land, often explored Taulus together. Their first child, the first dragon offspring, clawed his little red self out of his egg shell, and his parents named him Feinan.

Soon after, Railyn and Grawlth, the blue and the green, gave birth to a green son they named Taulin. A blue female followed for them, then another green.

Yalea and Feinor gave birth to a second red dragon, a female, then a male with orange scales.

A loud wave hit the rocks at the base of the cliff, and another followed. A soft wave receded gently.

A chirping gull stirred Lila.

The young dragons explored Taulus, at first with their parents and then on their own. The children claimed lordship of the lands most pleasing to them, and disagreements over who saw what first, and whether that even mattered, led to arguments, but all were settled peacefully with so much of barely explored Taulus to go around.

When the offspring of Railyn and Grawlth and Yalea and Feinor had grown old enough, they had children of their own, including the first purples. Dragons of the six natural colors, with one exception, began filling Taulus.

Lila imagined such a rainbow soaring over Taulus, seeing land—discovering it—for the first time. They must have made lists in their heads of spots they liked—plains and peaks and rivers and lakes—and then simply chosen their favorites as their own.

Lila yawned, curled her legs inward in the damp grass, and wished for vivid dreams of those dragons and those early days.

For Yalea, no tan-colored children came. As the years passed, her love for Feinor grew deeper, as did his for her. The two were rarely apart. But one after another, her children, whether male or female, hatched red colored, like their father, or occasionally orange. Though she loved each dearly, when Yalea had lived more than four hundred years, she sensed her time growing short and, longing to see a baby dragon with tan scales to match her own, determined she had no choice but to try a different mate.

Why not? Lila wondered. Why had Yalea not been given her tan baby?

In secret, Yalea went to Railyn and Grawlth's eldest son, Taulin, a green. Yalea and Taulin's first brief meeting set the plans for their second, to take place on a small island halfway around the world.

Lila cracked open her eyes—bright! She shut them and snuggled into Gorvenal. He brought his arm over her and breathed fire high above her that warmed her skin and the air buffeting it.

Lila thought of Yalus, the island named after what had happened there, and what those events led to, and she found herself so sad for Feinor, as always. Yet hope and joy for Yalea filled Lila, as well. How could Lila fault Yalea? But how could she blame Feinor for how he reacted?

After Yalus, when Yalea returned to Feinor, he didn't know Yalea carried a child of Taulin's.

Lila wouldn't think of it yet. She wouldn't let her questions spin in her mind and keep her awake. Sleep would be better—sleep, sounds of waves crashing into the Azure Cliffs, and dreams of the spectrum of colors filling the skies of the tranquil first days of Taulus.

5

Taulus

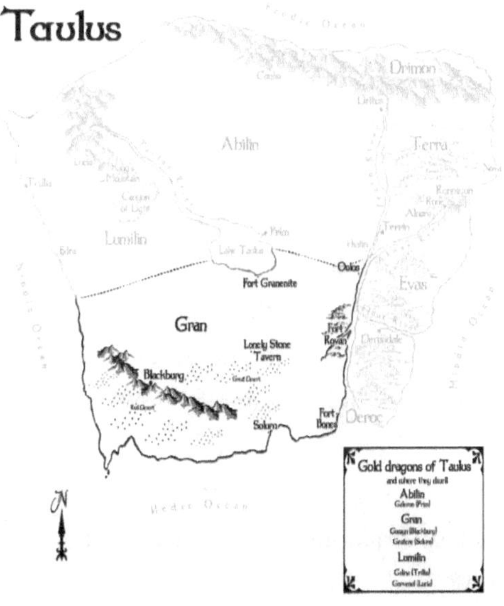

His head resting on his arm for a pillow, Gall rolled to his other side on the dirt floor. He was thirsty, his nose was stuffy and dry, and his forehead ached. The back of his skull throbbed. Gall opened his eyes: four worn stone walls, a tiny iron-barred window just below the ceiling behind him, a wooden door with a barred opening near the top and a panel at the bottom. A jail cell.

Gall sat up, rolled his neck, and squinted at a small ray of sunlight in the window.

He had won the tavern fight, he decided. The man who had provoked him had been flat on his back, bleeding from Gall's jab to his nose. The rat's two men had been lying on the floor, beaten and broken, unable to carry on. That the bartender had knocked Gall out seemed fair enough; after all, they had destroyed the table and those chairs… but Gall had won the fight.

Madine… she should have been fine. If the bartender cared to keep Gall from tearing his place apart, presumably he cared for the girls at least a little. Nothing Gall could do about it from jail anyway.

Gall pictured Madine's long skirt hiding her long legs. Nothing he could do about those, either.

Gall got his achy self off the ground and went to the door—no one in sight in the dim hallway past the iron bars. He called, "Can I get some water?"

A rustling of keys then footsteps came in response. A guard with a sword at his hip approached. "No water."

"Whisky?" Gall asked.

At the door, the guard said, "No."

"How about something to eat?"

"No food."

Gall leaned against the wall with outstretched arms. "But I'm hungry."

"You know"—the guard patted his belly—"so am I. Think I'll get me some breakfast." He swung a metal cover over the opening in the door.

"Hey!" Gall shouted.

The covering swung open.

"Where am I?" Gall asked.

"Jail."

"Where?"

"The Midlands. Near the scene of your crime."

"What crime?"

"Murder. Lord Ivon's dead."

The covering closed, and Gall heard a latch being shut.

Gall pulled on the door—locked. He went to each of the other three walls and pushed against them—sturdy. He sat at the rear of the cell with his hands above his head. Ivon was dead? *Lord* Ivon. Not good. Gall tapped on the wall with his knuckle. Not good at all.

However, with Ivon dead, *no one* could say Gall hadn't won the fight.

―――――――――

At least it isn't unbearably hot, Gall thought, recalling the time in his life when he had often done stints in cells like the one he lay in. Judging by the changing light in the small window, much of the day had passed. Gall had yet to receive any water or food. Or liquor or beer. His head's aching had died down, and the throbbing at its back had gone away, but a lump remained.

He tapped his knuckles on the wall behind him and debated if he could smash the door down. With a running start, he'd throw his shoulder into the effort. Or he could kick it, endeavoring to make a hole, which he could then rip wider until he fit through. He considered attempting to pull in his window's iron bars and climbing out that way, or if he couldn't fit, using the bars to destroy the door. He'd try something, eventually.

And sooner rather than later if they didn't feed him.

—————————

Gall figured it would be a chilly night and decided the chances of the guard coming by with a warm, cozy blanket were about zero.

He inspected the bars covering his window, noted rust where they met the stone in the wall, then ran through his few escape ideas again. How long should he wait? Which should he try first?

The panel at the base of the door opened. A wooden board with a thick turkey leg and a chunk of bread slid into Gall's cell, followed by a large cup.

"Finally." Gall went to the door. He grabbed the tray, chomped the bread, and chugged half the water. "Ahh."

The metal cover over the window in the cell door swung open, and a head appeared—that of a young man, not a guard. Gall stepped close, chewing his food. A thin girl stood beside the youth. Pretty. He recognized them from the tavern.

Gall held up the turkey leg before biting through the skin to the meat. "Thanks," he said around a mouthful.

"Your name's Gall?" the boy asked.

"It is," Gall said. "What's yours?"

The boy glanced at the girl.

"She your sister?" Gall asked.

The boy said, "You're in no position to ask questions."

"No?"

"You're in jail." The boy crossed his arms.

"So? Ain't the first time." Gall bit off and chewed a mouthful of bread. "I always get out."

The girl spoke up. "How will you this time?"

Gall looked around his cell. "Dunno."

"I'm Avery," the boy said. "This is my sister, Avril. Do *they* know your name?"

"*They?*"

"The guards."

"What's it matter?"

"It just does," Avery said. "Do they?"

"Don't think so. Not unless Madine told them."

"She didn't," Avril said. "She's smart."

"You know her?" Gall asked.

"Yeah."

"She all right?"

"Yeah. We talked to her this morning." Avery unfolded his arms. "She was our father's favorite… lately. We got to know her a little when she'd come home with him. He treated her better than the rest."

"*Was* his favorite?"

"Until you killed him last night," Avery said.

"Hm." Gall tried to peer down the hall through the opening in the door. "And where are those guards who don't know my name?"

"Asleep," Avery said.

"Drugged," Avril added.

Gall put his food down and swallowed hard.

"Your turkey's fine," Avril said.

"Sorry about your father," Gall said. "I didn't mean to—"

"Don't be sorry," Avery said. "We're not."

"No?"

"He hurt our mother," Avril said.

Gall paused his chewing. "What about you two?"

"No." Avery looked at Avril, who made an encouraging face. Avery held a ring of long keys up to the cell door window. "We can get you out of here."

"Good." Gall took another bite of his turkey leg. "Go for it. Proceed. Begin."

Avery shook his head. "If you will help us."

"How?"

"Well," Avril said. "You're headed to Blackburg?"

"I am."

"Take us to Trillia first."

"What's in Trillia?"

"Our mother," Avril said.

Gall gnawed on the long turkey bone, looking for more meat. "That's north of Blackburg. It's not on the way."

Avery looked fierce, suddenly, and no longer quite so young. "So go *out* of your way."

"Hmm." Gall sipped his water. "It seems I've already done you a favor, taking care of your father, who you tell me I was correct to judge as a rat. And I don't like going out of my way."

Avery glanced at his sister. "What choice do you have?"

"What do you mean?"

"You're in jail!"

"Shh." Avril grabbed her brother's arm.

"I'll get out."

"How?" Avery asked.

Gall tugged on an iron bar in the window. "Told you, dunno yet."

Avery huffed.

"Blackburg first," Gall said.

"What?" Avery asked.

Gall stuffed the end of the bread in his mouth. "I'll take you to Lumilin." He chewed loudly. "But Blackburg first." He swallowed so he could explain more clearly. "It's on the way, and I have business there to attend to."

"No." Avery shook his head. "We need to go straight to Lumilin."

"What choice do *you* have?"

Avery and Avril both folded their arms.

Gall shrugged. "How many honorable former knight commanders do you have lined up waiting to take you to Trillia? You've played your hand. You're out of lowlife fathers to set up to fight passersby. I have questions for you two, and I'm impressed. But it's still a fact: you've played your hand. Blackburg first."

Avery and his sister exchanged glances.

"I will get you to Trillia," Gall said.

"Swear it," Avery said.

Gall leaned closer. "I'm a man of my word, boy."

"How do we know that?"

"Why would me 'swearing it' satisfy you? They'd just be words."

"I want to hear them."

Gall put down the bare turkey bone and empty cup. "After Blackburg, I swear I will get you to Trillia."

Avery slid a rusty key into the door lock and turned it quietly. He pulled the door open. "What now?"

"Do you have horses?"

"Out front," Avril said. "With yours."

"Have you packed?"

"Packed what?" Avery asked.

"For your trip. It's a week to Blackburg, and farther from there to Trillia."

Avery's gaze fell, and he shook his head.

"Your place far?" Gall stepped past them.

"No," Avery said.

"Let's go." Gall led the way down the dingy hall. He pointed at each of them. "Be quick when we're there. Then we'll head west."

———————————

With the sun setting over the plains, Gall, Avery, and Avril raced south from the jail to the twins' home. They tied their horses in front of the long main house.

"Nice place," Gall said.

"He was a lord," Avery said.

"A low one," Avril added. "He never even met the king and queen."

"He met the last ones." Avery led the way inside. "And he had some money."

Pots and pans spilled out of open cupboards and drawers. Furniture had been knocked over and pushed out of place on the wood floor. Hooks and fasteners with nothing on them covered the otherwise bare walls. On the floor in front of the fireplace, a painting of a fox hunt lay with a metal poker sticking through it.

"Osric and Penton, probably," Avery said.

"The two men with your father at the Tavern?" Gall asked.

"Yes," Avril said. "Not very loyal. Not very surprising."

"The sheriff's men," Avery said. "Our father paid them so they'd let him do as he pleased. At the tavern, in town… here."

Gall assumed he meant how he'd hurt their mother, or what he did to other women he brought home, but he judged it the wrong time to dig into such a delicate subject. "With your father gone, do you think they'll chase us?"

Avery shrugged.

"They put you in jail," Avril remarked.

"True," Gall said. "Gather your things."

Avery and his sister headed for a room to the left.

Gall asked, "Where'd you learn how to drug the guards?"

"Our mother," Avril called.

"How long you think they'll be asleep?"

"Depends," she said.

"On?"

"How much they ate." She followed her brother into their bedroom.

"Well." Gall made a face for his own amusement. "Let's hurry then."

"Aye!" they both called.

Gall surveyed the ransacked home. "Anything to drink around here?"

Avery answered, "There's water near the door."

Gall glanced at the pitcher. "Your *father* keep anything to drink?"

Avery stuck his head out of the bedroom. Then he got it. "The cupboard in the corner."

Gall checked and found a few cups and bowls. "Nope."

"Lift the floorboard," Avery said.

Gall did. His face lit up.

"He hid his best from his 'friends,'" Avery said.

Gall brought a bottle and a cup to a long wooden table in the center of the room. He righted a knocked-over chair, sat, and poured himself a big drink. He chugged the whisky to the last drop. "Ahhh."

Avery and Avril stuck their heads into the main room. Avery asked, "What do we need to pack?"

"Clothes." Gall poured another drink.

"Got 'em," Avery said. "What else?"

"Warm clothes." Gall gulped down some whisky. "It gets cold at night in the desert."

The pair disappeared into their room.

Gall asked, "How old are you?"

"Sixteen," they called in unison.

"Twins?"

"Yup," they both said.

"Have you ever been to Blackburg?"

"No," they answered, as he had expected.

"Have you ever left the Midlands?"

"No."

"Hm." Gall finished his cup and refilled it.

The twins' heads appeared in their doorway again. Avery asked, "What else?"

"Blankets."

The twins vanished again, and Gall heard a chest open and close. They returned.

"Stolen," Avery said.

"The ones on your beds?" Gall asked, pouring a third cup of whisky.

They fetched them. "What else?"

"Money."

"Got it," Avery said. "Took that with us earlier."

"Food?" Gall asked.

"Dried beef and bread?"

"That'll work. How 'bout weapons?" Gall pulled his long knife off his belt. "Swords, knives?"

They stepped out of the doorway.

"No?" Gall asked.

The twins glanced at each other.

Gall tapped the flat side of his blade on the table. "What does that mean?"

Avery crossed his arms. "My father's would have been with him. There were some out in the stable."

"Let's go." Gall stood and put away his knife. "Get your things." He finished his drink, corked the bottle, then returned to the hollow in the floor and began filling his arms with bottles.

Avery emerged from his room with his brown sack. "How much do you drink?"

Gall added to his haul. "Enough."

"Every day?"

"Um." Gall widened his eyes. "Yeah."

Avril, carrying her own sack, gave her brother a concerned look.

Gall laid a bottle sideways atop the others he carried, but it fell. Glass shattered at his feet. "I guess that'll do, then. To the stable!" He stepped over crunchy broken glass and out the front door, his arms full.

Outside, in the last of the day's light, Gall squeezed the bottles into a sack hanging from his horse's saddle. The twins emerged from the house as he checked that his sword, blanket, and supplies were still in order. They moved silently down the path through overgrown grass toward the stable, and Gall followed them.

"Kind of a mess," he said.

Avery glanced back. "I didn't feel like cutting it." He swung the wooden stable doors open to dark and quiet inside. Avery led them in, and they found the four stalls vacant. "At least we got ours."

Gall went left and pulled a long, wide sword off the wall. He inspected its rusted edge. "No good." He dropped it in a pile of straw and noticed metal beneath the yellow stalks. He uncovered and picked up a medium-sized knife then gripped its handle—reasonably sharp blade, no rust. Gall flipped it around and held it out, hilt first. "Avery."

"No," the boy said.

"You can't fight?"

"I don't."

Gall held the knife out toward the girl. "Avril?"

She shook her head.

Gall gestured to Avery with the knife. "Take it."

"No."

"It's a long way to Trillia," Gall said.

"And you promised you'd get us there," Avery said.

"I aim to. But Blackburg's on the way, and it isn't the friendliest city in Taulus."

Avery crossed his arms.

"What if someone tries to rob you?"

The boy lowered his eyes.

"Take it," Gall said. "To defend yourself."

Avery looked up.

"What if you need to defend your sister?"

Avery watched her fold her hands in front of herself. After a moment, he walked over and took the knife.

"Right!" Gall clasped his hands. "Let's get out of here."

Back near the house, they mounted their horses and rode out the dirt path to a larger road heading west.

"We'll ride a few hours," Gall said. "See if anyone's following, then find a place to sleep off the road."

The twins nodded.

"Stay quiet," Gall instructed them. "Avery, you lead. Avril, follow him close." Gall reached back for a bottle of whisky. "Go."

They did, and Gall trailed them, liquor ever in hand, often at his lips. He checked behind frequently for pursuers from the jail. Night fell. The sliver of a moon in the clear sky gave a little light. Through the western plains of the Midlands, Gall reckoned they made good time. Not as fast as if he had been alone, but the youths rode well. Fortunate that their father had seen to that. Or maybe their mother had taught them, like the trick with the food. He wondered which.

The ride was quiet save for the sound of the horses' breath, the thud of their hooves against the ground, and the clattering of the supplies they carried. Avril and Avery pointed out small animals in the tall grass at the roadside, but they all ran off, scared of the noise and the horses. They saw the occasional owl hunting overhead. Gall assumed the twins had seen all the animals before, but tomorrow, when the sun rose and they found themselves farther from home than they had ever been—and then in the heat of the Great Desert—how would they react then?

A dragon glided by high overhead. Gall couldn't tell what color. The twins tracked it in between glances back at Gall. He took a drink and gave them a look indicating he would not be doing anything about the winged reptile in the sky. Avery and Avril kept quiet, as they had been told.

Would Gowyn have been sent looking for him? It seemed a bit much to catch one man. Once the twins stopped checking to see Gall's reaction, he gazed skyward— the dragon didn't seem to be deviating from its course. But one *murderer*? Surely the creature overhead spotted the three of them riding, or could have, if it cared to. Gall kept an eye on the sky until the dragon flew out of sight to the south.

"Avery," Gall called. When he got no answer, he called again, louder, "Avery!"

Avril and Avery slowed to a stop.

Gall rode up next to them. "Let's get some sleep."

"Was that Gowyn?" Avery asked. "Looking for you?"

"Looking for *us*," Gall said. "You broke me out of jail, remember?" He glanced at the sky. "But a gold dragon for the three of us… nah."

The twins appeared relieved.

Gall continued, "If memory serves, and there's a reasonable chance it does, over that hill, across the field, there's a stream." He led the way, found the small stream near a clump of tall shrubs, and stumbled as he dismounted.

"Is it safe?" Avery glanced behind him. "I can see the road."

Gall swapped his empty liquor bottle for a fresh one from the sack on his horse's side then led the animal to the shallow water to drink. "Eh." He waved his hand. "If they were following, they'd have caught up by now."

"Are you sure?" Avril asked.

"Nope." Gall took a rolled mat and small pillow from his horse. "But I'd rather fight than run."

Avril looked at her brother. He dismounted. After they tied up their animals and Avery checked his sister's knot, they sat near Gall, who lay on his mat.

"Build a fire?" Avery asked.

"Nah." Gall propped himself up, sipped his whisky, and pointed. "We *are* pretty close to the road. If the guards are following, no point in leading them right to us."

The twins exchanged worried glances.

"Why won't you fight?" Gall asked Avery.

He turned away.

"How 'bout you, Avril?"

"I could never hurt anyone," she said. "No matter what they did, even our father, I just… couldn't."

Avery added, "*Hurting* him wouldn't have been enough."

"That's why you needed me?" Gall asked. "How'd you know I'd kill him?"

"We didn't," Avery said. "We figured when you walked into the tavern that you'd sit at his table if we got up from it. Then you'd fight him when he challenged you over it, and you'd end up in jail. We'd talk to you there, tell you our story. *Then* you'd kill him."

"Hm." Gall nodded. "Good plan. What would you have told me? To convince me."

"That he hurt our mother." Avery's gaze became steel. "That he beat her and beat her. He drank a lot, but he beat her sober sometimes too. And when she went to the sheriff, he and his corrupt men ignored her. They ignored her bruises and breaks. And our father kept hurting her."

Gall recalled the look on Madine's face in the tavern when she had told him of the rat.

"And he threw her out of the house some nights," Avery said. "When he got tired of hitting her, I guess…" The boy's voice trailed off. He breathed deeply. "He said she could go, that she could leave, but that she couldn't take us with her."

"He needed us," Avril said softly.

Avery continued, "And she would never leave us, he

assumed, or leave his money. She had none of her own. So she came back every time, and I think in his mind that meant she accepted what he did. That it was all right."

"I woulda killed him," Gall said.

"I don't know why she always came back," Avery said. "Probably because of us, I guess." He glanced at the ground. "Then one night, almost a year ago, he shoved our mother out the front door, screaming that he needed her gone so he could drink in peace. Avril and I ran out to her, like we always did, but it was different. She was different."

"She was done," Avril said. "Done with him, done with that life."

"Our mother knew we saw it," Avery said. "Knew that we understood what had to happen next. We all cried on our front porch"—Avery's unblinking eyes searched inward—"hugging, until he yelled at us to keep quiet. He told us to spend the night in the stable with the horses. We recognized the opportunity and headed for them. Our mother said she'd send word when she got where she was going. We said our good-byes, and when all had quieted in the house, she left."

"And she says she's in Lumilin?" Gall held his bottle of liquor firmly to the ground.

"Yes," Avril said.

Avery added, "Which is why she wanted us to try to reach her ourselves, rather than her organizing something from outside the kingdom."

"Uh huh," Gall said.

"She wrote that it's one thing to hire men to travel across a border and commit murder," Avery said, "and quite another for children to organize their own escape. The former is not only murder, but a custody battle with a lord. The latter may result in death, but at its heart is children fighting for their future."

"Smart," Gall said. "Why'd she leave you behind? Why not try to take you with her when she ran?"

"She believed him," Avery said. "That he'd never let her take us. He'd hunt us all down. He'd been saying it for years."

"And he couldn't hurt us," Avril said. "Avery and I together. We *all* believed that."

"So where is she?" Gall slurred the words together.

"A place called Pinnacle, in Trillia," Avery said. "We asked around at The Lonely Stone. Pinnacle's sort of like that, but nicer, we think."

Gall asked him, "Why didn't you do anything to stop your father? You're strong enough."

Avery said softly, "We did this, didn't we?"

Gall drank, then offered the bottle to Avery.

"No," he said.

Gall held it out to Avril.

"No."

"Why do you drink so much?" Avery asked.

"Why not?" Gall said.

"Our father hated himself," Avril said. "He hated that he wasn't an important lord, like he thought he deserved to be, so he drank. He sobered up and hated what he had done to our mother, so he drank again and did it again. Now *you're* drinking his whisky. Do you hate yourself?"

"No." Gall rolled away from the twins. "S'time to sleep." He *didn't* hate himself. He loved himself. Bounty hunting was a good life. Fun. Better than taking orders from idiot knight officers. And he enjoyed fighting, and he got to do plenty of it. The kids were smart, but what did they really know? About him *or* the world. They had never even been away from home. "Drinking's fun," Gall spat. "You'd know if you tried it. Go to sleep."

Gall's head hurt. Above his nose mostly. He opened his eyes. Dawn. Hazy plains. He clutched an almost-empty bottle to his chest. Avril and Avery slept under blankets off to his right. Gall needed water. He stood.

Horseman. Crossbow.

Gall ducked. A rod shot over his head. Avery and Avril stirred.

Gall ran for his horse, tied near the twins', and a shot from a second horseman whizzed by. Guards from the jail, their dress told Gall. He ran around his horse and grabbed his sword.

Thunk. A crossbow rod sank into his steed's side. The animal let out a shrill whine, snorted, and crumpled.

Gall cut the rope to Avery's horse, got on it, and spun to the attackers—four on horseback, surrounding him. Gall rushed at the one charging him.

Their blades met high—Gall's hit harder, driving his foe backward. Gall cut low—fast—across the guard's midsection. The guard fell from his horse, a gaping wound in his belly.

"No!" Avery called, trying to pull his sister away from a rider who held her.

"Ya!" Gall sped that way. "Ya!" He rose from his saddle and leapt, throwing his shoulder into the guard. He, Avril, and the guard all toppled to the ground. Gall got to his feet, and as the guard tried to rise, Gall used both hands to drive his blade into his chest.

The two remaining horseman charged.

Avril staggered to her feet.

"You all right?" Avery asked her.

"Get back." Gall tightened his grip and readied his sword above his head.

"Yeah," Avril said.

The lead horse neared. Gall turned to his side, and the twins rushed backward.

The lead rider swung. Gall parried, ducked, and chopped low across the trailing horse's shoulder. The animal stumbled and crashed to the ground. Its rider flew forward, landing with a thud. Gall pounced, but the guard avoided his stab. His sword blocked Gall's swing from above, but the guard couldn't stretch his arms to attack.

Gall swung—the guard blocked weakly.

Gall swung harder—the guard's block was softer still.

Harder—a meek block.

Gall stabbed the guard in the stomach and kicked the sword from his hand. Blood poured from the man. Gall kicked the blade farther way. A red puddle formed around his boots.

Avery and Avril ran behind Gall. The last guard cautiously rode near.

"Go!" Gall shouted. "Leave us be." He pointed at a fallen rider's horse. "Avery, to replace mine."

"You've committed murder," the approaching guard called.

"Ivon was a *rat*," Gall said. "A monster."

The guard stopped. "Now you've killed these men."

"You attacked us. After that, the fight was fair." Gall lowered his sword. "Ivon deserved to die."

Avery grabbed the reins of the animal he had been sent for and called, "He hit our mother."

The guard shrugged. "A domestic concern."

"He beat her," Avril yelled. "He beat her and beat her."

The guard shook his head. "That doesn't—"

"The night she left," Avril said, her voice loud at first then becoming quiet, "he told her he'd keep going, a little farther each time, let her heal, and see how badly he could beat her without beating her to death."

The guard shifted in his saddle.

"He would never have let us leave," Avery said. "He told us, all the time. He swore it to us, and he swore it to God. We had no choice."

"Look at your friends!" Gall implored the guard. "You want to end up like them over the life of *that* kind of animal?"

He didn't answer.

"I don't lose fights." Gall stepped toward him. "I just don't." He readied his sword. "And I've already killed three men today. I'll kill you and whoever else comes. Happily. With ease." Gall gestured to the east. "Or leave us be. Get out of here. Realize it isn't worth your life."

The guard glanced toward where he had come from then pointed at Gall. "Leave the Midlands and never return." He shifted so his gesture encompassed the twins. "All of you." He kicked his horse's side and, keeping well out of Gall's long reach, rode for the road.

6

Taulus

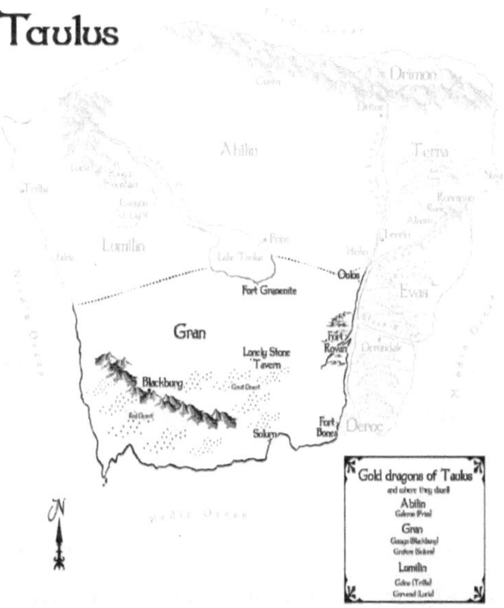

The sinking sun in the clear blue sky warmed Taylan more than he liked. Broken and burned wooden walls, roofs, and furniture lined both sides of the road leading to Fort Granenite. Where the wreckage had been cleared, men hammered flat nail ends, driving the fasteners into wooden beams and boards.

Clang, knock, knock, knock, clang!

Taylan's headache didn't appreciate the clamor of metal on metal. Fathers swung their tools harder than the sons they instructed. Most wives and daughters brought water to the thirsty men. Others joined young boys moving lumber and supplies from site to site. No one gave more than a passing glance to Taylan, the half-elf dressed in black, riding his dark-brown horse to the fort.

He wiped his brow. A large fire, clearly, had burned the houses to the ground.

More than houses—family *homes*, with all their furniture and possessions—had been reduced to ash. Taylan was all too familiar with that kind of destruction.

Yet hope abounded. The constant noise ruined the sensation for Taylan, but he found himself riding through an energetic air of resolve—of rebirth—not one of townspeople mourning all they had lost. Before the journey to Fort Granenite, how long had it been since Taylan had been filled with such optimism? Over the years, brief flickers had lit inside him when seeing Valencia or receiving one of her letters. But the sparks died fast at the sight of the latest knight kissing her or holding her, or when her letters mentioned the dashing options she couldn't decide between. But her latest letter included no such thing. It asked for him to come to her. And she sounded eager to see him. Taylan brimmed with such excitement that he could hardly believe it. But the sound of construction was the latest annoyance spoiling his mood.

Mercifully, beyond the open gate, inside the fort, the commotion faded to background noise—still constant, but it didn't pierce Taylan in the same way. The long stone halls on the fort's three sides still stood strong, as expected, and it appeared the fire hadn't reached inside the fort at all. Guards spaced evenly atop the high outer wall kept watch. Taylan tied up his horse and entered the long hall at the west wall.

Inside, a pair of sweaty men in dirty clothes with various tools hanging off every inch of their belts conversed with a knight while pointing at different sections of a tabletop map showing the fort and the town.

Beside the table, with her back to them, tall Valencia, wearing a white tunic with a long knife on her belt, spoke to a short woman dressed in a white robe. "And Randal's fine?"

"He is," the emote said. "Both arms healed. Good as new."

Valencia noticed Taylan and raised a finger to indicate she'd be a moment. "Where is he now?"

"Out with his friends, I think," the emote said.

"*Out.*" Valencia shook her head. "Causing more trouble, I'm sure."

The emote smiled.

"I'll find him and talk to him, eventually," Valencia said. "Thank you, Shaela."

The woman nodded and headed Taylan's way. She smiled as she neared him, and a warmth reached Taylan's skin. Then she passed, and he cooled completely, quickly, as always.

"Taylan." Valencia approached.

"Val," he said. Would she hug him? Surely. It had been so long. She had sent for him, and he had come.

"Val*encia*." His friend slid her eyes side to side. "Here anyway." She grasped his arm. "Thank you for coming."

"Of course." Taylan knew the hug would come later. It had to. He pointed his thumb behind him. "What happened out there?"

"Beore," Valencia said.

"Was anyone hurt?"

"Not permanently."

"Why'd he do it?"

"One of the boys picked his flowers."

"Ah." Taylan cracked a small smile. "Beore…"

Valencia rolled her eyes. "Uh huh."

"Is that why you sent for me?" Taylan asked. "Trouble with him?"

"No." Valencia took Taylan's arm. "Let's go for a ride."

West of the fort, far off the main road in a rocky clearing in the grassy plain, Taylan set a log on their pile for later.

"It'll be a cold night." Valencia laid a blanket between their tent and the fire then sat, leaning on her elbows behind her, and stretched out her long legs. She gazed at the canopy of stars, full in the absence of moonlight.

"It will." Taylan sat beside her. High above, a slender dragon with long, outstretched wings glided by. The randomness of nature—or a cruel force beyond his control, Taylan often thought—had made him far more human than elf, but his eyes still saw a bit better than pure men and women's. "Red."

"Yes," Valencia said.

"Friend of Beore's?"

"Don't think he has many."

Taylan doubted anything would come of the red. Flying through another dragon's land—even stopping to rest—was no crime or offense. Tampering with the land or staying too long was a different story, of course, and one that could lead to a very violent confrontation. But such conflicts had been rare for some time, as dragons understood whose territory belonged to whom. Though when one died without clearly bequeathing their land, the ensuing fights for control could be quite fierce.

The field surrounding the clearing where Taylan and Val sat, like the land around the fort itself, was similar to the Plains of Abilin, where Taylan had grown up with his mother. There, the same grass grew as high and swayed the same way in the steady breeze. In truth, they camped not far from that original home of the first men and women of Taulus.

While the people of Gran held a very different view of the world than those they had left behind ages before, faced with greater threats than each other, the first human kingdom had never been an enemy of the second kingdom. The plains were no place to mount a defense, the Granans had decided, and they held sound defense above all else. While the Abilinians clung to their precious homeland, the Granans had dreamed of a home markedly different than those plains and a great distance from them. Their leader returned from a daring exploratory expedition with word of a broad mountain range in the southwest, and only when the long journey there had proved too perilous did Gran set their capital at Granenite. There it remained until centuries later, when they could finally complete their relocation to the mountains—to Blackburg.

But that had all been settled long ago. Eager to satisfy his lingering curiosity, Taylan asked Valencia, "So, an ogre, you say?"

"Yes, out east. Two or three, we think. They shouldn't be so far north. We're going to find them and find out what they're doing there."

"What do they have to do with me?"

"Actually, I sent for you before word had come of them."

"Oh?"

"Well…" The warrior scooted closer to him. "Maybe I just wanted to see my old friend."

Taylan smiled.

"Do you remember the summer when, the instant my family got to your mother's sister's, you and I disappeared into the woods and we didn't see the rest of them the whole week?"

"Of course." Taylan's heart raced. He leaned close.

"I miss that."

"What?" Taylan regretted letting the dumb word slip past his lips.

"Getting away," Valencia said. "From everything."

"Me too." He kissed her—his dumb question hadn't robbed him of it.

She smiled and put her hand on his shoulder. "How are your headaches?"

At the mention of them, pangs beat from his heart up into his mind. "I still get them." The beats crashed harder against his skull. "From time to time." With Taylan's parents gone, none but Val knew the true cause of his most poignant pain.

"I saw the way you looked at Shaela earlier," Val said. "Could she help you?"

Taylan leaned away and watched the fire flicker high and low. Throbbing waves slammed into his forehead.

"Could she?" Val repeated. "Could any of them? The king's sister in Blackburg is a gifted emote. I've seen her heal soldiers with the deepest wounds and bring the most gravely ill men back from the brink of death."

"I am not ill, nor wounded." Taylan gently shook his head. "Some say God returned the emotes' healing magic to them because the Creator could not bear to see humans, his frailest children, suffer after battles and linger with disease. I believe that, despite my own suffering. But not even a renowned emote of that eternal line can help me. My curse, it seems, is more powerful than that magic."

Val nodded.

Taylan leaned close to her. "One thing gives me some peace." He kissed her—enough of the fire, enough of the headaches—and kept kissing her. He brought his arms around her and held her strong body. She held him—finally, he had his embrace.

"Happy to help." Val pulled him to the blanket.

7

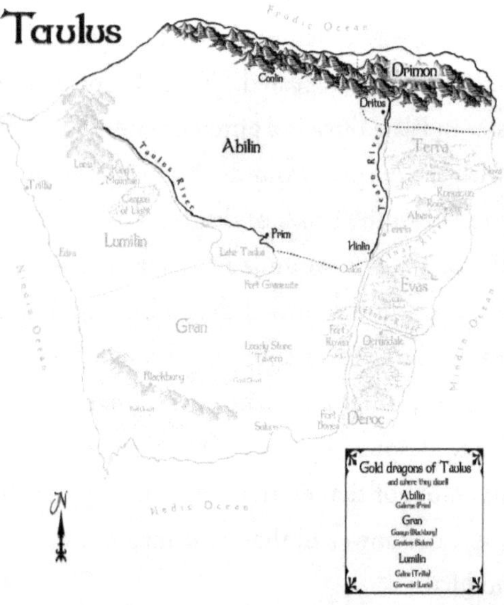

Ri had learned at a very young age, like most everyone else in her kingdom, that when God created humans, before the people of Gran struck out on their own, he set the men and women of Taulus to live on the Plains of Abilin, in the town of Prim. The men learned the names of their land and their town from God himself, for he dwelled among the people then for a short time. While he did, no dragons threatened the settlement. None flew the skies above. God's presence protected the Abilinians while he taught them of the world.

More than a thousand years later, Ri sat in Prim, in Charles Hall in Castle Mikannel, at a long table with her three older brothers—Kalen, the oldest, Chance, and Gregory, the youngest. Kalen and Chance's wives sat beside them and Gregory beside Ri. King Kenrick—her father— occupied the far head, and around the table, opposite the children, sat her mother—the queen—and the royal advisors. Ri leaned forward in her high-backed chair and sipped a spoonful of creamy soup. Bright red and yellow banners hung off the sharply cut white stone walls in the great room.

Galeron, lord of the gold dragons, dwelled nearby in the center of the circular city and likely rested while they dined. The huge dragon traveled less as he grew older, and Ri had seen him earlier that day. She had asked, but he hadn't mentioned any important business he had to attend to. He had no uprisings to quell, no councils to preside over, no troublesome dragons to deal with. Ri tilted her head back and looked up at the high ceiling. Were Galeron off on any errand, they would rely on the stone, for the long outer walls of Mikannel and all the walls inside had been built of granenite by master dwarven craftsmen to protect those inside from dragon fire.

Ri's father said, "It will be a gift to King Doxton and to all the dwarves."

His chief advisor, Norwell, glanced at the square dark-ruby gemstone. It was as large as the mouths of the goblets they drank out of and sat on a white satin pillow on a table behind the king. "We only just recovered it from the Thorns. Rubies so large are rare, and it's cut perfectly. Why give away such a fine stone?"

"To express our gratitude." Kenrick bit a piece of chicken from his shiny silver fork.

"For what?" Norwell asked.

The king made eye contact with all enjoying the meal, saving his sons for last. "For this castle. For all the castles and forts they constructed for us." He pointed down the table with his fork. "For the security they have provided us, so we may dine like this, in peace."

"Haven't we expressed that gratitude already?" Chance asked.

Kenrick shrugged and chewed.

"We paid them long ago, when they did the building. Gold, silver"—Gregory pointed at the especially flat ruby being debated—"jewels like this one. Did we not pay them in full?"

"We did," Kenrick said, focused on his plate of food.

"And Dritus," Gregory added, "their capital city, and all the lands of the north that we ceded to them, along with what the elves gave to the east."

"Yes, yes," Norwell said. "Surely that land is sufficient payment. Forever."

"I do like the ruby. It is our color." The king turned to his queen. "Madeline, if we kept the stone in Abilin, would you like to have it?"

Ri's mother wore a small bright ruby hanging from a

golden necklace and sitting delicately at the base of her slender neck. She placed her hand on her husband's shoulder. "It is exquisite, dear. Thank you, but I have no need for it."

Kenrick nodded and took another bite. "Corina? You have a birthday coming up." He held his utensils still and shifted his attention from his plate to her. "I think. Would you like the ruby?"

Ri leaned forward for a clearer view of the stone recovered in a raid on a thief hideaway in Conlin, largest of the cities in their kingdom's north. She grimaced. "No."

Her brothers smiled.

"I'm sure *someone* in Abilin would cherish such a gift," Norwell said. "Make it a present to one of the lords. Hadwin or Daegal. Don't waste it on the dwarves."

"It would not be a waste," her brother Kalen said. "The dwarves are our allies and our friends. Isn't that reason enough for the gift? And what if, one day, we need a new castle?"

Norwell leaned back and smirked. "I'm sure they'll charge us appropriately for the work."

"What if Gran or Lumilin wants a castle, as well?" Kalen asked. "Maybe this gets us to the front of the line."

"The dwarves don't work like that," Norwell said. "They'll build two at a time."

"But could they build three?" Kalen asked. "And what if the elves are also in need?"

"It's been centuries since they've built anything so large." Norwell rocked forward again. "They haven't built a thing of importance since then, and… this is absurd. The scale of construction you're describing… worldwide… it's absurd."

Kalen said, "It would be a mistake—"

"Kalen." The king put down his knife. "Norwell, as you say, we will not be in need of dwarven construction anytime soon. But the dwarves are our allies, and they will appreciate the ruby more than we would. Kalen, will you take this gift to them?"

"Of course."

The king looked down the table. "Gregory, accompany him?"

"Certainly," Gregory replied.

"Corina?" her mother asked. "Will you go?"

Ri gave her a puzzled look. "Why?"

The queen shrugged. "I thought you might like to take the trip."

"Madeline," the king said, "she's just returned from Terrin."

"I'll go," Ri said. "Nothing going on around here, anyway." Plus, a ride on Galeron sounded fun.

"Nothing *going on*?" Her father shook his head and got back to his food.

———

Twenty hours of the twenty-one-hour journey from Prim to the cold northern dwarven kingdom of Drimon lay behind them. Their departure had been uneventful and unexciting. When Ri was younger, seeing the Vitus River running through the concentric circular walls and spoke streets of

Abilin's bustling capital from high above had never failed to bring about at least a small smile. The outer-ring Great Wall reached far enough to contain all of the city's markets, homes, shops, theaters, tournament grounds, and even its countless farms. That had always impressed Ri and made her proud to call the city home.

While the days when she'd wondered at the sight of Prim from the air were long past, Drimon had not become so commonplace to her. Galeron flew low, but Ri and her two brothers nevertheless wore thick jackets and wrapped themselves in heavy blankets for warmth. The wind buffeted her face in the space where her cap and scarf didn't quite meet. Ri couldn't wait for the roaring dwarven fires that would follow their arrival. And despite the chill that reached her gloved fingers, she always preferred to be very cold for hours on the back of a dragon than to be fairly cold for days, journeying on horseback to the northern lands.

In the distance, Ri began to make out the peaks of the Endless Mountains, which spanned hundreds of miles of Abilin's north and continued east to the north of the forests of the Red Elves. The Frodic Ocean lay beyond the mountains and the Mindin to the east.

Their destination, Dritus, the great dwarven capital city, had been built in the foothills of those ever-snow-covered mountains and dug deep into their rock. The land it occupied, and all the lands of the dwarves, had been gifts from Abilin and the elves. In return, the dwarves had pledged to use their engineering and stone-working expertise to build castles and fortresses out of granenite for the humans and elves of the world, beginning with Abilin.

On the back of golden Galeron, Ri imagined the time, long before, when men and women had the magic to protect themselves from dragons and their fire and could even take the fight *to* the great wyrms. The dwarves came when that time had ended, and luckily for men, elves, and dwarves alike, the newcomers to Taulus could build with granenite stone, which none had been able to do well before. Especially lucky for the dwarves, Ri thought, because otherwise she doubted anyone would have ceded land to them, or at least not as much.

Ahead, a big blue dragon flew high above the sharply cut, intentionally fire-grayed walls of Dritus. Smoke rose from the large outer hall of the long castle and from a wide chimney at the far end. Ri had no doubt countless other fires burned deep inside the mountain, where the fortress extended. A few of the intricate stained glass windows of predominantly blue and purple stood swung open, despite the crisp outside air.

Inches of fresh snow covered the stone cottages before the castle walls. Narrow streams of smoke rose from each and every chimney. Ri, her brothers, and the lordly dragon approached, and dwarves came out of their homes to watch.

What the newest race of inhabitants of Taulus lacked in height relative to men and elves, they made up for in strong, stocky bodies. Living in the cold north of Drimon, working in the mountains and the mines, clearing the snowy forest for fuel to feed their fires, the dwarves were a hard race.

Hardy, Ri decided, fit them better. While they could be

gruff or serious when the need arose, most all dwarves Ri had ever met hid a comforting warmth somewhere, whether shallow or deep, beneath their rough appearance.

Dwarves from behind the castle walls ran to see the arriving gold dragon. Rare were males without full bushy beards; rarer were those with cleanly shaven faces. Dwarves with completely clean clothes were non-existent. Dust and dirt from the mines or the mountains covered their warm layers, either from working themselves or from sharing their homes with those who brought the dirt and dust home with them.

"How long since you've been here?" Ri asked Galeron.

I've flown the skies, but not so low for a year, he answered her and her brothers in their minds.

Dwarves in the crowd called, "Galeron!" Open windows exposed glowing fires in every home. "It's Galeron!"

Doors swung open, whole families—parents, typically one or two children, and often grandparents too—hurried outside, and the crowd grew. All gazed skyward. The gold descended, the dwarves quieted, and their eyes widened.

Galeron landed on the crunchy snowpack outside the castle gates before the crowd. The dragon leaned low, and Kalen slipped off. He offered a hand to Ri, but she ignored it. Gregory dismounted last, and Galeron brought his wings in close around him.

From the crowd, a child broke forward from his parents' restraining arms and pointed. "Ga… Ga… Galeron."

The dragon craned his neck to bring his head inches from the wide-eyed little dwarf. Gasps came from the crowd.

Ri glanced at Galeron, who nodded. She went to the child, knelt, and whispered into his ear. His face brightened, and he nodded rapidly.

Gregory, lift him onto my back.

Gregory picked up the dwarf and set him at the front of the saddle. "Hold on tight."

The crowd murmured. Many grinned. From beside the same parents, an older child stepped forward.

"Are you his brother?" Ri asked.

"Yes," he said.

Ri motioned toward the dragon. "Hop on."

The dwarf ran over and, with the dragon's help, climbed up as five horses galloped out of the castle gate. Sunlight reflected off Galeron's extending wings. The older child sat behind his brother and repositioned the younger boy's hands for better grip. Galeron leapt into the air. The horses recoiled. The big dragon flapped his wings and rose. The crowd clapped and cheered. The dwarves on horseback steadied their animals.

Even from below, Ri could hear Galeron inhale.

A few dwarves noticed and pointed.

The dragon's head tilted skyward.

The crowd quieted.

Galeron spread his wings wide and let loose a stream of fire, deep orange and red at its source and ending in a swirling ball of brilliant flame.

The crowd roared. The horses remained restless. The younger brother closed his eyes and pressed his head into Galeron's neck.

Gregory watched the dragon rise. "He'll be out here all day giving rides."

"That will suit him just fine," Kalen said.

Galeron flew into the mountains, and the dwarven greeters from King Doxton rode to their company.

———

With her eyes long since closed and her legs hanging off the foot of her bed, Ri rolled her head to the side atop her thick comforter. Warm air, pumped from roaring fires at the lower levels of the castle up and through a vent at the base of the wall, brushed her cheeks. She breathed the heat deep into her lungs, and the glistening, cavernous mine she had visited earlier shimmered again vividly in her mind. The dwarves had been digging deeper—always deeper—and Ri had already felt like a tiny insect, standing on the overlook, gazing at the high, brightly lit ceiling and down to where that light reflected off the freshly exposed precious metals and gemstones.

Ri rolled her head the other way to cooler air and opened her eyes. Outside cracked-open hinged windows, pink hues from the low sun filled the clear sky and reflected off the white mountaintops. She sat up. The *too low* sun.

Ri slid off the bed, thankful she had changed into her long white-and-red dress for the ceremony before dozing off. She grabbed a thick fur shawl from the back of the chair at her mirror and slipped on her sandals.

Ri pulled open her door and walked briskly down the long, wide, echoing hallway. Her brothers would not be happy if she arrived late. *Later.* She should already have been there.

Pink to blue to purple filled the cloud-littered sky above the mountains out the tall, narrow windows, but Ri didn't have time to savor the view. She hurried up a wide staircase and jogged down the hall. When she rounded the corner, a group of dwarves interrupted their conversation to give her surprised looks. Ri slowed to a walk. If she missed the ceremony, Kalen would tell her parents, she had no doubt. Her father would certainly not be pleased. Nearly to the throne room, she jogged again.

Up another level, around another corner, with the entrance to the great hall in sight, Ri slid to a stop. Past the two guards at the entrance, Doxton, King of the Dwarves, was speaking with Bardric, the governor of Ronnigun, the dwarven lands to the southeast. Ri approached casually and caught her breath. She could almost hear them.

Then, at the doorway, Doxton said, "My answer has to be no. I am sorry."

"I understand," Bardric said. "Thank you for hearing me out."

Passing between the guards, Ri entered the hall and behind her the king said, "Of course, Bardric. Of course."

Unlike most of the castle, the very high ceiling had not been smoothed—the jagged rock of the mountain from which the room had been cut remained. A huge fire roared in a circular pit at the center, vented out a chimney above. The throne lay beyond the fire at the end of the hall. Dwarven guards stood near it and at the walls of the room.

Ri's two brothers gave similar disapproving looks while she made her way to their side, near the fire. Kalen held the ruby on the small pillow, covered in a white satin sheet.

Ri began quietly, "I—"

"King Doxton!" a guard at the doorway shouted, and all gave their attention to him.

"Princes of Abilin." The approaching king put out his arms. "Princess of Abilin. Welcome to Dritus. It has been too long."

Governor Bardric followed him.

"It has," Kalen said. "Thank you for having us here."

"You are always welcome." Doxton grasped Kalen's shoulder, and Kalen returned the gesture. The king glanced at the covered ruby, greeted Gregory as he had his brother, then took Ri's hand and kissed the back of it. "You all know Governor Bardric, I believe?"

"We do," Kalen said.

"How is Abilin?" Bardric asked.

Boring, Ri thought. Like these introductions.

"All is well," Kalen said. "The days are peaceful, our nights are tranquil. Our people are happy. It is a grand age in Abilin, as it is throughout Taulus."

Ri stood smiling pleasantly, as she knew she should.

"It certainly is a grand age in Drimon," the king said. "And how are your parents?"

"Very well," Kalen said.

"Good." Doxton clasped his hands and said solemnly, "Let's get this over with."

Kalen raised an eyebrow in surprise.

"I'm hungry." The king smacked his belly. "And our feast awaits!"

Ah, King Doxton. The greetings had been boring, but that he felt the same way she did, despite the unavoidable formalities, reminded Ri why she had always liked him.

Kalen uncovered the ruby.

Doxton and Bardric's respectful smiles deepened. They focused intensely on the square jewel.

"A gift from our family and the people of Abilin," Kalen said. "In hopes that our friendship with the dwarves will be ever as strong as it is now." He handed the pillow to the king.

"It is…" The King seemed to search for the right word.

"Exceptional," Governor Bardric finished for him.

Doxton nodded. "Yes. We have unearthed many fine gemstones in our mines, including rubies, large and small, but this one, dim as it is, stands out from the rest." He again grasped Kalen's shoulder. "Thank you. Truly, I share your wish that our kingdoms ever remain close friends and allies." He made eye contact with Ri and Gregory. "Thank you all."

A guard from the wall came and took the ruby from the king and the white sheet from Kalen.

"Now." The king rubbed his hands together. "Follow me." He led the group out through the hall's entrance. "I met with my cooks this afternoon." Doxton licked his lips. "The variety of meats tonight… no matter your preference…" He turned back. "But do try them all."

"We will be sure to," Kalen said.

"And his beer!" Doxton smacked Bardric's shoulder. "He brought a barrel from Rone. I had a mug earlier. The hall will be crowded, so it will go fast. Be sure to get some."

Ri preferred wine, but among the dwarves, and after King Doxton's enthusiastic recommendation, beer sounded pretty good. It would just be dinner, but Drimon was certainly proving more interesting than Abilin.

King Doxton led Governor Bardric, Ri, and her brothers down a staircase in one of his castle's many long hallways toward the feast. "We finished the hall last year. It's bright, and those spending all day in the mountains or the mines find the light very welcome."

"Is it cold?" Gregory asked. "With the window? I hear it is quite impressive."

"No," Doxton said. "You'll see. We can cover the window if we need to with just the pull of a lever, but the hall is warm. Our best engineers worked on it. Aside from some small projects for men and elves—infrastructure, statues, and palatial homes in Lumilin—we aren't so busy beyond our borders these days. And that's just fine. We mine our mines, work our forests, and build into our mountains, and as you'll see, our new hall is both bright and warm."

They turned the corner to sounds of a distant commotion.

"Kalen, Gregory, Corina," the king said, "I've arranged a table for you up front."

"Thank you," Kalen said.

A pair of guards stood at a wide, tall arched doorway at the end of the hallway.

"I'll join you at your table if I can," the king said.

Ri could make out singing beyond the door. "Is it always guarded?"

"Yes." The king looked at her. "For our most important guests."

The guards opened the door, revealing a small room with an identical closed door at its end. The singing beyond the door faded out to a loud, jubilant clamor.

The king entered the small room, the others following him, and while Ri glanced at the high ceiling, the doors behind them closed, snuffing out all light.

From the total darkness, King Doxton sighed. "They forgot to set the torches afire."

The doors before them swung inward, and evening light rushed into the room from the hall's famous window and over the long rows of tables crowded with merry, short, dirty dwarves.

The crowd let out a roar at the king's arrival, beginning with the dwarves nearest him and rolling to the rear of the hall. Ri stared past them, past the sparse columns supporting the roof, to the mountains framed in the tall window that wrapped around the spacious room from the far end to just to her right. Only a column in the corner interrupted the panoramic view. Blazing torches lined the walls and hung atop the columns.

They stepped into the hall. Warmth hit Ri—not the cold northern air of the twilit landscape she marveled at, but the rich heat she recalled from visits to confined dwarven halls in her youth. Beer mugs rose, and the dwarves raising them broke into earnest song.

A hard day's work, they sang, meant a night of hard drinking in reward. Their king beamed at them while Ri surveyed the scene.

They had entered opposite the shorter of the wraparound window's two sides. Small cutouts dotted the longer wall to her left—a flame flickered in one, and another farther along the wall. The heat came from there, Ri reasoned.

A singing dwarf on that side of the room, near one of the tables covered with a variety of partially sliced slabs of beef, made eye contact with Ri. She smiled back at him. Some dwarves worked harder than others, his song went, and some drank harder as well.

Someone poked Ri's arm.

She turned to Governor Bardric.

"We vent heat from the columns, as well," he explained. "Clever, no?"

Ri spotted small openings up and down the stone ceiling supports, and agreed it was, indeed, a clever way to maintain the room's warmth with the wide-open window.

The song ended with a shout. "King Doxton!"

The smiling king made his way into the crowd and accepted a mug of beer from an eager dwarf.

Governor Bardric said to the Abilinians, "You're over here." He pointed right, toward a table near the window quickly emptying of dwarves carrying their meals and drinks away.

"They can stay," Ri said.

"Absolutely," Gregory added.

"Well," Bardric said, "they're already going."

Ri sat with her brothers, and without another word, Bardric launched into conversation with nearby dwarves and disappeared into the crowd.

"I like it here." Ri took off her fur shawl. Cool air from outside touched her bare arms, but the heat emanating from a nearby column did more than enough to keep her warm.

"Me too," Kalen said.

A young dwarf with only a little dirt on her face came to their table. "What can I bring you all?"

Gregory opened his mouth, but Ri answered the child first. "No, please, that won't be necessary." Ri stood. "But can you show us to the food?"

"Yes!" the dwarf said and took Ri's hand.

Kalen smiled at Gregory.

"She's terrible at being a princess," Gregory said.

"She really is." Kalen got up with his brother.

They followed Ri and her guide to the tables near the heated wall. They were covered in the kind of variety of meat Ri had only ever seen on previous trips to Drimon. Dwarves in line for food tried to let the royals from Abilin go ahead, but as much as they could without making a scene, Ri and her brothers waited their turn. The three filled their plates with spoonfuls of roasted potatoes and all manner of beef: lean slices, marbled fatty slabs, and thick chunks of the finest cuts. Kalen and Gregory piled their plates noticeably higher than their sister.

Ri filled her mug with ale and began to make her way through the crowd to their table. A fat dwarf bumped Ri in the hip.

Ri shuffled her feet to maintain her balance and keep from spilling her plate and drink.

The dwarf turned to her. "Apologies, m'lady." He motioned to the brown dirt mark he had left. "About the dress." A few of his friends turned to see.

"It's all right," she said. "In truth I wish I weren't wearing this thing anyway."

The dwarf raised his eyebrows. "Me neither."

After a moment, Ri rolled her eyes and resumed her trip to her table.

One of the dwarf's friends shoved him. "You can't say that!"

"What?" the dwarf protested and laughed.

Ri's brothers joined her at the table.

"What was that?" Kalen looked at the group of dwarves.

"Nothing at all." Ri took a bite from a strip of juicy beef. "Mm."

"Yeah," Gregory said. "Doxton doesn't disappoint."

Ri savored another bite, and the commotion in the room seemed to quiet while she watched the puffy clouds drifting above the mountains outside in the darkening sky.

"Out of the way." The voice brought Ri back inside.

"Move," a female dwarf said.

At the opposite side of the table, two dwarves shoved through the crowd.

The scruffy dwarf who made it first addressed them. "Your Highnesses, my name is Halbert. This is my wife, Halfryth."

A female dwarf emerged from the crowd and joined him.

She and her husband both held clear jars filled with some kind of thick liquid. Halfryth's was darker than her husband's. "'Allo!"

"Hello," Kalen said. "What's in the jars?"

"Sauce. For the meat."

Gregory rubbed his hands together.

"We need to know which you prefer," Halbert said. "Mine or my wife's."

Kalen put out his hands. "I'm sure they're both wonderful."

"Aye," Halfryth said. "But mine's *more* wonderful." She took an old wooden spoon from her pocket and dropped a glob from her jar onto the edge of Kalen's plate. Her husband hurried to do the same.

Kalen's siblings both motioned for him to get to tasting. He poked his fork into a small piece of beef and dipped it in the dark sauce Halfryth had spooned onto his plate.

"Really get it on there," she said.

Kalen ensured he had covered the meat then ate it. He nodded approvingly.

"Now mine," her husband said.

Kalen took another piece, dipped it into the lighter sauce, chewed it, and again nodded. "Mmm."

"Aha!" Halbert said.

Halfryth's face fell.

"No." Kalen put out his hands. "No, no. I cannot choose."

Halfryth brightened some. "You must."

"I cannot," Kalen said. "They both complemented the meat so well, in their own way."

"Please," Halbert urged him. "It's all right, just pick. Which did you prefer?"

Kalen shook his head. "I'm—"

"I will." Ri grabbed Kalen's plate, dunked a piece of beef from hers into Halfryth's sauce, and chewed. "It's thick, flavorful… it's good." She ate a piece with Halbert's. "Spicy… it's good too."

"See," Kalen said.

Halbert began, "M'lady—"

"Hers is better," Ri said. "Yours is *too* spicy… at least for me."

Halfryth beamed. "Haha!" She held up her jar. "I win!"

Halbert frowned. "I'll adjust the recipe. Try it again tomorrow?"

"Of course," Ri said.

"Thank you, m'lady." Halbert headed off after his jubilant wife.

"You shouldn't have done that," Kalen said to Ri.

"Why not?"

"We're here as friends. We're not here to pick favorites."

"It's a condiment!" Ri threw up her hands. "And I said I liked both."

"Even so," Kalen said.

"Who wants allies so averse to conflict, or to ruffling any feathers *at all*, that they won't even decide between sauces when their makers beg them to?"

Kalen got up. "I'm going to get more ale."

Ri called after him, "There are winners and losers in life, Kalen." She said to Gregory, "At least there ought to be."

"It's just not that kind of age," Gregory said. "Unfortunately for you."

"Well… I can pick another one here, at least." She stood. "I'm going to try some of the beer Governor Bardric brought." She raised her voice to add, "And if anyone asks, I'll be happy to share my opinion of it."

After the feast, out in the cold on her room's balcony, Ri held a cup of hot cocoalan in both hands. She sipped the dark, sweet drink made of ground beans imported all the way from the far south of the world—the warm, wet bottom of the White Forest.

Ri watched small fires flicker in the watchtowers on the snow-covered mountaintops surrounding the castle. In the starry night sky, she imagined dragons climbing over the peaks and swooping low into the valleys—reds, blues, and all the natural colors that had filled the skies of the first ages of Taulus, as well as the blacks and golds that had joined them in the Dark Wars.

In the foothills of the mountains, opposite the lines of Dark Elves and their corrupted creations, Ri pictured the Red Elf army in formation, radiant in their elegant, gold-accented armor, with bows and swords at the ready. The proud men from Abilin formed rows of shining steel chainmail, plate armor, and swords, with cavalry eager to charge. The sturdy dwarves came to the battle wearing steel that had been dimmed in color and wielding long, two-headed axes. Powerful gold dragons flapped their wings to hover over the allied forces.

Except that hadn't happened, not exactly, and not in Drimon. The dragons Ri pictured had filled the skies of Taulus, but not so far north. Dwarves only came into the world after the first Dark War and in the second played no large role, as the fighting had stayed to the south.

Back in reality, a dragon glided high above the mountain peaks. Maybe Galeron, without the saddle from their trip. Ri couldn't be certain in the darkness.

Two unexpected knocks came at her thick wooden door.

She went inside and opened the door halfway.

"Corina," a white-haired, long-bearded dwarf said.

She tilted her head down to him, trying to place the face. "Dunmore," he said.

"Dunmore." Ri smiled. "Of course." She opened the door wider. "How are you?"

"Well," he said. "I am well. It has been a long while—since you stood shorter than me. I came to see how all is with you."

"I am well. Come in, please."

She stepped aside and the dwarf—one who had kept her company when she visited Dritus as a young girl—entered.

"You've grown tall," he said. "And even more beautiful."

"Oh," Ri said. "I'm not *that* tall."

He chuckled. "How was the feast? Word is Bardric brought beer from Rone."

"The beer was fine." Ri shrugged. "He and the king had built expectations pretty high by the time I tried it."

"I see."

"Wonderful food though." She held her stomach. "And I ate too much of it."

"Good," Dunmore said.

"I was outside." Ri motioned toward the balcony with her cup. "Admiring the mountains."

"Hm. None near Prim," Dunmore remarked.

"Exactly." Ri headed out.

The dwarf followed.

Ri gazed out at the mountains. "I didn't realize how much I missed them—their majesty, their strength... how massive they are, even rising into a limitless sky." Ri sipped her warm drink.

"Do you remember the story of the first battle of Blackburg?" Dunmore asked.

"I do. I remember when *you* told me that story."

"I told it more than once," the dwarf said. "At your stubborn insistence to hear it over and over."

"I liked battles."

"And that was a big one."

"Do you think there'll ever be another like it?"

"I hope not," Dunmore said. "And no, I do not believe there will be. There are no more black dragons. The rest of the evil forces in the world are weak and confined to Deroc. There is no more aggressive magic, nor defensive..."

Ri's shoulders slouched.

"At least some men and elves can again heal," Dunmore said, referring to the emotes. "Do *you* think there will be another battle like Blackburg?"

"No," Ri said softly.

The same dragon glided by. In the darkness, it appeared black, and like the savage beasts of old—stronger than all the dragons that came before them and able to belch flame that melted granenite.

"Galeron," Dunmore said when fire on the mountain illuminated his wings and golden scales.

Mighty Galeron… the first of his color, devoted to protecting mankind, and the first to match the black dragons' power.

"He won," Ri said.

"We all won." Dunmore looked up at her. "Write your own story."

"Hm?"

"Make up a story. There won't be a war, but you could write one."

Ri considered it. "I'm not much of a writer."

"Start with a single battle."

"Oh…" She gently shook her head. "I don't think so."

"Write of brave knights. Write of handsome ones and the fair princesses they come to rescue."

Ri raised an eyebrow.

"And write of swords with names and bows that shoot arrows with purpose. Write of dragons laying waste to castles with their terrible fire."

Ri nodded. "That's more like it."

Galeron glided by the other way.

"Who knows?" Ri took a sip. "Maybe when I'm older."

"If you do," Dunmore said, "be sure to write well of the dwarves."

8

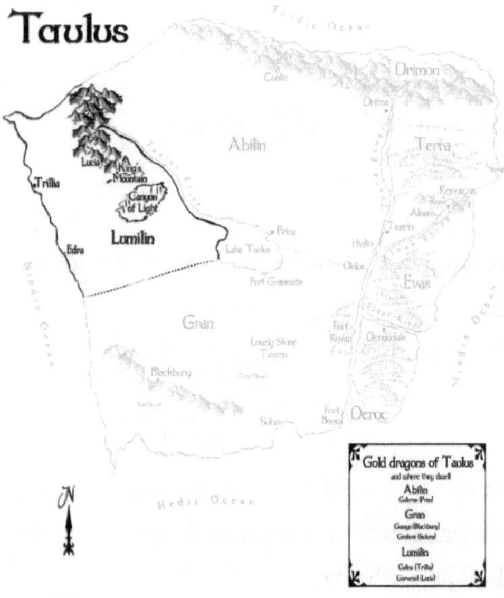

Lila placed a thin cloth marker in her book—a volume of a history of the elves, the events of which had taken place on the other side of the world. She closed the worn leather cover. A warm ocean breeze hit her tan skin softly. Sitting in lush grass, she rested her head against the old tree behind her and saw Trillia far down the hill, radiant in the low sun at the northern end of the Azure Cliffs.

Homes, shops, and administrative buildings concentrated near the ocean spilled to outside the high walls of the long, narrow capital of Lumilin. Silver and gold accented the white stone walls and most of the buildings inside. Ruby, sapphire, emerald, topaz—the decorative jewels glistened atop columns and roofs and would shimmer spectacularly in the coming night's firelight. The palatial dwellings situated atop the rolling hills in the city and overlooking the great ocean would be especially magnificent.

The wars of ages past against dragons and Dark Elves had left the cities and towns of Gran and Abilin burned, battered, and needing to be rebuilt. Lumilin, nestled in the northwest of Taulus, enjoyed a history free from such destruction. In fact, when the dwarves came to Taulus, Lumilin had razed its own cities of softer stone so they could be remade entirely of granenite. The riches of the mines within King's Mountain and the Canyon of Light, which lay within the kingdom's borders, funded the construction with ease.

Lila watched as two golds rose from behind the city walls. Gorvenal flapped his wings and headed for Lila, and the larger of the dragons, Gorvenal's mother, Galina, went south. Soon Gorvenal would be near enough to speak into her mind. He glided.

As an awkward, skinny, orphaned child, Lila had dreamed of someone standing up for her and protecting her from other kids. A little older, a little less skinny, and a lot less awkward, Lila didn't expect she would have trouble finding a knight to play the part. But Gorvenal had found her before any knight she cared to be found by had, and no knight—not even Sir Beal, the renowned champion of Lumilin—compared to her dragon.

Gorvenal landed.

No knight could fill Lila's days with such wonder. "Can we stay here?" she asked. "The sun will set over the city soon."

Of course. Gorvenal lay on the hillside.

Lila held her book in her lap. "How is your mother?"

Fine. She thinks I spend too much time with you.

Lila half smiled.

But she likes you. Gorvenal rested his head on the ground. *And she knows why I like you. Her eyes see the same beauty that mine do.*

Lila smiled fully at that and blushed. Galina saw the same Lila but did not see her in the same way. How truly lucky she had been to have been found by Gorvenal.

"Will you continue the story?" Lila asked.

Certainly. Gorvenal, who had seen Trillia countless times and had witnessed hundreds of years of suns setting into the Nindin Ocean, fixed his full attention on Lila. *After leaving the remote island Yalus, where Yalea, the first tan dragon, went in secret with the green dragon Taulin, eldest offspring of the first blue and green, she returned to Feinor, the red. Feinor didn't know where Yalea had been or that she carried Taulin's child.*

Lila closed her eyes.

When tan-colored Yalia was born, Yalea wept, wept with a joy that could only come after hundreds of years of giving birth to beloved dragon children who all lacked that one simple trait. And proud Feinor cried. A lifetime of subtle but constant disappointment gave way to overwhelming relief at having finally given Yalea the tan-colored baby she had always longed for.

Then…

Then… Lila wondered what she would have done.

… seeing the powerful dragon's pure happiness for her, Yalea could not hide the truth. She told Feinor that he had not fathered the baby. Rare tenderness drained from him, most say never to return. Feinor grew enraged. Though a dragon had never murdered another in Taulus, Feinor threatened to kill the baby Yalia and demanded to know the father's identity. Only after receiving assurances that he would not harm anyone, Yalea revealed that Taulin had fathered the tan child.

How different would Taulus have been, ages later, if Yalea had kept her secret?

Feinor spent days in the Red Desert with Yalea, fuming while she cared for her newborn daughter. Then, when the pair of tans went off in search of food, Feinor flew northeast over the mountains, out of the desert, and found Taulin in his lands on the southwestern shore of Lake Taulus. The green dragon argued that he had acted at Yalea's behest and that he had nothing but respect for Feinor, but the conversation was short, and the fight barely longer. Feinor tore Taulin apart, left his lifeless body to rot, and returned to his red desert.

One of Taulin's sisters spotted Feinor flying from Taulin's lands then found her brother's mangled carcass. Taulin's parents, blue Railyn and green Grawlth, flew south with most of their kin—a rainbow of scales—to confront Feinor and to learn why he had committed murder when none had done so ever before. They intended to demand justice.

Not surprisingly, Feinor and Yalea's offspring noticed the host flying south. They got word to Feinor and gathered their ranks. Reds dominated their side. The confrontation between the families took place north of the Red Desert, near the grasslands of the long-disputed border currently separating Gran and Lumilin.

As she did every time she heard the story, Lila wondered whether the battle been inevitable. If not for Yalea, would something else have sparked it eventually?

"Yalea was mine!" Feinor shouted as the full spectrum of dragons approached each other in the evening sky.

"I went to him!" Yalea called, racing ahead of her kin, little Yalia struggling to keep close to her mother. "So that I might see another tan before my days in this world had come to an end."

Feinor growled and sent a burst of fire at Railyn.

The blue dodged it with ease.

Yalia flew under Yalea's wing, and her mother clutched her close.

"If you were wronged, Feinor," Grawlth, the green, called, "blame Yalea, not our son."

"You must be punished for what you did to Taulin," Railyn said.

"Never," Feinor said. The two lines of dragons inched nearer. "YOU and your contemptible family will ALL be punished!"

Grawlth shot fire skyward. The lines halted.

"You have murdered, Feinor. You must be punished—but not with your life," Grawlth said. "One lost life—our son's life—is enough. He can live on in his daughter. That would satisfy me."

"And land," Railyn said. "You must give up some land. I will hate it, in place of our lost son, but I will settle for a tract in the north of your desert. We will keep it for Yalia for a time, then it will become hers when she is older."

"Yes," Yalea urged. "Please, Feinor. Take this good and fair offer."

"No land!" Feinor screamed to her. "YOUR daughter can find her own." He called to Grawlth, "And one life gives ME no satisfaction." He asked Railyn, "Do you think you are stronger than me?"

She leaned forward. "I know I am."

Feinor glanced at Yalea, then leaving the sea of red at his back, he darted at Railyn. The big blue came at him with all her speed, and the two dragons twisted to avoid each other's scalding fire as they drove their shoulders into each other's hard scales.

Grawlth raced toward them, but Feinor's eldest son cut him off.

Like massive waves colliding in a rainbow ocean, the lines of dragons met, feeding on the rage of the eldest in their ranks. While some fought reluctantly, most found themselves eager to act upon years of frustration built up while avoiding serious conflict. As the sun set on a more crowded sky than Taulus had ever known, every dragon punched and grappled, whipped their tails, and belched their awesome fire in combat.

Every dragon except Yalea and her daughter, who remained within sight of Feinor and Railyn's struggle.

And a great struggle it was. Other contests spanned miles of clear night sky, with combatants racing to and fro to gain an edge or to make space for planned attacks. Alliances formed, especially as the night wore on and the wounded and dead fell to the earth. But Railyn and Feinor sought no such space or company. Covered in each other's bright red blood, the pair grappled and punched and, when surprised to find themselves separated, dove into one another hard, biting and lashing out with their claws.

Railyn bit Feinor's red wing and tore a huge hole in it. Falling, Feinor sank his talon into the center of one of the blue's eyes. She shoved him and kicked him away.

Yalea, seeing Feinor struggle to stay airborne with his torn wing, left Yalia and helped Feinor control his decent. With blood pouring from Railyn's face and the sight lost in her eye, the blue darted toward them, drove the pair downward, and crashed with them to the ground.

Railyn chomped into Yalea's neck near her head. "YOU brought this on my son!" Railyn ripped her teeth away and blood poured from the tan.

Feinor roared and fire shot from him, scorching Railyn's side.

Railyn whimpered and jumped into the air, but Feinor caught her shoulder and slammed her back to the ground. He torched her neck and face and held her in the flame until nothing—no scales, blood, or bone—remained of her head except ash, and her body ceased moving.

Blood gushed from Yalea's neck as she lay alongside the blue who had bitten her so deeply. Yalia flew down to her mother.

"Keep her safe, Feinor," Yalea said.

"Yalea…" He nuzzled his mate.

She strained, trying to return the gesture. "Whatever happens, keep her safe." Her breathing stopped, and Taulus's first tan dragon was gone.

Feinor sent such a roar and stream of fire skyward that the nearby battles paused. Young Yalia jumped and flew backward.

Grawlth descended toward Feinor but remained in the air beyond his reach. "Enough death, Feinor."

"No!" Feinor roared and leapt.

Grawlth rose higher while Feinor struggled to land gently with his injured wing.

"Enough!" the green repeated. "Fight me, and you might prevail." He flew higher and cut a circle in the air to demonstrate his relative health. "Or you might not. And this battle, if it continues, may well take Yalia's life."

"How dare YOU threaten ME."

"Look at Yalia," Grawlth urged. "Look at her!"

Feinor's eyes settled on the young dragon.

Grawlth continued, "Killing me will not bring Yalea back to you. But without her last child, there will never be another tan dragon in Taulus."

Feinor growled.

"My firstborn is dead," Grawlth said. "And Railyn is dead. Care for the young one, and let the vengeance you have taken be enough."

Yalia landed beside Feinor and craned her neck up to the massive red.

Feinor snarled at Grawlth. "We shall see if it is enough." He turned his back to the green, and with Yalia, Feinor began the long walk south.

The other raging battles ended in short order, most indecisively.

Feinor returned to the Red Desert, and though his wing healed, he never left his land again. They say it is his scorching fire—born either from fury at what Yalea did, or anguish over how Railyn killed her, or both—that turns the sky above the mountains separating Taulus's deserts red with each day's setting sun. That is why they are sometimes called Feinor's Mountains of Fire.

After the first great battle between dragons, smaller conflicts—often over land and mates—became common, to the ultimate peril of one of the two combatants. Eventually the battles escalated until the Dragon Wars engulfed all of early Taulus.

Yalia, however, lived a peaceful life. When she had grown up, she moved northeast, and one of her uncles gave her a stretch of land near what would later become Conlin, in Abilin. There she—

"Had a lot of tan babies," Lila finished. She opened her eyes to see that night had fallen. "And it's a good thing, for your sake."

It is, Gorvenal said.

Lila had missed sunset, but brilliant Trillia, with fires set for light, warmth, and to brighten the jewels in the city, lit her horizon instead.

9

Taulus

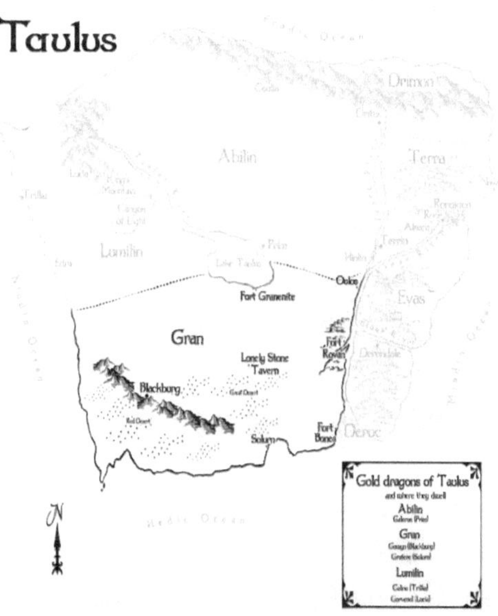

Gall, Avery, and Avril had been riding hard all morning, west toward Blackburg, Gran's capital city. Hours into the first day of their long journey, the tall grass of the plains became patched with tan, rocky dirt. Clumps of puffy clouds dotted the sky.

The position of the sun confirmed what Gall's growling stomach told him—lunchtime. He wiped his brow and swallowed. With the Great Desert in their path, it would grow significantly hotter and dryer, but he was already very thirsty. The stubble on his cheeks and neck was growing steadily toward a proper beard and that didn't help the heat, but he wouldn't shave yet. He surveyed the area and deemed it as good a spot as any nearby. "Avery," he called. "Stop."

Avery and his sister pulled up and circled back to him.

"Lunch." Gall reached into the sack on his horse for a bottle of whisky. He popped the top off, brought it to his lips, and when the twins shot him equally worried looks, decided to take a longer first drink of the day than planned. "Ahh."

"You were a knight?" Avery asked.

Gall dismounted. "Still am, actually." He twisted himself side to side to stretch his back. "Just not part of any kingdom's army."

"No shield?" Avery noted the absence amongst Gall's things.

"In my current line of work," Gall said, "speed is more valuable."

"You're after a thief in Blackburg who stole from an elf," Avery said.

"How'd you know?" Gall twisted in the other direction.

"Madine told us when you were in jail." Avery dismounted.

Avril didn't. "You like girls like her?"

"Very much," Gall said. "Not that I confine myself to one particular type."

"Why aren't you a regular knight anymore?" Avril asked.

"Wasn't for me."

"Which part?" Avril backed her horse away.

Gall quit stretching. "Smart. You hardly know me. But know that you are safe with me. You are too young, and besides, I only enjoy the… close company of women who are eager to enjoy mine." Gall took dried beef and a piece of bread from another sack.

Avril got off her horse with her own bread, sat with her brother, and gave him the bigger half. Avery gave Avril a bit of dried meat.

"Why are you after the thief?" Avery asked.

Gall joined the twins on the ground. "Because the elf he stole from wants his property back, ideally, and the thief caught, whether he still has the property or not. And the elf who hired me will pay me very well."

"Red or White Elf?" Avril asked.

"What did he steal?" Avery asked.

Gall pointed a finger at him. "Have you ever seen an elf?" He aimed at his sister. "Either of you?"

"Yes," they both said.

"A few times in the tavern," Avery added. "We sat with a half-elf the night we saw you there."

"Hm." Gall bit his bread and chewed loudly. "Hmm." He washed it down with water from his canteen. "Red Elf. Don't deal with the Whites much." He washed that down with whisky. "And the thief stole a sword and a shield from my employer."

Avery stopped short of a bite.

"A special sword and shield," Gall went on. "Perfectly balanced. Made to cut dragon scales and block their fire. In the right hands, impossibly light."

"What do you mean, 'in the right hands'?" Avril asked.

"They were not meant to be wielded by just anyone."

"They're magic?" Avery asked.

Gall shrugged. "The dwarves forged them long ago for a knight general of Gran, in the heat of the fiery breath of Galeron and his mate."

"Wow," Avery said.

"When the knight died, the sword, Rihtalt, and the shield, Rihtva, passed to his son. The son moved to Lumilin, and *his* son had no interest in combat or knighthood, so after his father died, he sold them to my employer, who collects that kind of thing."

"And you know who the thief was?" Avril asked.

"Yup," Gall said. "Another elf. Unusual but not unprecedented. He wants to sell them to a lord in Gran, but they're all balking at his price, so the thief wrote my employer and is trying to ransom them to him, or start a bidding war between the parties."

"You'll buy them?" Avery asked.

"No. My employer sent me as his negotiator, but the only thing I might negotiate is what I do to the elf once I've taken the sword and shield from him."

The twins ate their food.

"Why didn't either of you fight back there?" Gall asked.

They didn't answer.

"Hm? Not a thing to say for yourselves?"

"I don't fight," Avril said. "I mean, I tried to get free from the guard, but that's it. I won't set out to fight."

"You should," Gall said. "Girl or not, you really—"

"That's not it," she said. "It just isn't in me."

"How do you know? Have you tried? Ever practiced with a knife? Ever shot an arrow?"

"I couldn't hurt anyone," Avril said. "I watched what my father did to my mother and others, and I couldn't hurt him. *That* is how I know."

"Hm." Gall looked at her brother. "Avery? You aren't shy. You yelled at the guard, you set me up in the tavern. *You* didn't want to fight your father?"

Avery made eye contact with Gall.

"You couldn't hurt him either?" Gall asked.

"That's not it," Avery said.

"Are you scared?"

Avery turned away.

"No? You're a young man. Do you know how to use a sword?"

Avery looked back at Gall.

"I can teach you," Gall said.

Avery stood. "Let's go."

Avril went to her horse, and when she and her brother had both mounted theirs, and Gall had been sitting alone with his whisky for another couple sips, he huffed, got on his saddle, and caught up with the twins when they resumed their ride.

———————

The following afternoon, Gall spotted a small cloud of dust in the distance, in the otherwise still air of the hot desert.

Avery turned on his saddle back to Gall, who was watching the growing cloud, drinking whisky. Distinct figures on horseback emerged from the dust.

Gall took his bottle from his lips. "Three of 'em."

Avery and Avril halted, so Gall did too.

"Who are they?" Avery asked. "What do we do?"

"Well…" Gall hit his fist to his chest as he burped. "Y'already stopped."

"Should I not have?" Avery asked.

"Doesn't matter. They're thieves, and three's no problem. I've fought off many more than that."

"Drunk?" Avery asked.

Gall waved away the question. "Meh."

In the approaching cloud of kicked-up dirt, one of the riders behind the leader had a beard fuller than Gall's, the other a big mustache. The thinnest, the leader, had neared enough that Gall could see him smiling. One of the two in the rear held a sword, the other a bow and arrow. The leader wore a knife near his belt and had a sheathed sword and bow on the side of his horse.

"Thank you," the rider in front called as he slowed, "for not running away."

"Wouldn't dream of it," Gall said.

The one with the mustache went one way and the bearded the other way so that Gall and the twins were surrounded.

The leader relaxed in his saddle. "Headed to Blackburg?"

Avery looked at Gall but got no reaction.

"Hm?" The rider turned to Avery. "You, boy, speak."

"Yes," Avery said.

Gall finished a drink. "Shouldn't have told him."

"No?" The rider gestured to Avery. "The boy is smart to tell us."

"He's smart," Gall said. "But he has a lot to learn."

"Oh?" The thief raised an eyebrow. "Like what?"

"Nothing to be gained by telling you anything."

"And *you* will teach him this?"

Gall burped again. "Just did."

The thief squinted at Avery then shifted to Avril. "Not your children, I don't think."

"No," Gall said.

"What's your name?"

Gall flashed a toothy grin. Avril sat stone-faced. Avery kept his mouth shut.

"Well, sir," the thief said, "despite appearances to the contrary, you also seem to be smart. I hope that means you will empty your purse for us and instruct your... companions to do the same, without delay."

"In a hurry?" Gall glanced toward the sky. "Worried about someone?"

The thief chuckled. "Gowyn is not nearby. Nor Grafere." He shrugged. "But you never know."

"Right." Gall wagged his finger. "Ya never know."

"Your money then," the lead thief said. "You may keep your weapons. We have no need for them."

"You are *too* kind," Gall said.

The thief put out his hands. "Well..."

"But no," Gall said. "You get no more than the

information my young friend has already given you and our time that you are wasting."

The thief frowned. "I see." He shifted in his saddle.

Gall noticed the silver chain necklace under the leader's crisp shirt collar. "Not a common thief, I don't think."

"I'm common enough around here. A long list of travelers parting my company with lighter loads would attest to that."

"Not ordinary then." Gall sized up the other two. "Them maybe, but not you."

The leader put a finger to his lips and gave a slow nod. "Hm."

"What do you mean?" Avery asked.

The thief walked his horse to the boy's. Avery leaned away.

The thief brought up his hand. "Don't worry." He pulled his necklace out from under his shirt and, in his palm, showed the two sharp, narrow triangles hanging from it.

Avery leaned forward to see.

"A Thorn." Gall inched toward the leader. "A master thief. A thorn in the honest"—he pointed at the thief with his bottle—"upstanding society of Taulus."

The thief drew his knife. Avery leaned back again, and Gall halted his approach.

"I like you." The thief tapped his knife on his saddle. "But we *will* have your money now."

"I don't like you," Gall said. "And you will not."

"I do not enjoy fighting. Or even ordering my men to do so. I steal, and I love that—but if you make us, we will take what have come for by force."

"I *do* like to fight," Gall said. "Which is why you should let us be on our way."

The bearded rider huffed.

The one with the mustache flicked his fingernail against his sword. "Drunken bum."

The leader pointed at Avery. "Can *he* fight?"

"Dunno," Gall said. "Never seen him try."

The thief shook his head. "I just do not believe we have a choice."

"We do," Gall said. "Let me beat you at something else."

"Hm? What did you have in mind?"

"Anything. Pick a game. You said you don't enjoy fighting."

"Well…"

"I'm… not sober." Gall scanned the nearby ground. "And I bet I can still throw a rock farther than you." Gall looked behind him. "Any of you."

The leader nodded. "I bet you could."

"I could throw it *twice* as far," Gall said.

"I do not think so." The thief swung a leg over his saddle and dismounted.

Gall jumped to the ground and stumbled but held his liquor bottle high and safe. "If I win, you let us pass."

"No." The thief put away his knife. "But I want to play anyway."

Gall pointed at him. "You first then."

The thief found a rock that fit well in his palm then walked around, stopping to pick up a few more until he had one that satisfied him. He went to Gall and held out two similarly sized stones.

Gall paused in the middle of taking a drink. "Don't matter."

The thief gave Gall the one in his left hand then swung his arm in a wide arc, loosening his shoulder. "Twice as far?"

"Uh huh." Gall switched his rock to his right hand.

The thief crouched then got up and stretched his torso side to side. "Rufus." He pointed at his mustached companion. "Go see where this lands."

Rufus put away his sword and rode out into the desert.

"Whadda I get when I win?" Gall asked.

"The respect of Jaran of Solurn," the thief said. "And if you lose, you tell me your name."

"Oh… very well," Gall said.

Rufus stopped a ways away.

Jaran assumed a ready stance. He stepped forward, built his momentum, brought his arm back, and three steps later, launched his rock into the air. The stone shrunk as it flew straight away from them. Rufus followed it. The rock became tiny, slowed, and fell. Rufus rode to it.

Jaran wiped his hands together. "Not bad, I don't think."

"Eh." Gall took two steps, brought his arm back, and on his third step launched his rock high into the air. The stone soared out toward the waiting thief, high above him, becoming a speck in the blue sky.

Avril gasped. Avery grinned.

Rufus watched the rock sail overhead, tracked it as it kept sailing, then when it finally slowed, descended, and fell to the ground, he rode to the group and reported, "He wins."

"Indeed," Jaran said. "Indeed." He walked to his horse

and pulled a bow and arrow off its backside. "Beat me at this, and you may go."

"What?" the bearded thief called out.

Rufus said, "Let's—"

A raised hand from their leader cut him off. "I do not wish to fight this man."

"But—"

"I will *not* fight him," Jaran said. "However, I do not figure him for an archer, and I would like another chance at besting him."

"What's the game?" Gall asked.

"Give him your bow and an arrow," the thief said to Rufus.

Rufus rode over, pulled his bow off his horse, and gave it to Gall. Rufus grabbed an arrow from his quiver, and Gall extended his hand for it. Rufus looked at the leader.

"Give it to him," Jaran said, and Rufus held it out.

Gall took it. "That is a very fancy mustache."

Rufus drew his sword.

"Ride," Jaran said. "Go set your drinking cup out on the ground."

Rufus glared at Gall and sheathed his sword. "How far?"

"Far." Jaran motioned him away.

Rufus rode into the desert and took out a worn pewter cup.

Gall set down his whisky then pulled the string of his bow twice to gauge its tension. He nocked the arrow he had been given then let it slip off the string. "Whoever's closer?"

"Indeed," Jaran said.

Rufus spun and called to them, "Here?"

"Farther," Jaran called, and Rufus rode on. Jaran asked Gall, "You shoot often?"

Gall grabbed his bottle. "S'been years."

"Here?" Rufus yelled.

Jaran glanced at Gall in the middle of a long drink. "Farther." He waved Rufus on. "Much farther."

Rufus galloped away from them.

"Ahh." Gall wiped his mouth and put down his bottle.

Rufus glanced back but kept going.

"All right!" Jaran yelled. "Set it down!"

"What?" Rufus yelled.

"Down!"

"What?" He cupped his hand to his ear.

Jaran pointed at the sandy ground. "Down!"

Rufus hopped off his saddle and placed the little cup on the ground.

Avery and Avril squinted and leaned forward to see it among the rocks and low plants.

Gall nocked his arrow, pulled it back, and aimed at the target.

"It's where the arrow stops after it skids on the sand." Jaran turned to Gall. "Would you—"

Gall loosed his arrow, nodded, and then, while Jaran, his bearded companion, and the twins watched its low arc, threw his bow to the bearded rider and picked up his bottle of whisky. "Let's go."

Clang! The arrow smashed into the side of the cup. Rufus jumped back.

"But—" the bearded thief said.

"No," Jaran said. "It's enough. He wins."

"But—"

Jaran raised his hand. "We will find someone else to rob."

Gall mounted his horse and motioned for the twins to lead the way. They did, and Gall trailed after them, a smile on his face.

When the thieves disappeared into the dust in the distance, Avery called to Gall, "Why two thorns on his necklace?"

"Rank." Gall hiccupped. "For skill, not seniority. One, two, or three thorns. Three's the highest… ain't many of those." Gall paused with his bottle just short of his lips. "And then there's their leader, in Conlin—the *only* one with four. Happens to be old, but if all they say about him is true…" He hiccupped again. "Or even half, he's earned his four."

"Are most of them in Conlin?"

"Some," Gall said. "There and Solurn in the south. No shortage in Blackburg. They're all over, and they've been around forever." Gall wiped his mouth with his arm. "They stay hidden, that's their game, but… s'plenty for them to steal *everywhere*."

10

Taulus

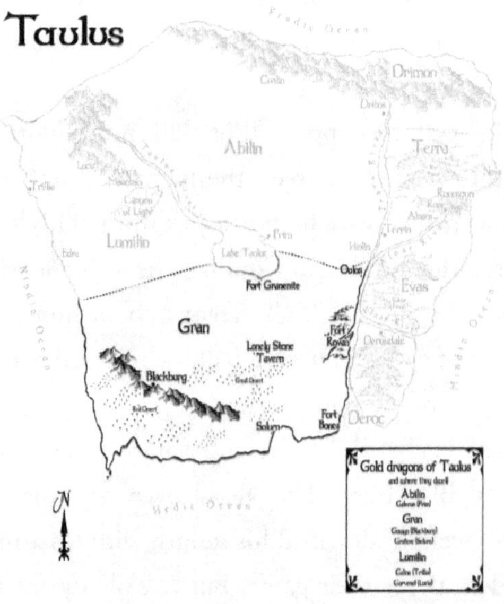

Golden Gowyn could have flown some of the company from Fort Granenite over the plains to the southeast. Rsyc, the red dragon, or Jala, the orange, would also have come had Valencia asked. Any one of the dragons could certainly have dealt with the situation themselves, Taylan had no doubt.

Instead, he, Valencia, the emote Shaela, and a dozen knights from Granenite—eight men and four women—rode on horseback. Investigating trouble caused by a few ogres was a far from glamorous mission, but it was also far more than no mission at all, and Valencia had decided her knights could use the experience. Plus, one dragon couldn't carry them all, and enlisting multiple had seemed like overkill to her. So they rode, the knights wearing their plate-and-mail armor through peaceful Gran for practice.

With luck, Shaela's healing abilities would not be needed, but Taylan figured the mission would be good experience for her as well. And the knights would need to practice ensuring Shaela's well-being. Like all emotes, she could not heal herself if wounded, whether in battle or otherwise; her power could be directed only at others.

Shaela cared for the pair of white homing pigeons that traveled with them. The birds had been trained to fly back to the fort if needed, carrying a message calling for reinforcements or to get word to Gowyn. He spent much of his time near Blackburg, and from the fort, another bird could be dispatched to reach him there. The pigeons were standard procedure, but Taylan couldn't imagine they'd be needed on the mission.

A day away from the first of the farms that had reported ogres on their land, they stopped for water at a brook.

Taylan's head throbbed. He had spent the night before with Valencia in her tent, and his head hadn't hurt then. They had hardly talked. She hadn't offered much, and Taylan hadn't known what to say, despite desperately wanting to say something—something of substance, something about *them*. But no such words passed his lips because of his fear that he would ruin his precious few moments so close to the woman he had so often longed for from afar.

Early the day before, an aching stomach had been his dominant ailment, and it had made the jostling of riding extremely uncomfortable. But at present, his head tormented him. He sipped his water, tried to think of things to say to Valencia, and wished for nightfall, for the sun to cease beating on his brow. Cooler air would calm his throbbing head, Taylan assured himself. And the nightmares that might otherwise come later—the torturous replays of his past, of what he had lashed out and done—being with Valencia would keep those at bay.

Valencia knelt and filled her leather canteen. She noticed Taylan noticing her and flashed him a smile. She was the key. She was his answer, Taylan told himself. He would hold her, he would kiss her soft lips. *Oh, nightfall…* the powerful woman would lie on his chest, and he would run his fingers through her blond hair. She couldn't cure his pain in one night, but for the night, she would quiet it to a whisper.

A young knight called Spear approached them and asked Valencia, "Why would they have come up north? It's been years, decades, since any of us remember ogres this far north."

"I don't know," she said. "The boundaries set for them in the treaty are quite clear."

Hayle, Valencia's chief lieutenant, came over. "There should never have been a Treaty of Solurn, if you ask me."

"No?" Valencia asked.

"We shouldn't have stopped with the black dragons. We

should have wiped out the ogres, the trolls, and all the creatures the Dark Elves corrupted."

"And the elves along with 'em." Spear shot Taylan a look. "The *dark* ones."

"My elven father was not kind," Taylan said. "At least not to me. But he was not a Dark Elf."

"Good," Hayle said. "There is no place for that kind of evil in Taulus. Be rid of it all, I say."

"Well, the magic they used is gone," Valencia said. "And so are those dragons. We should all be thankful for that." She hooked her canteen to her horse. "As for the rest, it is not up to us. We are knights. Were we knights back then, it would not have been up to us either. We uphold the Treaty of Solurn, as the king commands."

Spear nodded.

"Without question," Hayle said.

Valencia mounted her horse, Taylan and the others returned to theirs, and they resumed their journey southeast.

———————

Early the next afternoon, a farmer emerged from his small brown-stone home. Valencia and Taylan rode out from the company to meet him and his wife and children, who followed just behind.

Valencia called to the farmer, "You've seen ogres here?"

He threw his arms in the air. "Killed my best cow!"

"How many did you see?"

"I ain't seen 'em," the farmer said. "One mornin' she wasn't eatin' with the rest. He found her." He pointed at his son. "Hole in her side. Took a bite right out of her. The rest left to rot." He pointed at Valencia. "Ain't no man or natural beast do that."

"Did it leave tracks?"

"Aye," the farmer said. "But you ain't need 'em. Reed's farm to the east and Paul's—they've seen 'em. Causin' them trouble like me."

"We'll find the creatures."

"Damn thing's here *one time*"—the farmer raised a finger—"and got my best cow."

"They won't be back," Valencia said. "We'll see to that."

"Two or three, I think. More than one for sure," Paul said to Taylan and Valencia, echoing the assessment of Reed, the second farmer they had visited. They sat at a long wooden table inside Paul's home. "They steal my crops. Poach my livestock. I'm glad you're here."

"They come at night?" Valencia asked.

"Yes."

"Every night?" Taylan asked.

"No, but most. I followed one, one night, for as long as I dared—for as long as I could stay hidden. Wound up near the river, in the woods near the old fort ruins." He shrugged. "Smart place for them to hide, actually."

"Yes," Valencia said. "We'll check there first."

Outside, standing beside her horse, Valencia explained the situation to her knights.

"We should have rebuilt and manned that fort," Hayle

said. "Or have *some* outpost nearer to here."

"It's been decades since we've had ogres on our land," Valencia said. "You said it yourself."

Hayle glanced at the sun sliding low on the horizon. "Camp here, see if they come? Or else head to the ruins tomorrow?"

Valencia looked over her company. "Twelve knights. Taylan, Shaela… They'd be crazy to fight us."

"They're ogres. They *are* crazy," Hayle said. "And they see better in the dark."

"What say you?" Valencia called to the group.

"Go," a few answered.

"Aye, let's go," said another.

"Kill 'em now, and be done with it," someone else said.

"All right." Their commander mounted her horse. "Let's go."

They started off, and Shaela rode alongside Taylan. "Do you think the ogres will fight?"

"I hope not." Taylan imagined the battle, and the ache in his side returned, thrumming in rhythm with the trotting animal beneath him. "But who knows? They're ogres."

After night had fallen, near where the Rovan branched from the Tearn River, in the woods where the elves' White Forest spilled west into Gran's lands, Taylan lay on his stomach on the dirt in a gully, watching two ogres. The eight-foot-tall brownish-green humanoids sat on long logs outside the entrance to abandoned Fort Rovan, hunched over a wide fire, waiting for their stolen beef to cook. Valencia lay next to Taylan and kept her head low, as he did. Four of her knights crouched beside her. Hayle had led a second group of knights, with Shaela among them, around to the other side of the ogres' fire. Another group covered their backs in the woods.

Spear, who held a spear, whispered to Valencia over the constant chirr of the forest insects. "Big mace."

"Iron head," she said. The ogre's weapon reflected firelight in the darkness.

Taylan couldn't see a weapon within reach of the far ogre, but one might have been hidden by its seat. Massive arms and chests along with muscular but smaller legs gave the ogres their characteristic shape. One's face stretched wider than the other's, and both faces slanted from recessed heads out to pointy chins. They wore brown, tattered pants, and one's chest was bare. The other's was crisscrossed with suspenders.

While not scholarly by any stretch, ogres had more going on upstairs than the notoriously dim-witted trolls and fought much more fiercely. Those sitting at the fire had never been human, but their ancestors—the first ogres—had been. The first trolls had been too. Taylan recalled his research on the Dark Elves of the southeast, what they had done, and why.

Whether from the kingdom of Abilin, Gran, or Lumilin, a man or woman of Taulus might live eighty years or a hundred. A dwarf could live two hundred fifty. The natural dragons all had five hundred years to fly the skies of Taulus and settle among its most magnificent nooks, peaks, and plains. Their golden and black relatives lived longer. And blessed with a thousand years to make their mark on Taulus, the elves lived longest of all, though Taylan did not think he would see a hundred fifty years, so human was he.

But the pure elves, over their long lives, seemed unable to avoid acquiring a great deal of experience and knowledge. Most lived lives of balance—including education in either the arts or the ways of war, or both. But some elves, like some men, spent their years wholly focused on the study of different emotions and the magic that could be channeled from them. A thousand years allowed for a lot of learning, and the ranks of the strongest healing emotes in Taulus were filled mostly with elves.

At their fire, an ogre rubbed his hands together, and the other licked his lips.

Ages ago, when men and elves, in addition to healing magic, could also channel defensive and aggressive magic, some elves became devastatingly powerful emotes, capable of causing vast destruction and death. Fueled by their anger, rage, or lust to rule others, such elves had, from time to time, tried to overthrow their kings, or attacked the human kingdoms to their west. Legendary emotes like Kysa, Rayce, and Thain had been bent on such conquest. Upon those elves Taylan focused most of his research.

An ogre rotated their meat to expose the other side to the fire. He said something to his companion that Taylan couldn't make out.

Other emotes, armed with defensive magic born from

their compassion, commitment to righteousness, and love for those dear to them, had opposed and matched the aggressors. Attacks against mankind's kingdoms left a great many men and women, including occasional kings and queens, dead; castles destroyed; and the very earth changed in their wake, yet always the aggressors were ultimately defeated. When the script had played out the same way enough times, a group of elves took a different approach.

After their schism, the elves who remained north of the Alnar river became known as the Red Elves. Those who moved south became the White Elves. No different in physical appearance or origin from those from whom they separated, they nevertheless held a distinct opinion of their standing in the world and, in the case of many, a distinct temperament. The White Elves, whose kingdom would eventually be named Evas, claimed the forest from the Alnar to the southern shore of Taulus as their own, and the Red Elves did not dispute the claim. Very soon after, a small group of White Elves, including most of their oldest, most powerful emotes, continued their journey and settled in the swamps near the Hedic Ocean at Taulus's southern shore. Stories say that even before what happened between King Elric and Queen Evelyn and led to the elf schism, those disdainful emotes already considered themselves superior to the men to the west. The royal affair turned that notion into unwavering contempt in the Dark Elves of Deroc.

Nevertheless, the elves hadn't moved to the swamps to rush into an attack on mankind in the name of that contempt. They settled those secluded lands to experiment, to push the limits of their magic, and to build an army for a war unlike any Taulus had ever seen.

"Ogress!" called a knight in the woods behind Taylan.

The female ogre's swinging club cracked the side of the smaller knight's head, and his skull exploded in a bloody, chunky mess.

The ogres at the fire stood, and the ogress behind Taylan charged. Hayle's knights and the others charged the fire.

Valencia and the four with her yelled as they attacked the roaring ogress. Taylan turned and watched from the gully.

The ogress dodged Spear's spear, took a crossbow bolt to her shoulder, then smashed her club first into Spear's chest and then low on his leg. He crumpled to the ground. Behind Taylan at the fire, amidst the yells and roars, blades clanged and blunt weapons smacked. In front of him, Valencia slashed open the ogress's wounded shoulder, which bled and hung lazily.

The creature swung her body toward Valencia, the ogress's limp arm whipping into her, driving her away, while the beast's club knocked another knight out cold. Two remained fighting the ogress.

Taylan stepped forward. His heart pounded. His mind raced. He focused on the ogress, and a swirling ache filled his stomach.

The ogress took a stab to her side. Driving the blade in farther, she smashed her head down through the collarbone of the knight who had wounded her. She bashed him with her club.

With a sword still stuck in her, the ogress seethed at the

last knight standing before her.

Away from the pair, Valencia lay on the ground, trying to collect herself.

The ogress was large, Taylan thought. His forehead throbbed as if lightning sparked in his temples. But not *too* large, he told himself... he *assured* himself. He walked toward the creature and stared at her, and the combat in front and behind him quieted.

The ogress swung her club at the knight—who ducked it.

An image—charred corpses—shot to Taylan's mind. He stopped walking. The memory of four burnt, lifeless boys in the dirty alley behind the tavern hit Taylan hard. Sounds of the commotion of the battle rose. But those boys had deserved it!

The ogress swung and missed the knight again.

No, the punishment hadn't fit the crime.

Or had it?

He watched Valencia the knight struggle to her feet and remembered Valencia the vibrant young woman, as she had been on that day years ago. He could hear the crass boys bothering her—the lewd things they said because she sat with a half-elf. They refused to leave her alone when she asked them to, so Taylan had accepted their invitation to settle it outside. They would have followed if he and Valencia had left the tavern, he had told himself—he still told himself.

It wasn't his fault his father had been an elf!

He had just wanted to talk to Valencia... to be with

her… to see her smile and hear her laugh.

But they wouldn't let him. They wouldn't allow him those brief moments of joy in his miserable life. And they had died because of it.

Maybe the punishment had been exactly right.

Valencia, the grown-up commander of Gran, ambled into an attacking run.

The ogress parried the other knight's strike with her club then spun and swung at Valencia.

She halted short of the club and lunged to slash across the ogress's thigh.

The creature roared and fell.

Valencia swung at her neck on the way down, cut clean through it, and watched her ugly head slide off her green body. Valencia leaned on her sword for support.

Taylan's images of the burned bodies at the tavern receded to the corner of his mind. "You all right?"

"Yeah." Valencia took a deep breath and stood straight. "I'm fine."

At the fire, Hayle pulled his sword out of an ogre lying on the ground. The other lay unmoving beside it.

Valencia helped Spear, with his smashed leg, up onto his good foot.

"Can't ask them why they were here," Taylan remarked, walking to her, while his churning stomach calmed.

"No." Valencia passed Spear to Taylan. "Get him to Shaela."

"Easy…" Taylan brought taller Spear's arm over his shoulder. "Here ya go."

"I'm all right." Spear winced. "Take care of the others first."

"Fine." Taylan strained to help him limp to the group gathering at the fire. "But we still need to get you there."

A knight lay on the ground with his eyes shut and his head propped on the log where an ogre had sat.

"Firth," Spear said, reminding Taylan of the knight's name.

Taylan got closer and saw the pool of blood where it had run out from beneath Firth's smashed, reddened chainmail. The other knights watched as Firth's chest rose and fell very slightly with slow breaths. Taylan judged him to be moments from the end, and for a knight of Gran, that meant moments from a real and true end. Most of them believed they had their life on Taulus to make of it what they could, and nothing came after. Taylan helped Spear sit down among his companions, and as Firth quietly bled before him, such finality sounded so peaceful to Taylan.

Shaela's white robes and ever-warm face glowed in the firelight as she approached. She knelt beside Firth and held his hand. Shaela placed her other hand on his side and closed her eyes. Her smile yielded to a resolve Taylan had never seen in that particular emote.

Firth's eyes cracked open.

Shaela leaned lower and focused further.

Firth blinked and blinked wider. He breathed deeply.

Shaela leaned up, and seeing his progress, she smiled fully.

Firth breathed easily.

Knights murmured. A few smiled wide.

"You'll be all right," Shaela said.

Firth lifted his head and brought his hand to his healed side. "Thank you."

Shaela nodded and stood. "Who else is suffering?"

"Wilda." A knight pointed. "Over here."

The emote headed that way.

Valencia and another knight reached Taylan, carrying one of their slain companions.

"Shame she cannot help him," Valencia said.

"Aye," the knight beside her said.

Two of the twelve knights, Danon and Hollis, lay dead, beyond the reach of any emote. The rest Taylan watched Shaela manage to heal significantly, if not completely. She had begun with the worst off because with each, she grew wearier. The compassion and love that Shaela drew upon ran deep, but as with any emote's, it had its limits. By the time she reached the last injured knight, she had strength enough only to improve a shattered wrist to the point of a very bad sprain—a shortcoming Shaela promised to correct once she had rested, the next day.

Firth helped exhausted Shaela to a nearby tree. She rested her head against the bark. Firth remained to guard her.

The knights had surely all seen emotes at work before, but because real battles had grown so rare, it was unlikely any had seen one rendering herself as emotionally drained as Shaela had, tending to such gruesome injuries or to so many in such short order. They all expressed their heartfelt gratitude for her services.

With the ogres' fire already burning for them, the company made camp at the fort entrance. Valencia took the first watch, sitting on the log with her drawn sword beside her, looking out into the woods and stretching her neck.

Taylan sat with her. "You all right?"

"I'm fine." She pushed on her neck with her palm to stretch it farther.

"You should tell Shaela."

"I'm *fine*," Valencia repeated.

"All right," Taylan said. "What now? Back to your fort?"

"No. We head south."

"To Deroc?"

"Yes. To see what those Dark Elves have to say about this."

"I'm sure the ogres set out on their own."

"Maybe."

A twig snapped in the forest. A rabbit bounced away.

"Probably," Valencia conceded. "But they killed two of my knights. I want to personally deliver the news and remind King Eldred of his obligation to keep control of their ogres, their trolls, and *all* of their abominations."

11

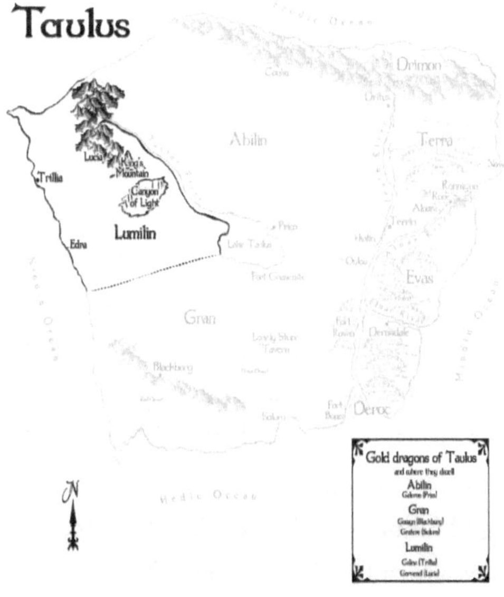

Gorvenal jumped and flapped his strong wings. On his bare back, Lila clutched his golden scales tight. They rose from Lucia, the second city of Lumilin—a rich city lacking the capital's royals and whose residents, without the politics that came with the king and queen's court, could focus even more on art, luxury, and all the pleasures of life. Lucia had been built in the foothills of the Lordly mountain range running from the north, and Lila and Gorvenal headed east toward King's Mountain, which sat at the end of the range.

The Lordlies to the north rose from the Frodic Ocean, each peak higher than the last. People considered the southernmost, mightiest mountain king because it stood the tallest of all in Taulus. Some viewed it as a king specifically because of how it presided over the rest of its range. And to many, that particular peak, which overlooked the Canyon of Light, where the first dragons had hatched into the world, deserved the name 'king' for the Creator who had set the four dragon eggs there to hatch.

Gorvenal, who dwelled in Lucia, was making his routine patrol around the mountain and then out over the canyon. In ages past, rule of King's Mountain had often been contested among some of the most powerful dragons in Taulus. And portions of the canyon, overflowing with colorful rocks, streams, and forests, had been constantly claimed, counterclaimed, and battled for by those dragons who cherished such beauty. In Gorvenal's age, Eilig, an old blue, made King's Mountain his home. Like all his ancestors before him, Eilig was friendly with Lumilin. On his watch, and on Gorvenal's, the numerous dragons holding territory in the hotly contested canyon remained content with the status quo.

As they neared King's Mountain, Lila called to Gorvenal, "When can we go to Yalus?"

Soon, he answered, without looking at her.

Lila longed to set her feet in the island's rarely stepped-on sand, where so long ago the tan dragon Yalea had gone to be with Taulin. "How far is it?"

A day and a half, in the middle of the ocean, halfway around the globe.

"I can't wait." King's Mountain impressed Lila as always, and doubtless the Canyon of Light would as well, but she had seen them before. At Yalus for the first time, she and Gorvenal could be completely alone, removed from the world, with nothing but each other, the sand, and the ocean. She would bring her recorder, she decided, for Gorvenal. He always enjoyed the soft melodies she played.

Shall I go on with the history? Gorvenal asked. *After the dragons' first battle.*

Below, Lila noticed a team of climbers wrapped in warm coats and scarves descending the mountain, nearing its base. "Please."

After the battle, Grawlth kept his family from banding together to attack descendants of Feinor and Yalea. And with Feinor in retreat in the Red Desert and none of his oldest offspring willing to follow any of the others, his family never united as one force. Instead, minor battles for territory became common. Individuals fought others, and occasionally small groups formed based on geography and common interest.

In time, tensions cooled, and the two great families mated amongst each other again. Centuries later, when the dragon armies formed and fought, they did so across those old family lines.

"Can you skip to when we came to Taulus?" Lila asked.

Gorvenal curled his neck to her. *You do not care to hear of the dragon wars?*

"They are exciting. But… dragons fighting dragons, over

and over… I've heard it, and I'll ask to hear it again someday. Just not today."

Of course. I do enjoy telling those stories of legendary dragons, their celebrated deeds in the skies above Taulus, and how they fought fervently for the land below that they held so dear, but I'll gladly skip ahead.

"Thanks." Lila saw the expansive Canyon of Light off to her right, but they were turning to circle King's Mountain before flying out that way.

Thousands of years after the first dragon eggs hatched, men and women stood on a grassy, windswept plain in the middle of Taulus. Far to the east, elves found themselves beholding the majesty and wonder of a wooded valley, the mountains that made it, and the river that ran through it.

The humans gazed across their plain at the clear blue sky and at each other for the first time. At the same moment, hundreds of miles apart, the same rider, on a gray horse, approached both the men and the elves. The rider smiled warmly, and said, "I brought you here."

Gorvenal turned to Lila. *Men or elves?*

"Men," she said, agreeing it would be confusing to detail the stories of both kingdoms at the same time.

All stood in silence, Gorvenal continued, *until one man said, "Thank you."*

"You are welcome, Charles." The rider made eye contact with him and then with every other man and woman in the plain. "We are in the middle of a land called Taulus with vast oceans on all sides. You and the land you live on will be the kingdom of Abilin. Together we will build the first town of men

and women, Prim, right here."

"I will teach you for a time." The rider's smile faded. "Though you are the only humans in Taulus, you are not alone, and the dragons that came before you will not be glad to see you on territory they claim as their own. But they will not know of you until I have gone."

"Dragons?" Charles asked.

"My first great creation, after Taulus itself and the lesser animals that inhabit it. Dragons roam the skies and dwell in the places most appealing to them. In different ways, both you and the dragons are very beautiful to me." He dismounted. "And they have been here, battling and warring, for an age. They will not share their land willingly, so you must learn how to fight them if you are to survive."

"Do they look like us?" Charles asked.

The Creator gazed at the sky, and a red, winged, reptilian creature with a tail soared high overhead. She flapped her wings, squealed, and shot flames from her snout.

"She cannot see us," the Creator said, watching with the others. "She will not see us, nor will any dragon, and you will not glimpse another, until I have left you."

The red flew out of sight.

The Creator showed the men and women of Abilin how to farm their land—which seeds to plant, when to harvest, and how to prepare for each season. He led them in gathering mushrooms, berries, and herbs, and taught them to cook and bake bread. The Creator gave them horses and rode with them to the small forest west of Prim, near the great Lake Taulus. He taught them to fish in the Vitus River nearby.

He instructed them on how to build homes from mud packed with sticks and straw and, with his own hands, helped them build their first one, along with a great hall for them all to gather in.

A strong gust hit Lila. She clutched Gorvenal tighter.

When the first thick clouds the men and women of Taulus had ever seen darkened the plain and the wind that blew them strengthened, the Creator beckoned his people inside the hall and sat with them.

As raindrops fell on the straw roof, the Creator led the men and women in a song, then had those he had given the most glorious voices lead the next. All joined in. While the storm outside intensified, with flashing lightning and booming thunder, inside the Creator fashioned a flute from a piece of a tree branch. He demonstrated how to blow into its end to make soft music. A simple drum beat followed.

In the morning, after the rain had ended and the clouds had moved on, the Creator led the people to a building he had filled with bows, arrows, swords, knives, and different kinds of armor. He showed them how to make more and told them where they could find the raw materials they would need. The Creator led a group of those most suited out into the plains on horseback for the first hunt. While their Creator did not fire an arrow or wield any weapon, the men and women of Abilin learned fast and returned to Prim with a plentiful bounty of meat for dinner.

Lila spied Eilig, the big blue dragon who was lord of King's Mountain, descending from its top, headed west.

Eilig called out to them.

Gorvenal returned the loud greeting then continued his tale.

Before a feast that evening, the Creator showed the people how to dry some of the meat to keep it from spoiling.

At the feast, around a wide fire, some men and women played music, others danced, and many talked and laughed as the fruits of their hunt roasted. The Creator set two wooden barrels on the ground. "Beer and red wine," he said to those within earshot.

Bron, another man who had asked the Creator a few questions already, posed an important one. "What are they for?"

"For drinking." The Creator poked a hole in the top of a barrel, poured a cup of the red liquid, and handed it to Bron. "For relaxing. For fun. Maybe for getting to the truth of a matter."

Bron sipped it.

"Try it with roasted deer," the Creator said, and Bron went happily to do as he'd been instructed.

Charles, who the men and women had come to rely on to pose questions they feared asking themselves, went to the Creator, who motioned for Charles to walk with him. Away from the group, in a bare patch of ground near a big log, a small fire suddenly rose. The Creator bade Charles to sit then joined him.

Charles said, "Thank you for helping us on the hunt today."

The Creator nodded. "You are welcome."

"And for showing us how to build such fine homes."

"I enjoyed our productive day."

"As did I, truly." Charles shifted on the log. "Will… will the

homes protect us from the dragons when you are gone?"

"Do you think they will?"

"Against creatures that can breathe fire…" He shook his head. "I am sorry, but I fear they will not."

The flames before them flickered.

"They will not protect you," the Creator said.

"And the weapons you showed us… against the grouse and the deer… they worked well. I thank you—we all thank you. But they are small weapons. The dragon we saw when you first came to us was quite large. Are they all that size?"

"Many are larger," the Creator said.

"Are we to use those weapons to fight them?"

"They may do some good." The Creator shrugged. "And you might build more powerful weapons like them. Think of the bow. Think of arrows, but bigger. You could launch a heavy spear to meet a dragon."

Charles nodded. "How long do we have until we must fight them?"

"Not long."

"Oh… we need to prepare."

"You do," the Creator said. "But just as homes of mud and branches will not protect you from them, heavy spears will not be your chief weapon against my dragons."

"What then?" Charles asked.

The Creator smiled. "I know how you look at Catherine, how you hold her hand and gaze into her blue eyes. I know the care you took earlier, cleaning dirt from the scrape on her arm."

Charles stared into the fire and, in the blue hot hues at its base, saw those pale eyes—the exposed expressions of her soul that touched his soul so deeply, so uniquely. He was speaking to his creator, the creator of all of Taulus, and tried to keep his focus there, yet he wished he sat with Catherine, laughed with her, and saw her soft blue eyes instead.

Gorvenal turned to Lila, and his big brown eyes met her blues. She smiled warmly. He headed out toward the long, deep Canyon of Light.

The Creator asked, "What would you do to protect Catherine?"

"Anything."

"Were she ill or injured, what would you do to ease her suffering, to return her to health, or to heal her wounds?"

"Anything," Charles said. "From the bottom of my heart, I would do anything for her."

"You have that power, Charles," the Creator said. "As a small number in Prim do. You can reach deep inside yourself to protect those you care for, to heal them, and when you need to, to attack without a sword, a spear, or any weapon like those I showed you today. That power is how you will fight the dragons."

Charles nodded.

"Go to Catherine," the Creator said. "She is sitting with a few others at the fire at the feast, her attention wandering from their conversation, in search of you."

Charles couldn't help smiling, and he went.

Lila failed to resist a fresh smile of her own.

The next day, Charles, Bron, and Catherine were among a group tilling a new field when Catherine screamed.

Charles ran to her where she knelt to the ground, and those nearby stopped their work to see.

"A snake," she told Charles, holding her bitten, swelling ankle.

Charles couldn't find the slithering serpent that had made the two pricks in Catherine's soft skin, nor could he find the Creator in the field with them. He held Catherine as her lower leg expanded to many times its normal size and sweat beaded on her brow.

"You'll be all right," he said.

"Charles…" Her eyes rolled up and closed.

"Help!" he called. "Help!"

The others nearby ran over, encircling Charles and Catherine.

"Charles…"

"Catherine," Charles whispered, "hold on."

"Cha—" Her body went limp.

Charles looked around the group. "Where is he? Where is God?"

"I don't know," a woman said.

"Has anyone seen him?" Bron asked. "All day?"

"No. I haven't. No," the responses came.

In Charles's arms, Catherine grew warmer and paler.

"Hold on." He hugged her tighter. Her skin grew hot. Her breaths became shallow.

"Help!" Charles took her hand and brought her fingers between his. "Help…" He squeezed her hand. He closed his eyes.

Lila clutched Gorvenal's neck tight and pressed her cheek into his scales.

A spark of flame inside Charles grew into a whirling stream at his core. Lightning crackled across the surface of a ball of thick, gray clouds enveloping the flame. Charles clutched Catherine. Inside him, a ray of white shone from the murk. He gripped her tighter, and the ray expanded.

Light burst!

The cloud parted within Charles, leaving a ball of glowing white light.

Catherine gasped.

Charles opened his eyes and saw the light inside him while at the same time watching her swollen leg shrink. Catherine's skin cooled. The light shone on, undimmed. Catherine stopped sweating.

Tears streamed down Charles's cheeks. Catherine's ankle gradually shrank to its normal size. The bite mark faded.

She opened her eyes. "Charles."

He kissed her cheek as claps and shouts rose from the surrounding crowd. Charles kissed her deeply as those nearby cried along with the couple on the ground.

Tears filled Lila's happy eyes. She and Gorvenal flew above the great canyon of Taulus.

With a loud roar, a tiger charged Charles and Catherine.

Men and women scattered.

Charles let go of Catherine and stood. The light inside him crackled.

The oncoming beast roared again.

Charles stretched out his arm. That animal would not hurt Catherine, he told himself. He would not let it!

From the tips of his fingers, lightning in forked bolts shot at the tiger. With a whimper, the big cat slid to a stop on the ground, a charred hole in its side.

"Charles!" Catherine grabbed him.

He held her. "It's all right." He called to the returning crowd of men and women. "It's all right." Charles let go of Catherine. "Last night, God revealed to me that this is how we will fight his dragons."

A roar split the air, and another tiger pounced from the high grass.

Bron stepped forward. A stream of flame flew from his palm and halted the animal in its tracks, its striped skin burned black.

While everyone watched for more tigers, a woman asked, "Can we all do it?"

"No," Charles said.

"What else do you know, Charles?" Bron asked. "What else do you not share with us?"

"Nothing, I swear."

Bron rubbed his chin. "Can the dragons do this?"

"No," God called, approaching on his gray horse. "Not beyond their fiery breath. A small number of you have this power." He smiled. "Along with a small number of elves."

"Elves?" Bron asked.

"Elves," God repeated.

That evening, in the great hall of Prim, God explained to the people of Abilin that the ability to heal, protect, or attack came from channeled emotions, and that among those with the power, not everyone could channel their emotions in all three ways. Some could only heal, others could only attack or protect, and some were capable of a combination of the three. Such people became known as emotes, and those like Charles, who could project their emotions in all three ways, were rarest of all.

God also told them of the elves, a race similar to mankind who lived to the east, in the kingdom of Terra, in the town of Terrin. Elves had fair skin, pointed ears, keen senses, a profound understanding of nature, and lived significantly longer than men and women, though God did not explain why he gave them the extra years. He suggested that the kingdom of Abilin would be wise to look to the elves as an ally against the dragons.

When it had grown late and God had said all he had to say, the Creator held the door as the men and women filed out of the hall to head to their homes for the night. Charles and Bron reached the door last.

Bron asked, "Why are we here?"

"I had to explain your magic," God said. "And to tell you of the elves."

"No," Bron said. "I mean, why are we in Prim—in Abilin, or Taulus at all, if dragons are already here? Why bring us to such a place?"

God clasped his hands. "If not here, then where?"

"What are we to do when you are gone?" Charles asked. "With this magic, I hope we can survive."

"I share that hope," God said. "And I will be watching closely."

"But is that it?" Charles asked. "We are to survive?"

God grasped his shoulder. "Charles"—he moved his hand to Bron's arm—"Bron, you and the men and women of Abilin are capable of much more than survival." God motioned for them to go, so they did.

Below, in the Canyon of Light, a young tan dragon rested near a crystal-clear stream. A green farther ahead took flight from a rocky perch above dandelion-littered grass and headed north.

The following morning, at dawn, a cry much louder and more shrill than any tiger's roar pierced the air. A red dragon bore down on Prim. Charles and Bron rushed out to confront it, knowing full well that seeing the creature meant the Creator had gone. They did not waste their breath calling for God.

With their minds and hearts set on protecting all those they cared for in their new settlement, Charles and Bron shot lightning and fire into the air, searing the scales of the stunned, winged reptile. To defend the others who had rushed out with swords, spears, and arrows, the two men produced waves of wind and river water as shields against the dragon's breath of flame.

The dragon learned its new foes possessed power far greater than their small size suggested and then fought more carefully, repeatedly swooping low to scorch the humans or knock them broken and bleeding to the ground, before quickly flying higher.

As the battle wore on, Charles and Bron learned to attack more forcefully, more accurately, and defend more fully. Others found they possessed the emotional power to join the magical battle. Those with traditional weapons began to evade successfully and occasionally inflicted damage themselves. Eventually the dragon fled, badly wounded, screaming its shrill cry for the rest of its kind to hear.

Bron found he did not have the power to heal the wounded, so Charles, along with emotes who discovered themselves able, attended to all they could. Despite their efforts, the first man and woman died in Taulus. They would not be the last to fall in the fire and fury of the dragons.

To the east, the elves slew an attacking blue that day while suffering their own loss in the fight. The age of the three races had begun.

12

Taulus

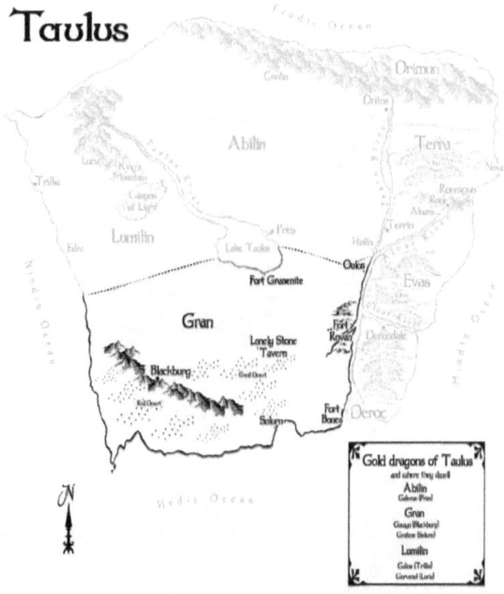

The blistering desert sun beat down on Gall and the twins. All three had stripped to their lightest, dirtied beige shirts. Avril had bunched her hair up high off her neck, and Gall had tied an even dirtier shirt around his head to try to keep cool. Avery said that he thought Gall looked ridiculous, so his brown hair baked as the sun shined directly on it.

The day before, they had passed twenty mounted, armed

knights riding east on the same road through the northern stretches of the Great Desert. Avery and Avril appeared terrified at the sight of the company, presumably fearing they had come because of what happened with their father back in the Midlands. The knights paid Gall and the twins no more mind than a nod from the lead rider. Gall hadn't been concerned and explained to the twins afterward that the knights had most likely been headed for a fort to the east or any number of small towns that way as part of a training mission.

The day before that, among those they passed had been a family on their way to visit friends in Abilin. Gall introduced himself jokingly as the twins' guide and never offered a more serious explanation. He simply was not worried about the events in the Midlands at all.

They were a day from Blackburg, the oasis city made by water running from high in the mountains. Gall made out hazy peaks far ahead with hints of green from the trees at their base.

He guided his horse between the twins and asked Avery, "You ever thrown a spear?"

"Why aren't you a knight in an army like all the rest?" Avery countered.

Gall wiped his brow and took a drink. "Have you ever kissed a girl?"

Avery veered to the right. "Leave me be."

Gall turned to Avril. "Kissed a boy?"

"Yes," she said.

"Great." He called to Avery, "See how easy this is? *You*

tell me something, and *I'll* return the favor."

Avery motioned to his sister. "*She* told you something."

"Nope," Gall said. "The offer was for you. She's quiet but warming up. You're the stubborn one. Stubborn as a… as a…"

"Mule," Avril said.

"Thank you." Gall squinted at her. "You ever kiss a girl?"

"Gall!" Avery shouted.

"What?" He put out his arms. "It happens. It's just a question."

"No," Avril said, perfectly pleasantly.

Gall looked at Avery. "Boys for you? It's not my thing, but that's fine. Nothing wrong with—"

"No," Avery said. "I've kissed girls, all right?"

"Fine, fine," Gall said. "Just wondering." He leaned backward.

Avery pointed ahead at the broad, distant range. "Are those the Mountains of Fire?"

"They are," Gall said.

"Is it true that Feinor's fire is what makes the sky red?"

"Maybe," Gall said. "But it might be the sand in the desert behind the mountains and how it swirls into the air."

Avery's smile faded.

"Buuut… there's red sand and dust elsewhere in Taulus, and no sunsets are redder than the ones above those mountains." He gazed out at them. "The sky over the twin castles of Gran truly burns red some nights."

"Will it tomorrow?" Avery asked.

"We'll arrive during the day," Gall said.

Avery stopped. "Let's wait."

"Thought you were in a hurry?"

"I want to ride up at sunset."

Gall scratched his beard. "All right, but let's get a little closer. Might as well have a better view tonight, then we'll take our time tomorrow."

———

"Good thinking," Gall told Avery the next day, a day when Gall had hardly drunk any liquor.

"What?" Avery asked.

"Waiting until late in the day so we'd have this view."

The three of them rode slowly toward Blackburg and the bright crimson filling the sky over the broad charcoal-colored mountain range behind the city of dark stone buildings. Peaks rolled into peaks as far and wide as Gall could see, casting their shadows onto the long, thick walls and sturdy towers of Castle Enduran and its twin, Auderon.

"It's just desert past the mountains?" Avery asked.

"Pretty much," Gall said. "Until the Dead Horn, at the southwestern tip of Taulus. One of Feinor's descendants has always lived there."

"Who does now?"

"A temperamental female dragon named Fria."

"Why are there two castles?" Avril asked.

"Because they took so long to make it here," Avery said.

"I don't get it."

"When they left Abilin," Gall said, "after men and women first came to Taulus, the ones who split off intended to go all the way to Blackburg, but they couldn't because of all the dragons. So they stayed where Fort Granenite is located now. It served as Gran's first capital."

"I know *that*," Avril said.

"Well, hundreds of years later, when they finally made it, with the red dragon Ferron's assistance, they found themselves so overjoyed to have made it, and so set on securing a permanent foothold on the territory, that after they finished their first castle, they kept building and wound up with a second."

"Are they exactly the same?"

"Pretty much but not *exactly*." Gall glanced from her to her brother. "Kind of like you two."

Avery rolled his eyes.

Gall knew well the stories about the twin castles. Enduran, built to the north of and after Auderon, in its current incarnation of granenite and constructed by dwarves, had been named for how Gran had endured and intended to endure always. The wide castle in the trees overlooked the city with its twin from low on the mountains at the west end of Blackburg and guarded an entrance to tunnels linking a series of chambers under the mountains. Enduran stood as a testament to both the kingdom's unbroken line of kings stretching all the way back to Bron the Rock and to its rock-hard men and women who had defended that line and their homeland since Gran's first days.

Gall, more focused than he had been in days, rode into

Blackburg with Avril and Avery. They entered through a gate in the eastern wall, which had been moved farther east when the city became overcrowded. A new wall and expanded irrigation were being planned for even farther east and would protect those already living beyond the current wall and accommodate further growth.

Block after block, city buildings grew more densely packed, and their stone proudly showed the wear of more years' weather and use. The sun had set, and the streets were not crowded. Most people had settled into their homes for the night as reward for a hard day of work or training—or had settled into a spot at a tavern to drink a reward for their day.

Gall and the twins passed a tall building that blocked Enduran from their view. Auderon to the left remained in plain sight, a fire alight at the top of its blackened wall. The shades of red in the sky above the mountains were being overtaken by a fierce purple and ultimately descending darkness. Avery watched a knight light another fire farther down the wall.

"Pay attention here," Gall called to Avery.

Avery sat up straighter in his saddle, taking visible notice as shadier characters emerged from unlit side streets and alleys.

Avril guided her horse nearer to her brother's. "Here?" She pointed at a worn wooden tavern sign that showed mugs of ale.

"Let's see." Gall hopped off his horse, led it to Avril, and passed her the reins. "Wait here." Gall pulled open the wood-and-iron door and went two steps inside. He scanned the crowded room and then left.

As he emerged from the tavern, he saw a man with tattered clothes and a filthy face lingering near the twins. Avril was huddled in close to her brother. Gall glared at the filthy man, who lowered his head and continued past.

"No." Gall climbed onto his saddle. "Not there."

"Are we safe here?" Avery asked.

"Should be," Gall said. "But night's falling in a hard city full of hard people, so you'd better stay sharp."

"All right," Avery said.

"To the next tavern." Gall motioned up the road.

"What are you looking for?" Avril asked.

"We'll see." He gestured again for them to ride on.

The twins led, remaining very close together. But by the time Gall came out of the second tavern and they rode on for a third, the two seemed more relaxed. The appearance of the characters on the street and those heading in and out of homes, inns, and taverns must have ceased being so new to them.

At the fourth tavern, Gall emerged to see Avery staring up at firelight-illuminated Castle Enduran.

"Hey," Gall called.

Avery looked at him.

"This is the place," Gall said.

They tied up their horses around the side of the building. Inside, Gall led the way through a sizeable raucous crowd to a small table near the rear. He sat facing the bar on the long bench shared by eight similar tables, and the twins took rickety wooden chairs across from him. The sweaty clothes they wore fit the scene well. Avril let her hair down.

Gall watched Avery for a moment. "You look nervous."

Avery scooted in to avoid a passing pair of armed knights.

"Yeah, ogres out east," the one in front told the one behind.

"Dumb shits," the other said. "I wish they were here so I could call 'em that before I chopped 'em down and sliced their heads off."

Avery said, "I'm not nervous."

Gall shrugged.

A short buxom waitress came over. "Your kids?"

"No, no." Gall took her hand. "Not my kids."

She smiled and leaned into Gall. "Whatcha drinkin?"

"Whisky. Bring a bottle, my dear." He rubbed the back of her palm with his thumb.

"Three glasses?" she asked.

"Not for us," Avery said.

Avril sat very straight. "Do you have wine?"

"We do, love," the waitress said. "Red or white?"

"Red."

"Good girl," Gall said. "Bring a short glass for the boy." The waitress slid her fingers from Gall's and started away, but Gall grabbed her wrist. "And bring that third whisky glass."

She went off to the bar.

"For a game," Gall explained to his tablemates.

"We don't want to play," Avery said.

"*Shut up*," Gall said. "Please."

Avery slumped in his chair.

"Maybe your sister wants to play. Maybe you will later." Gall pointed past Avery. "Maybe that guy over there does. Or the waitress." He leaned forward. "Have I made you do anything you haven't wanted to?" He leaned closer. "Have I?"

"You made me take the knife from my barn," Avery said.

"Ahhh." Gall leaned back then pointed at Avery. "But I never made you use it."

The waitress returned and set their drinks and glasses on the table. "Food?"

"Yes," Gall said then put out his hands defensively. "But nobody has to eat if they don't want to."

The waitress gave him a surprised look. "Chicken or beef?"

"Beef," Gall said.

"Chicken," Avril said.

"Beef," Avery said, and the waitress went off.

Avril had a tiny sip of wine.

"Like it?" Gall asked while he poured himself a drink.

"It's all right."

Gall poured whisky into Avery's glass.

Avery nudged it away.

Avril sipped her wine. "What's the game?"

"I used to play with my friends all the time." Gall brought a silver coin up to the table and placed it beside the extra glass. "Bounce it off the table and land it in the glass and you win."

"Win what?" she asked.

"Well…" Gall looked at Avery. "I want you to answer my questions, and you want *me* to answer *your* questions. Make it in, I'll answer. I make it, you answer. Miss, take a drink. Shoot when and *if* you want."

"I'm not playing," Avery said.

"The glass and the coin will be there," Gall said. "I'll talk to your sister until you feel like being part of the group." He fixed his gaze on Avril. "Where your mother worked, before she met your father, it was a place like this?"

"Yes," Avril said. "It might have *been* this place. It was in Blackburg."

"There are a lot of places like this one," Gall said. "A lot of knights who like to drink. A lot of knights who like the company of a good woman." He made a face. "Sorry."

"It's fine." Avril shrugged. "It was her job."

The waitress set their plates of food down—the ordered meat, along with a chunk of bread and a clump of mixed vegetables for each. She left then returned quickly, put a stack of cups on the table, unstacked them, and poured them all water from a pitcher.

"Thank you." Gall gave her a big smile as she slowly turned away and headed to the bar. He bit his bread and asked Avril, "Why'd your mom pick Trillia to go to?"

"I don't know. But it's supposed to be so wonderful there."

"It is a magnificent city." Gall drank his water. "What if your plan hadn't worked? If your father hadn't picked the fight or if I—or anyone—hadn't… taken care of him?"

"We would have tried something else." Avery glanced at

his sister. "Maybe poisoned him." Avery speared a strip of beef with his fork. "But then we would have had to get to Trillia on our own."

"Right," Gall said.

Avril spoke up. "Eventually our mother would have sent someone. We didn't have a set plan, but she would have."

"If she could," Avery added.

While they finished their meals, Gall found the twins far more eager to discuss their mother than themselves. He didn't need his game with the coin and the glass to learn that their mother, Isabel, was much younger than their father had been. She had been born into a poor family and had worked hard to become respected in a line of work so often devoid of that sentiment. Avery and Avril said their mother was the smartest person they knew.

Isabel had met Ivon when he traveled to Blackburg to see the old king. Ivon had been happy then, their mother had told them, when he brought Isabel back to his home in the Midlands and married her, and for the first few years of the twins' lives. And then things didn't go the way Ivon expected them to in Blackburg. Other lords, many younger, received substantially more of the new king's favor than he. Ivon was never truly happy after that.

The twins' mother taught her children all kinds of things—how to mix different medicines, drugs, and poisons and how to read when their father proved uninterested in educating them. Gall imagined Isabel to have been a very warm, very wise woman, and certainly a strong one to have endured Ivon as long as she did. She must have been pretty to capture the lord's attention, and confident—confident that she had taught her children well and that they would find her, or else survive until she could send for them.

The waitress returned and cleared their plates. "More wine?"

"Please." Avril drank the last bit in her glass.

Gall filled his empty whisky glass for the third time.

Avery sat with his arms crossed in front of his untouched liquor.

"Take a drink," Gall said. "You're on your first trip away from home—and you'll never have to go back there."

Avery turned his head to the side.

"All that past... forget it," Gall urged. "At least for the night. Have some fun." He motioned to Avril. "Your sister seems to be enjoying herself."

Avery shook his head.

"Play my game," Gall said.

Avery looked at him.

"Afraid you'll lose?"

Avery picked up the coin from near the empty extra glass.

Gall nodded. "Thatta boy."

"It wouldn't be fair," Avery said. "I've never played before."

"You know what?" Gall tapped his fingers on the table. "You're right." He stood and went to the bar. He returned with a small shot glass, which he held to the coin in Avery's hand.

"It won't fit," Avery said.

"It might." Gall set the shot glass next to the much larger extra glass.

"Bounce it off the table?" Avery asked.

"Yup," Gall said.

"How?"

Gall took the coin. "Like this." He held it flat between his thumb and index finger, faced Avril, then, fast, brought his wrist down to the wooden table and let go of the coin. It hit the table and spun into the air end over end at Avril. She leaned away, cupped her hands, and caught it. She handed the coin back to Gall, who handed it to Avery.

He held it like Gall had. "Practice."

"One," Gall said.

Avery aimed for the large glass in front of him, brought his arm down and, like Gall had, slammed his wrist into the table. The coin hit the wood, then flipped high, end over end, up and over the rim of the glass, and rattled off the far side to the bottom.

Avery and Avril grinned.

"I *would be* answering a question," Gall said. "If it hadn't been practice."

Avery grabbed the coin and tried to hide his smile. He shot again—the coin flipped well past the glass and onto the floor.

Gall retrieved it and set it on the table. "Drink."

Avery lifted his whisky glass, took a deep breath, and sipped. He made a face as he swallowed.

"Not so terrible," Gall said.

Avery chugged his water.

"Don't," Gall said. "Or do. Do what you want. But water'll leave a bad taste in your mouth, that's all."

Avery wrestled to return his contorted face to normal.

"Have you had whisky before?" Gall asked.

Avery shrugged.

Gall grabbed the coin. Softer than Avery had, he hit his wrist off the table. The shot spun, lower than Avery's had, and with a solid *clank*, it stuck in the little shot glass, at the very top of the rim. "It fits!"

Avery's shoulders slouched. "I've had whisky before. A little." He shot at the larger glass. The coin hit the face and landed on the table. Avery had a small drink. He made another pained face but didn't wash the liquor down.

Gall took his shot, and it landed squarely in the small glass. "Ever throw a spear?"

"Yes."

"At anything?"

Avery shrugged.

Gall rolled his eyes then shot—*clank*. "A spear, at anything living—a person or an animal?"

"No," Avery said.

Gall voluntarily drank some whisky. He noticed an elf at the far end of the bar leading a redheaded woman through the crowd toward the staircase.

Avery shot and missed off the far rim of the glass. "Dammit."

Gall smiled while Avery drank. The elf and the woman went upstairs.

"How are you so good at this?" Avril asked.

Gall looked at Avril. "Hm?"

"Getting it in the glass," she said.

Gall slid her the coin.

"Uh uh." She shook her head. "I'll sip my wine when I want to."

Avery shot and watched the coin rattle to a stop in the larger glass. "Well?"

"I'm good at everything," Gall said.

Avery's smile faded.

"Ask a better question next time." Gall refilled both their drinks. He shot and made it. "Ever use a sword… in practice or against anyone?"

"No," Avery said. "Well, I practiced in the barn." Avril raised her eyebrows as Avery said, "A little."

Avery shot, and the coin dropped into the glass. "Where were you a knight?"

"Gran."

"I mean specif—"

"Blackburg mostly." Gall glanced from side to side. "It was a while ago. I recognized one guy on the way in, but I don't think he noticed me." Gall scratched his cheek. "Never grew a beard back then."

"What happened?" Avery asked, his sister watching intently for the answer.

Gall dumped the coin out of the glass.

Avery's shot went long. He drank and swallowed it fast. His next shot fell in. "Well?"

"I was"—Gall leaned back—"a talented knight of Blackburg."

Avril grabbed her brother's arm. "He doesn't lose fights! *Remember?*" She turned to Gall. "You mentioned it—a lot—

and we've only known you a few days. Madine told us you told her too."

"Seemed relevant," Gall said. "Each and every time." He pointed at Avril. "When that glass is empty, please do order more."

She turned a softer shade of the color of her wine.

Gall continued, "So I was a good knight. Things came easy for me. They made us run long distances most days, and if we weren't fast enough for their liking, they punished us until we were. My friends and all the other knights had to train hard to make the times, but not me. I never trained. They told me to run, I ran and made the times. I drank every night—and some days—but it didn't slow me down.

"They told me jump, I jumped the highest. They told me punch, I punched the hardest. I fought the best with a sword, the best with a lance, and I never missed throwing a knife. I was a crack shot with a bow." Gall took a long drink. "They set harder goals for me than anyone else and were annoyed when I met them all and broke all their old records with ease."

"How could they be *annoyed?*" Avery asked.

"A few weren't, but most were. In this age, with no real fighting to do, they clung to their tournament triumphs and their records like nothing mattered more in the whole world. And they set those records when they were younger, but they weren't *getting* any younger. And to be honest, in this age of peace, it wasn't much fun being a knight around here. Not to me anyway. Drills, and even tournaments, aren't that exciting to me."

"So you quit?" Avril asked.

"Basically. I annoyed them *so* much—did I mention being a bit of a smart ass about it all?"

"No," Avery said. "But…"

"Exactly," Gall said. "Not hard to imagine. My friends liked it, but not the officers. And I kind of stopped listening to them too. I did some short stints in jail for that. No big deal. I just didn't care. I was the best knight in Gran, which meant likely the whole world. And I didn't need to train to be. Lying in jail suited me fine. Sometimes I broke out early." Gall drank his whisky. "I didn't like giving orders either, when they tried putting me in charge of units of knights. I always hated drilling and found I hated planning and ordering others to drill all the same."

Gall sipped and swallowed slowly. "So… right, what happened? I made a deal with my commanding officers. A fair bit of money in exchange for not sticking around and breaking all the rest of their records. They were thrilled to pay and get back to ordering around an obedient core of the best knights in Taulus—except me."

"Do you miss it?" Avril asked.

"Nope. It was never for me." Gall emptied his glass. "Even being the best." He pointed at Avery. "I told ya you were lucky *I* took your table at The Lonely Stone."

Avery dumped out the coin and slid it over.

Gall left it. "Why don't I just ask you a question?"

"What question?"

"You can't guess?"

Avery said to the table, "Why don't I fight?"

"Uh huh."

Avery drank, stared into his glass, then drank some more. "I'm scared."

"That's normal," Gall said.

"No. Not scared of getting hurt or dying." He glanced at his sister then started to tear up as he explained. "I'm scared that once I hit someone, or cut them with a sword or knife, that I won't know when to stop."

Avril sniffled.

"I'm scared I won't be able to stop." Avery gulped. "I'm scared I'll be like our father."

Avril wiped her nose with her wrist. "You're not." She put her hand on Avery's shoulder. "I know you're not. In my heart, *I know it.*"

Gall set down his glass. "I don't see that man in you, Avery. I looked into your father's eyes before we fought, and I'm looking into yours now. I'm telling you, I don't see it."

Avery shrugged. "Maybe."

"Let me teach you to fight." Gall leaned forward. "We've got a long road to Trillia after this. We can practice when our horses are resting or in the evening. We'll buy you a sword before we leave Blackburg."

Avery drank his whisky.

"Better you learn from me than from anyone else."

"Because you're the best," Avery said with a sneer.

"Yes, I am," Gall said. "And I'll be around, in case... well, in case..."

"In case anything happens?" Avery asked.

"Yes. And it won't, I'm telling you. But you're scared it

will. And I understand. I really do. It's all right to be scared about it. It's all right to be scared about anything—but not forever. Let me teach you, so you can get past this."

Avery looked at the table again. "Maybe."

"Hear that?" Gall asked Avril. "I'll take that as a 'yes' from this one."

She smiled, then Avery did too, a little.

13

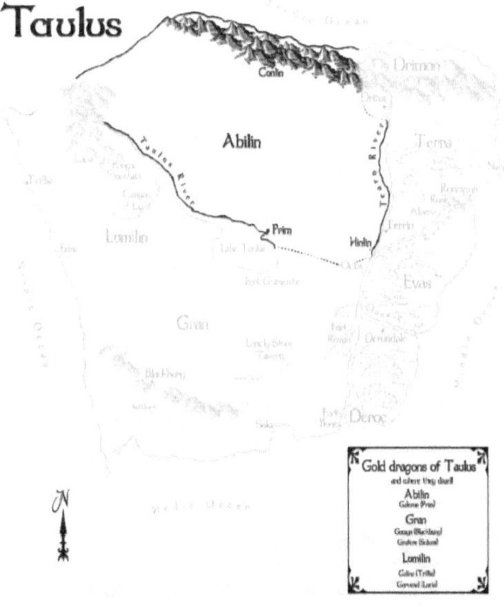

Sitting on a red, cushioned stool, in Mikannel Castle in Prim, in a room typically used for larger classes of younger students, Ri watched a bird pass out one of the open windows and plucked a string on her harp—the wrong one.

"No," her teacher said, spinning on her heel to face her pupil.

"I know." Ri stopped playing. She sighed. "I know."

"I know you know," her blond-haired but graying instructor said. "So what keeps you from playing the correct notes?"

"Because I don't care." Ri had told her teacher as much before, but not in a while and rarely as frankly.

The woman's shoulders slouched. "This is important."

"So am I," Ri said. "I'm the princess." She brought a finger to her lips. "Can I fire you?"

"No."

"Are you sure?"

"No," the woman said again. "But I think your parents would find you another teacher."

"Hmmm… maybe."

Her teacher threw up her hands. "What would you rather be doing?"

Shooting an arrow. Fighting a battle. Being with her elven scout team. All of a sudden, those uneventful missions didn't sound so bad to Ri. "I don't know. Something else."

"But you're good at this."

"I'm good at a lot of things."

Her teacher crossed her arms. "Do you understand *why* this is important?"

"Yes?"

"This"—the instructor pointed at the harp—"and all our music, like our paintings and poems, is what makes Abilin great."

"Not the fact that we're still in Prim?" Ri retorted. "Not the fact that so many years later—after the wars, the battles, and the countless dragon attacks of ages past—we're still here?" Ri motioned to the walls. "That this castle is built where mankind's first king reigned? That I can go outside and stand on the same spots where God explained magic to Charles and where Charles saved Catherine from the snake and the tiger? Everyone has songs and music. The elves, of course, but even the dwarves. That we are *in Abilin* isn't what makes us great?"

"It is that, dear, all those things. And the elves do make fine music and sing lovely songs. But the rest? The dwarves play bellowing music to mine by—"

"That's not all."

"But mostly. Lumilin's songs are rich and bright, like their opulent cities and their lives. The people of Gran left Abilin because they didn't consider the arts important."

"That's hardly the only reason," Ri said. "That's not really the *main* reason."

"But it *is* part of the reason. And it is that part which makes Abilin the greatest kingdom of men and women. We have our army, and our knights are no less mighty or noble than those of Gran. We mine deep into the mountains in the north and have been mining since before the dwarves first came to Taulus. We have songs and stories and paintings. Our arts—their importance never doubted, never questioned—run the entire spectrum, touching highs, like this glorious age we live in, and lows, like the devastating battles, the wars, and the struggle and the loss we've endured on these plains."

Ri shrugged. "I still don't want to play the harp."

"Well, you have to, because you are the princess and it is

one of your duties to play as occasion necessitates. Since it is my job to teach you, how you play will reflect on me. Try the song again."

Ri relaxed her arms and got her hands to the strings, but her mind wandered.

———————

That evening, after another stately dinner with her family, Ri lay on her back on the thick comforter atop her bed. She had almost asked her mother if she could stop her music lessons or if she could fire her teacher, but she doubted quitting was an option and figured the old woman correct that they'd simply find someone to replace her. And Ri didn't *actually* dislike her teacher. Arguing with her had been the high point of the day's lesson—maybe of the entire day.

Ri gazed out her open window—the sky was partly cloudy, and the sun had nearly set. She noticed no hint of wind.

She rolled the other way and buried her face in her feather pillow. Nothing going on... not even air moving quickly enough to be considered wind.

Ri usually waited about a month to ask her parents to let her return to the elves, but she wondered if she could bear waiting so long. She would tell her parents that she wished to play the harp with their master musicians. Even Ri's teacher had to agree that the elves had no equal with the instrument in all of Taulus. Her parents would say she could go. They always did. It pleased her father that his daughter was so fond of his close allies.

She definitely wouldn't wait a whole month to get back to the elves.

And *then* she'd have something to *do*. A patrol with her team would have an actual purpose. A small one. Or they'd compete—hunting again or target practice at tremendous lengths between a ridiculous number of trees.

No matter what, it would be better than home. Ri smiled. Old Launfal might want to race again, to redeem himself, after his loss to her last time. She'd have to come up with a new way to beat him.

And then her visit to Terra would end. In the blink of an eye, she'd be back in Abilin. Ri's smile faded. She'd be back at dinner with her utterly satisfied family and back in her perfectly comfortable bed.

Ri turned to her side.

She had to attend a knighting ceremony the next day. She'd maintain her pleasant smile the whole time, assuming she managed to stay awake. And she'd smile through the wedding she had no interest in being at the following day, and at the party afterward, and at whatever ceremony, ball, or royal event the next days and nights brought. Ri cringed at the prospect of having to play her harp for others then at the thought of petty conversations with the same noble men and women she'd been surrounded by her entire life, though the idea of fresh nobles did nothing to change her mood.

Something else had to change. Ri rolled over and stared at her ceiling.

She didn't want to write a story, but Dunmore's suggestion had merit. It excited her *a little*. Creating her own world—or setting a tale in the Taulus she knew—with her own villains and heroes and knights and dragons didn't sound *terrible*. Maybe her story needed a new color dragon that the world had never known. Maybe new magic, from a new source. Perhaps an irresistible weapon, discovered by good, that simply could not be allowed to fall into the hands of evil.

But all that didn't sound like the answer either. Ri wasn't a writer. She could imagine characters in an epic war, she could play out battles in her mind—vividly—and she frequently envisioned made-up conflicts to go along with the history she had been taught. But putting it all to paper? Too tedious. She needed to be out there living it, not stuck to a chair with a quill in her hand.

Except there was no war to live. No battles. Nothing epic about dinner with her family. And nothing really epic to be said for out-hunting Launfal either.

Nothing mattered.

A troll had been found in the Red Forest, King Ervain had said. But Ri hadn't found it. The conversation in Dritus between the Dwarf King Doxton and Bardric, the governor of Ronnigun, had seemed important to them, but Ri hadn't quite caught it.

She wished she had been outside the great hall minutes sooner. Even seconds might have revealed enough. The king had regretfully declined Bardric's request. But what had the request been?

Additional resources to work his mines, probably. Dwarves, supplies, or both. Maybe money. Nothing interesting to Ri.

Nothing that affected the rest of Taulus.

But what if it *had been* something interesting? What if their conversation had been a vital component of a grand strategy? And that very conversation set in motion unexpected events, unsettling events…

Bardric sought more land! Seemed logical. The king could grant him more to control. Take a tract in the north from a less senior governor. But what if Bardric hadn't wanted it gifted to him, like Ronnigun had been by the Red Elves? And perhaps he didn't want dwarven land at all. No… he intended to attack the Red Elves to his west, or the White to his south. He would take their land, take it by force! Bardric hadn't decided which elves to attack first, but he had plans for both, and for both plans, he needed a dwarven army and his king's blessing.

Ri stopped there. Attacking the elves could never work. For all their skill in music, in writing, and with nature, the elves had also earned their place among the greatest warriors in Taulus. While not as plentiful as humans, each individual elf fought with speed and skill honed over lives ten times as long. And many dragons of Taulus would respond to Bardric's aggression. A few *might* side with the dwarves, but most would not, and certainly not the golds. No way. Galeron had another war in him, and with his son and the others, he would crush any threat to the peace that all had fought so hard to achieve and had sacrificed so much for.

Ri spotted a triangular cloud out her window that resembled an arrowhead. Unless Bardric had a secret weapon. Or King Doxton did, and Bardric had asked to use it. Offensive and defensive magic were long gone from Taulus, but say Bardric and Doxton had found a way to bring it back and bring it to the dwarves for the first time? Could the elves survive that magic if the dwarves alone possessed it? Doubtful. Could the dragons stand up to it?

Ri sat up straight. What if she had overheard a little more of Bardric and Doxton's conversation and what she heard had worried her?

What if it still worried her? If so, she would be obliged to tell King Ervain of the Red Elves. If she wrote to him, he would have to at least investigate. Bardric's territory, Ronnigun, bordered elven land.

But why wouldn't Ri tell her parents? The king and queen of Abilin should know… Although, after Ri's trip to the dwarves in the name of friendship and alliance, perhaps she didn't want to upset that relationship over something she had heard only in small part, in passing. And Ri could be honest with Ervain, telling him that she wanted to check it out with the elves as a scout instead of staying behind in Abilin while others investigated.

It might have been nothing, she would tell Ervain, and she didn't want to trouble her parents with something so uncertain.

The letter Ri actually wrote to the king of the Red Elves would be far shorter than her entire imagined plot, but if she told it right, it would get her out of Abilin and hopefully on a reconnaissance mission to Ronnigun's capital, Rone. That would be a *real* mission, beyond the elves' borders, with a *real* purpose.

Ish. A real*ish* purpose. But more real than all the rest of the missions she'd gone on.

Ri swung her legs off her bed, went to her desk, selected a piece of parchment, and grabbed the quill that had sounded so unappealing mere minutes before.

14

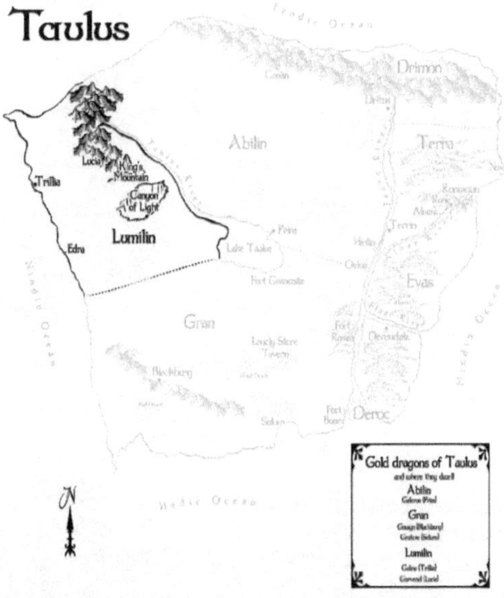

In the king's courtyard in Trillia, with His Highness Adrian
and his young queen, Kiara, looking on from above, Beal
held his trusty broadsword in one hand and his shield in the
other. With a long looping swing, he smashed his blade
against his opponent's shield. Sir Windell lashed out low
into Beal's shield, causing a thunderous crunch, then
smashed Beal's shield high and advanced. Beal parried and

stepped back, then parried again and back, and back again.

Beal lunged into a swing—hard into Windell's shield—then swung and sent blocking Windell stumbling to the tall white wall behind him. Their swords met high. Windell couldn't retreat farther, and he blocked and blocked, finding no time for attack.

From the corner of his eye, Beal saw Queen Kiara stand for a better view.

Windell's shield stopped a strike then another. His sword blocked Beal's onslaught, but Beal's powerful swing loosened Windell's grip on his weapon. Windell parried, and his blade flew to the ground.

His back pressed against the wall, Windell clutched his shield to absorb Beal's attack.

And his next.

Windell moved off the wall.

Beal shoved his opponent back into it and maneuvered past Windell's shield to thrust his blade to Windell's throat.

Clap-clap-clap. "Well fought, Sir Beal," Queen Kiara said.

Beal lowered his sword and smiled up at her. "Thank you, m'lady." He pulled his countryman away from the wall. "Well fought, Windell."

"I got in a few good swings," he said. "I'll take that, against you."

"Learn from it. You came at me hard, and it worked. Don't be afraid. Stay on the attack. Don't stop."

Windell nodded.

The king placed his hand on Kiara's shoulder as he rose.

"Beal, you are Lumilin's greatest knight."

"You are too kind, my king," Beal said.

Adrian waved his hand. "No, no, it is true. No one would deny it. My advisors laud you, saying they remember no greater knight in all of this age. My eyes have certainly seen none finer." He glanced at the queen. "You look the part, and it is a joy to watch you fight."

"It is my honor to fight for you, m'lord."

"We shall have a tournament," the king said. Kiara lit up. Adrian continued, "Close combat, jousting, archery—it has been too long since our last. And…" He grinned. "We'll hold it to bestow the honor of second finest knight in Lumilin, since there is no doubt as to who is the first."

Beal chuckled. "You are too kind!"

"It will be soon—a week or two from now, not more," the king said. "Come inside, both of you, and we will set the plans."

Beal nodded and retrieved Windell's sword.

"High praise." Windell took the sword from Beal. "Don't let it go to your head."

Beal raised an eyebrow. "May be a little late for that."

They both laughed as they headed inside.

Beal rode for his home.

"Sir Beal!" A merchant pulled his mostly empty cart of fruit away from the market.

"Good sir," Beal responded.

The merchant threw an apple to Beal, who caught it.

"Thank you!" Beal took a big bite. When he had passed, he checked behind him to ensure the merchant wasn't looking, then shoved the apple in his pocket, for he was not hungry at all.

A group of children fighting with small wooden weapons quit their play to shout, "Beal, Beal, Beal!"

"Hello!" he called down as he passed.

"Beal!" they yelled again.

He whirled his horse around. "What are your names?"

"Oliver!" one shouted.

"Ronald!"

"Sam!"

"Well," Beal said, "let me ask you wise children this. Which is the greatest kingdom in Taulus?"

"Lumilin!" they shouted.

"And its greatest city?"

"Trillia!"

He leaned low to them and asked quietly, "Its greatest knight?"

"Beal!"

He shot back up, extra surprised. "Oliver, Ronald, Sam… thank you. You have made my day." He turned. "Hya!" And rode off.

"Beal!" they continued shouting. "Beal!"

Up the hill, around the corner, and up the hill some more, at a long, single-story home made of finely cut granenite, Beal dismounted and let his page take his horse.

Inside, Beal called for his wife, "Lorelei?" He headed through the largest room, filled with paintings and sculptures that had been gifts from the city's nobles. He called into the kitchen. "Braden?" Beal set the bitten apple next to a vase of colorful flowers on a small mahogany table.

"He has not returned," Lorelei called from out back.

Beal found her on the balcony, weary-eyed, looking out at the ocean beyond the high city wall their hilltop home sat above.

"On a long march with his company, I think," she said.

"I see." Beal kissed Lorelei's cheek then brought his hand to her waist and kissed her lips. "So no one else is home."

She softly pushed him away. "That is not so rare."

"No," he said. "S'pose it isn't."

She gently pulled him to her for another kiss. "I am exhausted, my love."

"All right." He covered her hand with his on the ledge. "Hard day?"

She sighed. "The young ones struggle to focus. There is no shortage of aptitude. They will be fine healers, but not without considerable work."

"They are lucky to have you to teach them."

She flashed a smile. "Yet I grow tired of it."

"They need you," Beal said.

"Do they?" Lorelei asked. "There are other teachers." She moved her fingers between his. "*I* need you. And not when I'm spent at the end of the day."

"Lorelei… we've talked about this. You and I are lucky. We are talented, and we each have a responsibility. We have to do our part for the city and for our king."

She gently shrugged.

"And for the people," Beal said. "You know I fight for them, above all."

"I know." Lorelei searched his eyes. "And I know that we are lucky." She gazed out to the ocean. "How was the king?"

"Full of praise, as always."

"As he should be. His people adore you, his queen adores you."

"She just likes to see a good fight," Beal said.

Lorelei waved her arm. "Oh, I am not threatened by that girl."

"There is to be a tournament, to name the *second* finest of the knights of Lumilin."

"Hmph." Lorelei brought Beal's arm around her waist so he held her. "Second finest… ensuring everyone adores the *finest* even more."

———————

Gorvenal's spacious dwelling at the outer wall of the city of Lucia offered a roof over his head to protect him from the rain, a bed of straw to rest on, three solid granenite walls, and an entrance large enough for his big body. A curtain could cover the gap and keep in the heat generated by a fire which sometimes burned in the corner. A long awning ran outside, should the dragon seek nothing more than relief from the rain.

Inside with the curtain open but out of the blustery wind and steady raindrops, Lila rested on the straw near the fire. Soft notes from her recorder rose and fell as she lifted and dropped her fingers to open and cover holes in the fine elven instrument Gorvenal had brought back from Terrin for her. He lay just within her reach on the same bed.

The tune shifted higher. The fire's flames crackled. The low wind howled outside. Gorvenal closed his eyes. The song slowed as Lila held each note longer.

Air rushed into Gorvenal's dwelling. His eyes snapped open. Thick blue legs landed at the entrance, then a wing folded down. Lila took the recorder from her lips.

Eilig stuck his wet head inside. *Hello, Gorvenal! Hello, Lila!*

Gorvenal lifted his head. *Eilig.*

I was on my way home to my mountain, it began to rain, and I noticed smoke rising from here. Eilig stretched his neck in farther. *I wondered if you were with Lila, telling a story.*

Gorvenal looked at her.

She placed her recorder in her lap.

Oh, Eilig said. *I'm interrupting!*

"Nonsense," Lila said. "Please, join us. We *are* in the middle of a story."

Eilig squeezed inside.

"May I ask you a question, Eilig?"

Of course! Eilig settled himself against the wall near the entrance.

"How old are you?"

I am four hundred sixty-seven. How old are you?

"Nineteen," Lila said. "And if you're older than Gorvenal, shouldn't you know these stories better than he does?"

Eilig rose. *If you'd rather I leave you alone—*

"No!" Lila sat up straight. "No, not at all. You're one of the oldest dragons I've ever met. I've been curious, that's all."

Eilig relaxed. *I know the stories—each and every one of them.* He pointed at Gorvenal. *And I'll correct this one if he makes any mistakes. But I have told the tales many times over my long years, so I prefer listening to them these days.*

Gorvenal said, *I was telling of the first days of Abilin. When dragons attacked the men and women constantly.*

Bloody days, Eilig said.

Indeed, the gold agreed. *The battles raged furiously in Abilin, those first years. By all accounts, almost every day brought another dragon to Prim, or more than one. Initially they were curious about the new creatures there who spoke aloud to each other and planted fields and built homes among the tall grass.*

Lila settled back against the straw.

Bloody nights as well, Eilig added. *Fire lit the starry sky over the plains, they say, and not only that produced by our kind. Charles—who had been made king after he healed Catherine and killed the tiger who attacked them—and Bron, and the other emotes who were able, fought with all the magic they could muster.* The big blue stopped. *I'm sorry, I'm stealing your story.*

It's fine, Gorvenal said.

No, please, Eilig insisted.

Gorvenal continued, *Along with the fire, lightning was shot, boulders were hurled, and men and women moved the very earth to fight the dragons who threatened them and their homes.*

And spears, and swords, Eilig interrupted. *It takes a*

particularly strong throw to pierce our scales, or a powerful swing or perfectly timed thrust, but it happens, and among those first men were mighty warriors.

Aye, Gorvenal said.

Eilig went on, *You have not had the unfortunate experience of being cut by such a weapon, Gorvenal, but little men and elves have, on occasion, bested some of the mightiest among us without their magic.*

I know, Gorvenal said.

Now. Eilig pointed at Lila. *They would not have survived the first years without their magic. They might have taken a dragon or two with them, but they would not have survived the first month. I'm not sure they would have made it without the elves, either. Don't forget them, Gorvenal.*

Of course not.

And the healers! Eilig said. *It wasn't just Charles and Bron shooting lightning at dragons. It was emotes rushing to wounded warriors and holding their lives in their arms. With humanity's very survival at stake, the emotes learned to dig deep within, to harness every ounce of their feelings, to bring Abilin's warriors back from any injury, so long as the injured clung to even the tiniest bit of life.* Eilig stretched his head close to Lila. *The defense of Abilin took all they had: cunning plans, courage, and caring for one another.* Eilig looked at Gorvenal. *It was caring for their homeland that shaped their strategy and what would happen next.*

Yes, the gold said. *I was getting to that.*

I'm sorry, Eilig said. *I just don't want you to leave anything out.*

Understandable. So the elves… far to the east, the elves fought to defend their own homeland, Terra. Almost identical in appearance to humans, save for their pointy ears and uniformly pale skin, the elves had not been on Taulus any longer than mankind, so their long life did not yet offer them the advantage of combat skills and magic honed over centuries. They were, however, quicker of foot than humans and could see farther, which helped them become finer archers. Then, as now, their calm demeanor also helped them aim precisely.

Eilig interrupted, *They were also more in tune with nature.*

I was about to mention that.

Sorry!

The gold resumed the tale. *The elves, probably because they came into the world in a forest, moved among the trees quickly and quietly. And it went beyond the woods. While the men of Abilin lived on a plain—a beautiful one, but a plain—the elves' home, Terrin, was situated in the foothills of the Green Mountains, near the banks of the mighty Tearn River. Those surroundings, and the elves' close bond with the land and the animals that inhabited it, made it very hard for dragons to engage the elves in decisive battles. Trees provide excellent cover, and a bird singing a particular song would herald the coming of the winged attacker it fled.*

But no such cover existed for the men of Abilin. Not long after the dragon attacks began, King Charles, judging their situation to be dire, and heeding the advice he had been given by the Creator, sent two riders east, to find the elves.

Weeell… Eilig interrupted. *Times were hard, but not so dire, I don't think. Not yet. After the first full day and night without a dragon attack, Bron suggested sending riders to search for a more easily defensible location. Charles had no intention of leaving Prim but did seek to take advantage of the lull in attacks by sending riders to look for the elves. Bron disobeyed Charles and, with a like-minded healer, set off to the south.*

I see, Gorvenal said. *Please, continue.*

Eilig did. *The riders headed east, for days and nights following the flight of dragons to Terra, barely fighting off those who swooped low to attack. More than once they considered abandoning their journey and turning back for Prim, but eventually they found themselves too far away to be confident they would make it back, so they pressed on. From across the Tearn River, a lone elf spotted the wounded, weary riders. He swam across, healed them, and brought them to the city of Terrin.*

The first king of the elves, Elric, and his queen, the radiant Evelyn, greeted them warmly, for God had told them of the men living to the west. In the fresh green forest, absent its later red and white hues, they shared a feast of finer food than the men had ever tasted while listening to finer music than they had ever heard. The men marveled at the pleasing appearance of the elves—while they varied, the Abilinians judged all to be no less than pretty or handsome and most deserving of much more eloquent praise.

The riders thanked Elric and Evelyn profusely for their hospitality and asked how the elves managed their relative success in dealing with the dragons. Elric noted that nature served as their close friend and ally, especially the forest. Dragons had bashed trees aside and ripped others from the ground in pursuit of elves, but they had always refrained from using their fiery breath to torch the forest on a large scale. Elric surmised— correctly, the elves would later learn—that the dragons cherished those forests too dearly to destroy them, even to regain control of them.

Evelyn explained the importance of sacrifice. While each elf's life was a precious thing, she said, there seemed to be many more elves than dragons on Taulus, and there would be significantly more elves as time went on, so to lose a small number to defeat such a powerful enemy was a sacrifice that had to be made.

Before the human riders departed, they gave the elves a painting of Lake Taulus, which the elves had never seen. The gift survives to this day in Terrin. Elric and Evelyn gave the men sheaves of finer arrows than the men of the plains made and the promise of friendship between man and elvenkind. The people of Abilin were welcome in Terra any time and should especially call on the elves for assistance if circumstances grew dire, Elric said.

The riders returned to Abilin and shared what Elric had told them. While Elric's explanation of nature's role in the elves' battles against dragons did nothing to sway Charles' opinion about leaving Prim for a more easily defensible location, the elven arrows, which flew truer than any others, proved quite useful to the Abilinians.

They did, Gorvenal said. *And Bron had returned long before the riders, having not made it far, and without his companion, who an orange dragon had killed.*

They're lucky the riders made it to the elves, Eilig said.

Agreed, Gorvenal said. *And the near disaster of both*

excursions settled Bron for a time, outwardly. Months passed. Attacks remained constant and cost men and women their lives most days. Rarely did dragons follow them to the grave.

Then, a year after the dragon attacks had begun, when others used lulls in the battles as a welcome chance to rest, Bron seized the quiet as an opportunity to act. Maintaining that the flat plains were an impossible position to defend long term, and adding the argument that stone to build better defenses was in short supply near Prim, he set out to explore to the south again, alone save for his horse.

A month passed, then another. Bron was gone for so long that most assumed he had been killed, but eventually he returned. In addition to broken bones, severe wounds, and tales of terrible dragons he had fought and fled, he brought news of a broad mountain range in an oasis from a vast desert far to the southwest, whose peaks he had glimpsed bathed in red sunset.

Healed in Abilin, Bron began in earnest to persuade others of his desire to move to the mountains. Another year later, he decided he had convinced enough of them and brought the matter to King Charles.

"Look at the elves," Bron began, in the great hall of Prim, where everyone quieted to listen to the latest round of the old argument. "Nature is their ally, and with the mountains at our backs, it would be ours as well. These plains offer no protection, but a cave in a mountain of rock would put us beyond the reach of dragon fire and talon."

"Are you certain," Charles asked, "that mountain rock will withstand dragon fire?"

"Better than mud," Bron said. "Of that I have no doubt."

"This is our homeland. God put us here."

"But he did not command us to stay. He did not command us to do anything. He hoped we'd survive the dragons, I think. He didn't even promise we would!"

Charles found a few emotes and smiled at them. "He gave us magic." The king's warm face settled on each and every person in the hall for a brief moment. "He gave us each other that we would help each other survive."

"We are barely surviving, Charles, and I do not know if it will last. Not here."

"He gave us the elves as allies nearby," Charles said. "You think it is wise to relocate so far from them?"

"How have the elves truly helped us? They sent a healer and a warrior, sure. They brought their fine arrows, and they did some good. But the elves returned home and their arrows, try as we did to reuse and repair them, only lasted so long."

"Children are being born," Charles said. "Should they not be born in the land where God set us? Where he taught us and guided us?"

"Better they live longer in the south than die young here," Bron said.

"God taught us to sing and play music in this very hall."

"Fine." Bron took a turn, making eye contact with those listening as he spoke. "Keep your songs, keep your music. Those of you who wish to, keep your homeland. Stay here. Those that will, come with me to the mountains."

"Bron—"

"Charles, I understand that your mind will not be changed. Nor will mine. I had hoped you would see things as I do, but I

had prepared for you not to."

"*Separated, we may all perish,*" Charles said.

"*My friend, I believe we will all perish if we stay here.*"

After two days of preparation, Bron and about half the population of Prim began their journey to the mountains, hundreds of miles away. His company included the majority of the knights and most of the emotes capable of aggressive magic—those men and women who considered survival their sole priority.

Eilig looked at Gorvenal. *Do you think Bron was wise to leave Abilin?*

I suppose. His line endures to this day, while Charles's does not. Gorvenal tapped a talon on the floor. *Bron was certainly wise, in the face of the dragon attacks on his migrating people, to accept that they could not make it all the way to the mountains in the southwest as planned.*

Begrudgingly accepted, Eilig said.

Quite, Gorvenal agreed. *Stopping south of Lake Taulus was vital, though he did not expect to remain stuck there until the time of his death, those distant peaks a memory his waking eyes never again glimpsed.*

15

Taulus

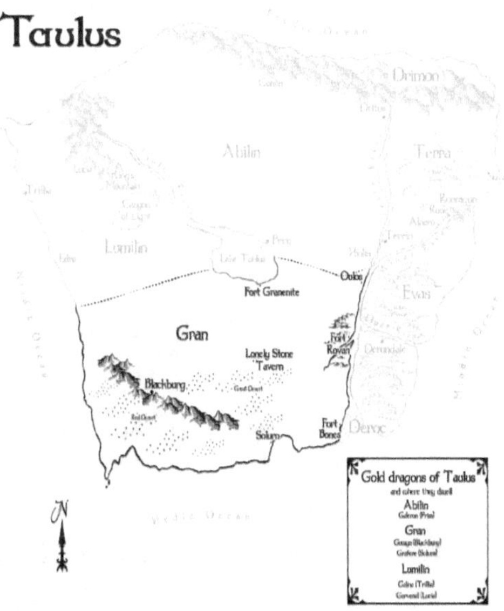

Upstairs in the tavern in Blackburg, Gall cracked open his eyes to the early morning light. "Avery…"

On a cot on the other side of the room—his sister lay in the other bed—Avery shied away from the same light. "What?"

"You didn't close the curtains."

Avery sat up, clutched at his head, and then lay back down. "What?"

"You said you'd close the window curtains. Last night. Avril was going to…" Gall glanced at her. "But she went to bed instead."

"I don't remember." Avery pulled his blanket to his chin and moaned. "I think I'm sick."

Gall buried his face in his pillow, and his explanation came out muffled. "You're hungover." He lifted his head. "Shouldn't have missed so many shots last night."

Avery sat up straight again. "I need to throw up."

"Down the hall."

"Water." Avril lifted her head and squinted. "Bring water."

Avery stumbled off his cot, grabbed a big cup from the bedside table, and left their room.

"How do you feel?" Gall asked Avril.

"Bad." She blinked. "But all right. How 'bout you?"

Gall grunted.

"I'm sorry about the curtains," she said.

"S'all right." Gall spoke into his pillow. "Avery's fault."

Their door opened, and Avery stepped in. "I feel a little better."

Gall lifted his head. "Hooray."

Avery brought the cup of water to Avril.

She held it with both hands and gulped until it was half empty. "Thanks."

"When do we find this elf thief?" Avery sat on his cot.

"Soon."

Avery finished a drink of water. "Where?"

Gall stretched his neck. "Two rooms down the hall." He

paused. "Or three? I asked the waitress…"

Avery's eyes grew wide. "What?"

"That's why I picked this tavern."

"I figured you had seen old friends in the other places," Avery said. "Friends you wanted to avoid."

"Well, you figured wrong."

"So what are we waiting for?" Avery asked.

Gall rolled onto his back. "You to bring me that water."

Avery peeked into the cup. "It's empty."

"Fill it up."

Avery slid off his cot and went out to the hall.

"What are you going to do?" Avril asked.

"If he doesn't have the sword and shield with him," Gall said, "I'm going to make him tell me where they are."

"Make him how?"

Gall looked at his palms and made fists. "I will punch him until he tells me."

"What if he won't talk?"

Gall punched softly into the air. "I will continue punching him."

Avery returned. "I threw up again."

"Well done." Gall reached for the cup.

Avery brought it over. "Is the elf a Thorn?"

"Dunno." Gall took the cup.

"What are you going to do to him?" Avery asked.

While Gall sat and drank the water, Avril said, "Punch him."

"Why?" Avery asked.

Gall emptied the cup. "Why not?" He swung his legs off

his bed, rubbed his face, then grabbed his boots.

"Why don't the golds do anything about the Thorns?" Avril asked.

"They do sometimes." Gall pulled on a boot. "But Thorns aren't easy to catch, and I don't think dragons enjoy spending their days scouring Taulus for thieves who are smart enough not to be in possession of evidence on the rare occasions they are caught."

Avery nodded. "What should we do?"

"Keep throwing up." Gall slid his foot into his second boot.

"No," Avery said. "About the elf."

"Oh, uh… if he escapes the tavern—and he might, which won't be fun, because I haven't had breakfast yet—watch where he goes." He pointed at them. "Don't let him grab you or anything like that. I'll catch him eventually, but if he has one of you two, that'll complicate things."

"Right," Avery said. "He won't get us."

Gall stood and stretched side to side. He glanced at his sword then put his knife on his belt. At the door, he said to the twins, "I'm going to go to take a piss, but I'll be back."

They hurried to put on their boots.

After a groggy trip down the hall and back, Gall slowly swung the door inward. He pointed at Avery's knife on the table. Avery shook his head. Gall nodded, more demonstratively. Avery grabbed the knife.

Gall motioned the twins out of the room and for them to be quiet.

In the hallway, the twins stayed behind him as Gall

paused two doors down and raised his fist to knock. He made an unsure face then proceeded to the next door.

There, he gestured for the twins to stay where they were then rolled his neck. He drove the door open with his shoulder.

The red-headed woman in bed with the elf, Meldrick, screamed, covering her bare chest with the blanket and sheet. She pulled more sheets around her, yanking them off the pale elf, who wore nothing but black shorts.

"Where are they?" Gall yelled.

"What?" The elf sat up against the headboard. Two thorns hung from his silver necklace.

"You know what. The gold dragons' sword and shield."

"So," Meldrick said, "you're Lairgnen's 'negotiator.'"

"I am. But Lairgnen decided he'd rather pay me to retrieve his property *and* beat the crap out of you—if you don't cooperate—than pay your ransom. So tell me."

The elf formed a smile. "They aren't here."

"No?" Gall stepped toward him. "Then where?"

"I will not tell you."

Gall made a fist with his left hand, cracked the knuckles with his right, then switched and cracked his others.

Meldrick grabbed a knife from the bedside table, pulled the woman close, and with his hand over her mouth, brought the blade to her neck. "I'll kill her."

"No…" Gall walked forward. "You're a thief, not a killer."

Meldrick ignored the woman's muffled screams. He pressed the sharp steel into her skin until blood trickled. "I am both, I assure you."

The woman quit trying to scream.

Gall stopped. "Then I guessed wrong."

"Indeed." The elf glanced at the curtains ruffling at the window. "What now?"

Gall grabbed his knife handle.

"Ah, ah!" The elf pointed with his weapon. "No."

Gall slowly unsheathed the blade.

"I'll do it." The elf clutched the woman closer. "I'll kill her."

Gall flipped his knife over to hold its metal. "Better hurry." He brought his arm back and above his head.

The elf moved the woman in front of him as a shield and stuck his head over her shoulder. He repositioned his knife on the woman's neck. "Your aim is that good?"

Gall focused on the elf's forehead. "It is."

The elf sliced into the woman's skin.

Gall threw.

Meldrick darted for the window.

Thunk! Gall's knife embedded in the headboard.

Blood poured from the woman's neck.

The elf leapt through the curtains and out the window.

The woman crumpled to the bed.

Avery and Avril rushed into the room.

"Get her help," Gall said to them. "Gimme your knife." Avery threw his to Gall, who caught it, ran for the window, and jumped out through the curtains.

Two stories below, the elf paused a block down the quiet morning street as Gall landed and went to a knee. The elf ran. Gall chased him uphill toward the castle, thankful to be dressed but concerned that being barefoot wouldn't actually slow the *elf*.

Gall followed Meldrick around the corner. The elf's legs pumped faster and faster. Gall considered throwing his knife to end the chase immediately but decided he wouldn't risk losing the chance to interrogate the thief. Outside a bakery, they passed a woman sweeping the entranceway. A city knight groggily walked past in the opposite direction. Two children watched and pointed from a second-story window.

Meldrick looked back then turned right, and Gall followed. The castle lay behind them, a small market ahead. The elf grabbed a street cart of bright fruits and vegetables, and pulled it down.

"Hey!" the merchant yelled.

Gall stomped tomatoes, grapes, and berries as he maintained his pursuit past other merchants setting up carts and tables with their goods for the day. Meldrick snatched a log from a startled old man's stack and flung the wood at Gall, who ducked under it.

The elf went left, uphill again, toward the edge of the town and the woods up the mountain beyond. They ran past the last houses. The road dissolved into a grassy path. Gall considered his knife again—he didn't want the elf reaching the cover of the trees.

Gall reached his weapon back, picked a spot on the elf's bare back, and without breaking stride, threw the knife hard. End over end, the knife spun.

Meldrick veered right, into the woods.

The blade embedded into a tree trunk at the forest's edge.

Gall growled as he ran. He got to his knife and pulled it free on the way past. He spotted the elf weaving between trees, uphill, toward… a cliff, as the forest on the next mountain was not near.

"Are they in Conlin?" Gall called.

The elf didn't slow.

Gall jumped a fallen branch. "You are a Thorn!"

"Yes!" the elf called, racing to the cliff.

"Are they in Solurn?"

Meldrick stepped into brighter light beyond the woods. His foot pushed off the edge, and he flew out toward the mountain in the distance then descended.

Gall ran hard but lost sight of the falling elf. The edge of the forest neared, Gall burst out of it, stepped on the ledge, and pushed off. And as he flew down behind the elf toward a thin mountainside ledge above a rocky, raging river, Gall wished he had thrown his knife before he leapt.

The elf landed, hit the mountainside hard, and spun toward his airborne pursuer.

Gall descended with his knife in hand.

Meldrick reached his knife high, awaiting Gall's imminent arrival.

Gall slashed at the elf, and the elf slashed back. Their arms met, neither weapon drawing blood. Gall hit the mountain with a thud. Meldrick sliced Gall's side—shallow.

Gall swung his knife. The elf ducked and swung at Gall, who blocked with his arm and reoriented himself on the ledge. Gall punched up into the elf's gut, launching Meldrick off his feet and forcing the elf's knife to miss high and hit the mountainside.

Gall stabbed down into Meldrick's shoulder.

"Ah!" Meldrick cried. Auburn blood flowed out of him.

Gall grabbed the elf's knife hand and smashed it into the mountain.

The elf cried out again.

With his knife still in Meldrick's shoulder, Gall smashed the elf's hand into the mountainside once more, then he twisted his blade, bashed Meldrick's hand, and ripped the elf's knife handle from his fingers, letting it fall to the ledge. Gall kicked the knife to the river. "Solurn or Conlin?"

Meldrick pushed against Gall and grimaced.

Only a slight smear of red seeped through Gall's shirt where Meldrick had cut him. Gall brought his blade out and stabbed the elf in the shoulder again.

Meldrick screamed and strained to get free.

Gall held firm. "The elves spotted your messenger coming to Terrin from the north. But he left to the south."

Blood streamed from Meldrick's shoulder. "Solurn. Conlin." He shrugged with the uninjured shoulder. "It's one of those."

"Which?"

The elf's wry smile returned.

Gall let go of his wrist and punched Meldrick in the stomach. "I don't need to kill you, but I do need the sword and the shield. Which city?"

Meldrick tried to catch his breath.

Gall punched him again. "Which?"

"Stop," Meldrick choked out. "I will take you to them."

"Nope. Tell me." Gall hit him a third time. "I know the jailers in Blackburg personally. I won't pay you a thing for what you stole, but I'll gladly pay them to lock you up."

Meldrick coughed blood. "I won't tell."

"Then you'll die."

"But I don't want to die." The elf kneed Gall in the groin and forced him away. Meldrick lunged for the ledge and pushed himself off.

Gall spun and grabbed for the elf's arm.

Meldrick's wrist and fingers slipped through Gall's hand, and the elf's dive toward deep water became a spinning fall to nearer rapids. He flailed.

"Conlin!" he shouted before his head hit the edge of a protruding rock. His bloody, cracked skull bounced before his limp body slid into the water.

Gall took a deep breath as he watched Meldrick drift down the river then saw where the ledge reached the trees. He felt the cut in his side, took a close look, and decided it would be fine. He put away his knife and headed to the forest then back to the city outside Castle Enduran. Blackburg had woken further by the time he returned, and the streets had grown more crowded. The last of the spilled fruits and vegetables were being picked up when Gall got to the market. A sweeper helped clear the mess. Bruised tomato in hand, the merchant gave Gall a mean look.

Gall shrugged on the way by. Around the corner, Avery and Avril approached on their horses, with Gall's behind them. Gall's things were packed on it.

"Thought it'd be best to get out of here," Avery said.

"Emhm," Gall said.

"You catch him?" Avery asked.

"Yes. But he fell."

"The sword and shield?"

Gall took hold of his saddle. "In Conlin." He pulled himself onto his horse. "North Abilin. In the mountains."

"He told you?" Avril asked.

"The second before his skull smashed into the rocks in the river," Gall said.

"Why?" Avery asked.

"Why what?"

"Why'd he tell you?"

"Wasn't looking forward to dying," Gall said.

"Telling you helped?"

"Maybe he thought it would." Gall shrugged. "Somehow. That woman dead?"

"No," Avril said. "It wasn't as bad as it looked."

"Really? It looked pretty bad."

Avery shrugged. "You all right?"

Gall glanced at the red on his shirt. "But a scratch."

Avery pulled a loaf of bread from his bag and threw it to Gall. "From the tavern. Got leftover chicken too."

"Ah. Good," Gall said. "Give me some of that."

Avery threw a wrapped piece of the previous night's meat to Gall. "To Trillia, not Conlin, right?"

Gall held the bread under his arm and unwrapped the cold chicken. "Yeah. Trillia ain't close, but it's closer than Conlin." He took a bite then led the twins down the road. "And before anything else, we need to buy you a sword."

16

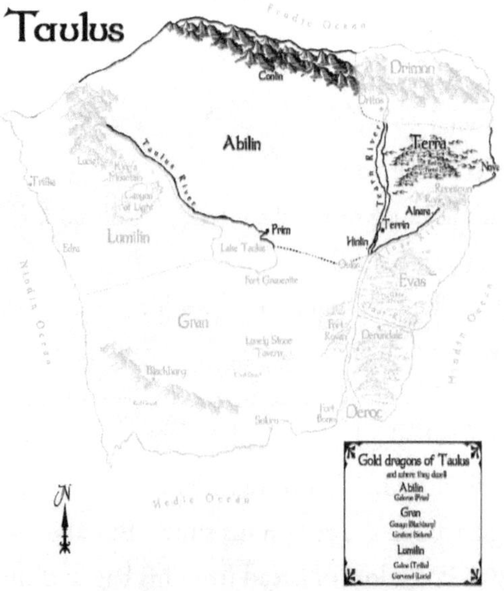

Farlan, the red dragon who dwelled in Terra, had come to Abilin in the morning, and Ri, set to fly with her to the elves in the afternoon, hastily packed for the trip—or so she had told her parents and everyone else. She had packed most everything she needed days before, leaving her little to do but lie on her bed, staring at the ceiling, waiting.

Ri had written of the fictional events she had settled on to the king of the Red Elves:

> *King Ervain,*
>
> *I hope this letter finds you well. On a recent trip beyond the borders of Abilin, I overheard a portion of a conversation I was not meant to. Elven lands were mentioned. I fear there may be cause for alarm. I wish to speak with you in person about these matters and would gladly travel to Terra, as soon as you would have me.*
>
> *Ever your friend,*
> *Corina*

Three knocks came at her door. Ri slid off her bed and answered it.

Her brother Gregory stood before her. "A two-week-long arts festival?"

"Yes!" She pulled him inside and shut the door. "The elves' idea, but Mother and Father bought it. And knowing the elves, it might actually be going on when I get there."

"What *will* you be doing?"

"Scouting, same as always." Ri had not shared details of her plan with her brother.

Gregory crossed his arms and raised an eyebrow. "And they needed *you,* specifically, for this scouting mission?"

"Apparently," Ri said. "Maybe they just like having me around."

"I find that highly unlikely."

"You don't care." Ri waved her hand. "Tell me you weren't glad when Father asked you to go with me. Tell me how you're going to miss all the 'excitement' around this place."

He uncrossed his arms. "Oh, I'm happy to go."

"Which of your elven lady friends are you most excited to see? Silana? Kattrina?" Ri tapped her finger on her chin. "Or Kacee?"

Gregory smiled. "Our friendship with the elves is strong, and I have many reasons to be thankful for it. *Surely* the company of a particular elf in Terra interests *you*."

"I'm sure one could. I can think of one or two who might… but here or there, it's just not a priority."

"Why? My friends ask me why you—"

"Your friends ask me too. But a real relationship means Father would push me to marry, and that means children, which means no more scouting."

"You can't scout with them forever."

"Exactly," Ri said.

"Don't you ever tire of it? I do all I can to skip my training here."

"We have more fun." Ri disregarded her growing boredom with her missions for the sake of the argument. "We compete and hunt and play games. We test ourselves out in that forest."

"It's still training."

"What if one day it isn't?"

"One day it may not be," Gregory said. "But we won't see that day."

"You never know."

"I do know." Gregory opened the door. "And I'm glad for it. It means you're free to have your fun, while I have mine."

He left, leaving Ri even more set on convincing King Ervain that the fabricated danger to his kingdom had to be investigated and that Ri and her team were the ones to do the investigating.

In Terrin, Ri—itching to change out of her dress and into her scouting attire—waited on a red cushioned chair at a round stone table inside a gazebo secluded from the heart of the palace by shrubs and leafy trees. Gregory had already run off with Silana and Kacee, who had greeted the Abilinians upon their arrival.

Ri accepted that Gregory was handsome but found it odd that three- and four-hundred-year-old elven beauties took such interest in him. He was a prince, Ri reminded herself, which probably excited his admirers. And while elves shared the same emotions as men and women, people said that things like love and hate did not run as hot in the longest living of Taulus's beings, and that humans excited some elves because of it. Ri struggled to believe that time, however long, put limits on the depths of any emotion, but a lot of smart people, in every age of Taulus, had suggested exactly that.

Marriage among the elves was rare, except among royals. And married or not, elven parents hardly ever had more than one child. Gregory could never marry one of his friends from

Terra. Only pure humans could ascend to the throne in Abilin, and even though Gregory had older brothers, Ri's father would never consent to Gregory wedding an elf who could only give him half-elf children, if she gave him any children at all. Half-elf births—all called half-elves, no matter how elven or human the babies turned out—were extremely rare.

However, other than making it clear that Gregory would have to pick a human wife eventually, his father didn't object to him enjoying the company of elves. The exception at the highest levels of royalty aside, elves and half-elves alike were warmly welcomed in Abilin, even in the knighthood, unlike in Gran or Lumilin, where both inhuman races—and especially the halves—were seen through wary eyes. The Red Elves had no problem with the halves at all and many lived in Terra, while most White and Dark Elves resented the half-breeds' very existence.

King Ervain approached on the long path with his son, Erwyn. Ri stood.

"Please." The king motioned her back down. He sat across from her, and his son, himself a hundred ninety years old, sat to her right. The king said, "Despite the circumstances, I am glad to see you, Ri."

"And I you, Your Grace, as always." Ri glanced at the prince. "And you, Erwyn."

"Likewise, Ri," Erwyn said. "How are you?"

"I am well."

Erwyn smiled. "I am glad."

"As am I," Ervain said. "Now, you overheard part of a

conversation? You suggested time was somewhat of the essence."

"Yes," Ri said. "Thank you for sending for me." She shifted in her seat and began the story she had practiced in her head the whole trip. "In Dritus, on the way into the king's hall, I passed King Doxton talking to Governor Bardric of Rone. I was late going to the hall because I had fallen asleep in my room by accident, so they mustn't have expected me then."

"What were you doing in Dritus?" Erwyn asked.

"Giving the king a gift," Ri said. "A gemstone we recovered from the Thorns. I went to Drimon with my brothers to present the gift on behalf of my father, as a token of Abilin's friendship with the dwarves."

"Most generous," Erwyn said. "Please, what did you overhear?"

"Well…" Ri folded her hands together on the table. "Bardric said, 'The elves won't see it coming.' King Doxton responded, 'Soon. Return to Rone and be ready.'"

Ervain glanced at his son.

"Anything else?" Erwyn asked.

Ri shook her head. "No, I went into the hall and couldn't hear any more." After a pause, she added, "I couldn't believe what I had heard. I'm worried, but I couldn't think of a reason to stay out in the hallway to keep listening."

"Of course," Erwyn said.

"This is troubling," Ervain said. "And comes after reports of goblins in the White Forest."

"Goblins?" Ri asked.

"A scattering," Ervain said. "Happens from time to time. And none north of the Alnar. Nevertheless, it seems we ought to take a closer look at what's going on in Rone."

"Yes," Ri said.

Both elves raised an eyebrow.

"That's what I thought made sense," Ri added.

"I'll ask Farlan," Erwyn said.

The king put up his hand. "No. I want to do it more quietly. More discreetly."

"Scouts from Alnara then?" Erwyn asked.

"No, my best scouts are here. Naelon's company, which means you, Ri."

Ri smiled.

"If you'll go."

"Of course," she said. "Anything I can do to help."

"Good."

"And it may be nothing," Ri added. "Or maybe I misheard them."

"I hope that proves the case. Thank you for bringing this to us." Ervain motioned to the pathway. "We'll see you at dinner."

"You're welcome." Ri stood.

As she walked away, she heard Erwyn ask, "You wouldn't rather send Farlan?"

Ervain brought his finger to his lips to quiet his son while Ri left. Once she had passed the point where the path curved and was out of sight, the king waited a few seconds more.

"Asking Farlan to fly over Rone would be wise. And if not that, sending scouts from Alnara would be the obvious choice. Or it would be, if Ri had not fabricated this story."

Erwyn nodded. "I had the same suspicion. Why would Bardric and Doxton have a conversation like that out in the open?"

"Exactly," the king said. "And that is aside from the nature of the conversation itself. I've known those two dwarves their whole lives. I knew their fathers and their families. They are no enemies of ours."

"Why play along? It's a waste of Naelon's time, and of the others', sending them out there."

Ervain shrugged. "Why not? They *are* my best scouts, and what else are they doing?"

"Training, games," Erwyn said. "I'm starting to see why Ri set this ruse in motion."

"Indeed. I fought in my wars, and in your long life, you may fight in one yourself."

"I do not wish it."

"Nor do I, for you. And maybe, if you are to know war, yours will be exclusively political, of a nature that does not bring widespread death and destruction. But regardless of the form it takes, you may live to see such a conflict. Ri is a quarter of the way done with her short life. She is an accomplished scout and fighter—for a human, quite accomplished. But her years at the peak of those abilities are such a short portion of that brief lifetime..." He rubbed his chin. "I will let her play her game."

"That is most kind of you, Father," Erwyn said. "What

will you tell the rest of the company?"

"The same thing Ri told us, plus my insistence that they keep this mission secret from the others because of its sensitive nature." The king paused. "And that they look out for goblins, though we would surely have noticed them already were they in our woods." Ervain rose from his seat. "When they return, I will ask Ri not to send us on another made-up mission." He tapped his finger on the table. "Maybe."

————————

Ri lay in her bed, unable to sleep despite the pleasant chirr and buzz of nighttime insects outside and the earthy scent of forest air she so loved.

Her plan was working! She imagined, in intoxicating detail, being out on the scouting mission she had succeeded in securing.

Her mind had wandered at dinner as well. The meal had been nice—and contrasted starkly with the dwarven feast. Nine elves and a half-elf poet, all of notable standing and importance, had sat around the long, finely carved wooden table in Terrin, compared to the crowd of workers who had packed the hall in Dritus. Wine filled fancy goblets, instead of beer brimming to the top of plain, well-worn mugs.

In Terrin, outside on the warm evening, a waterfall peeking out from the forest ran far enough in the distance not to drown out the violinist's soft strokes while they'd eaten. Ri had wondered how the melody sounded to the elves' sharper sense of hearing. Had what Ri found so pleasant been nothing short of exquisite to the others at the table?

The king, the queen, and Erwyn had been there. Kacee and Ri's brother had shared countless whispers and giggles. Ri had glared and rolled her eyes, but she hadn't succeeded in stopping him.

Launfal, Ri's scouting companion, hadn't been able to attend, as he was away bird-watching with friends, but he would return in time for the mission's departure in the morning.

Two teachers, a painter, the poet, and two singers had rounded out the group. The courteous conversation centered mostly around the elves' occupations, especially their upcoming projects and performances. The king and queen assured the artists that they looked forward to every bit of their work. Ri answered a number of questions about the goings-on in Abilin, and Gregory was kind enough to interrupt his whispering with Kacee to help field a few.

To an onlooker unfamiliar with the elves, the meal might have appeared overly reserved and its participants uncomfortably restrained. But Ri had been in Terrin enough to understand the genuine warmth shared among all in attendance.

In her bed, thinking back on it, Ri smiled. No one had run to the table asking her to judge anything, and she had never had to fetch her own food or drink.

Thankfully, no one had asked Ri about her mission, either. If the king had, she would have come up with whatever lie necessary to reiterate what she had heard in

Drimon. To anyone else, she would have politely declined to comment.

But none of those questions had come, and her mission remained set for the morning as planned, so Ri closed her eyes tight and tried to force herself to sleep.

———————

The next morning, Ri tied the thin laces of her leather boot tight, verified that her quiver contained twelve arrows, and threw its strap over her shoulder. She grabbed her bow, pausing for a moment to admire the engraving of her name in small black lettering in the dark wood below the handle. Launfal had given her the fine weapon for her birthday years before. He explained to Ri that it had been made by the elf he considered most skilled in such work in all of Terra and that it was of the quality that the elves reserved for gifts. A bow like that would not be produced for sale. Ri pulled on its string to check the tension.

She smiled as she pictured her scout team chasing a pack of goblins scurrying through the forest and tried to force her happy face away. But goblins! A real threat out there. *Please, let one have made it north into the Red Forest. Please, just one…*

Ri had been unable to find Gregory earlier to inform him of her departure and decided not to bother trying again. She headed to the stables, where an elf named Ren sat downhill from the horses, leaning against a tree, reading.

He closed his book on his finger. "Ri."

"Ren."

He stood and whistled—high pitched and short.

A finely groomed chestnut mare trotted out of the stable to them.

Ri took her reins. "Secra." She petted the horse's nose.

"Where you headed?" Ren asked.

Ri smiled. "Can't say."

"No?" Ren crossed his arms.

Ri's smile grew to a wide grin. "Sorry."

"This secret pleases you too much."

"It pleases me because it displeases you." Ri led Secra away, down the path.

"Hah. I suppose I should wish you good luck, in any case," Ren called after her.

"You don't have to," Ri called back.

"Good luck."

———

Launfal was waiting near Terrin's main gate with Egan and Addis and their horses when Ri arrived. Two elven guards stood watch atop thin towers.

"How was the venison?" Launfal asked.

Ri's smile washed over her. "I savored each bite." She shared a hug with the elf, who more than any other had taken the time to teach her to be a good scout.

Egan and Addis were the youngest in the company, both around one hundred fifty years old. Of the two, Egan fought better at close range, had a sturdier build, and was shorter, though no elves stood especially short. Ri embraced him then Addis, the team's emote, who possessed a sharper mind for tactics and shot better with his bow, though no elves performed especially poorly with that weapon.

Emlyn arrived. "Ri."

"Emlyn," Ri said. The three-hundred-fifty-year-old elf had been like a mother to Ri when Ri first joined the company years ago. But Ri had grown up and proved herself, and the days she had needed a mother out in the woods had passed. They hugged.

Naelon came down the path. "Glad you could join us, Ri." He hugged her.

"Glad to be here," Ri said. *So glad.*

"Ri tells us that something may be amiss in Rone," Naelon said to the group. "Shall we go find out?"

"Aye," Egan and Addis responded.

Launfal nodded.

"We should," Emlyn said.

"After you, young one." Naelon motioned toward the gate.

Ri mounted her horse and grinned. "And be on the lookout for goblins!" She kicked Secra and rode away fast down the path while her team was still mounting their horses.

Taulus

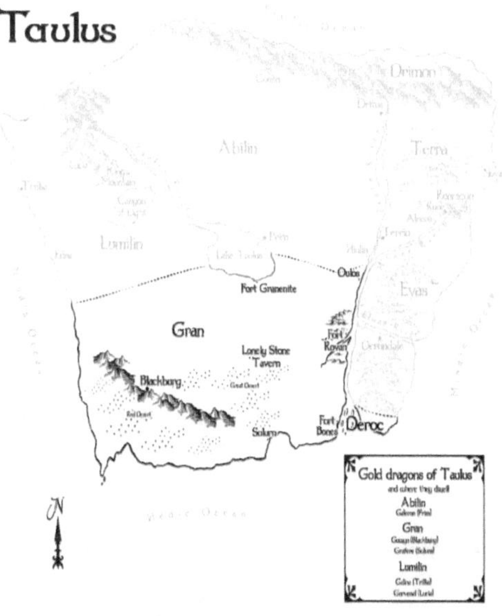

After laying their two fallen knights to rest near the site of the battle with the ogres, Valencia's company rode south to confront the Dark Elves of Deroc. The swamp at the southern end of Taulus spanned the wide mouth of the Tearn River. The land had belonged to the White Elves until their dark cousins had settled there. Deroc bordered Gran on the west and the White Elves' forest to the east. Even before the elves brought their dark magic, the swamp had been a gloomy place, and on more than one occasion, when thinking about that ultimate destination, Taylan felt the hairs on the back of his neck rise.

The knights stayed on the western side of the Tearn, in Gran, with forest of white-barked trees to their left the entire journey and ever-grayer clouds thickening overhead. Golden Gowyn's arrival on the third day lifted everyone's spirits. While they all rested from riding, ate, and watered their horses, Valencia and Taylan moved away from the others to speak with the dragon.

Valencia. Gowyn bowed his head slightly.

"Gowyn." She returned the respectful gesture. "This is Taylan, my friend."

Gowyn nodded to him. *Hello, Taylan.* He looked them over quickly. *Did you find the ogres?*

"Three of them," Valencia said. "They attacked before we could ask what brought them up north and west of the Tearn."

You killed them?

"Yes."

And you're headed for Deroc to ask Eldred, now that you cannot ask the ogres?

"Yes."

Would you like me to go with you? Or to take you?

"No, but thank you. I want answers for me, not me and the dragon who could incinerate them all with a few bursts of flame." Valencia looked at Shaela and the resting knights. "And they could use the experience."

Then I will find you after Deroc, Gowyn said. *To hear what King Eldred and Queen Jadira had to say for themselves. Send for me if I can be of assistance sooner.*

"We will."

And ask the elves about goblins in the White Forest. Grafere spotted fifteen running across a clearing, and that's fifteen more than should be there.

"I will ask them," Valencia said.

Taylan watched as Gowyn flew to the rest of the company, wished them good luck, then headed east over the White Forest. Taylan did not see Grafere, the golden dragon from Solurn, anywhere in the sky.

The company resumed their ride south in a column two abreast, following the eastern border of Gran. The sun grew increasingly dim behind thickening clouds, until near Fort Bones just north of Deroc, an opaque blanket of gray capped the warm, sticky air.

Fort Bones stood as the nearest guarded position to Deroc. The dreary clouds that usually covered the swamp had earlier in Taulus's history been ever present and coal colored. The power of the hateful emotional magic the elves had employed at the time seemed the explanation for that eerie canopy, and the darkest clouds had dissipated along with the disappearance of that type of magic.

Taylan watched Valencia as they rode and appreciated that the sun did not beat upon him. He imagined the upcoming night in the fort on a soft bed with Val, instead of another in a tent. He imagined holding her tight.

Unless the fort meant he would not share her bed, he

realized. Taylan's throat grew dry. He grabbed his canteen and wet his lips. They dried immediately, and a gulp hurt his throat. Valencia bounced up and down in her saddle. Taylan needed to be with her. *Surely* she could not wait to be with him either.

However, whether because her position as commander dictated discretion or because his pointy ears demanded discretion among those outside her own company, Taylan could see Valencia deciding against being with him in the fort, even after their last few nights together.

The Tearn River ran louder off to Taylan's left. He drank more water. The sticky air grew heavier. Taylan's thirst would not be quenched. He stared at Valencia as they neared Fort Bones.

So beautiful, so strong, he thought. So many years without her… Such long, lonely years without his dear friend, his confidant… his love.

Valencia dropped back in the line of horses and nodded for Taylan to follow her all the way to the rear.

When they got there, she said to him, "Tonight, our own tents."

"Why?" Taylan asked.

"This close to Deroc, with Commander Algar nearby, it would be for the best."

Taylan gulped, irritating his dry throat. "All right."

Taylan could not bring himself to watch Valencia as she rode to the front of the column.

———————————

Shortly before nightfall, Valencia and Taylan stood atop the wall in the fort with Commander Algar, looking out at Deroc. "Notice anything unusual out there?" she asked Algar.

"No. Thick clouds most days," he said. "But the sun peeks through plenty."

Taylan asked, "Any ogres, goblins, or any of the elves' other creatures up this way?"

Algar raised an eyebrow. "You some kind of expert on that stuff?"

"Hm?"

"You ain't a knight," Algar said.

"No, I am not a knight. And I'm no expert either."

"He's a friend," Valencia said.

"Hm." Algar studied the view for a moment. "Some of their birds fly here, but we always see a few. Nothing else. No ogres or goblins. You found yours near Fort Rovan?"

"Yes," Valencia answered.

"Must have stayed east of the river in the forest and went north. Crossed near the fort."

"Right," Valencia said. "A group of goblins have been spotted in the forest as well."

"Really…" Algar grasped the hilt of his sheathed sword. "Take two of my knights with you to Deroc tomorrow."

"Thank you," Valencia said. "But there's no need."

"I insist," Algar said. "In case you don't return this way, I need to hear Eldred's excuse for violating the treaty."

———

Valencia led the knights in a single-file column of horses slowly down the narrow dirt path through the outskirts of Deroc. Taylan rode behind her, one of Algar's knights followed, and the other brought up the rear. Hayle rode behind Shaela in the middle. Mud, puddles, and tall grassy patches lined the path. The thin, white-trunked trees were sparse.

Taylan had put on gloves after the first few insects had bitten him, but they continued to buzz by his exposed face and increasingly agitated horse. A few of the knights had the focus to ignore the little nuisances, but Taylan and most of the rest swatted at the bugs constantly. Their horses flinched when the insects flew near their eyes and ears. The gray clouds became darker and darker.

While any bugs would have annoyed Taylan, wondering if those that pestered him had been changed, mutated, and *enhanced* like the other abominations of the Dark Elves unsettled him. Such unnatural things… but he had no real choice except to ride on.

A hummingbird beat its wings at a twisted tree ahead off the path. Or it *had been* a hummingbird. What should have been green wings had become pale and, most tellingly, longer and wider. Taylan had seen one like it when, as a youth, he had come to explore the outskirts of Deroc on his own. The elves had changed that species of birds back when they, like many emotes in Taulus, had commanded aggressive magic. Taylan didn't know what to call the thing anymore, and he hadn't seen one since. The elves of Deroc possessed as strong a connection with nature as any elves, and that allowed them to keep their modified creatures within their borders, as mandated by the

Treaty of Solurn. The incessantly buzzing insects reminded Taylan that he had never known himself to possess any special connection with nature.

He decided he had never before been as deep into Deroc when, to his right, a raccoon poked its head out from a hole in a crumbling stone wall—maybe an old watchtower. The animal's eyes were red, and the muscles of its front legs bulged grotesquely. An early experiment, Taylan reasoned—a start, like the hummingbird. But the elves hadn't built their army with such diminutive creatures.

The path grew thinner as the company rode on. The mud abutting it gave way to deepening water on both sides. The forest thickened.

"Croc," Valencia called calmly. "Left."

They passed the animal quickly, the knights with their spears at the ready and with arrows aimed at the top of the snout poking out of the water. *Crocodile… that's more like it*, Taylan thought. The powerful reptilian body hidden beneath the water surely also had been changed at its deepest levels by the elves. Its ancestors would have had the very fibers of their beings torn, tortured, and twisted, like the smaller animals and like the larger winged reptiles that terrorized the world before the golds were around to fight them. Eldred's father, King Ewald, and his emotes almost certainly practiced on crocodiles shortly before they made purple dragons into the first monstrous blacks.

The sound of galloping hooves preceded approaching riders. Huge black-haired horses carried two tall elves—pale skinned, and dressed in black, navy, and gray. They both had long white hair.

Taylan halted with the rest of the column. The elves pulled up when they got close.

"Valencia," the lead rider said.

"Fyren," she said. "Darrin."

They nodded, and Fyren asked, "What brings a renowned knight of Gran away from the safety of her fort and with such a company to as dismal a place as Deroc?"

"Ogres," Valencia said.

"Ogres?"

"Near Fort Rovan. They shouldn't have been there."

"No," Darrin said. "They should not have been."

"They should have been here," Valencia said.

Taylan had no doubt other ogres were spread throughout Deroc, along with ugly trolls and little goblins.

"We dealt with them," Valencia said. "And I came to discuss the matter with King Eldred."

Fyren nodded once. "In ages past, I might have told you that our king is too busy to attend to such requests personally. Three ogres is no great matter. But in this age, in these sunny years, we both know that would be a lie. Eldred, confined to this dying land, is not busy with the same matters of state as other kings. We will take you to him."

"Thank you." Valencia followed when the elves turned and headed back the way they had come.

With the others, Taylan trailed her, curious how the elf knew the exact number of ogres there had been.

———

Through thickening forest and air that smelled of ocean salt, they rode for the southern shore of Taulus. Taylan noticed a few elves up in trees off the path, watching the company pass. No one spoke.

Taylan had never seen a black dragon—no one his age, including any living humans, had. But picturing one was not difficult. And numerous paintings showed the creatures, and stories described them. A little larger and stronger than the natural dragons and more aggressive, the monstrous, terrible reptiles had sharp scales and fierce, reddened eyes. The mutated animals in the swamp served as living reminders of the angry beasts. God had been so upset at how his gift of magic had been used to warp his creations that he had taken away the emotional powers of men and elves, and Taylan understood why.

When Taylan could hear ocean waves in the distance, the path widened. The elves led them on, and Taylan spotted a smooth black wall ahead. A little farther on, he noticed where the granenite had been melted. They entered a clearing, and Castle Derindom's ruins, overgrown with trees and vines, came increasingly into view. Galeron, full of rage over his very personal loss in the second Dark War, had destroyed it. After the elven forces had been beaten and none of their dragons remained to protect it, in a prolonged bout of fury, he had used his fire to melt the castle until only a few battered sections remained.

Fyren stopped and said, "Wait here. Darrin will bring water for your company and your horses. Valencia may come with us to the shore to meet King Eldred."

The riders halted.

Valencia said, "Taylan, come with me." She pointed at the knights from Fort Bones. "You two, and Shaela."

"As you wish," Fyren said.

Everyone dismounted.

Fyren led Valencia and the others on the muddy, narrow path through dense plants and trees. While Taylan cringed as his boots sank into the mud and he pulled hard to free them, the Dark Elf seemed not to have the same trouble. Thorns caught Taylan's clothes and scraped his cheeks. As comfortable as he usually found himself in darkness, Taylan felt very glad to have come to Deroc during daytime.

Finally they escaped the wilderness. Small waves sloshed onto a thin, dull beach of packed sand. Near the tree line, two elves sat holding their knees. Halfway to the water, crownless King Eldred and Queen Jadira—both slim and tall—lay on their backs, staring at the clouds.

"My lord," Fyren said. "Valencia of Gran, and those she felt needed to accompany her."

"Valencia." The white-haired king didn't move. "It has been a while."

The queen sat up. Wet sand covered the powerful emote's shoulders and arms and stuck to her long raven-black hair. A few clumps of sand fell to the ground.

"Please," Eldred said. "Sit. Join us."

Valencia led her group in front of the royals. "Thank you, but we'll stand."

Still lying in the sand, Eldred said, "Suit yourself."

Jadira stared at Taylan. Fair skin, thin lips, sapphire-blue eyes—the mud did not dim her beauty, nor Eldred's.

Jadira tilted her head. "You are in pain, half-elf."

All looked at Taylan.

"I'm fine," he said.

"No, you are not." A clump of sand fell from Jadira's shoulder. "But that is not why you are here."

Eldred's silver eyes shifted to his queen, then to Valencia. "What brings you to Deroc? Can't you see I am *quite* busy?"

"Ogres," Valencia said, looking down at him. "On our land near Fort Rovan. The treaty is very clear. They shouldn't have been there."

"How many?" he asked.

"Three. A number Fyren knew exactly."

"Did he?" Eldred tapped his finger to his chin demonstratively.

Valencia crossed her arms. "He did."

"Well, they shouldn't have been there."

"Right. And they killed two of my knights."

Eldred put his hands together in front of him. "I am sorry for your loss, and I am sorry that the ogres caused any trouble at all. We will keep a closer watch."

Jadira cracked the smallest smile. The ocean breeze blowing her hair exposed a pointed ear.

"I hear of goblins in the White Forest," Valencia said. "Why?"

"Goblins?" Eldred's eyes shifted up. "Do you know anything about goblins in the north, Farek?"

"No," one of the elves sitting behind him said.

"Do you, Ivir?" Eldred asked.

"No, my king," the other said.

Eldred returned his gaze to Valencia. "I do not know why goblins are in the White Forest. May I ask from whom you *heard* of these goblins? Not a child telling stories of what they imagined in the night, I hope?"

"Grafere told Gowyn."

"Ah, Grafere… and of course Gowyn believed what he was told. He is not so young but is a child in his own right. It has been some time since I have seen Gowyn, as well."

Valencia crouched and said sternly, "He told me he would be happy to pay you a visit."

The king lifted his head from the sand. "You needn't a princely golden dragon to threaten me, knight of Gran. There are enough in your kingdom to wipe us out without him having anything to do with it."

Valencia stood. "Stop the ogres from going north. And the goblins."

"We shall do our best." Eldred laid his head down. "As ever we aim to." He motioned to the path they had come by. "Thank you for your visit, but I am afraid our time together is up. We have clouds that need watching and waves that need listening to."

Taylan took a long look at Jadira, who stared straight back at him, before he left the beach.

18

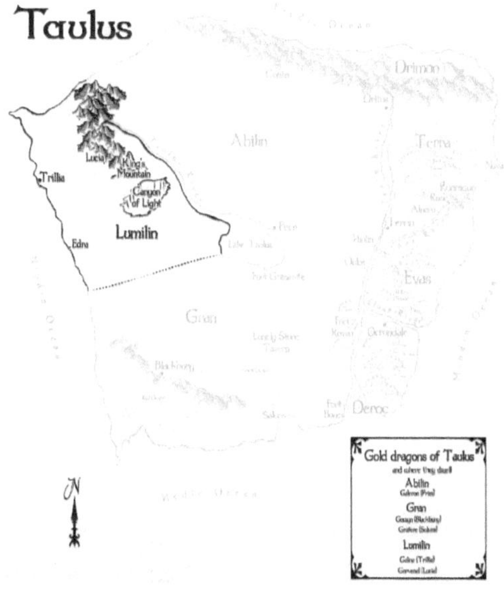

Salty water sprayed off the jagged rocks where Gorvenal had perched out in the ocean not far from Azure Cliffs. The rock face was so splendidly blue that Lila might have mistaken the sky for stretching all the way down to the beach at the cliff's base, were it not for Trillia's high white wall and tall castle with its spire-capped towers interrupting the color.

One after another, the waves Lila had asked Gorvenal to

fly her to crashed against the rocks, and a refreshing mist reached her up on the dragon's back. Lila pointed along the narrow white-sand beach at a rider on a big brown horse. "Someone's coming."

Gorvenal looked at the rider. *Sir Beal.*

"Can we go to Yalus soon?" Lila asked.

Yes. I promise.

She lay on his scales. "I can't wait."

Beal dismounted and, stepping gingerly from rock to rock, made his way out to them. He waved. "Gorvenal."

Sir Beal. Gorvenal craned his neck backward. *This is Lila.*

"Hello, Lila," Beal called from a few rocks away. "I heard you might be out here with Gorvenal. How are you? How are you both?"

"Fine," she said.

As am I.

"Good. What, ah—" Beal flinched when a splash of water hit him. "What are you doing out here?"

I was telling Lila of the birth of the kingdom of Lumilin.

"Ah." Beal looked up at the big dragon. "When Charles's line was broken in Abilin three hundred years after it began, when help from Gran could not stop Prim from being leveled, and when the dragons of the world were poised to decimate that first kingdom entirely."

That is the story.

"We are not like the dragons, Lila," Beal said. "Not even knights like me. We are not built for constant battle and war like they are. Thankfully, mercifully, a few dragons realized this, hated seeing us suffer, and in what could have been

Abilin's final hour, those dragons came to its defense and saved the first kingdom of men."

Beal leaned to the side, avoiding most of a splash. "Then when the fighting had calmed down and the knights from Gran had returned to their capital around the lake, the men and women of both kingdoms found they could communicate with dragons for the first time. We have been able to ever since. The people of Gran, under the protection of the ferocious red, Ferron, in return for acknowledging his lordship of the desert beyond the Mountains of Fire, finally completed their journey and relocated their capital to Blackburg.

"Abilin needed a new king and a new line of kings. Their choice, though it eventually proved a fine one, angered many, and that, plus the allure of unsettled lands to the west, the judgment that such an opportunity would not last, and the aid of the blue dragon, Edra, led Luscious to bring our people to settle this breathtaking land."

Lila sat up. "You tell it considerably quicker than Gorvenal."

"Oh?" Beal said. "You already know the story?"

"I do."

"Then apologies"—a splash of water soaked Beal—"for rushing it."

"Not at all," Lila said. "Thank you for getting to the heart of it."

What brings you out here, Beal?

"There is to be a tournament next week." He wiped water from his face. "I am not sure if I will be fighting. I suppose it is likely I will, some, but... anyway, King Adrian wants me to make a grand entrance to open the games. He suggested I arrive from the sky, the sun shining upon me, carried on your mother's back."

Not subtle. But the people will love it, Gorvenal said.

"Adrian's idea, not mine," Beal said. "But they will love it." He rubbed his chin and motioned to the dragon. "However, your mother said she'd rather you fly me in to start the tournament. Said it rather forcefully, to be honest. And since you are here today, I rode out to ask you."

No.

"No?"

No. Tell my mother that were the games in Lucia, I would do it, but as this is her city, she should make the grand entrance.

"I see." Beal brought a finger to his lips. "And I understand. I may take a more suggestive approach, but I will relay your message." He brought his hands together in front of him. "Gorvenal, thank you. Lila. Enjoy the"—another splash hit him—"warm ocean water."

Good day, Sir Beal. As the knight jumped from rock to rock to leave, Gorvenal said, so Lila alone could hear, *I won't be attending the tournament at all. I will be with you, out on Yalus.*

19

Taulus

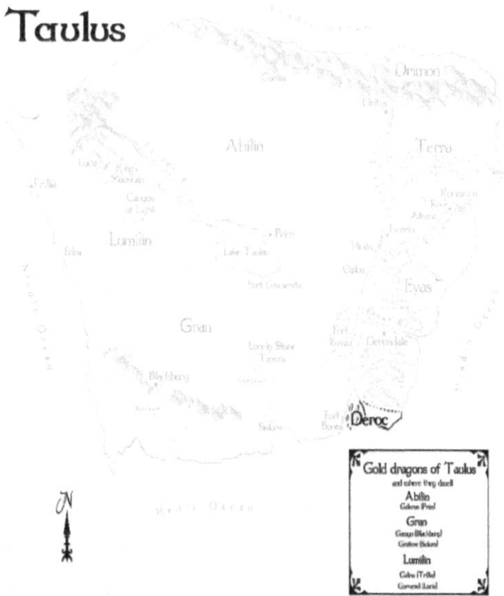

King Eldred followed his queen onto the breezy beach on the southern shore of Deroc. A single torch lit the sands. His chief strategist, Ivir, and most trusted advisor, Farek, both much older than the three-hundred-year-old king, sat where they always sat, up the beach beyond the reach of the water of the Hedic Ocean.

Jadira, herself two hundred fifty years old, walked close

to the waves running up the sand, but for a change, remained standing. Eldred didn't sit either.

He took her hand and brought it to his lips for a soft kiss, then he turned it for another, and another. Toward the swamp, he whistled—high pitched and short—then whispered over the churning waves into Jadira's ear, "You will be queen of so much more."

She wrapped her arms around him, and her lips met his. He held her with one hand and ran his other through her blowing hair, finally settling on her neck. Their tongues found each other's, and they clutched one another more tightly.

A loud wave crashed, and warm water ran onto their feet. They ended their embrace and turned to Ivir and Farek, who rose.

"Time has come," Eldred said.

A male Dark Elf approached from the same pathway the king and queen had, and a second followed. A female stepped out from the woods onto the sand. Another three elves came, and on and on—more males than females, no children—until the Dark Elves packed the whole of the small beach except for the space they gave their king and queen.

"Patience," Eldred said to the crowd, "has brought us to this night. Patience has served us well. I am saddened that our kind does not live so long that *all* of us could be here to see the fruits of our patience." He glanced at the sand. "But we made that sacrifice knowingly." He looked at his elves. "And I have been considerably more than *saddened* these long years in Deroc, watching the world outside our swamp… our prison."

Eldred pointed north. "*That*, beyond our borders, is no world worth living in. *That peace* is absurd. It is a joke. Those *knights* who visit us here, what have they done to earn the title? Drills? Tournament games? When have they truly fought or struggled, and for what? When have they suffered real pain?" Eldred lowered his arm. "We have suffered, here in our prison. Yet we have also struggled to plan a way out, to be free, to *earn* a better life.

"The world beyond Deroc is a gilded fantasy that should never have been and one that will never again be. Word has come from our friends that we are ready to begin." He scanned the crowd. "I am tired of waiting, dejected. Tell me, are you also so tired?"

"Yes," the elves all responded.

"Are you ready to put an end to this peace—to this detestable *age*?"

"Yes."

Eldred nodded. "Begin your final preparations." He and the queen sat in the sand facing the water. The elves, including Ivir and Farek, left the beach. Jadira, the youngest elf in Deroc, rested her head on her king's shoulder and watched dark waves roll ashore.

20

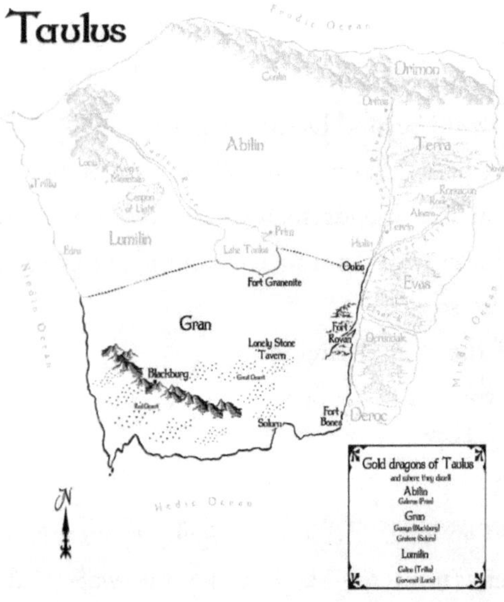

On the second night of their long journey northwest from Fort Bones to Fort Granenite, Taylan lay beside Valencia in her tent, as he had been so thankful to do the day before. Crickets chirped outside. He held Valencia's hand and rubbed his index finger against her palm.

Taylan recalled summer nights full of the same sharp insect sounds when they had been younger and had run off from the adults' boring conversations at his mother's sister's home to be alone in the woods together. He remembered their first kiss—it had been his first ever, but not hers.

Taylan remembered the nights they had hardly spoken, when their long kisses rolled into longer ones, leaving no time for any words. He remembered the first night that those kisses had led to clumsily pulling off each other's clothes and had left them naked in their tent. A fire had burned and crackled outside, and they were truly together—Taylan's first time with anyone, but not hers.

He remembered, almost as vividly, when her family's visit had ended that year and she had ridden away from him with her mother and father, home to Gran. Taylan could do nothing but watch her go and then head home with his mother—and without the elvish father who, though he continued to send his mother plenty of money, Taylan had not yet met at that point.

A flash of flame burst in his mind's eye—a memory of the fire that had burned years later and killed his parents. Taylan didn't want to remember any more.

He let go of Valencia's hand. "How are your parents?"

"Fine. Father drills his units hard in Gran. Hardest of all the generals, some say. Mother is out there helping him most days."

Taylan propped himself up on his arm. "Think that'll be you one day?"

"Commanding units in Blackburg? Or helping a husband command his?"

Far more female knights served in Gran's army than in

any other, and Taylan knew Valencia would have any opportunity she earned there. "Either."

"Oh… I don't know," she said. "I could lead units. I could lead an army." Her eyes shifted from spot to spot on the ceiling. "Someday, I could lead an army." She turned to Taylan. "I don't wish to be married today, or soon, but eventually? Maybe. I like where I am. I like my fort. It's the right size for me right now. My knights are good knights. And after this…" She gently shook her head. "After losing two, I won't have any trouble getting them to train with purpose."

"I'm sorry about Danon and Hollis. I could have helped."

Valencia shook her head. "It's my fault. And theirs. But not yours. Real combat is so rare, and like them, I proved unready."

"You'll learn from it, I'm sure."

"Oh, I will," Valencia said. "I already have."

Taylan returned to his back and spoke to the ceiling. "And maybe you proved wiser than you give yourself credit for, bringing me along. I just failed miserably."

Valencia rolled to her side and propped up her head. "That's not why I asked you, Tay."

He looked at her. "Why did you ask me?"

"What I said in my letter. I missed you. I missed nights like this, like when we were young."

Taylan's face softened. "Me too."

"*We* can handle the fighting."

"I know, but… there I was, and I did nothing."

"I know it's hard for you," Valencia said. "I know it hurts you. In your travels and your research, have you figured out *why* it hurts you? In the stories it wasn't so."

Taylan's travels, funded by the money his mother had left behind, had taken him to every kingdom, shore, and corner of Taulus, to the pages of old books and to ancient scrolls. He had met more men, women, and elves than he could remember, and even some dwarves. Many whose paths he crossed he found interesting, some eccentric, plenty reclusive and stubborn, plenty more a waste of his time, and a few wise and eager to share all they had learned over their lives. "Would they include such pain in the stories?" Taylan asked. "Would anyone talk about it?"

Valencia shrugged.

"I don't know," Taylan said, so glad that Val had written him and given him a rest from that endless search. "I haven't found any answers. I don't know how it was for everyone, but I know how it is with me. I know how it stays with me. Day and night, constantly, I see and I feel my pain." Images from inside his burning house filled his mind. "I don't know why I can't stop it, but I can't."

She took his hand. "That's why I understand you not helping with the ogres. It's not fair, the burden you carry."

Taylan looked into Val's eyes. "I would have saved *you.*"

Val turned away. "I didn't need to be saved."

Taylan leaned in and kissed her cheek. "But I would have." He kissed the side of her mouth. "If you did."

She kissed him. "I know," she said and kissed him again as she slid on top of him.

Taylan rode a few horses behind Valencia the next day. He had woken beside her in the night in a sweat with inhuman visions—tall, inky figures oozing into fat blobs—laughing and fading in and out of his head. Of his many recurring terrors, those ranked among his least favorite. Before Taylan began riding, he had separated from the group to throw up and didn't think Valencia—or anyone else—had seen.

The company crested a hill. The same amorphous specters waited for Taylan at the top until he blinked and they instead invaded his thoughts. Shame poured over him—but for that he had no need, no desire. Taylan rode with the woman he longed to be with more than any other in all of Taulus, yet shame or an irritation he could not pinpoint haunted him. It was always something. Always!

"I know," Valencia had said the day before. He would have saved her, and she knew it. It was good that she knew it.

But the way she had turned away before saying it… and she had *nothing* else to add? No kind words to say to him? None at all?

But what did he expect her to say? That she loved him? He would have welcomed it. He would have cherished it. *He* loved *her*. He had always loved her. He had never loved anyone else. But gentle words like that were not her way— not the warrior's way. And Valencia was a warrior above all else.

And why should she have professed her love for him in that tent? He had not said those particular words to her. It had been a wonderful night. And the coming night would be as well. *Stop,* Taylan told himself. *Stop it and enjoy yourself. Enjoy the nights… and the days! She sent for you to come to her.* Enjoy it, dammit. Just… enjoy it.

"Gold!" Hayle shouted. "West!"

Taylan spotted the dragon descending toward them.

"Gowyn," Valencia called out.

"Aye," Hayle agreed.

Valencia stopped, and the company followed suit. "We'll rest here," she said. Most of the knights dismounted as Gowyn landed.

Valencia waved, riding to him. Taylan, Hayle, and Shaela rode over as well.

Valencia, Gowyn said. *Hello, all. What did you find in Deroc? What did Eldred have to say?*

"Not much," Valencia said. "He acknowledged that the ogres and the goblins shouldn't have been out of Deroc. He said they'd keep a better watch."

Nothing else?

"No. And Commander Algar at Fort Bones had nothing out of the ordinary to report. Have you seen more goblins in the White Forest?"

No.

"Think Eldred's bored?" Hayle asked. "Think he's playing with us?"

Bored? Yes. Playing with us? Not likely. In my experience, he would not find such a game worth his effort and attention. I think he's getting lazy.

Hayle nodded.

Nevertheless, Gowyn continued, *we should be more*

vigilant in these parts, and more ready to respond until we are sure. Grafere and I will increase our patrols in this area. Valencia, can your knights remain out here in the east for a while?

"Another group," Valencia said. "I agree we should have a larger presence. I'll go back to my fort and return with fresh knights."

Good. Gowyn gazed south. *And it is Eldred's laziness. Or he is bored and you are correct, Sir Hayle, that he aims to annoy us. He is exceedingly good at that.*

This may be excessive in response to a few ogres and a small number of goblins, but I prefer to be safe rather than sorry when elves of Deroc are involved.

"I agree," Valencia said.

Gowyn leapt into the air and flapped his wings. *I'm off to relay this plan to Grafere. I will find you on your way out here from the fort, Valencia.* He headed south toward Solurn.

21

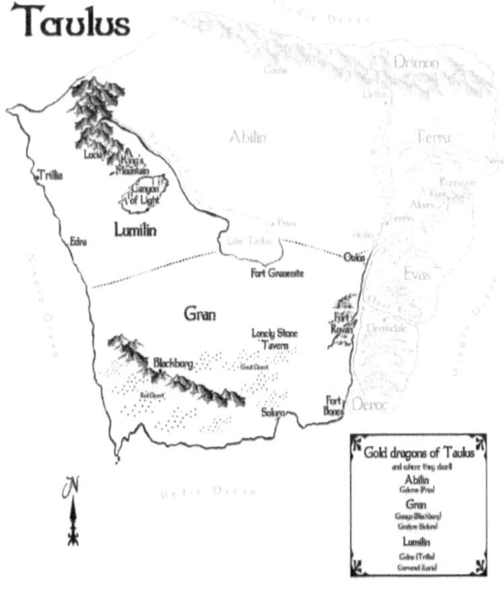

In late afternoon six days into their journey to Trillia, Gall—
the knife wound in his side healing without complication—
corked his whisky, which he hadn't been hitting particularly
hard, and returned it to his bag. He and the twins had
entered the disputed territory at the northern border of
Gran. Both Lumilin and Gran claimed ownership of the
three-mile-wide strip of brown prairie. Ahead, off the road,

four knights sat outside their tents, eating. Gall, Avery, and Avril slowed their horses to a walk.

"They're from Gran?" Avery squinted, peering past the knights. "And way out there, those are from Lumilin?"

"Yes," Gall said. "They keep a constant presence on the land. Neither will leave it."

"Do they ever fight each other?"

"Not really, since their war, when Gran and Lumilin first settled the lands west of Lake Taulus and no natural border separated the kingdoms at the north and south. Then they fought. But you must know about the war."

"How long was it?" Avery asked.

"The war?"

"Yeah."

"Five years. During which, both kingdoms also fought countless dragons—to the death in some cases, to terms in others—to establish themselves and their towns and cities within their borders. So even with their dragon allies, their forces had to spread thin. Out here, a few big battles took place, especially at the beginning, but the rest were small and infrequent. Once they dug in, neither side ever advanced their line much at all. The war ended because both kingdoms needed to focus inward.

"Since then, it's been nothing but small skirmishes, and, oh… three hundred years since the last. Galeron and the other golds intervened back then. They didn't want the two kingdoms at war, least of all over this little stretch of land."

"Why do they guard it then?" Avril asked.

Two of the nearby knights stood with their food and

watched the riders approach.

"It's a point of pride," Gall said. "And anger… and resentment. Five hundred years ago, in the first Dark War, the knights and emotes of Lumilin massed here, at their southern border, ready to come to Blackburg to fight alongside Gran's army. But they waited when the attack on Blackburg began and kept waiting while the city burned and its people suffered. Not until the tide had already turned and the worst of the fighting was done did Lumilin head south. Then, when the fighting ended completely and the Dark Elves returned home, Lumilin's army stopped within the borders of Gran, farther south than this, claiming the land as payment for their assistance in battle. The king of Gran marched his army here, and weary as the battles to the south had rendered them, they forced Lumilin's army all the way to this point, but no further."

"Ho there." A knight on the roadside raised his hand. The one standing beside him bit into a chunk of bread. Two others remained seated, scooping stew out of bowls.

Gall rode into the lead. "Good day, sir knight."

"Where are you headed?" the knight asked.

"Uh…" Gall motioned up the road. "Lumilin."

The knight smiled. "*Where* in Lumilin?"

"What's it to you?"

"Just curious." The knight shrugged. "Bored, actually." He glanced at the other knight. "We've nothing left to talk about."

"Nothing," the other knight said in between bites. "At all."

"I see," Gall said. "But our business is our own."

"*That*"—the knight sighed—"is fine. There is the *business* of the toll, however."

"Toll?" Avery asked.

"Yes, toll," the knight shot back.

The second knight chewed his bread. "King Rion's decree."

The first knight added, "Decided that if we're going to be on this border all the time, might as well collect some silver."

"What if we weren't on the road?" Avril asked. "We could have crossed the border anywhere else."

The first knight walked over to her. "We would have seen you."

"What if we went *really far* away?" Avril asked.

"You didn't." The knight shrugged. "You are crossing here, m'lady."

Gall threw the knight a silver coin.

He caught it and put out his thumb. "One."

Gall reached into his pouch and produced another two coins. He threw them to the knight.

He caught them. "Two and three. Tell our fine friends to take it easy on their perfumes and incense. We're tired of the odor downwind."

"We will." Gall rode on.

"M'lady," the first knight said to Avril as she passed.

Gall let her and her brother into the lead as he and the twins galloped farther into the disputed territory. Gall had seen plenty of Gran and more than a little of Lumilin, so as they went along he frequently found himself watching Avery and Avril taking in the grassy landscape instead of paying attention to it himself.

Avery gazed into the big blue sky to his left, then switched to the right.

"Green grass, finally," Avril said, noting the color mixing in after all their riding through brown grasses, and desert before that. She watched a pair of prairie dogs scamper into an underground burrow.

A knight ahead stood, and Gall and the twins slowed to a walk again. A seated knight lowered a telescope from his eye. All four of the knights' armor was shinier.

The one standing smiled more warmly, and when he called out, "Welcome, good sirs and fair lady," his voice sounded kinder.

"Knights of Lumilin," Gall called to them as they neared. "There a toll here, too?"

The knight who had greeted them shook his head. "Not here, my friends."

Gall and the twins stopped.

"The coffers of the kingdom are as full as ever," the knight said. "Welcome to Lumilin."

"Thank you," Gall said.

"Thanks," Avery added.

"Are you headed to Trillia?" the knight asked.

Gall gave Avery's answer of, "Maybe," an approving nod.

"Well, you should," the knight said. "A tournament begins in a few days. You might catch part of it."

Gall glanced at Avery.

"Regrettably, Sir Beal won't be taking part," the knight said.

"Why not?" Gall asked.

"King wanted someone else to win for a change."

"Ah."

The knight asked, "Any message from our friends to the south?"

The twins looked at Gall.

He sniffed, caught a hint of sage, and briefly searched for its source before answering, "They bid you a fine day."

The knight rolled his eyes. "I'm sure."

Gall gestured for Avery to go, and the three continued up the road.

When they had distanced themselves from the knights, Avery asked, "Who's Beal?"

"The finest knight in Lumilin," Gall said. "Ever seen a tournament?"

"Nah."

"Ever seen proper knights in battle—or competition?"

"No."

"Well then, that tournament could be fun, eh?"

"I guess," Avery said.

Gall had been hoping for more. "We should practice tonight." Gall noted that Avery's new sword, strapped to the side of his horse, had not been unsheathed since the boy put it there.

"We'll see."

"You've gotta learn sometime," Gall said.

Avery looked at the sky. "It's getting late." He kicked his horse and galloped ahead.

22

Taulus

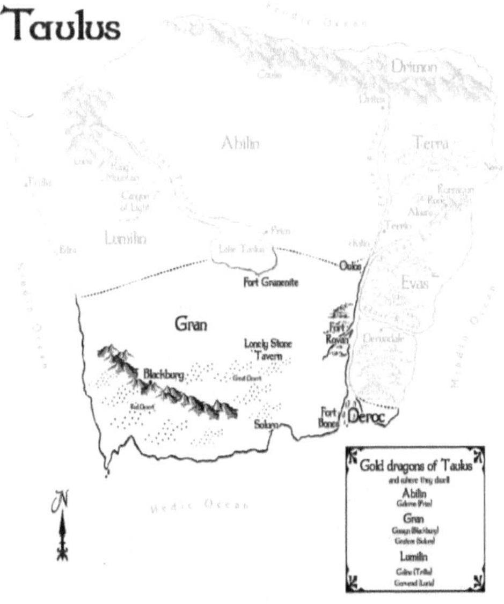

The sun rose on central Gran. Taylan, Valencia, and her company rode for Fort Granenite, which they expected to reach before the day's end.

From two horses behind her in the column, Taylan watched Valencia's long blond hair bob up and down her back. He had run his fingers through her soft hair each night, and as she rode, he traced it with his eyes down past its tips to her waist. He pictured her bare skin there and his arms wrapped around her. Taylan's stomach didn't ache. His forehead hurt but appreciably less than it often did. Yet his throat had dried so completely that it protested at every swallow.

The last nights and days had been good ones because he had been with Valencia. She hadn't professed her love for him—nor had he for her. But she wouldn't say it until he did, he kept telling himself. He had almost shared his feelings once or twice but each time decided to wait.

He stared at Valencia. He wouldn't rather be riding with anyone else in all of Taulus. He couldn't ruin the moment, or the moments that would come later in her tent. Time to discuss their relationship would come eventually, perhaps on their ride back east from the fort to continue their patrol. But he would not risk what was finally his after so long in order to hear but a few words from her.

Taylan spent the morning lost in a ceaseless cycle of those thoughts and different rationales leading to the same conclusions, all the while keeping his gaze fixed upon the gorgeous warrior who finally cared for him and apparently didn't mind that part of him was elvish—or that he harbored another pain. Of all the men, elves, or half-elves in Taulus who would surely have answered her call, she had sent for *him*.

Thank the Lord for her, Taylan thought. Whatever else God had done to him, despite the suffering and darkness the Creator had thrust upon him, Valencia shone bright through it all.

They stopped for lunch.

"Valencia," Taylan called while the others dismounted near a partially shaded stream. He motioned for her to follow him farther ahead.

She did, and when they could barely hear the rest of the company, she guided her horse under the cover of the same tree as he had. "What is it?"

He leaned over and kissed her. "That."

She smiled then gestured to her horse, who watched the stream. "She needs water."

When Valencia turned back, Taylan had already leaned in close. He kissed her until she put her hand on his cheek.

She slid her hand to his shoulder and gently pushed. "What will you do when we reach the fort?"

"What do you mean?"

"Where will you go? Will you return to Prim or continue your research elsewhere?"

Taylan slumped. His head ached.

Valencia gave a sad smile. "I have to head back east."

"I'll come with you."

"No. We could be out there a while."

"All the more reason."

"Taylan…" She shook her head. "It's been fun… the last couple weeks. Just how I hoped—"

"Gold!" Spear shouted from behind them.

Valencia looked at the sky. "Gowyn."

"Gowyn!" Spear shouted. "I think."

"Yes," Valencia called to her knight. She glanced at Taylan then rode toward the descending dragon.

Taylan followed her—followed her long blond hair bobbing away from him. Why couldn't he stay with her? Violent pangs shot down his spine. Fun? It had been that, and so much more to him. So much more…

No clouds blocked the sun, yet shadows swept over Valencia. She rode miles ahead of him.

She shot back into view—close, bright… beautiful. No! He would not give up! Their conversation had been cut short—not ended. He would stay with her. He *would* convince her. They would have more fun when he rode with her after Fort Granenite.

Gowyn landed between them and the company.

Hinlin was attacked in the night, Gowyn said, referring to the trading town in southeast Abilin.

"How? Who?" Hayle asked.

I do not know. There were no survivors. I have just been there. Piles of stabbed and sliced bodies, but no witnesses.

"Eldred," Hayle said.

Maybe. Galeron is headed from Prim to investigate, and I am going to Deroc to pay King Eldred a visit.

"Take me," Valencia said.

Taylan couldn't finish his conversation with her from afar. He urged his horse forward. "And me." He could not bear being parted from her so suddenly.

Valencia glanced at him before turning to her knights. "Hayle, lead the company to Oulos. Take my horse and Taylan's. Send word to Granenite for a dozen more knights to meet you out there. Oulos is not far from Hinlin, and we will not have our town caught off guard. I will join you after Deroc."

He nodded. "Shaela, send the message."

Shaela went to prepare the note for one of her pigeons.

Let's go. Gowyn lowered his neck.

Valencia climbed on first then helped Taylan up behind her. The dragon leapt into the air, flapped his wings, and rose fast.

Strange footprints filled Hinlin, Gowyn said.

"Strange how?" Valencia asked.

Three long toes on each foot. A short stride. Like none I have ever seen before.

"Not goblins?"

No.

"What then? Animals?"

Perhaps. Perhaps my father can identify them when he arrives.

————————

Taylan held Valencia. She held Gowyn at the base of his neck in her sleep while eastern Gran slid by below them in the darkness. Taylan should also have been sleeping; the trip to Deroc was long, and their next opportunity for rest was not guaranteed and likely depended on what King Eldred revealed.

But Taylan could not relax, let alone sleep. Valencia had put her hair in a bun to keep it from blowing wildly in the wind, and from inches away, Taylan stared at the loose, short strands that had come free… when he wasn't staring at her bare neck, wishing he could kiss it.

His arms wrapped around Valencia, holding her body to

his, yet he already missed her. He wouldn't be able to convince her. He would hate life without her, as he had for all those long years. He remembered that pain vividly. But life after being with her again as before—even better than before—only to have been so abruptly sent away? That would be something new… and far worse.

He had to tell her he loved her. Their time together *had* been fun, but it had to have been more to her as well. Taylan knew it. Hope remained. He'd tell her he loved her, and then maybe those short words, for him, would pass her lips.

———

Gowyn glided lower near Fort Bones. Knights atop its walls watched Deroc, and a few practiced archery inside the outpost.

"There's Commander Algar," Valencia said.

"Everything looks fine," Taylan said.

It does. Gowyn flapped his wings, and the fort shrank behind them as they sped on to the swamp.

Taylan noticed the changed birds first. The trees thickened. Beneath their leaves he spotted a pack of red wolves surrounding a larger brown bear. The pack attacked, and then treetops blocked Taylan's view of the action behind him. From their altitude, Taylan could not determine exactly how each of the animals on the ground and slithering through the water had been changed—improved, made more savage. But they had been, all of them. Meek, natural animals would not have survived in Deroc.

Taylan pictured Xodon from paintings and drawings of

the first purple dragon the Dark Elves had changed into a black. Massive and terrible, with harder scales than any dragon before him and fire hotter than any dragon in Taulus had ever breathed, Xodon led the other blacks the elves made against mankind in two devastating wars. Though hardly meek, the natural dragons proved no match for the ferocious blacks, just as the unchanged animals of Taulus had no chance against the changed.

Salty air hit him, and Taylan saw the ocean ahead. Gowyn descended. Corners and broken walls of ruined Castle Derindom jutted out from the leaves.

"No guards," Valencia said. "No sentries at watch."

No. Gowyn flew lower.

The end of the tree line neared. Ocean waves, as dreary as the cloud cover, rolled toward them. On the small beach… no one.

Drab, desolate sand. A burnt-out torch. Nothing more.

Gowyn landed. He inhaled deeply. *No scent of Dark Elf. Did you see any?*

"No," Valencia said.

"No," Taylan echoed.

Nor did I. We will search on. He leapt into the air. *Though I do not expect we will find King Eldred, Queen Jadira, or any of them.*

They flew over Deroc—first on the Gran side. Gowyn stayed low then repeatedly swooped lower, yet they found no elves. Taylan recalled Jadira's sapphire eyes, how they had stared into him, piercing his composed veneer—or his attempt at one. She had known his suffering. How truly had she understood it? Had she known its cause or merely sensed his tormented soul?

Taylan clutched Valencia tighter. She glanced back at him with a soft, sad smile. Gowyn headed east, crossing into the portion of Deroc which had once belonged to the White Elves. Changed hawks and eagles soared and screeched louder than their natural kin could. Angry animals roamed the swamp. Huge ogres sat in groups, a pack of goblins chased a raccoon, and a troll tried to hide from Gowyn's view behind a tree trunk far too thin for the purpose, but they spotted no Dark Elves.

"To Hinlin?" Valencia asked. "Or Derundale, to see what the White Elves know of this?"

Neither. Not yet. To Fort Bones.

"Gone?" Commander Algar rushed up the stairs and looked south toward Deroc. He called down to the middle of the fort, to Gowyn, Taylan, and Valencia standing beside the dragon, and to all the knights who had interrupted their usual duties to listen. "All of them?"

Yes, Gowyn said. *You saw nothing?*

"No." Algar yelled out to the fort, "Ready yourselves. We ride for Deroc!"

The knights hurried to finish last bites of food and to gather weapons, armor, and horses.

"Are they responsible for killing everyone in Hinlin?" Algar asked Gowyn.

Footprints there suggest not.

"Then where did they go? How did they go?"

Where exactly, or how, I do not know. Likely hidden under the shroud of the White Forest. But of that I cannot be certain either.

"Will you accompany us?" Algar asked the gold.

No. Valencia, Taylan, come. He leaned low, and they climbed on. Gowyn stood. *Conduct your search, commander. If you find anything, report it without delay. But I am satisfied that the Treaty of Solurn has been broken, deliberately and egregiously. I head north to tell my father and to seek his council regarding how to respond.*

23

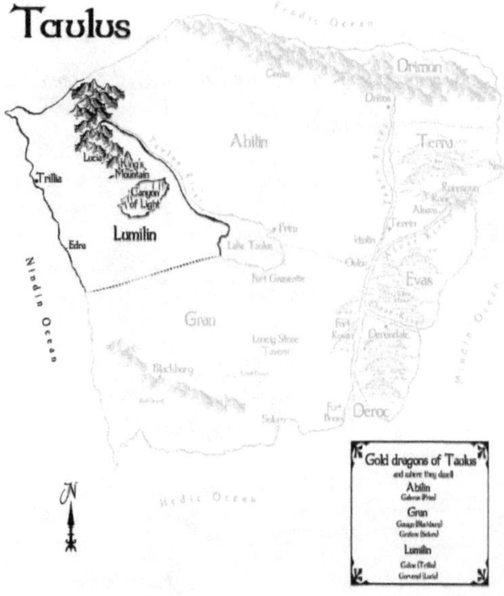

Under the cover of darkness, Lila and Gorvenal headed east from Trillia toward Lucia before turning north and flying for an hour. Then Gorvenal went west, out over the Nindin Ocean. He kept that course for a while and didn't turn southwest until his keen eyes could not make out the shore behind him. The indirect start, intended to disguise their destination and minimize the chances of being seen from the coast, meant flying through colder air but added only a little time to their day-and-a-half-long journey halfway around the globe.

Small islands were scattered near the shores of Taulus, but few dotted the vast ocean that stretched longer than the mainland itself. Yalus stood out among the remote islands because of its place in history and because it lay nearly equidistant from one end of Taulus to the other.

The dragon turned back to Lila, who huddled under thick blankets, a scarf, and a heavy hat. *Are you cold?*

"I am fine." She smiled. "I am wonderful."

He nodded and faced forward.

Over the ages, a small number of men, elves, and even a couple of dwarves had made the voyage to Yalus by ship, and many times more had perished trying. Out in the middle of the ocean, storms were common while assistance from the mainland was not. Since the feat had finally been accomplished, such expeditions had become rare. There simply wasn't much to be gained, especially not when compared to the significant risk.

Adult dragons could make the flight, and those who did typically went for the same reasons that lured Gorvenal and Lila: escape from Taulus to complete isolation, appreciation of the historical significance of the island, and the beauty of the remote tropical setting. But those trips were also rare. Peace and quiet and striking landscapes could be found in abundance throughout Taulus, without the taxing flight to Yalus. Even Gorvenal, a mighty gold, would be exhausted by the time he reached the island.

He flapped his wings. *Where did I leave off?*

"The Dark Elves had just changed the huge purple into Xodon, the first black dragon."

Ah, yes. After him, with the promise of leading them in war to conquer Taulus, the Dark Elf King Ewald and his most powerful emotes used their aggressive magic to slice, stretch, and warp the fiber of other purples until they became terrible blacks. And once they were changed and evil, Xodon and his dragons shared the sinister elves' lust for lordship over the men of Taulus—all of them—for they found the short-lived race inferior and so unworthy of all they possessed.

King Ewald and Xodon waged their war. The kingdoms of mankind were to be destroyed, the royals would be killed, and the rest of the men and women of Taulus would kneel before the Dark Elves or meet their own deaths.

The endless rolling waves below them, the sight of night giving way to day, and the rising sun's warmth distracted Lila from Gorvenal's story. In the light, she could see schools of fish beneath the clear water. Lila had brought food and water for the long trip, but Gorvenal would occasionally swoop low and dip his head into the ocean for a bite to eat, as he would at the island. Out there, heat from Gorvenal's fire would turn salty sea water into all he and Lila needed to drink.

A pod of six dolphins took turns breaching in the rolling waves. Later Gorvenal flew over massive whales, and that excited Lila most of all. One exhaled beneath them, and the resulting mist nearly reached them. Lila's attention to Gorvenal's story came and went. She had heard it before, and she knew the tale well.

King Ewald, his Dark Elves, and the goblins, trolls, and ogres in their army moved west across Gran with Blackburg in their sights. Xodon and all the blacks, who flew significantly faster than the land forces traveled, sped north for Abilin with elven emotes in the saddles on their backs.

The world had never seen black dragons, nor endured dragon fire as hot as the inferno that spewed from their maws. Before reaching Abilin, Xodon—the largest dragon in Taulus since he had been changed into a black—and the others decimated Fort Gran, the precursor to Fort Granenite. With no golds yet in the world, Gran's handful of dragon allies fought bravely, but the bigger, stronger blacks tore the natural dragons apart.

Magic-wielding emotes slowed the evil dragons, blocking their fire and wounding some of the beasts, but the blacks' elven riders summoned magic of their own, both in defense and on the attack. The abilities of those so old and powerful proved another advantage over the relatively young humans.

Prim burned three hours after Fort Gran. The old Great Wall around the circular capital of Abilin did nothing to stop Xodon and his dragons from sweeping into the city and raining fire onto frantically fleeing citizens and hopelessly fighting knights and emotes.

Prim's emotes made shields of the plain's wind, water drawn from the Vitus River, and earth from their ancient homeland, but against the black dragons' furious flames, those defenses failed fast. Prim's aggressive emotes failed too. They shot fire and lightning up at their attackers, hurled boulders and clouds of small stones, and flung tree trunks as spears but found their efforts blunted by the Dark Elves.

The black dragons perched atop tall buildings and watchtowers and torched everything below. Flesh and bone turned to ash. The city's stone walls and homes melted. Then the black dragons destroyed their own perches.

The first natural dragons to come to Prim's aid rushed to confront the blacks and, for their desperate haste, were rushed to gruesome deaths. The blacks punched their foes harder, held their foes tighter, and yet still moved more swiftly than the natural dragons. The fights were not fair. The naturals were bitten and torn apart, limb by limb, wing by wing. The destruction of the city and the slaughter of its men and women continued.

Dragons from all corners of Abilin raced to Prim, and once the power of the terrible black monstrosities became clear, the natural dragons who didn't flee fought more carefully and in groups. With the blacks occupied, the heavier defenses of the city could finally be readied by brave knights. The dark assault was slowed. Abilinian emotes, refusing to accept their city's doom as certain, reached deeper within themselves to produce their strongest efforts.

And black dragons fell, crashing to the burning streets with scorched, jolted, bloody scales; crushed bones; ripped wings; and slain elven riders. Some of Abilin's people made it to the castle. Others ran out the city gates. Those moments—those fierce battles that won glimmers of hope—lived on in stories and songs of valiant men, women, and natural dragons.

Yet each tale and tune ended on sad notes. The black

dragons and the Dark Elf emotes proved too powerful. Prim, its army of knights and emotes, its dragon allies, its king, queen, and nearly every single one of its men, women, and children burned in the fire of Xodon and his minions. Those fleeing beyond the Great Wall did not get far, and the city's central castle, unable to withstand the dark beasts' fire, melted to the ground. The black dragons took care to level the entire city.

Xodon led his forces south to rejoin Ewald's land army. Many natural dragons followed the lord of the blacks obediently, hoping to be spared his wrath and seeking a share of the inevitable spoils of his conquest. They saw Xodon's power and saw that nothing in Taulus could match it.

Ewald's combined air and ground forces laid waste to towns and cities across Gran. Again, human emotes mustered the strength to slow the Dark Elves in furious battles of magic and emotion. But again, against the older elves, mankind's emotes eventually fell, and the attackers had their way.

How are you? Gorvenal asked. He and Lila had been flying for a while.

"Fine," Lila said. "How are you holding up?"

Perfectly. Gorvenal continued the tale, and Lila paid better attention.

Ewald, long weary of Gran's boasts that their line of kings stretched back through the ages to the first men, took care to be thorough in his conquest of all of Gran's cities, towns, and villages as he made his way west, just as he intended to thoroughly end the eternal line in Blackburg.

While Ewald and Xodon occupied themselves traversing Gran, a young but strong tan dragon named Galt flew from Conlin in the north of Abilin to Prim to survey the destruction. Among the rubble, ash, and smoldering fire, he found two emotes desperately searching for survivors to heal—Mikael and Siann, a husband and wife who had kept each other alive during the attack. The couple had found and tended to but a handful of saved souls. Galt returned the emotes and those few to Conlin on his back.

The Dark Elf army and their dragons amassed at Blackburg in the foothills of the Mountains of Fire. King Ewald gave Gran's king a day before they would attack and told him that he and all those of his line should say their good-byes to each other and good-bye to Taulus.

Knights and emotes of Lumilin headed south but, fearful of the dark army, waited on the kingdom's border with Gran. The Red Elves, distraught over their inability to lend assistance during the sudden attack on Prim, yet also divided over whether they should stray farther from the protection of their home forest, remained camped far from Blackburg, at the eastern border of Gran. The White Elves sent no army.

In Conlin, Mikael and Siann, recovered from their exhausting efforts in Prim, found Galt sitting near the top of snow-covered Mount Conel, staring to the south. The big dragon noticed the emotes and flew down to them.

When Galt landed, Mikael asked him, "Would you help the good people of Taulus fight the black dragons?"

"Yes," Galt said. "It would kill me, but I have thought of little else since Prim."

"Wait," Lila said.

Gorvenal looked back at her. *Hm?*

"I love this part, but I'm falling asleep. And we have so much time together out here. Save Galeron's story for when I wake."

Of course.

Far from Taulus, and still a long way from Yalus, with the midday sun warming her, Lila closed her tired eyes and slept.

24

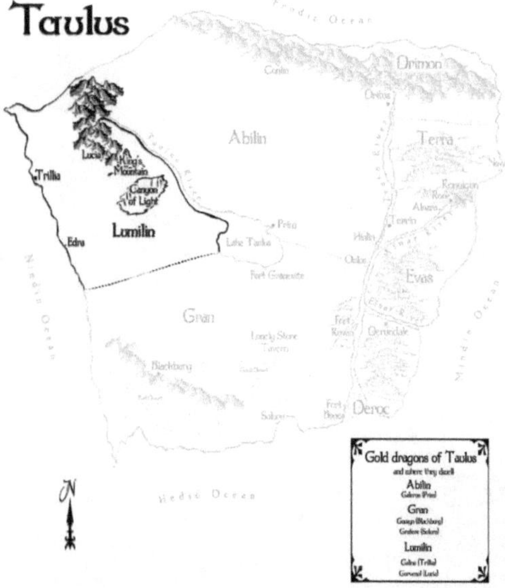

About halfway between Lumilin's southern border and Trillia, Gall, Avery, and Avril rode north from Edra, the port town where they had stopped the night before. In a welcome change from sleeping on the ground, they had secured rooms in Edra at a reasonable inn. Gall had finally shaved his beard, telling the twins that he was glad to be rid of it and that he did not intend to let it return anytime soon.

With the city's low cliffs behind them, they had sat on a dock in Edra, watching the ships coming and going and the hustle on the docks as cargo was loaded and unloaded. Conversation frequently drifted to the twins' mother, Isabel. Avril and Avery wished with all their hearts to find her well, they told Gall, though the sentiment would have been obvious even if they had said nothing about it. They recalled aloud the hope in her eyes for the future on that same night when she had abandoned hope that her old life could go on.

If the twins made it to Trillia and were reunited with their mother, all would be well, they said. They would have had a hard childhood, and their mother a harder marriage, but with a little luck, it could all work out all right. So more than anything, Avril and Avery wished for their journey to be completed without incident.

Gall had assured them it would be and was so confident that he even suggested diverting east to see the Canyon of Light and King's Mountain. But as they neared their ultimate destination, the children's longing to be with their mother trumped their curiosity to see the birthplace of dragons on Taulus. Those historical sites could wait.

As they rode, Gall noted the darkening clouds in the sky and, deciding something else could no longer wait, slowed to a stop. He slid out of his saddle and stumbled before catching his balance.

"What is it?" Avery asked.

"Time to practice." Gall took a drink of whisky. "You persuaded me against it yesterday. You persuaded me every day before. But you won't today."

Avery motioned ahead. "We need to keep going."

"We will. When we're done here."

"Come *on*," Avery protested. "We just had lunch. It's going to rain."

Gall got his broadsword off his horse. "Let's go."

"I never said I'd do it. I said maybe."

Gall rubbed his chin. "I distinctly remember a 'yes,' later in the evening, just before you tripped heading upstairs."

Avril dismounted.

"Want to join us?" Gall asked.

She shook her head. "I'll watch."

"Want a drink?"

She grabbed a blanket. "No."

Gall called to Avery, "Bring your sword."

Avery dismounted and held his brand-new sword low at his side in his right hand. "I said maybe."

Gall swung and with a loud *clang* knocked Avery's sword to the ground. "Hold it in two hands."

Avery picked up his blade. "You aren't."

"I have to hold this." Gall shook his liquor bottle. "Plus, you don't have a shield for your other hand. Two now. We'll practice with one later."

Avery glanced at his sister then did as instructed.

"Swing at me," Gall said.

Avery did, with a looping attack from his side.

Gall parried it.

"Stop." Gall dropped his sword and put down his whisky. "Left foot forward." He got behind Avery and covered the boy's hands on his sword hilt with his own then brought his arms high. "Hold it here, move your foot and"—Gall nudged the boy's right leg forward—"swing." He led Avery in the motion of cutting down with his sword. "Like that."

"Shorter?" Avery asked.

Gall let go of him. "Yes, exactly."

Avery tried one of his own.

"Better. Start higher."

Avril watched intently as Avery swung again.

"Faster." Gall retrieved his sword. "Maybe you reach for the big swing when your enemy is lying wounded or not looking, but otherwise, you need to strike quick."

Avery held his arms high. A big raindrop landed on his nose. He cut faster.

Gall shot his sword up to block it. "Again."

Avery cut, and Gall parried.

"Switch your legs, step toward me, and strike from the other side."

Avery swung his blade.

Avril leaned back on her arms, and while the warm rain gradually picked up, she watched Gall give her brother his first real instruction on how to properly wield a sword.

25

Taulus

Ri and her team rode on a path in the Red Elf forest for two days from Terrin to the city of Alnara, where they left their horses. With the constant lookout for goblins, tensions were higher than on any other mission she had taken part in. Ri kept vigilant and sensed a heightened sharpness in the others.

On a few occasions, when she heard noises in the woods

she could not identify, Ri signaled her team to stop and find the source of the sounds. While each time the searches yielded nothing, or nothing out of the ordinary, it wasn't just Ri who was on edge. The elves with her claimed to see or hear unexpected things as well.

Ultimately, they encountered no goblins or any other dark creatures along the way, but Ri thoroughly enjoyed the threat of them.

From Alnara, the dwarven city of Rone in the mountains of Ronnigun lay a day's trek through the woods. Ri carried her quiver on her back, her bow across her body, and her small knife on her belt along with her canteen and other supplies. Her companions had equipped themselves similarly, except Naelon, who had a sword on his hip in addition to his bow. With Rone a few hours ahead, they took a break.

Addis, ever eager to learn because he sought to lead a scout team of his own one day, sipped from his canteen. "What's the plan when we get there?"

Naelon said, "We'll approach using the woods as cover. When we're close, Emlyn"—he pointed at her—"and Egan"—he pointed at him—"will head out to the road. The rest of us will watch the city, but you two head for the front gates. They'll let you in, and you can snoop around inside."

"Why should we say we have come?" Egan asked.

"Tell them you are headed for the ocean and need a place to spend the night." Naelon shrugged. "Tell them you wish to buy dwarven presents for children at home in Terrin. Tell them you are *scouts* and need a place to rest. They may guess that you are, and a lie could raise suspicions."

"Or we are lovers." Egan looked toward Emlyn, his expression pleading. "And we have so tired of rolling around on the dirty forest floor that we need a soft bed to express—"

Emlyn laughed. "I'm sorry, no. I could not stand at their gates and say that with a straight face." She motioned to each of the other males in the group in turn. "Addis, Launfal, or Naelon… for the sake of the mission, I could. But you?" She shook her head. "I am sorry."

Addis grasped Egan's shoulder. "I would be your lover. For the mission, I would tell any story. I would *live* any story."

Egan shrugged Addis's arm away.

"The two of you, rolling around the forest floor," Launfal said. "Such passion…"

"For the mission," Emlyn added.

Ri smiled. "For the mission."

Egan grimaced. "Ri!" He turned to her. "Sweet Ri… what if—"

"No," Ri said.

Egan slumped his shoulders. "A dwarf, then. A little, tiny, ugly dwarf. It is all that is left for me."

Everyone laughed.

"Have fun, Egan," Naelon said.

"I doubt it." He frowned then lit up. "But I will try!"

"Soo…" Addis lost his smile and waited until the others' had faded out. "In the city, what are we looking for?"

"The prettiest little dwarf," Launfal said. "In all of Rone."

"Yes, that"—Naelon flashed his old friend a smile—"and

for whatever is out of the ordinary. We've all been to Rone. See if things have changed in a peculiar way. Are there places you two are not permitted to go? Are things kept hidden from you? Look for dwarves engaged in any kind of preparation, and if you find any, try to tell what for."

"All right," Addis said. "Ri, what you overheard, it was nothing specific?"

"No," Ri said. "I heard 'soon,' but nothing about what the 'it' was."

Addis nodded.

Naelon said, "Launfal and you, Addis, will be up in the trees watching the city. Ri, too, with the looking glass—you could use the practice."

"Definitely." Ri checked and found the short, extendable, leather-covered brass spyglass secured tightly to her belt, exactly where it should have been.

"I'll be keeping guard below," Naelon said.

"Think we'll find anything?" Addis asked.

"No, but we are here to be certain."

Launfal spoke up. "I do not see how the dwarves could be so foolish as to mount an attack. They might catch us off guard and take Nova to their north, perhaps Alnara… perhaps not. With our assembled army, we would drive them back regardless—it would not take long."

"Aye," Emlyn agreed.

"No offense," Launfal said to Ri. "After what you heard, I do believe it is prudent that we investigate. But there must have been context missing from that conversation in Dritus."

"No offense taken," Ri said, a little pained that her friend was basing so much on her lie. "That all makes sense to me."

––––––––––––

With a few hours of sunlight remaining in the day, and after another joke about them as a couple and another good laugh, Emlyn and Egan had decided their story would be that they wished to purchase dwarven souvenirs from merchants inside Rone, then headed for the road to the city.

Quietly, with faces painted in dark, earthy camouflage, Ri and the others crept through the forest toward Rone and the mountains. Bow and arrow in hand, Ri took each step lightly. She had never been so tense, so alert. She scanned left and right and up into the treetops, ready to fire in an instant. She had never felt so awash with purpose. They would spy on a foreign city! She beamed, only forcing her smile away when she feared the others might see. Her little lie—her simple plan—had worked. The mission—the pressure—was *real.*

The edge of the forest lay close ahead and the base of the mountains not far past it.

At Naelon's instruction, the four team members came together. He pointed at a wide, leafy tree, and whispered to Ri, "Think you can get up there?"

"Yup." She unnocked her arrow and put it away then slung her bow across her body to free both hands for climbing.

"Addis, go south, not far, and make sure you have a good view of the gate," Naelon said. "Emlyn and Egan should already be inside, but see who else comes and goes."

"Got it," Addis said.

"Launfal," Naelon said, "north."

He nodded.

"Meet here in an hour. I'll whistle like the warbler's song for two seconds when it's time. I'll whistle one second if there's trouble beforehand," Naelon said. "Go now."

Addis went right, Launfal left, and Ri straight for the tree picked out for her. She didn't smile, just focused on the trunk and branches she needed to climb. And she needed to climb quietly. She *couldn't* be caught spying. Word would reach her parents. The dwarves wouldn't harm her, because there wasn't *really* any dwarven plot in motion, but her parents and then all of Abilin, eventually, would know Ri's secret.

She jumped, grabbed a thick branch, pulled herself onto it, then leaned against the trunk of the tree. If she were not allowed to be part of her elven team any longer, she did not know how she would cope with the boredom in Abilin. Dense leaves blocked her view of Rone—the semi-circular front wall, the tall mountain near the front of the city, and the lower peaks behind it running to the east. The same leaves blocked the city's view of her. With both hands, she grabbed a knot farther up the trunk then pulled until she got her legs onto another branch. Ri let her weight shift there and reached higher to steady herself. She would not be seen. She would not be caught. She simply couldn't be.

Higher she climbed. One jump, branch, pull, and knot at a time, and the leaves began to thin. The last thick branch seemed the place to stop, so she got her feet onto it and steadied herself, kneeling, with a hand back against the trunk. Through the leaves, on the high, curved stone wall Ri could now see over, a dwarf with a long, double-headed battle-ax stood sentry. Around the wall, a second guard stood, as did a pair farther around, past the closed main gate—but they all watched down at the road and the forest floor.

Ri pulled the spyglass off her belt and extended it. The elves had no need for the magnified view it offered, but she certainly did. She pointed it at Rone, closed one eye, then put her other to the glass at the thin end, and found herself disoriented, staring at zoomed-in stone wall. She took her eye from the glass and pushed and pulled on the branch beneath her—sturdy, she concluded.

Ri pulled off her bow and quiver. With its shoulder strap, she tied the quiver securely to the tree trunk and hung her bow around it so that she could quickly grab it and an arrow if need be. Ri lay with her stomach on the branch.

She looked through the glass again, and despite blowing leaves occasionally obstructing her view, Ri could see well, over the wall, into the city. Without the glass, she saw the guards hadn't moved. They didn't appear to notice her. Ri let herself smile. A real mission, and she had made it to her watch post.

She put the telescope to her eye. In the city, at the foot of the big mountain, two dwarves sat leaning against a small stone building, talking. To the right, road, more road, then a dwarf on a small horse talking to two standing dwarves beside him. To their right, a dwarf sat, eating bread.

Snap—the sound came from below Ri.

A doe nibbled at high grass.

Ri wouldn't find anything in Rone, she reminded herself. She had lied to get herself out there. But she peered into the city anyway. She refused to let her moment be ruined.

She found the dwarf on the horse—still talking with the others. Then laughing. She scanned left, up the main road, up the mountain. Dwarves walking. Smoke rising from chimneys. Dwarves entering homes and shops. Higher on the mountain—a cave or, most likely, an entrance into the mountain. Dark—she couldn't see inside. She kept her view there. A dwarf emerged and headed down the road. Ri scanned higher.

Another cave—light flickered inside but no other activity. Higher up, a longer dark entrance, smooth ceiling and sides, clearly unnatural, cut into the mountain. A hooded, cloaked figure emerged—very tall, not a dwarf— and then a dwarf did appear—Governor Bardric.

An arm reached out from the cloak—a pale arm. The slender fingers of its pale hand grasped Bardric's wrist. Bardric grasped back, the two shook, and the tall figure turned toward Rone, smiling.

Ri jerked her head away from the telescope. No…

She peered back through. King Eldred wore a wry smile on his face. The Dark Elf nodded to Bardric before heading into the mountain. Bardric went down into the city. Eldred had gone out of sight, but Ri had seen his smile. And she had seen it before. She had traveled to Deroc once as a child.

Eldred had been kind to her in that murky place, as all his elves had been to the entire delegation from Abilin and to their Granan escorts. But Eldred's smile had unsettled her then—it had been too full, too frequent.

Ri's stomach sank as she stared into her telescope, waiting for him to reappear from the mouth of the mountain cave. What was he doing there? He should not have left Deroc. He hadn't been away from his prison homeland in hundreds of years. Not as far as Ri knew. And he wore a hooded cloak, meaning he wanted his presence in Rone to remain unknown. Had he come as part of some… sanctioned visit, secrecy would not have mattered.

Ri's stomach churned. Below her perch, the deer had gone. To the left, she could not see Launfal, but he was out there, in his own tree. And Addis watched from the right. Had *they* seen Eldred? Had they seen other Dark Elves? Was her team in danger? *Real* danger?

Snap!—Ri couldn't find an animal that had made the noise. She scanned the forest floor but found no one and no creature. How long had she been in the tree?

She peered through her telescope at the wide cave mouth. Her view jerked up and down with her fast, uneven breaths. Would Eldred emerge again? Ri could not see inside—she saw nothing except darkness.

And she continued to see nothing but black in the cave. Ri scanned a little higher on the mountain and a little lower. She did not see where Bardric had gone, and she kept returning to the wide cave mouth.

Chirps rang out—Naelon's whistle. One second—as if

from a bird, undulating higher and lower. Two seconds—no danger.

Ri took a deep breath. She fastened the spyglass to her belt, crawled backward to the tree trunk, strapped her quiver over her shoulder, then slung her bow across her body. Limb to trunk knot to limb, she made her way down and landed softly on the ground.

She checked side to side—no one. She began jogging to their meeting point then slowed to a quieter walk. Every sound *did* matter. Launfal jogged to the north of her. She spotted Addis to the south. *They* could keep quiet enough moving at that speed, so they reached Naelon first. He asked them a question, and they shook their heads.

"Ri," Naelon said softly, as she neared, "anything to report?"

She looked at Launfal, then Addis. "Did you see him?"

"Who?" Addis asked.

"I noticed lots of dwarves," Launfal said. "As is usual."

"King Eldred," Ri said. "Shaking Bardric's hand."

"No..." Launfal scowled. "Here?"

"Where?" Addis asked.

"A cave—er, an entrance into the mountain, it might have been. Eldred wore a cloak. I only saw his face for a second, but... it was him."

Emlyn and Egan approached.

"Did you see Eldred?" Naelon asked them.

"No," Emlyn said. "*King* Eldred?"

"Yes. Ri says she spotted him on the mountainside with Bardric."

"We spoke to Bardric," Emlyn said. "He rode by and said a quick hello."

Ri crossed her arms. "I hardly believe it."

"But you're certain?" Naelon asked.

"Yes. I think so." She uncrossed her arms. "It looked like him, and then when he smiled, I had no doubt. I've seen that smile before. He went inside after that and didn't come back out."

For the benefit of the last to arrive, Naelon pointed at the other two watchers. "They noticed nothing unusual." He asked Egan and Emlyn, "And you two, inside the city, anything out of the ordinary?"

"No," Egan said. "I bought a little statue." He displayed a tiny stone Galeron in the palm of his hand. "She bought a silver ring. The dwarves were friendly—very welcoming. Nothing unusual at all."

"Go back," Naelon said. "Quickly, while we still have daylight. At the gate, tell them you forgot something. You need to buy another gift. Then try to get inside that mountain. Be careful, but take a look."

Egan and Emlyn nodded.

Naelon turned to the others. "You three resume your watches. When Egan and Emlyn return, whether they find anything or not, we'll head for Alnara. Or half of us will, while the others stay here. That I will decide, but we must get word to Terrin." He said to Egan and Emlyn, "You two, don't take long. And you three"—he looked at the watchers—"keep an eye on the sky. If Eldred's really in there, unless he came through the White Forest or on a ship up the coast, he came by dragon, and if he leaves, he'll leave that way too."

"Right," Addis said.

Ri nodded.

"Everyone stay sharp," Naelon said. "If King Eldred journeyed from Deroc, I doubt he did so alone. Let's go."

Emlyn and Egan headed for the road. Addis made for his tree.

Ri gave Launfal a look and considered telling him that she had made up the conversation from Dritus.

But why? What would telling him change at that point? Launfal gave her a confident nod and went on his way.

And Ri went on her way, back to her tree, quietly but quickly. She had to get up there. She had to return to her watch—a watch that *really mattered.*

Ri jumped and grabbed the first branch. She pulled herself up then climbed higher, using the same route as last time. She hung her quiver and bow as before, out of the way but within reach. Spyglass in hand, she lay and stared into the blowing leaves.

Unbelievable, she thought. So... *unbelievable.* She brought the glass to her eye, and when her view bobbed as before, she did her best to calm her breathing.

Ri found the dark cave entrance that had clearly been cut into the mountainside. No one stood outside, and she still couldn't see in, but in her mind, the sly smile formed. The elf towering over the dwarf governor seemed... excited.

Ri scanned up and down the road—no one. Could she have seen someone else? A different elf in a cloak? Could she have seen nothing at all? Without the glass, Ri searched through the leaves to the sky. Eldred *never* left Deroc. Could she have imagined him? Could she have craved real danger that badly?

Thunk—thunk—arrows sank into a body south of Ri.

Two hit to the north.

Rustling leaves to the right and the smacking of tree limbs culminated in a crash to the forest floor and a short moan.

To the left, a body fell—Launfal!—through the tree, smashing to the ground.

Behind Ri, blades clashed.

Someone groaned, possibly Naelon. Metal hit metal—faster the strikes came. "Dark Elf bastards!" Definitely Naelon. Metal sliced flesh. Another groan.

Ri clutched the tree, frozen, holding her breath, waiting for the sounds of her fallen friends fighting back. *Get up, Launfal. Get up…*

"The two at the gate are dead," a voice said. "Three here. That's five."

Ri heard a sword being sheathed. "That's the team," someone else said. "Back to the city. Bring the bodies."

She heard horrible sounds, like sacks being lifted, that must have been the bodies being moved. Heavy footsteps faded to the south. Ri chanced a quiet breath.

Dark Elves had left Deroc and come to Ronnigun. Every member of Ri's scout team was dead, their lifeless bodies being carried into the dwarven city. Ri's friends were gone. And they had only been out there at all because of her lie.

26

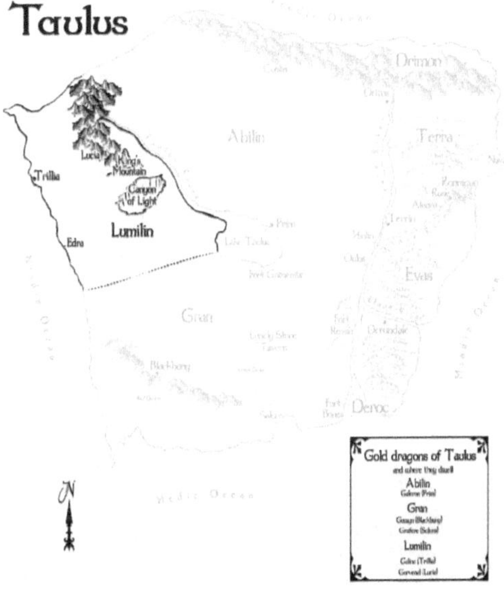

High above southern Trillia and the throngs of fans cheering in the sun-drenched tournament grounds and the rows of tents outside the city walls, Beal held the saddle at the base of Galina's neck with one hand and his gleaming broadsword with his other. The gold completed again the same circle out over the ocean that she had just flown then looped around to the knights standing tall before the king in their shining armor and arrayed in their units on the jousting track.

My son will pay for his absence, Galina said to Beal.

Horns blared, drums beat loudly.

"I am sorry," Beal said. "I could not find him when I went back with your command."

I do not blame you. He is too fond of that girl. I've told him as much, and I will go to Lucia to tell him again as soon as I am done here.

"Ah, Lila," Beal said. "She is very beautiful."

Galina craned her neck to Beal, forcing him to lean backward to avoid her snout. She shook her head, inhaled deeply, then when the horns quieted and the drums softened to a low rumble, she shot a long stream of flame into the sky. *Boom!* A fireball burst at the end. She darted downward.

"Well done!" Beal yelled over the loud music and rushing air. Galina flapped her wings, flapped again, and drove them lower.

The frenzy below grew. Spectators pushed themselves as close to the track as possible. The well-off sat on bleachers on one side, and the richest occupied a line of boxes on both sides of the royal box opposite the bleachers. Knights from every city and town in the kingdom—and those Trillian knights not in the formation on the track—watched from a large tent at the end of the dirt strip, where they would prepare for the games.

The few eyes not already aimed skyward looked up as the dragon flew closer. They cheered loudly, and as Beal neared them, they got even louder. Merchants who hadn't yet left their shops rushed out of the tent city that had sprouted outside the capital's walls and served as home to visiting spectators who could not afford better accommodations or had not secured them in time.

Galina closed in, and Beal raised his blade.

The crowd cheered.

Beal held tight when Galina paused their descent in order to expose her impressive golden body to those below. She shot fire upward.

The crowd cheered again, calling her name, and then she swooped close to them.

Beal pumped his sword skyward.

The crowd screamed for him.

Galina and Beal flew over the king and queen, who stood and clapped with Beal's wife, Lorelei; his son, Braden; and the nobles and special guests in the royal box. Galina's shadow covered them and then the rest of the wealthy, jewel-laden crowd as they passed.

Beyond the end of the tournament grounds, Galina flew a long, gradual turn, rising before gliding lower toward the track separating the crowd. They neared the dirt, and Beal leapt off, landing perfectly.

"Beal!" the crowd yelled while the dragon touched down.

Beal raised his blade skyward and shouted, "Trillia!"

"Beal!"

He motioned toward the dragon. "Galina!"

"Galina!" the crowd echoed.

"Queen Kiara." Beal bowed to her. "King Adrian."

The spectators clapped and cheered while the royals

smiled and waved at them. Adrian brought up his hands, and the crowd slowly quieted.

"Sir Beal, thank you!" the king called out. A smattering of cheers followed. "And thank you, Galina!" More cheers. "We are lucky to have such a champion as he and such a protector as she in this illustrious city!" A little softer, he said, "Not that we don't deserve them."

Laughter rolled through the crowd.

The king continued, "Trillia, the brightest star of the cities of Taulus, filled with its finest families, should have *no less*."

Applause came.

"Such a city deserves a champion like Beal." The crowd clapped and yelled their approval until the king quieted them. "But what if Beal were unavailable?" The king shrugged and looked down the box at Lorelei. "Perhaps busy at home with his lovely wife? What then?" He smiled. "We will find out who is second best. Once we have, Trillia, and all of Lumilin, will have *two* great champions." The king opened his arms to the crowd. "You deserve no less." Their cheers drowned out his call of, "Let the games begin!"

While the track cleared and workers raked the lanes for the opening joust before the archery competition, Beal climbed the wooden steps to the royal box where his family sat and kissed Lorelei's cheek.

Galina leapt into the air and flew east toward Lucia.

27

Taulus

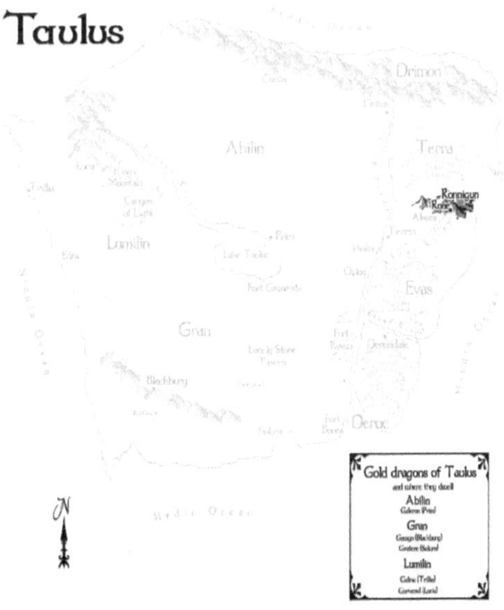

Ri's arms wrapped around her tree branch. Her cheek lay on its rough bark. Tears slid slowly down her face, where they had streamed hours before, making tracks in her camouflage paint. She had wiped her cheeks with her sleeve, but her nose continued running because she wouldn't sniffle. She couldn't risk making the noise. Firelight illuminated quiet Rone beyond the blowing leaves in front of her. She hadn't moved from her watch post above the dwarven city when the Dark Elves shot Addis and Launfal out of their trees and butchered Naelon on the forest floor.

The fight hadn't been long. Naelon had had the sense to yell out information about his attackers, in case Ri survived. And she had, and she might have been able to make it to Alnara to tell the Red Elves there, but she hadn't been able to get herself out of the tree to start the trip.

Naelon hadn't seen them coming, Ri realized. Their old leader, one of the finest Red Elf scouts of all, hadn't seen his attackers until they were upon him. And the Dark Elves seemed to take not a second's pause before killing him. They were not supposed to be in Rone, or Ronnigun at all, and they had refused to let that secret get out.

Ri had to stay in her tree. On the ground, Eldred's elves would find her. They'd hear her making noise. Naelon hadn't stood a chance, so Ri would die even faster.

Egan and Emlyn were dead, slaughtered at the gates. Slaughtered because Ri's lie had brought them out there.

Egan had been so young and full of life... poised for such a long, vibrant life, that because of Ri would never come.

Emlyn—motherly Emlyn—had always been so kind to Ri.

Naelon had accepted Ri onto his team, had given her a chance and then his respect once she had earned it.

Addis, the emote who had hoped to lead his own team, couldn't heal himself, and dead, he couldn't heal anyone else, either.

And Launfal. Dear Launfal—her teacher, her mentor. Ri

loved her family in Abilin—her brothers, her caring mother, and of course, her father, the king. But Launfal had been the kind of father Ri would have picked if she had been given the choice. The way he instructed her, pushed her, and demanded her best—Ri had loved it. She had loved him because she had craved exactly that kind of teacher.

Emlyn had helped a great deal. They had *all* instructed Ri, at least a little. But without Launfal, Ri would never have deserved her place among the scouts. And Launfal was dead. Ri's years of happiness, of escape from the mundane in Abilin—she owed so much of it to Launfal.

And escape… from what? From a peace that had been broken within earshot, on the forest floor beneath her. She knew not what Eldred and his elves planned to do, nor what Bardric had to do with it, or if any other dwarves were involved. Ri didn't know what was going on, yet when her friends died, with them went any peaceful explanation for why Eldred had left Deroc.

Ri wiped her face.

Surely Eldred meant to wage a war.

Unless he judged aggression on that scale to be beyond what his small number of subjects and Bardric's dwarves were capable of… perhaps instead he planned some measure of revenge. But what if *all* the dwarves were involved, those in Drimon with King Doxton along with those in Ronnigun?

In any case, Eldred couldn't wait long. His absence from Deroc would not go unnoticed. The age of peace in Taulus would end any day—any moment.

Ri teared up again. She whimpered.

That peace had ended when her team had been killed.

Why had Ri lied? *What had she been thinking?* It wasn't a game. It was the lives of her friends she had played with!

Scouting inside the Red Elves' borders, *that* had almost been a game. Hunting and racing against the others had truly been sport. But a fictional conspiracy requiring a mission to a foreign city? Lying to the king of the Red Elves? A child might dream of such a plot—a little girl playing with her toys or drawing on paper to show her mother or father.

Ri lifted her head and stopped herself from slamming it into the branch. Such a plot should not have been hatched by a young woman. She lay her head down gently. The princess of Abilin should not have put her elven scout team in harm's way for her own amusement.

Ri sniffled and hugged her tree branch. The princess of Abilin had no place among the scouts after all.

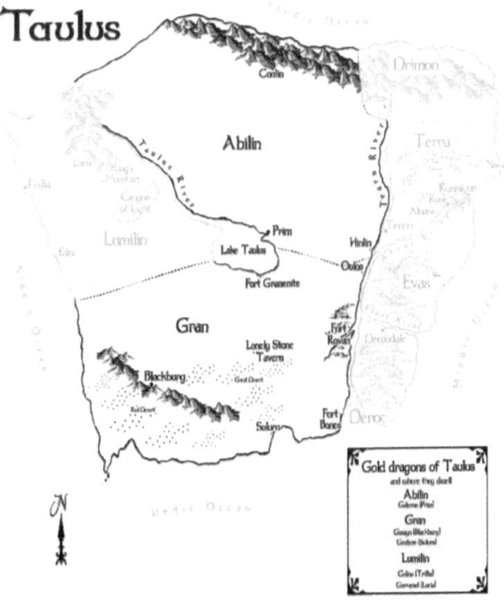

28

Gowyn agreed to take Valencia and Taylan with him north
to Hinlin, in Abilin, where he was meeting Galeron. The
trading town stood near the junction of four kingdoms—
Abilin, Gran, Terra, and Evas—known as the Great Divide.
Valencia's presence meant representation from someone in
authority from Gran and that Gowyn wouldn't have to relay
the news to her later. For all the dragon knew, Taylan just

happened to be along for the ride.

Outside the desolated town, Galeron was speaking with knights from Abilin who had come to survey the aftermath of the attack. Taylan could see them shielding their eyes from the sun to watch Gowyn's approach.

And? Galeron asked as his son landed among them. *What did the little king have to say for himself? Did he massacre these people?*

He did not say. Gowyn leaned low, and his passengers slid off.

"General Merton," Valencia said to one of the older knights of Abilin.

"Commander Valencia," he said.

I did not speak to Eldred, Gowyn said. *He was not in Deroc.*

The Abilinians murmured among themselves.

And his elves? Galeron asked.

Gone.

Galeron nodded. *Then the treaty is broken.*

Yes, Gowyn said. *I did not search the White Forest, but it is possible the Dark Elves are there.*

Merton stepped forward. "Will there be war?"

Perhaps, Galeron said. *That Eldred is not in Deroc after what happened here in Hinlin leaves no doubt that he had some hand in killing these people, though I do not know how he will wage a full-scale war with so few.*

"We must get word to Prim," Merton said.

Yes, Galeron agreed. *Send word, then when we have made our plans here, send word of them without delay.*

Merton pointed at a young knight. "Go, now."

The knight stumbled as he took off for a group of horses tied up a short way away.

Merton looked at Galeron. "We should see what's going on with the White Elves in Derundale, yes?"

At altitude, Gowyn said. *If Eldred is in Derundale with all his elves, it may be dangerous, even for me or my father, to investigate closely.*

Agreed. Galeron motioned toward the decimated town. *And I worry about the unusual nature of this attack.*

"The strange footprints?" Valencia asked.

Yes, Galeron said.

"The bodies were piled neatly in the center of town," Merton said. "We buried them yesterday. Their wounds were numerous, suggesting multiple attackers, but otherwise not unusual. But the footprints… They're little." Merton put his hands apart to approximate the length. "Smaller than a man's."

"Show me." Valencia headed into Hinlin, and the whole group followed.

From over by the horses, the young knight released a homing pigeon, which headed west.

Merton pointed ahead of Valencia. "There."

The young knight jogged to the group.

Valencia crouched and inspected prints on the ground. Taylan joined her.

Merton motioned outward. "And everywhere."

"Never seen these," Valencia said.

"Me neither," Taylan said.

"Ever read about anything of the kind?" she asked him.

"Hmm…"

Gowyn asked his father, *Who did this, do you think?*

I've no idea, Galeron said. *Elves, or even men, along with whatever these unknown creatures or animals are, could be responsible.*

Valencia looked at Taylan then at Galeron. "Could the elves possess some new magic?"

Anything is possible, he said. *And that is why we cannot rush to the White Elves with questions. Yet we cannot do nothing.*

General Merton rubbed his chin. "What in the world made these prints?"

"A pack of animals?" the young knight suggested.

"The prints are in pairs," Valencia said. "From something that walks upright—but not very tall with such short strides. Perhaps dwarves?"

"Or *changed* dwarves." Merton scooped dirt from a print and rubbed it between his fingers.

"Or a new breed of goblins," the young knight said. "Or a new breed of little trolls."

Merton pointed at the knight. "Or very young trolls."

Taylan stood. "Or… or…"

The prints are unlike any of those things, Gowyn said.

"'Orc,'" Taylan said. "Not 'or,' but the word 'orc,' and with these footprints, I am reminded of something I saw in Derundale."

Merton raised an eyebrow. "Are you?"

"From a parchment… a fragment of parchment. Years

ago, I was in one of the smaller libraries, and—"

"Why?" Merton asked. "Why were you there?"

"Looking for… other things entirely."

Go on, Galeron said.

"It was late," Taylan said. "I was tired… in a foul mood. But I remember taking time to study the parchment carefully because it was incomplete and thus unclear. A print was drawn, like these." He motioned toward the ground. "With three points, but I didn't know it was a print then. It was circled. The word 'orc' was written under it in large letters. And smaller, part of a sentence, 'with the right heat, they sprout fast.' So the three points, the sprouting… I concluded 'orc' was a flower, and at that, I wasn't interested. I left and went to sleep."

"You're sure the drawing matched these prints?" Valencia asked.

Taylan knelt to the dirt. "Quite sure."

"And there was nothing else?" Merton asked. "About these… *orcs*?"

"Nothing," Taylan said. "And when I returned to the library the next day, that piece of parchment I had set atop the pile I had been reading was gone. I found it strange, as everything else remained exactly where I had left it. But I didn't dwell on it for long. I didn't care about a flower. I never came across anything else like it, and I hadn't thought of it since."

"No flowers killed all these people," Merton said.

Taylan rose. "No."

Galeron said to his son, *Go with Grafere and fly high*

above the White Forest. Stay safe, and see if you can spot any Dark Elves or anything unusual below.

Gowyn nodded.

Galeron continued, *I will go to Terrin, deliver this news to the king and Farlan, then spend the night patrolling the Red Forest.*

"We're patrolling the riverside," Merton said. "More knights are on the way. We'll send an update to Prim and to Trillia."

Good, Galeron said. *Gowyn, meet me back here in the morning.*

"And Derundale?" Merton said. "Flying at altitude may prove useful, but surely we ought to ask the White Elves about these orc creatures, if that is what left these prints."

Don't worry. Galeron brought his head down close to the general. *I will not forget about Derundale.*

Gowyn said to Taylan and Valencia, *I will take you to Oulos, where you can rejoin your knights.*

At Oulos, Gran's trading town near the Great Divide, Valencia shared the news with her company and explained that they would remain there, ready to defend the town or respond to threats nearby if need be. She dispatched a message to Blackburg with the news and the suggestion that knights be sent east to reinforce defenses near the White Forest. Valencia ordered Hayle to advise Oulos's traders to suspend operations for a few days as a precaution. Then she walked to her tent with Taylan.

Outside it, she said, "You need to set up your own tent."

"No." He stepped close. "I want to be with you."

"Not now." She moved away. "And not after this. You should head back to Abilin tomorrow." She shrugged. "Or wherever you want to go."

"But I love you." Taylan's throat dried.

Valencia sighed. "I understand that now, since we last spoke. I should have known before I sent for you. I shouldn't have sent for you." She met his sad gaze. "I care for you, Taylan—I always have, since we were young. That's why I didn't leave you in Hinlin. I couldn't embarrass you like that. But had I truly understood how you felt, I would not have sent for you in the first place."

"But I could help you here."

"No. I have my knights, and more on the way. You are unpredictable. I cannot rely on you in battle, as I can them."

Taylan took her hand. "You *can* rely on me. I promise."

She pulled away from his grip.

"Whatever Eldred is planning," Taylan said, "I can help."

"Help your kin. In Abilin or Terra."

"I want to help Gran."

"Then go to Solurn," Valencia suggested. "Or Blackburg. If war is indeed coming, and history is any guide, we could use you there."

"But—"

"Stop." She put up her hand. "I'm sorry for causing you more pain. I truly am." She turned to her tent then glanced back. "Good-bye, Taylan." She pushed aside the flap and went in.

Taylan stared at the settling cloth blocking him from Valencia. A sharp sting shot down his neck. He stepped backward, and his ankle twisted when his foot landed on a rock. He groaned and grimaced at the stretching and snapping of ligaments then looked at the shut flap. Valencia must have heard him, but she did not come out to see.

Taylan limped away to set up his tent.

29

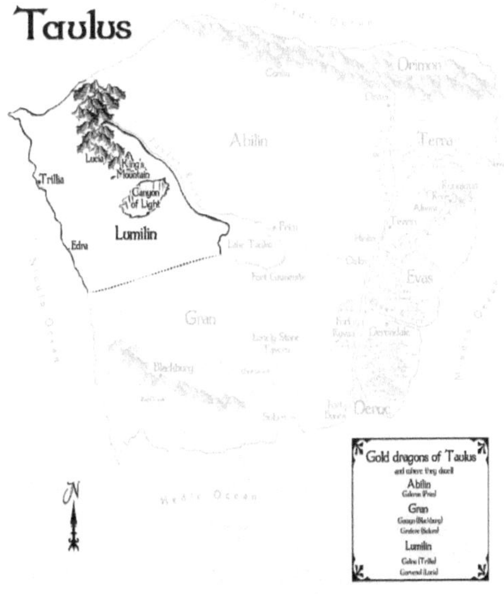

In the morning of another day dominated by riding north into greener, lusher land, a pair of young riders raced past Gall and the twins, shouting that they were headed to Trillia for the tournament and that it would be crazy for anyone not to hurry there too. Gall and the twins rode steadily on.

By mid-afternoon, with Avery and Avril in the lead as usual, Gall found himself thinking back to the second night of their trip. Around the fire, Avril had asked him, "Have you ever been married?"

"No," Gall had said.

"Ever close?"

"Not really. I've moved around a lot. Never wanted to be tied down."

"Not even in Blackburg, when you were a knight there?"

"Why get married? I didn't want to be a father." Then they had ridden on, and Gall's thoughts had drifted to his old friends from Blackburg who *had* settled down with wives and husbands to raise families. Their kids would have been pretty grown up by then.

Gall sipped his whisky and let go of that recollection of those old memories. He recalled his favorites from among the many women during his days in Gran's army, and since. He had had plenty of fun.

Gall jumped down from his horse.

Avery turned to him.

"Practice." Gall placed his bottle on the ground. It fell, but he righted it before much had spilled.

Avery's shoulders slumped, but he dismounted. He got his sword and commenced with the drills Gall had taught him—footwork, defense, and cuts and thrusts into thin air. To Gall's eye, Avery's form was improving, though the fact that Avery was holding back was just as noticeable.

They moved on to sparring, which Gall occasionally stumbled through on account of his whisky.

Their blades met high with a *clang*. They met lower, softer.

"Harder." Gall swung his sword.

Avery blocked then swung. He couldn't have matched Gall's strength if he tried—not remotely—but he didn't even seem to be trying.

Gall dodged Avery's slow effort, stepped in, and shoved him away. "Swing like you mean it, boy!"

Avery got his footing and clenched his jaw. He tightened his grip on his sword and stepped forward as though he might finally charge with a purpose.

Gall beckoned to him. "Come on!"

"You're drunk." Avery threw his sword to the ground. "You're always drunk." He walked away into the brush.

Gall fetched his whisky bottle and crouched next to Avril. "Any ideas?"

She shook her head.

"I'm not *that* drunk."

Avril smiled very softly.

Avery sat, facing away from them.

"My parents hated when I drank like this." Gall plopped to the ground and dropped his sword. "'Specially my father. And my mother."

"What was she like?" Avril asked.

"Me," Gall said. "She was happy. She didn't take things too seriously. She didn't have to, not in this age."

"Was your father a knight, like you?"

"A knight, but not like me, and he was not like my mother. He was stern—serious. Always serious." Gall shook his head. "*Always*, about everything. I hated it. I hated him for the same reasons I hated my commanders—all the orders and strict rules."

"He seems a strange match for your mother," Avril said.

"Aye. And no." Gall let out a deep breath. "My father was stern, and… unyielding. But he was also honorable and good. He was a *knight*, for everything that meant."

"So he treated your mother all right?"

"Always. And that always felt right to me too."

"What did?"

"That part of it," Gall said. "Even after my father screamed at me upon learning of my latest insubordinations, and after he disowned me for leaving Gran's army, that one piece of my father sat well with me. I hated the knighthood—the organization—but I never argued with my father about the merits of being honorable and just. He explained it to me once when I was very young, why those virtues mattered so much. I had questions, and he took care to answer them clearly." Gall huffed. "The only conversation I recall enjoying with the man… and we never spoke of it again!" Gall pulled a clump of grass out of the ground. "I guess he never had to remind me." Gall tossed the grass away. "He knew his son well enough to know that."

"But why drink so much?" Avril asked.

"Why not?"

"Your parents? You said they hated it. Your friends? Do you *have* any friends?"

"Eh. My father's hated my attitude my whole life, drinking or not. My mother doesn't approve, but oh well. My friends never minded… I don't think. And I've hardly seen any of them in years." Gall shrugged. "Maybe I just like the challenge. I won every contest and fight sober, however long the odds, so I wanted to see if I could win when drunk. Maybe cost me a few extra bumps and bruises, but turns out I still win, so I never stopped drinking."

Avril nodded.

Gall noticed Avery glancing at them. "If your brother won't practice, you should."

Avril's gaze sank to the ground.

"Not everyone is as honorable as me."

Her face softened.

"In this age of peace, thievery and crimes of passion have not died out. How'd you feel in Blackburg before the tavern, after the sun went down and the city grew dark?" Gall didn't ask how Avril felt when Ivon was being cruel to her mother. "Remember those unsavory folk who came out of the alleys and side streets like they had been waiting all day for—?"

"Defense only." Avril looked at him. "And no weapons."

"Deal." Gall figured any way to defend herself would be better than nothing, especially if Avery couldn't be counted on to fight hard on her behalf.

He set his bottle on the ground, and they got up and got to practicing.

30

Taulus

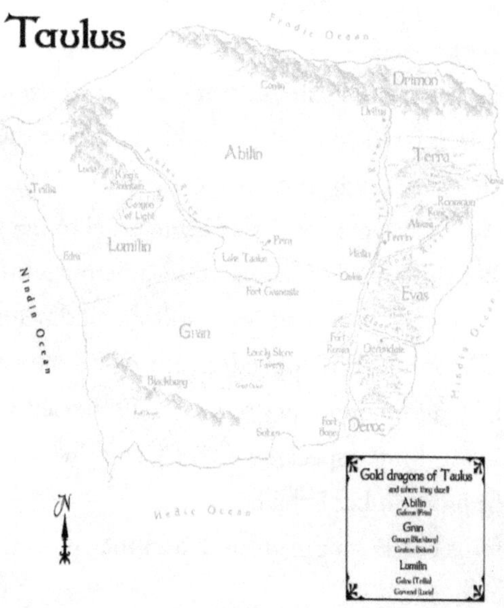

Lila awoke on Gorvenal's back. Under the dense canopy of stars, a small, round spot of land with a patch of trees at its center interrupted the tranquil ocean. She had been in and out of sleep but roused herself to see Yalus.

The island grew as they approached. Smooth sand—pale tan in the nearly full moon's light—surrounded the circle of lush vegetation at its center. So thick were the trees, high grass, and vines that Lila could not see into them past their outer line. Massive Gorvenal touched down gently on the pristine beach. No other footprints marked the slight slope inland from the slowly rolling waves. The island was a little larger than she had expected.

"We made it." Lila unwrapped her blankets and scarf and let them fall off the heavily breathing dragon.

He leaned low.

Lila untied her boots and chucked each one into the sand. She slid off Gorvenal. Her feet sank into softness, and she beamed, looking up at her dragon. He craned his neck to her. She wrapped her arms around his neck and nuzzled her cheek against his.

Lila gazed at the stars overhead, then to where they touched the ocean at the distant horizon. "It's incredible." She let go of Gorvenal and ran down to the water, which ran up the shore, warmly covered her feet, and lapped at the bottom of her long, heavy skirt.

Lila spun to Gorvenal, who was taking their cases and sacks of supplies off his back and setting them in the sand.

She walked to him. "Yalea was here, on this island, so long ago."

Yes.

"Incredible." Lila went to the water and breathed in ocean air. "I slept as we flew and do not need to sleep any longer. Would you tell me of how Galeron came to be?"

Of course.

"Wait," Lila said. "Are you tired from the journey?"

I am glad to be done flying, but I am fine.

"Good." Lila bunched her skirt up above her knees and sat with her side against Gorvenal, smiling wide and looking out at the water with him as his breathing calmed. "I cannot think of a better setting."

Nor I. Gorvenal let his head rest in the sand and began as he had concluded, after Abilin's capital had been destroyed and the dark army laid waste to Gran as it moved west. *In Conlin, Mikael and Siann, recovered from their exhausting efforts in Prim, found Galt sitting near the top of snow-covered Mount Conel, staring to the south. The big tan dragon noticed the emotes and flew down to them.*

When Galt landed, Mikael asked him, "Would you help the good people of Taulus fight the Black Dragons?"

"Yes," Galt said. "It would kill me. But I have thought of little else since Prim."

"Why?" Siann asked.

"For the same reason dragons first came to mankind's aid: to avert a catastrophic loss for humanity. Then Abilin would have fallen and, without its ally, maybe Gran not long after. This latest threat endangers all of mankind.

"Defensively, on the move, I might survive the black dragons. Or I could organize with others of my kind and try to come to terms, dividing the world between Xodon's dragons and the rest.

"But any settlement would be a tenuous one. And that world would not include mankind, or at least not a free mankind, unless under our protection, and I do not believe Ewald and Xodon would allow us to offer that.

"Among the creatures in Taulus who speak and think and

who the Creator brought here to be masters of his land, men and women are the most fragile. Yet you are also its most dynamic, its most interesting—its most beautiful, inside and out."

A gust of wind blew falling snow into the unflinching emotes' faces.

Galt continued, "Dragons love and hate, but we do so from a position of physical strength over the creatures of the world—at least we did, before these new terrible versions arrived. The elves' long lives—longer even than ours and spent with a youthful appearance—mean they have decades and centuries to consider and make choices and make new ones if their first prove misguided. But you humans have such a short time on Taulus that you have to be decisive. You cannot afford contemplative years and decades, no matter how important the decision."

Galt glanced at the peaks above him. "I cherish nature's beauty, as all of my kind do, and for me, it has always been the mountains. Yet I found, years ago, that I could care for my mountains and yet have room for more, because I deeply cared for the men and women of Taulus and their lives of triumph and tragedy and, most of all, love.

"Nothing is more beautiful or enthralling to me than your love, because its absence is so hard on your kind. The way short-lived humans experience that emotion moves me beyond the sight of any perpetually majestic peak or valley. The lucky find love fast and love hard; others ache without it or love the wrong ones as their lives and their youth slip away. Many find true love late, and cherish it and clutch it tightly, remembering their long years without it."

Galt craned his neck lower to the emotes. "I cannot stand by and let such wondrous life be snuffed out of Taulus by Xodon or be enslaved in it by Ewald. The black dragons will attack Conlin and its people eventually. I would rather there be fewer with Xodon when they do, so I will fly south to Gran, or maybe to Lumilin. The dark army will be weaker, and their dragons fewer after Blackburg. When I go, and which others I ask to join me, is all I have left to decide."

Siann asked, "What if we could make you like the black dragons? Only not like them. A little larger, a little stronger than you are now… Mightier than all the natural colored of your kind in Taulus, but not full of the rage that drives those black abominations."

"How would you?"

"We have guessed how Ewald and his emotes did what they did to the purple dragons," Mikael said. "In fact, we are quite sure. For Siann and I have also long pondered what our strongest feelings, the deepest of our emotions, could accomplish. We believe the elves tested those depths and made their savage creatures full of their own deep-seated malice and hate." Mikael took Siann's hand. "Together, we can give you the power to confront that darkness."

"What will you do?" Galt asked as the snow fell harder.

"You will be changed," Mikael said, "as Xodon and the others were, at the very fiber of your being. You will still be you, but you will also be something different. Something greater."

"You are certain you can do this?"

"We are confident. We will draw upon a power Siann and I rarely use, for we take no pleasure in aggression against others. But this is no attack for our gain. This will be an assault on you,

at your core, because there is no other way. There will be pain—agony—for the change we mean to cause is not trivial. But that we pour that hurt into you from a place of love—our truest and deepest—I believe you will feel, and that will give you comfort."

"You are worthy," Siann said. "We do not know how many we can change, so we must start with the most worthy, the most devoted to fighting for mankind."

"Think on it," Mikael said. "But please, not for long. Time is not our ally."

"I have decided." Galt leapt and flapped his wings. "I will do it." He rose into the snowy air. "I will return with another I hope you will find as worthy as I."

Lila watched a white bird with long, black-tipped wings land atop a tall tree in the middle of the island. A second followed and perched alongside it.

In short order, Galt returned with Tidra, a young, quiet tan dragon he had spent considerable time with and who shared his concern for and love of mankind. Out of the intensifying storm, they joined the emotes inside Mount Conel.

Galt's fire lit a pyre that the emotes had prepared. He sat beside Tidra. The high, jagged ceiling and uneven walls glowed in the blaze, whose crackling interrupted the howling of the wind outside.

Mikael asked, "Are you ready?"

"I am ready to give whatever I can for the men and women of Taulus," Galt said.

"As am I," Tidra said.

Siann took Mikael's hand. "This may take every bit of us. We have not practiced. We have not written a script or instructions for what we aim to do, because we do not know the words to describe it. We will succeed. You will be changed. But if this kills us, you will be Taulus's best hope against this new evil."

"You must not fail," Mikael said.

The dragons nodded.

Mikael stepped forward and placed his hand on Galt's leg.

Siann reached out for Tidra's. "Move closer." The tans did, until Siann slid her fingers onto Tidra's leg.

The dragons grew warm.

The emotes closed their eyes, Galt took Tidra's paw, the dragons shut their eyes as well, and all moved closer together. All grew hotter.

Flame swirled within the emotes, then the flame ever within the dragons roared.

Mikael's thoughts drifted to the warm spring morning when he had first glimpsed Siann. He had loved her every second since.

Siann knew she loved Mikael later, at some point during a week by the lake in the mountains, when the weather had been perfect, the conversation wonderful, and the moments of silence a delightful time to reflect upon it all. Their evenings by the fire had been magical, their time together in bed even more so, and their mornings in each others' arms before breakfast had served as an exquisite dessert before their next marvelous day together.

The fire inside the dragons burned hotter than either of the mighty creatures had ever known.

The blaze burst!

It built anew in them both. Flame flicked and exploded. The furnace at their bases glowed rich hues of red, orange, and yellow.

Galt wanted to make a child with Tidra. In their years together, full of both playful times and serious, he had almost told her of his wish many times. He would soon, at last. He would wait no longer.

Mikael had hated every moment apart from Siann since he had met her, and after that week in the mountains, Siann couldn't stand being without her Mikael.

Tidra longed for a little baby of her own, but she was shy and the other dragons would not be patient with her—except Galt. He had always been so. And of all the dragons he could have gone to, he had come to her on that day hoping she would join him in a new life that lay ahead. She would ask him if he would give her a child. And he would say yes. She did not want anyone else, and she could not bear it if he said no.

Mikael and Siann could not save Prim, and they had saved so few of its people. They loved each other so much—so completely. They loved the people of Abilin, yet they had failed them. They would not fail them again!

Flames ripped through Galt. His eyes shot open, and the powerful dragon raised his head to roar but held it in when Tidra, her eyes closed, her face scrunched in agony, pushed her cheek into his shoulder. Galt shut his eyes, held her, and did not fight the vibrant fire rushing from his core to his scales, out to his limbs, down his tail, and out to the tip of his nose—and then into his bones.

Galt clutched Tidra, and when Galt felt his bones tearing and twisting inside him, he prayed he had not brought Tidra to her death at the hands of the emotes.

Mikael's soul told Siann that he was ready and willing to

die, if he had to, in her arms, for the sake of the good kingdoms of mankind. Siann's answered that she was prepared as well, so long as she and Mikael did it together.

Galt had to fight for mankind, but he had to be with Tidra, just the same. The mountains did not matter. Their size and splendor had not been diminished, but their worth to him had. Tidra could not die. And so that he could be with her, he could not let himself die.

Tidra resolved to share her feelings with Galt. Finally, she would do it. If only she survived the emotes and the inferno destroying her insides.

Mikael and Siann's minds shared with each other their happiest moments since they had met, and if those amounted to all the times they were to be allowed, they would not complain. That they had found each other at all was such a gift to be thankful for.

The dragons' pain lessened. The fire within settled.

Mikael and Siann collapsed in each others' arms.

Galt held Tidra tight. His opening eyes saw golden scales for the first time, and hers beheld his, shining in the light of the glowing fire beside them.

On the ground, Mikael opened his eyes, then Siann did. They shared a deep kiss and, together, turned to their gold dragons.

"Galeron," Siann said.

Mikael nodded. "Gaiva."

The golds took their new names. Inside and out, they had changed.

Galeron and Gaiva exited the cave and flew to convince another young tan, a particularly strong female, to return with *them to Conlin to be changed as they had been. She agreed immediately. The male tan with her took a little persuading, but he came and committed himself to protecting the men and women of Taulus. Considering the toll taken on Mikael and Siann during his transformation, Galeron judged that they should try no more than two others.*

And he judged correctly. While the two tans became golden and powerful like Galeron and Gaiva, when Mikael and Siann fell into each others' arms, they did not rise. They did not share a kiss, nor did they speak, nor did they ever again glimpse the one they loved so dearly. They never saw the magnificent golds born of their ultimate sacrifice.

Galeron named Galina and Grafere, and together they were the first four of their kind.

Lila watched a loud wave crash against the moonlit shore. "And on this island, thousands of years before that, the mother of all tan dragons ensured her kind would live on." Lila let a handful of soft sand run out of her palm between her fingers. "Do you think a different color would have worked?"

Oh, maybe, Gorvenal said. *Though I doubt we would have wound up golden. And I do wonder if any other scales would have buoyed so well the men, women, and elves that rallied behind those first four with as fervent a hope in the face of such vile yet imposing enemies.*

I think of it like this: had Yalea never given birth to Yalia, and Yalia not mothered her family of tans, down the line, Galeron would never have been.

Lila asked, "Could we have won without him?"

That I do not know.

31

Taulus

Ri sat on her high tree limb, leaning back against its trunk. While the sun set behind her, mountainous Rone still lay before her. She took a piece of dried meat from the pouch on her belt and had a small bite. She sipped lukewarm water from her small canteen.

The city had been quiet that day. Ri had peered through her scope and found dwarves mingling about, not acting noticeably out of the ordinary. Little columns of smoke rose from the chimneys of some of their homes and shops. Governor Bardric had ridden up and down the big mountain, but she had not seen King Eldred or any Dark Elves. She did not know if they remained in the city.

But the evil elves had been there, and they should not have been. They were supposed to be far away, confined to Deroc, not in the north murdering Ri's friends and planning who knew what.

Well aware of her proximity to the White Elves' border, Ri had to tell the Red Elves in Alnara who was responsible lest there be any false suspicion or blame between the elves. Ri had only glimpsed Eldred for a moment. No one else on her team had seen him, so she couldn't imagine how anyone else in the world except her could know the sinister elf had come to Rone. She considered King Ervain her friend, as she did his queen, Kaelyn. The Red Elves had always been gracious and kind to Ri, and to all of Abilin. They had to be warned and know the truth about the attack.

Ri sipped more water.

She had to tell her parents. Ri had no idea what Eldred planned or how Bardric was involved, but the Dark Elves had destroyed Prim once before. Ri did not know how they could again. She could not think of any weapon of Eldred's that would enable him and his elves to defeat Abilin's large army or breach the high walls of Castle Mikannel, but she nevertheless couldn't stop seeing visions of Prim's people bleeding, burning, and suffering, as they had in the wars of old.

Ri checked her belt pouches and found plenty of food. She shook her canteen—half empty.

Perhaps Eldred merely intended to show his displeasure with the Treaty of Solurn. Maybe he meant no more than to stage a spectacle with a few of his elves and, for whatever reason, Governor Bardric had a role to play.

Ri sipped her water.

Probably not. Killing Naelon, Emlyn, Egan, Addis… and Launfal—that had been an act of aggression to which the Red Elves could never turn a blind eye. And Eldred's father Ewald had been ruthless in his efforts to dominate all of Taulus. He showed no mercy for any men or women who opposed him, common *or* royal.

Eldred's father had begun his wars by attacking the kingdoms of mankind first, and while he caused significant destruction and death, he had failed to achieve his grandest aims each time. Eldred must have been plotting something novel, something that would begin not by lashing out from the border of Deroc but from the cover of the forest. He had already killed Red Elves. From Ronnigun, he could strike the rest of them and also attack the White Elves to the south, if he so desired. Elves numbered fewer than men. Eldred launching his campaign against them by surprise seemed a reasonable plan.

Ri stopped halfway into a bite of dried meat.

After the elves, Eldred would cross the Tearn River and sweep west into Abilin. Gran would be in his sights, but Prim lay significantly closer than Blackburg. War would come to Abilin first.

Ri's eyes watered. She tore off the unbitten end of the tough meat and made slow work of it in her mouth.

She pictured her three brothers, swords drawn, back to back, surrounded by Eldred and his elves, fighting as their city was taken. Kalen and Chance were powerful warriors. Gregory was strong enough and the most cunning. But against the elves who had slain Naelon and his team, her brothers would fall eventually.

Tears ran down Ri's cheeks.

Her father could not protect her mother for long. He would fight to his end for her. He would give his last breath, but he would indeed be made to, and not in victory.

Ri swallowed hard, and the partially chewed meat stuck in her throat.

And what would become of them, her family, after they took their last breaths on Taulus? Ri had been taught that death in battle meant her family would be reunited with their creator to live with him for all time, as Charles, Catherine, and the first people of Abilin had on the great plain.

But really?

Most of Abilin believed in such an afterlife for the worthy, *but really?*

Launfal hadn't believed as the Abilinians did. He had told Ri of the conclusions he had reached centuries before.

Ri had never seriously dwelled on the subject, but suddenly it had become important. And she had no idea.

But she had to warn her family. She just *had* to.

A gust of wind rustled the leaves in her tree. Beyond

them, the sky grew dimmer. Ri looked at her bow and arrow. If she had any chance, it would be during the day. The elves' sight gave them an advantage over her then, but the difference would be even more pronounced in the darkness. If she would actually leave the tree, she would have to wait until morning. And then, Alnara still seemed the logical destination to run for.

Peace had been boring. Her boredom had been suffocating and crushing. But she missed those painfully monotonous days so much.

32

Taulus

At a round stone table in a small, dimly lit room under the tallest mountain in the dwarven city of Rone, King Eldred sat with an expressionless Queen Jadira to his left and his advisor Farek and strategist Ivir to his right. Bardric and his second in command, a relatively tall dwarf named Raff, completed the circle.

"At long last," Eldred said, "after all these years—after all our planning and all your impressive work here in Rone, in this mountain, and beneath your land—the time has come."

"What of the Red Elf scouts outside our walls yesterday?" Raff asked.

"Their disappearance can only help," Eldred said.

"The moonlight does not concern you?" Bardric asked.

"Better for all to see the show."

Bardric nodded.

"You trust your dwarves completely?" Eldred asked. "Every one of them? We've kept our secrets for so long, and we can ill afford dissent among us now. Not at this hour."

"They are all committed," Bardric said.

"They are all eager," Raff added.

"As they should be," Eldred said. "Never has our enemy been more green, nor more ripe for what is to come. They have never been more utterly untested." He motioned to Jadira. "We head east now." He looked at Ivir and Raff. "As planned, in three hours it begins."

Ivir nodded. "We are in place and prepared."

"So are we," Raff said.

Eldred stood. "Finally, my friends, we wait no longer." He put his hand out for Jadira, who took it and rose. "Please come with me to share the news with Xailyn."

Ivir walked to the opening of the wide cave mouth in Rone alongside a younger Dark Elf named Zia. With a long sword hanging off her hip like his did, she held her hands behind her back as he did, gazing at the clear sky.

Ivir located the curved string of stars making the great hunter's bow and the arrow he had shot across the heavens. He noted how the flickering lights had moved since last he'd checked. A gust of wind rustled the leaves before him. "Not long now."

The pair headed back into the cave.

The two dwarves guarding the mouth of a mountain cave at the northern border of Ronnigun noted how the stars making Dorran's hammerhead had fallen toward the horizon—a slow swing of the mighty tool in the celestial workshop.

"Almost time," one dwarf said to the other.

Near the mouth of a cave in southern Ronnigun, one of the short creatures at the front of the long line stretched his neck forward for a better view outside. "Now?"

Another of the creatures growled.

"Soon," the dwarf at the cave mouth said to the restless horde. "Very soon."

In the Red Forest, northwest of Ronnigun, a Dark Elf, camouflaged and hiding near an uprooted tree, looked away from the sky and reached through a small pile of sticks and leaves to retrieve a leather-wrapped bottle filled with an opaque, viscous liquid. He popped the cork and headed for the logs stacked on a dead, fallen tree.

Farther northwest of Ronnigun, deeper into the Red Forest, and at two locations to the southwest in the White Forest, three Dark Elves poured the same liquid onto branches and logs they had prepared and got ready to light blazes that would reach high into the night sky.

Far to the west of Ronnigun, at the entrance to a tunnel dug deep beneath the White Forest, a Dark Elf said to another, "It is nearly time." He called into the almost pitch black, to the first of a hundred rows of little fighters, "Run straight for the bridge, cross the river, and don't stop."

One of the creatures growled.

"Kill everyone you find!" the elf called.

Another creature pounded his sword pommel against the tunnel's stone wall and let out a bloodcurdling cry. He pounded against the tunnel again.

In the White Forest, on the southern bank of the Alnar River a little ways from where it ran into the Tearn, a Dark Elf carried a stuffed sack from the woods out to the westward-rushing river. He untied the string around the sack's neck and dumped large red seeds into the water.

The plume of red in the river expanded and thickened as the elf kept pouring. The bloody cloud flowed fast down the river and gradually spread to the opposite shore.

The elf watched until the red had darkened and spread far across the water, and then he ran to the east.

At the cave in northern Ronnigun, a dwarf smiled to his companion and stepped outside the entrance. "Go!" he yelled to the frenzied creatures as they began rushing past him. "Into the forest. Kill all who cross your path."

They roared as they ran out.

The dwarf blocking the cave mouth in southern Ronnigun stood aside. "Into the White Forest!" he called. "Burn and pillage!"

Standing at the western bank of the Tearn River, holding his horse's reins, Spear, the knight of Valencia's company on watch east of the town of Oulos, gazed at the Red Forest to the north and the White Forest to the south.

Whatever had happened to Hinlin had surely come through the White, he reasoned. But what *had* happened there? How had everyone been killed?

Spear, eager to perform better than he had against the ogres, preferred the notion of a fight to a watch. Much preferred, he decided. And Hinlin had been Abilinians… he and his countrymen would not have suffered the same fate.

Except… no one knew exactly who had murdered everyone in Hinlin—or what.

Spear looked at the southeast as a low rumble began in the forest.

His horse cried out and shuffled backward.

Spear yanked its reins, but it didn't settle.

"Whoa!" He pulled softer and got his hand to the animal's nose. It nodded its head down. "Easy." The horse shuffled its feet and nodded to the river again.

Red water. From the north and spreading south. Spear had never seen anything like it.

The noise in the White Forest grew so Spear could hear it over the commotion of his horse. He got himself onto his saddle. Backing up from the river calmed the animal.

Spear watched the river redden. He had never heard of the water of the Tearn turning so… bloody.

He pulled out a small scope and peered through the glass. He listened as the rumbling intensified, and marveled at how red the river had become.

He had to report to Valencia in Oulos without delay. Either another knight on watch would find the cause of the noise in the woods, or Spear would return to discover it.

Spear rode from the river, fast.

———————————

Thunder.

Ri awoke in the tree and saw Rone dark before her—darker than the night before. Thunder rumbled to her right.

Except she could find no clouds in the starry sky. She scanned the forest below—nothing.

Ri peered through her scope—a scant few fires giving light in Rone. She couldn't make out the cave openings from the rest of the mountain.

Thunder rolled on.

Dwarves, Ri assumed. Running from Rone, out the front gate on the main road. The sound was not galloping horses, and no elves—Red, White, or Dark—made that much noise, ever. Unless they played drums, though Ri could not imagine why elves would do that on their way out of the city.

She confirmed that her knife was on her belt then counted the arrows in her quiver. If a hundred jogging dwarves made that noise, she liked her chances better than if it were a handful of Dark Elves—especially in the woods.

And she had to find out. Ri collected her things and began climbing down. It might already have been too late. She might have waited in that damn tree for too long. But once she found the source of the noise, if she could warn someone, maybe her friends would not have died in vain. Her boots hit the ground. Maybe she wouldn't have led them to their deaths for nothing.

Moonlight occasionally peeking through the treetops helped Ri see as she jogged toward the source of the thunder. Her light steps paled compared to the booming coming from the road.

The thunder grew louder.

Weaving between trees, avoiding sticks and fallen branches, Ri picked up her pace. It had to be dwarves... a lot. Running to attack... Alnara?

A slow, consistent blur filled the space between the tree trunks ahead.

Ri stopped.

On the road, the blurry source of the noise jogged, its top hidden by branches and leaves. Ri didn't want to be out in front of it, in its view. She walked forward slowly, hoping to catch a glimpse of its rear.

Dark legs passed in front of her. Short legs. Not horses', but also… definitely not dwarven. The legs were thinner. The bodies and heads remained hidden.

Ri crept closer. Thunder rumbled louder.

Tattered clothes. Dark armor. A long column, two wide. What were they?

A variety of weapons came into view—maces, axes, and most commonly, one of a number of differently shaped short swords.

The column passed completely, so Ri crept closer. She reached the edge of the forest at the road and spied the end of the line. Ri peered out from the woods. She had never seen anything like them.

Gray, ragged, short. Not dwarves, not elves, and most definitely not men.

One of the last two whirled round. A squished face with yellow eyes—that spotted her.

Ri added an inability to stay hidden to her list of failures as a scout.

The creature smacked the one next to him and pointed at Ri. She grabbed an arrow from her quiver, got it on her bowstring, and aimed for the first creature's chest while pulling it back. She let it loose.

The sharp arrowhead sliced into her target. He fell to his knees, his face hit the path, and Ri learned the creatures could be hurt like any others of Taulus.

The second creature roared, and a pack at the column's rear broke off and ran at Ri.

She darted into the woods, grabbed an arrow, and checked behind her. She counted five chasing her. Ri stopped, shot an arrow into one's midsection, noted that the rest of the creatures had continued their jogging on the path—and that her four remaining pursuers appeared crazed.

Ri shot another in the chest. Knife! She ducked, and it sliced air overhead. She ran, dodged trees, jumped branches, and pushed deeper into the woods.

She glanced back—the three left hadn't gotten closer; the gap might actually have widened. She didn't need to stop and fight, she'd keep ru—

Ri screamed. Sharp stinging from high on the back of her left leg sent her tumbling to the ground. She rolled over and grabbed an arrow. She found a gray-skinned target, fired, and got him in the head.

Ri tried to stand, and pain shot up and down her leg. She couldn't put weight on it. Piercing waves radiated from where the thin blade stuck in her muscle. She pulled the knife handle, gasping at the pain, but failed to remove the metal.

Ri got to a knee, grabbed an arrow, and searched for the remaining two creatures.

A tumbling axe flew at her. Ri ducked to the side, and the sharp edge sliced the top of her left arm as she shot at the creature who had thrown it. He dodged her errant arrow and ran at her.

Ri grabbed an arrow. Leaves rustled to her left. She shot at the darkest spot—the rustling ended. She took a hand off her bow, grabbed her knife as she spun, and plunged it into the little creature leaping at her with his own knife in hand. She drove him to the ground.

Plum-colored blood oozed from his wound. He growled, and his eyes slowly closed.

Ri pulled her knife from him and let her shoulders slouch. The thunder rumbled in the distance, but she heard nothing nearby except her own heavy breathing. She inhaled deeply and slowed her breaths. Blood ran down her left arm from below her shoulder, under her long sleeve. Lifting the arm made her grimace, but that she could move it was promising.

Ri twisted for a better look at her leg—a lodged blade and blood seeping out onto her legging around it. She dropped her weapons, grabbed the handle of the knife, and because the noise would give away her position, vowed not to cry out in pain.

She pulled, and the blade shifted but didn't come out. Her blood streamed faster.

She gritted her teeth and pulled again—looser—and again until she finally ripped the knife from her leg.

Blood poured.

Ri took two strips of cloth from her belt pouch, one wide and brown and one red. She wrapped the thin red cloth around her leg, inches above the wound. She pulled it tight and let out a stifled, closed-lipped scream. The bleeding slowed.

With the long ends of the cloth, Ri pulled the tourniquet tighter and watched the blood slow further. She wrapped the brown cloth over the wound twice and tied it secure with a knot.

She caught her breath, then despite the pulsing stinging in her leg, gradually got up off the forest floor.

When she finally stood, she took a long look at the creature she had stabbed, the likes of which she had never seen before. It was short and not at all stout like a dwarf, but not scrawny, either. And such gray skin.

She felt blood running down the back of her leg and inspected her work. The bleeding gave her another reason to get to friendly lands quickly.

Ri grabbed her weapons, rotated her wounded arm, and grimaced. She took a slow, agonizing step toward Alnara.

―――――――――

Far to the west of Ronnigun, the little, gray-skinned creatures rushed out of the tunnel into the White Forest.

"Orcs!" The Dark Elf they passed called to them. "Run for the bridge! Find the blood-red river. Run for Gran! It is because of Gran that you and your queen had to live in darkness for so long."

The orcs growled and roared.

"Gran is your enemy!"

―――――――――

Northwest of Ronnigun in the Red Forest, the Dark Elf brought his torch to the uprooted tree and watched the dried wood ignite.

The fire spread along the bark and up the logs leaning against it. The flames rose and finally reached above the treetops.

Satisfied with his work, the elf ran to the east to meet up with his kinsmen, who had lit their own fires throughout both forests, Red and White.

Taulus

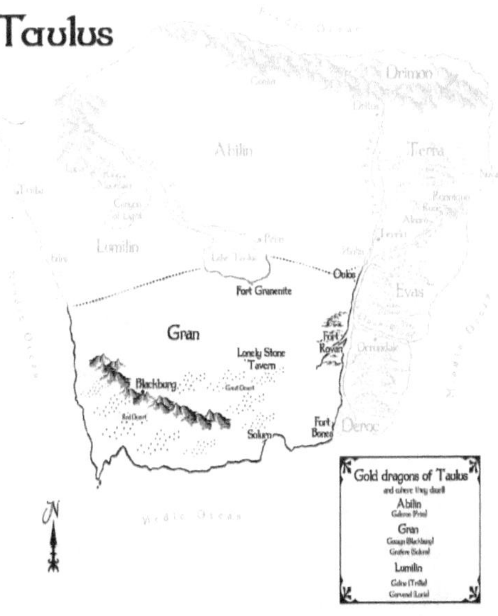

Taylan's tent blocked the moonlight. He lay on the grass in quiet darkness, staring at the apex of the cotton ceiling. The ten knights of Valencia's company must have been asleep, resting in their own tents, or out on the lookout. The trading town they had come to watch had a garrison of ten knights and, according to Valencia, about its usual number of traders, but commerce had long since ended for the day, so little sound came from Oulos.

Taylan closed his eyes to a different version of the same darkness, the same emptiness. Taylan was alone. Worse—far worse—he would be alone, without his love, without Valencia, forever. He would leave, he decided. Any second. Or in a few hours. Whenever he mustered the energy to get himself off the ground. Better to go than to risk seeing Valencia in the morning, wearing that look of indifference on her face—or one of pity.

"Fire!" The call came from a distance but clearly.

Taylan sniffed—a hint of smoke.

"Two fires!" came another call.

Taylan sat up, crawled forward, and pulled aside the flap at his tent's entrance. Flames rose over the top of the White Forest. The second fire burned to the north. Taylan stepped outside, grimacing at his first step on his sprained ankle, and watched the sudden fires along with Shaela, Valencia, and her armor-clad knights.

Spear raced his horse toward them from the direction of the river. "It's all red!" He headed for Valencia. "The river. It's blood red!"

"Arm yourselves!" Valencia called. "We protect Oulos." She ducked into her tent.

Taylan went into his and grabbed his knife. A fire might break out any time, he reasoned. But not two at the same time so far apart. And the river turned red? When Taylan emerged, Valencia had mounted her horse. She headed for the torchlit front entrance to Oulos as her knights and Shaela with her thin sword rode that way. Not even an indifferent glance from Valencia, Taylan lamented.

Though he would have despised the fresh reminder, had it come.

Taylan got to his horse, untied it, watched the knights assembling, and looked at the flames above the forest to the east. He turned to the west, to the quiet and calm. That was his path. He knew it, as truly as he hated admitting it.

But Valencia!

He wanted to ride to her, to be at her side. He gnashed his teeth. He longed to be there *because she wanted him to be there*, but she didn't. She didn't at all.

The company had reached the packed dirt before the main town gate. Half the knights donned helmets. The fires in the forest were spreading.

Valencia had told Taylan to leave because the mission had changed from training to uncertainty and danger. King Eldred had disappeared from Deroc. Times had grown serious. Taylan's throat dried. The time for playing with half-elven childhood friends had ended.

A rider—a knight of Oulos—raced from the river. "Dark creatures approach!" he shouted. "Small creatures, but many!"

Valencia shouted orders to her knights, and the six men and four women fell into a loose, wide line before the gated town entrance as the rider from the river went with Shaela inside the walls. From where he had come, a mass of short… orcs, apparently, ran toward Oulos. Taylan mounted his horse, tried to ignore his painful ankle, and slowly headed that way.

The ugly little orcs had angry eyes and carried an

assortment of weapons including dark swords, knives, and spears. And there were a lot of the creatures. More than a hundred… perhaps two hundred.

Out of Oulos, a white pigeon flew west, presumably carrying news of the attack with it. Taylan scanned the sky—no sign of Gowyn or Grafere. The reinforcements Valencia had sent for had yet to arrive, making it two hundred against Valencia's eleven, plus the ten in the town. And Shaela. As the dark mass neared the mounted knights, Taylan stopped halfway to them. He could help… but would it make a difference with such lopsided forces?

He watched as Valencia guided her horse out in front of her line of knights and turned to them. "We are bigger!"

"Yeah!" they responded.

"We are stronger!"

"Yeah!"

She glanced behind her at the oncoming horde.

"I do not know what those little orcs are or from where they come, but we will stop them. We will kill them all."

The knights yelled their agreement once more and pumped their weapons and fists high.

The orcs ran in a mob without formation.

Valencia waited for her knights to quiet. "For I know exactly what *we* are and where *we* come from." She raised her sword. "*We* are knights of Gran!"

"Yeah!"

Valencia spun into a charge with her company. The knights towered over the short orcs rushing straight for them. Dirt kicked up by the horses' hooves rose higher than the dirt brushed into the air by the small orcs' feet. Taylan walked his horse toward them. He had never been in a battle like the one before him. This age had seen none like it. Taylan wondered what it would cost him to help.

The lines neared, and Valencia's ranks closed. Her focused face hardened. Taylan remembered her indifferent one. Why should he bother? But Taylan continued his walk toward her.

The knights burst into the mob, trampling, swinging swords… and slowing as the orcs struck back. Four knights fell. The other seven made it all the way through and spun round. Half the creatures turned to them. The others rushed on to Oulos, many not slowed at all. Three archers atop the stone town wall fired down at the attackers.

The knights on foot struggled against their smaller but more numerous foes. Valencia led a second charge. With little room to gain speed, her horses pushed into the mass, but not far, and without knocking many orcs to the ground. Another two knights fell.

Taylan neared but couldn't locate two of the dismounted knights from the first charge. He watched a short sword thrust into the third. A mace smashed a knight's back, and the woman fell and disappeared in the mob. The little creatures swarmed the remaining five mounted knights.

Valencia shook an orc off her arm, spun her horse, and swung her sword wide to drive others away. They rushed back at her, and she hacked one while taking a slice to her side. She cut down the attacker and didn't seem badly hurt. Off his ride, Spear took a spear to the gut and fell to his knees. A sword sliced clean through his neck.

A crossbow bolt sank into Taylan's horse, and the animal reared. Taylan had ambled closer to the battle than he'd realized. He spotted the orc who had shot the horse beneath him as the animal bucked and crumpled and Taylan fell to the grass. Past the orcs charging at Taylan, an axe chopped a knight to the ground.

Fire broke out in Oulos.

Taylan got to his feet, grabbed his knife, and limped backward. Three orcs closed in on him, and more followed. Against one, he might use his blade. Two—maybe, but while they were short, up close they appeared quite muscular. A cloud swirled inside Taylan. He put away his knife. The cloud grew, and lightning crackled over it. Taylan hated doing it. *Hated it*.

He hated it so much…

The creatures growled and raised their weapons.

Taylan extended his hand. Could he do it fast enough? Why could he do it at all? Hadn't being born a mixed-breed been enough? Why had he been doubly cursed?

Lightning shot from four of Taylan's fingertips and struck the nearest orc, who fell backward. Darkness flickered in Taylan's mind. He raised his other hand and sent lightning at another—piercing jolts hit Taylan when his bolt hit the creature, who landed atop the first with a seared hole in his stomach. The third's short sword swung at Taylan, but he jumped out of its reach. He punched the orc away.

Taylan cried out as lightning from both his hands hit the orc's chest. Darkness exploded in Taylan's mind, and he screamed. Why didn't Valencia love him? Taylan seethed as his lightning charred the orc. The little thing dropped to the ground, and the four others coming at him skidded to a halt. Taylan stopped. His heart pounded. Three lay dead.

Taylan's throat swelled. Could Valencia not love a half-elf? Was it the dark power he possessed? *Why?*

The four fresh orcs charged. Taylan shouldn't have been in the battle at all—he should have ridden to the west. Why hadn't he gone? *Stupid!* Taylan scolded himself.

He extended his hands. Damn Valencia for writing to him, for asking him to come in the first place. Damn her!

Streams of fire flared from Taylan's palms toward two orcs and set them ablaze. They ran aimlessly, screaming. With a racing heart and eyes wide, Taylan moved the swirling flames onto the other two. They howled, fell to the ground as the first two had, then moaned as the inferno engulfed them.

All four quieted and ceased moving. Taylan let the flames recede and flicker out. His chest heaved.

Among a still huge pack of angry orcs, Valencia and Hayle, their horses nowhere to be found, stood alone before the burning town, covered in blood.

Taylan desired nothing except Valencia's love. He didn't want his magic. He never had. He didn't want to be an emote, able to lash out and kill. Visions of the creatures he had just jolted and burned to death shot through his mind. Taylan knew with dreadful certainty that those images and sounds, like all the rest, would stay with him forever. Even the smells would, like the smoke and charred wood and flesh from the fire that had burned his parents.

Hayle took a cut to his leg. An axe found his side. He fell forward into the swarm, and Taylan saw no knights except Valencia.

He walked toward her. Two days before, he would have torched the entire crowd of little creatures. It would have been terrible for him, but he would have done it. He had an older pain he would have drawn on for the energy to make it happen. Then he would have run to Valencia, to tell her he loved her, and to hold her, and to kiss her soft lips before bringing her to Shaela to be healed.

A fresh cut in Valencia's side let blood stream out.

Taylan froze. He *had* told her he loved her.

A mace smashed Valencia's shoulder from behind. She swung her sword lazily at the attacker.

Taylan had *finally* told her, and she told *him* to go away.

Valencia's flailing spin left her facing Taylan. A sword thrust into her back sent her body lurching forward. Her effort to swing her sword failed. Valencia's eyes found Taylan's.

A mace smashed into her ear. Her head caved. She fell into the swarm.

Orcs charged Taylan.

Valencia was dead, her head crushed.

A crossbow bolt sank into Taylan's quad. He dropped to a knee.

The orcs neared and raised their weapons. Taylan saw Valencia the moment before the mace had cracked open her head, and heard her heart's last beats, along with those of his, that she had broken.

A club rocked Taylan's cheek, and he fell. He stared skyward while the creatures kicked, stabbed, punched, and kicked him again. In the shifting spaces above, between gray limbs, angry faces with yellow eyes, and dark armor, gold scales swooped low.

Heat surged.

Shrill screams and guttural growls filled the air.

Gowyn stomped the fleeing little creatures, burning them and swiping them aside with his tail.

An orc kick to Taylan's head forced his eyes shut.

34

Taulus

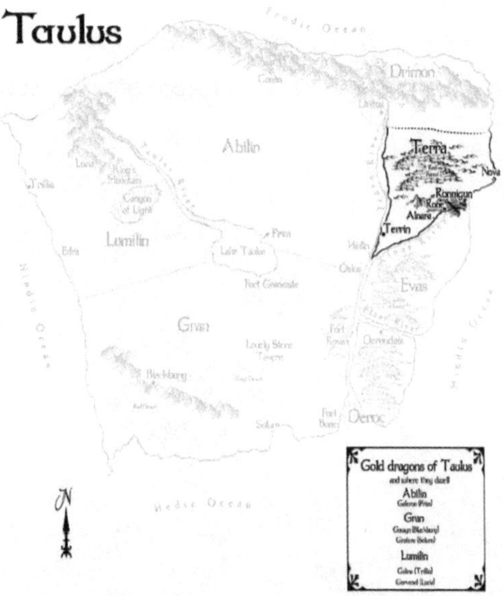

Ri held herself up against a tree barely sturdy enough for the task. Her bow hung across her body and her quiver loose on her shoulder. She caught her breath, exhausted from the effort of dragging her wounded leg through the dark woods. Two deer scampered by. The back of Ri's leg was soaked red. She loosened her tourniquet. The blood flowed faster until she gritted her teeth and let out a grunt as she pulled the strip of cloth tight.

She hadn't heard the thundering jogging of the little creatures for a while, so while she wasn't ready to head out onto the open path, she doubted the noise she had just made had reached them. Alnara lay a day away—longer, slowed as her injuries had rendered her—but she let herself rest a little more.

———

Hours later, Ri sat on the bank of a small stream, dipped her canteen into the water, took a long drink, then topped off her supply. She wetted her hands in the stream, rubbed her cheeks, and when she found no paint on her fingers, decided she had removed all the camouflage from her face.

She sat back on her elbows. The wound near her shoulder didn't hurt much worse with her weight on the arm.

Ri guessed the little creatures would reach elven territory soon—long before she could deliver a helpful warning. Life saving, she reminded herself. A *life-saving* warning.

After her life-costing lie. Ri choked up.

The elves would respond swiftly and successfully. Ri had been wounded in the process, but she had taken out six of the little creatures by herself. Elven warriors would have no trouble dealing with the entire pack.

And if the creatures were not headed to the elven city, Ri could still warn the elves, who could relay the message to her family in Abilin.

But what of the elves who had slain her friends? Where were they, she wondered. And where had the dwarves from Rone gone? She had spotted only a few in the city, when she had last spied from her tree.

The Red Elves had Farlan and other dragon allies. Plus Galeron, Gowyn, and all the golds were friendly with King Ervain. Ri couldn't see the sky past the treetops, but if any flew overhead, would they see her on the forest floor?

It stood to reason that those strange little creatures might be part of a larger group, perhaps an army. Ri shuddered at the thought.

An army might keep the dragons too busy to spot one person in the vast forest. She pictured Gowyn and Galeron soaring overhead, scouring the woods for the little things, and swooping low to spot Dark Elves in hiding. Such a search, spanning such a large area, would be far more important than her fate.

But there didn't have to be a whole army of the little things. And since Ri had hardly gotten any closer to Alnara and her leg had not quit bleeding, she had to hope there was no such army.

Ri's left leg dragged loudly through leaves and sticks. The throbbing from her wound radiated down her leg each time it hit something hard. The sound hadn't attracted anything dangerous, though—little creature, nighttime forest animal, or otherwise—so Ri had stopped trying to keep quiet.

In fact, she considered making more noise. It had been hours, and she didn't think she had made it across the border into Red Elf territory, but if the dwarves hadn't come after her yet, and Ewald's elves from Rone hadn't either, it didn't seem likely they would. Ri needed one of King Ervain's Red Elves to find her. An emote, ideally, but anyone who could help her with her leg. She felt woozy but not hungry or thirsty. She was losing too much blood.

Ri let out a gasp when her foot hit a stump hidden under leaves and long grass. She hopped on her good leg. She gently touched her foot to the forest floor and grunted. She lifted it again and looked around the forest—no one, nothing.

Carefully, she crouched, pulled her bow over her head, and let herself fall to the side. Leaning on her arm, she watched the rustling leaves and held her bow to her stomach. She would remain there for a little while. She needed to rest.

Ri awoke to a lightening sky—morning approached.

She smelled smoke and sat upright. She couldn't find any fire, but she sniffed—definitely smoke and maybe a haze along with it.

She twisted to see the wound on her leg—fresh blood on her legging and on the ground under her, but the bleeding had slowed. Perhaps not much remained inside her to seep out. She pulled the tourniquet tighter.

Using her hands to keep weight off the leg, she got to her feet—then fell to a knee among the blood where she had lain.

Slowly, carefully, she got up again. Ri reached her arms out wide to steady herself, and when her head stopped spinning, she took a painful step.

She took another step—the world spun.

She shuffled her feet and found balance.

But she couldn't keep walking. She couldn't even keep standing. She spotted a short piece of a fallen tree trunk, partially overgrown with high grass, at the base of a tall, wide tree.

She limped to it, deeming it better than no cover at all. Focused on her destination, she kept just enough balance until, beside the trunk, she fell and barely got her hands out to keep her head from smacking into the fallen tree.

Ri rolled onto her back and decided she didn't have the energy to tighten her tourniquet or pull her bow off her. Thick leaves rustled high above. Her eyes closed.

35

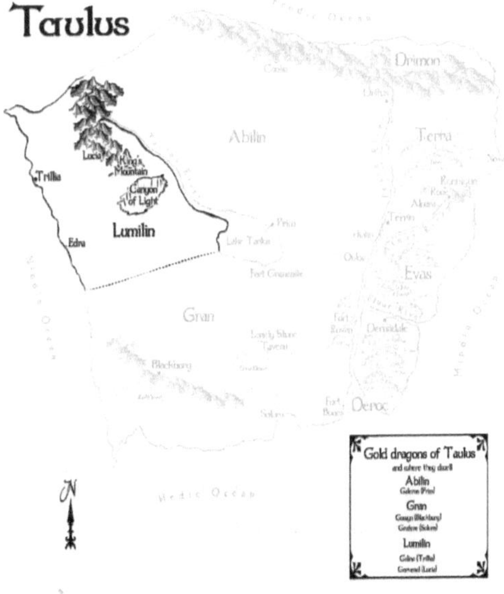

Gall, Avery, and Avril would reach Trillia before nightfall. The day's ride had been a quiet one. Though Gall hadn't drunk much liquor, and he looked forward to catching the end of the tournament for Avery's sake, he anticipated the festivities that would follow for his. The twins, so close to being reunited with their mother, showed little interest in the games.

When they had a few short hours remaining in their journey, Avery dropped back alongside Gall. "I'm sorry about yesterday. I'm sorry for calling you that."

"It's all right," Gall said. "I drink a lot. It's…" He turned up his palms. "Just what I do."

"I wish you wouldn't."

Gall shrugged.

Avery looked away from Gall for a moment then turned back to him. "How long will you stay in Trillia?"

"A night."

"Is that all?" Avril asked.

"Aye. Conlin awaits. I have to finish my job."

They rode on in silence, Gall in thought.

"You two could come with me," Gall said. "If you wanted."

Avery and Avril exchanged glances.

"Very few have ever seen Galeron's sword and Gaiva's shield. You could hold them."

"I want to see them," Avery said. "I… I really do. But we couldn't leave our mother so soon."

"I'm sorry," Avril said.

Gall nodded. "I understand."

36

Taulus

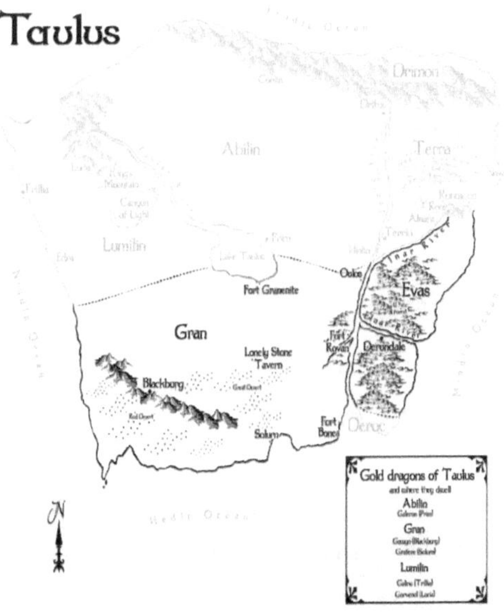

After a breakfast he had skipped and before a lunch he had no interest in, Taylan sat outside the large white command tent that had been erected after the battle at Oulos. He held his knees, looking out at the forest beyond the Tearn River. He told the knight beside him, "I'm leaving." He shifted, starting to stand.

The knight grasped Taylan's shoulder and held him down. "Not yet."

A cloud coalesced at Taylan's center. No, he told himself. He didn't want to focus on his hate. He couldn't bear to again so soon.

The knight held firm.

Lightning flashed inside Taylan.

Or could he use that anger? Just once more...

Taylan took a deep breath. "When?"

The knight let go. "General Bannan should not be long."

Taylan nodded. The fires had been mostly put out in the forests, but smoke rose from where they had burned up and down both the Red and the White. Taylan had watched the flames reach high into the night sky after he had been healed. He wished the emote hadn't done it. He wished he had been left to die with everyone else who had been at Oulos—left to die like Valencia.

But the emote had been brought by Grafere before daybreak, and then natural dragons and knights had followed. Taylan had been the sole survivor of the attack. Every knight inside and outside the town had been killed. The town's traders and inhabitants who had ignored the warnings and stuck around had been hacked apart by the orcs, as had Shaela. At least she died with her sword sunk in an orc who lay at her feet.

When Taylan had awoke after the battle had ended, he'd cried. The emote who cared for him did not know that he cried for only two people—himself and Valencia—for what he had done, and for what he had failed to do.

Then with the fires burning above the treetops, Taylan gave his account of the battle to Gowyn, in full detail, save for two facts—that he had used magic to kill the orcs who attacked him and that he had decided not to save Valencia before that heavy mace smashed her skull.

Gowyn reported that he had spotted the same little creatures in the south of the Red Forest. Elves, despite being outnumbered, had battled them successfully at a few locations. Since then, the orcs were scattering throughout the woods while the elves hunted them.

But the scattering meant a lot of groups had to be hunted. And as of yet, none had shared useful information about where they had come from, or their goal, other than offering different explanations of their enemy. The orcs in the forest seethed when mentioning the Red Elves. The orc Gowyn had gotten to talk cursed the word "Gran" as he said it.

After recounting his story, Taylan had packed to leave. West made sense, to get as far from the forest as possible. West, where he should have gone the night before… but he wasn't certain. What would he accomplish by going that way?

Since he no longer had a horse, he'd have to walk, but he didn't care. He was not in a hurry. He hadn't settled on where he'd go when the knights told him he could not depart until he told his story to General Bannan, who was on his way from Blackburg. Word had been sent to the general to divert him to Oulos, before he reached his original destination, Hinlin.

With darkness dominating his mind, Taylan had protested, to no avail, that he had to go immediately. So he had sat outside the tent and watched the forest beyond the Tearn River, as he still did, waiting.

He had seen Gowyn fly for the Red Forest in search of the source of the orcs and, in the meantime, to assist the elves in fighting them. Taylan had watched other dragons rise high over the treetops for a wider view and then swoop low to take action. Galeron went south. Grafere had stayed to the north. Blues, reds, tans, oranges, greens, and purples—dragons of every natural color—had flown into Taylan's view. Something unprecedented was going on, and they wanted to see for themselves.

Taylan just wanted to leave. He looked at smoldering Oulos and saw Valencia smile at him before the mace struck her. Except she hadn't. She had seen Taylan—she had found his gaze—but she had not smiled. He only wished that she had. If she had, would he have had time to save her? He would have tried. All she had to do was smile. Just… the tiniest curve of her mouth.

And then tell him she loved him, as he had loved her.

Soft little hearts beat in Taylan's mind. Seven of them. He brought his hands to his temples. The orcs' hearts beat louder. Taylan pushed on his skull to no effect.

"Are you all right?" the knight beside Taylan asked.

Taylan grimaced up at him and shook his head.

The knight looked away.

In Taylan's mind, the seven little creatures formed out of their twisted hearts, their bodies ripped open and burned from the emote's lightning and fire. And they laughed. They pointed and howled with laughter. He had killed them, but he had not killed more to save the woman he loved.

"Taylan," the knight said. "General Bannan."

The general stood before them. A big red dragon had landed. "Taylan," the knight repeated.

"Half-elf." General Bannan crouched before him. "Are you all right?"

Taylan blinked. "I'm fine."

The general stood straight. "Then get up."

Taylan did. The newly arrived red sucked in air fast and breathed it out hard, recovering from the long flight.

General Bannan clasped his hands behind him. "They tell me you call Abilin home."

"Yes," Taylan said.

"What were you doing here?"

"I…" Taylan wished he had already prepared an answer.

"Hm?"

"I'm a friend of Valencia's."

"Uh huh." The general's eyes shifted left and right. "I didn't know she kept such friends."

"Well, she did," Taylan said.

"How did you survive when she did not? How is it that the single survivor of this surprise attack happens to be not a knight of Gran but a scrawny half-Abilinian half-elf?"

"Luck?" Taylan ignored the General's insult and suspicion. Cackling laughter rose within him from the seven he had slain. He just wanted to go. "If you can call it that."

"What do you mean?"

"I don't know." He crossed his arms. "I was late to the battle. The orcs didn't see me until the end. They got to me, they surrounded me, but Gowyn showed up before they finished me."

"What can you tell me about the orcs?" the general asked.

"Did Gowyn tell you what I told him?"

"His report was relayed to me, yes."

Taylan shrugged. "I don't know that I can add much."

"Try."

Taylan glanced at the knight beside him, as if he might say something to get him out of there sooner, but no assistance came. Taylan pointed past the general. "They ran from the river in a huge pack. Valencia's knights charged and did well, but there were so many orcs. They swarmed the knights, and each of Valencia's force killed a few of the little things before falling." Taylan recalled it vividly. "But the knights all fell." How could he have stood by and watched it happen? "Just... too many orcs."

A knight galloped to them. "Reports of more orcs in the forest. Near Alnara and Ronnigun's northern border."

"Headed this way?" the general asked.

"Not sure."

"Find out. Quickly."

The knight rode off.

"May I go?" Taylan asked.

The general rubbed his chin. "You know nothing else that could help us?"

"No."

General Bannan squinted. "You knew nothing of this attack beforehand?"

"No. I swear it. Valencia was my dear friend."

The general nodded. "You may go." He glanced behind him at the forest. "It is a shame. This war is hardly begun, and we have already lost a great warrior in Valencia."

"War?"

"I've no doubt," the general said. "Eldred would not have left Deroc for less. We'll kill him for this." The general faced the forest and again clasped his hands behind his back. "He's out there somewhere. This is just the beginning."

Carrying a dead, raggedy-clothed, gray-skinned, three-toed creature in his talons, Galeron descended into Derundale, the capital city of the White Elves. He landed with a loud thud in a small clearing in the woods at the foot of the long steps leading to the palace.

A White Elf in a long silver robe appeared from behind thick tree leaves with hints of white running through their veins. He calmly descended the stairs.

The golden dragon roared at him.

The elf stopped.

Galeron let the little creature roll out of his grip. *What is this?*

The elf folded his hands. "You are upset."

Galeron roared and shot fire high into the sky.

Another elf, in a white robe with a silver-and-sapphire crown sitting low upon his head, emerged from the trees. "Galeron."

Queen Isylle, with her own intricately detailed crown, joined King Cyric, and the pair stepped lightly down the stairs together. They remained higher than the elf who had greeted Galeron.

A dragon's call sounded from behind Galeron and another from the woods past the palace. A slender purple dragon slinked out from the trees behind Galeron and a larger one from in front.

Brine, Galeron said to the larger and glanced backward at his mate. *Briaxa.*

Galeron, the slender purple said.

We've not seen you in the skies above the forest of late, Galeron said.

No, Brine said. *You would not have.*

"Galeron," King Cyric said, "we wondered when you would come."

Tell me what you know of this. Galeron nudged the creature he had brought with him. *Now.*

"Yes," Cyric said. "We have been dealing with those as well. Strange to see a new species seemingly crop up out of nowhere."

You know more, Galeron said.

"They refer to themselves as 'orcs'," Cyric said. "Our interrogations have yielded nothing else of substance about them."

Do not lie to me.

"We know nothing more."

Galeron stretched his snout close to the king on the stairs. *Was Eldred in your woods?*

"Yes."

Why?

The purples stepped closer.

"With his elves," Cyric said, "he made his way through our forest from Deroc."

The Treaty of Sol—

"Forever," Queen Isylle said, "was too long a time in that prison. Too long for him, too long for Jadira, and too long for our cousins."

Galeron roared and sent flames into the air above the royals.

Brine lunged at Galeron, who dodged him. Briaxa tensed her hind legs to pounce.

"Please." Isylle raised her hand, and the purples paused. "I understand Galeron's frustration."

The golden dragon growled. *You know how dangerous Eldred is. Whatever he's planning.*

"We did not know what he had planned," the queen said. "Or that he had planned anything at all. We do not know what he plans now. His father deserved to be punished for what he did—for the wars he waged—but for Eldred to suffer a lifetime confined to a tiny prison for those things was wrong. When he asked for safe passage through our lands, I only wished he had asked sooner.

"I knew Jadira's mother well. She lived among us for most of her life. This 'white' forest grew dimmer when her beauty and her power went to Deroc. Seeing Jadira in these woods, I saw something of my old friend, and joy filled me—for Jadira, and for my late, dear friend—that Jadira might spend the rest of her years somewhere better than a swamp."

That was not for you to judge, Galeron growled. *Where did they go?*

"We do not know," the king said.

You lie.

The king and queen stood firm.

Galeron spun and smashed Brine across the face. The gold jumped into the air, rose over the purples and elves, and called to them, *You should have told me Eldred had come.*

Brine rubbed his snout, and Briaxa walked to him. Galeron flew higher.

We do not serve you, Galeron, Brine said.

And we never will, Briaxa added.

37

Taulus

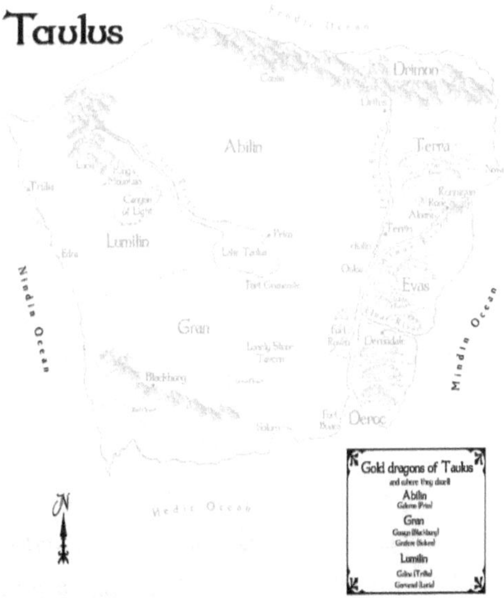

Lila lay on her side in the sand, resting against Gorvenal's warm body, looking out at the ocean they'd just flown over. She had changed into a light white dress the night before, and the rising sun in the cloudless sky had just woken her. Birds sang, and low waves crested, softly fell, and receded. Gorvenal spoke into Lila's mind.

The four gold dragons were outnumbered by their black

adversaries, but when they raced south from Conlin into Gran to join the battle that had already begun at Blackburg, Galeron, Gaiva, Galina, and Grafere came as such a glorious shock.

The golds brought hope to the men and women of Blackburg. Hope from above with wings to rally behind. The golds meant the evil dragons no longer terrorized the skies unmatched, so victory lay out there, somewhere—some way—and was worth any cost in battle to find and seize.

The golds convinced the Red Elves not to retreat to the cover of their home forest. Their doubt faded away. They had to come to the aid of the men of Taulus. Dragons that could match the blacks meant the elven emotes had a duty to go to Gran, to counter the powerful magic of their dark cousins. The Red Elves raced west from Abilin to join the battle.

To Xodon and his dragons, Galeron and the others were fear, the first fear they had ever known. A power that could match them had come to Taulus.

The golds rattled the Dark Elf King Ewald's confidence and dimmed his will, even before he felt the heat from a single burst of Galeron's righteous flame. The villainous king had underestimated mankind and the strength of their emotes. He had never imagined that they could produce anything like the gold dragons.

Blackburg, in the first Dark War, was a battle in three parts. King Ewald's taunting of the king of Gran came first, then once the fighting began, the men of the city fought as hard as they could, but facing a seemingly inevitable fate, they struggled to manage their best. And then the gold dragons came. The sight of them stunned the dark forces, who fell into disarray as the men rallied and found new focus.

From Blackburg, Ewald's army and dragons retreated east. The Red Elves racing west across central Gran forced them south, back into Deroc, and the borders of that land were pushed far toward the shore, giving Deroc its current—fitting—tiny size.

Lila made eye contact with Gorvenal. "And after that, Galina gave birth to you."

Indeed, he said. *And Galeron and Gaiva had Gowyn.*

"It's a shame that it took centuries of battles and a second war for the world to rid itself of black dragons. Gaiva and your father would still be alive."

Surely. That second Dark War—Ewald's race to Blackburg— seemed born of revenge from the outset. And while he and Xodon failed again to end Gran's eternal line or even conquer its capital city, they did wound Galeron and Galina by taking those they loved from them. A lot of men and women died, and that led to the strict terms in the Treaty of Solurn. Of course, no treaty could replace lost loved ones, so the hurt for Galeron, Galina, and many others lives on.

"I cannot imagine," Lila said.

Gorvenal brought his head to her, and she petted the top of his snout. *You will never have to.*

A shrill, distant cry pierced the tranquil air. It came from the other side of the island.

Gorvenal looked up quickly then leapt, flapped his wings to rise over the tree line, and stared.

Lila rolled onto her back, on her elbows.

Quiet, her dragon said to her, without looking down.

"Wha—"

Quiet! Not a sound! He landed. *I do not believe what I see.*

Lila got to her feet and whispered, "What is it?"

Gorvenal grabbed their bag of food, water, and supplies and threw it at Lila's feet. *Gather your things.* He went to the sack with her clothes and threw it to her as well.

Lila put a blanket into the sack. "Gorvenal, what is it?" She shoved in the scarf and hat she had worn on the journey.

Evil. Gorvenal sat tall. *And there are too many. They would chase me down. We cannot escape.*

Another cry came louder from the sky beyond the mess of trees and overgrown plants at the center of the island.

Run into the jungle. Gorvenal's chest heaved.

"What is it?" Lila begged.

Shh! Take your bags.

"What's going on?" she whispered, throwing one sack onto her shoulder and carrying the other.

Survive, somehow. Gorvenal leapt into the air and flew high. *If they see you, they'll kill you.* He flapped his wings. *If they don't…*

A tear ran down Lila's face.

A roar came loud and close.

Gorvenal's face strained. *Ration your water. I do not know what else to tell you. I hate myself for bringing you here. Run straight into the jungle. Go NOW!*

Lila stumbled with her bags through the sand while keeping her eyes on Gorvenal. What was going on? She glanced in front of her at the wall of thick tree leaves, strange-looking plants, and tall grass.

He landed and called, *Don't come out until they're all gone.*

Shrieking cries and roars neared.

What, so far from the mainland, made those screams in the sky? What in the world could scare Gorvenal? Lila stopped at the edge of the jungle—so dark inside. She turned to her dragon.

Our time is up, dear Lila. I loved each moment of it. I love you. I am sorry.

Gorvenal kicked and used his wings and tail to sweep sand over her footprints on the beach. He sucked in a huge breath, flapped his wings, and headed over the island toward the source of the noise.

Above Lila, he flew out of sight and roared.

A pair of roars answered.

Gorvenal's golden scales shone through the thick canopy. Flame burst out, and two—maybe three—other dragons flew after him. Dark ones. Lila stepped into the jungle. She had never seen dragons that color.

Lila stepped farther into the plants and trees and tried to follow the action in the sky but found her view blocked. She frantically searched for an opening above her but could only hear the roars and then bodies smacking together. She heard tearing and screaming. Bright fire revealed an opening for Lila to see through. Gorvenal spun across it. Dark dragons swarmed above him. Lila lost sight of the golden scales then found them plummeting like a stone until jungle blocked her view. She covered her mouth to keep from screaming. A loud splash came in the distance.

Shrill shrieks filled the air.

Lila dropped her bag and let the other slide off her shoulder.

The disturbed ocean water settled.

Lila crouched low, her heart racing.

A pair of loud thumps sounded in the sand, then two more. A big dragon with jagged scales and a saddled rider flew around the shore in front of Lila—a *black* dragon. Lila crouched lower, freezing completely. Elf rider. Long black hair. Female.

Gorvenal was dead. That dragon had killed him, had killed a *gold* dragon!

The evil beast dove its snout into the water and emerged with a long fish between its sharp teeth. The creature touched down on the sand to Lila's right and swallowed its catch.

Her dragon was *dead*.

The rider hopped off, glanced at the jungle, then walked out of sight farther to the right.

After another set of thumps, Lila heard, "Jadira, it is magnificent."

"What of Gorvenal being here?" a female voice—presumably Jadira's—said.

"Good fortune," King Eldred—Lila assumed, considering he was with Jadira—said. "One less for us to deal with."

"But *why* was he here?" Jadira asked.

"Look around." Eldred huffed. "Compare *this* to our swamp."

Air rushed under folding wings, and Lila heard the sharp sounds of breaths rushing in and out of large nostrils— dragon nostrils.

"One hour," Jadira said. "We have waited so long… I am tired of waiting."

"One hour!" Eldred called out. "Rest while you can."

Lila crept backward, cracking twigs and thick leaves, squishing her bare feet into mud. She stopped, crouched, and wished she had gone deeper into the jungle before.

A male elf walked into view on the shore to her right. She recognized King Eldred from drawings in her books. Why was he not in Deroc? Lila had not been gone from the mainland long… What had happened back there?

Eldred kept walking away from Lila, toward the water. A gigantic black dragon—larger even than Gorvenal— swooped into view then out of sight. Eldred sat in front of Lila, just beyond where the waves ran up the sand.

No, Lila urged him in her mind. *Keep going… to the other side of the island.*

Jadira walked over and sat beside him.

A black flew by.

Lila's quads burned from crouching.

Two elves walked into view and up to the king. They had a short conversation, then the pair walked back out of sight.

Jadira put her head on Eldred's shoulder.

What in the world were they doing all the way out here?

Minutes passed. Lila didn't move a muscle.

Low waves rolled onto the pristine beach. Other elves came to talk to the king or merely strolled by on their own or in pairs. Black dragons with angry, pale red eyes flew past and dove their heads into the ocean for food. Eldred and Jadira held hands, held each other, and kissed, frequently and deeply.

Lila lost track of time. Her aching legs had numbed. She

would not move to stretch them. She'd not been seen yet. She would not risk changing a thing.

She couldn't tell how many dragons had come to the island, but based on the number that had murdered her poor Gorvenal, she guessed at least three.

The scenes Gorvenal had just described played through her mind: the long-ago battles at Granenite, Prim, Blackburg... tan Galt becoming Galeron the gold... the dark forces retreating to Deroc... the second time only making it as far as Solurn. The swamp was to have been their prison for all time. The blacks were supposed to have been eliminated. It should have been an endless age of peace... peace maintained by unrivaled golds like Galina and her son Gorvenal.

Lila had never known her parents. She hadn't worried about it in years. Growing up, she had had no friends and hated feeling alone, all the time in the orphanage. Yet she was alone again. She had cried and sobbed at being teased and picked on by the others until she had learned to stop because of the satisfaction her tears gave her tormentors. But the tears had never stopped completely on the inside.

While Lila watched the royal elves on the beach, memories continued rushing back to her. When she had grown older, some of the boys bothered her less, but only because they all wanted one thing from her. And she had never found one boy she wanted to give that to.

Then, even though she could not be with Gorvenal as a man can be with a woman, he had been her answer. The gold dragon had loved her, and Lila had loved being so loved. She had loved him, loved being with him and being under his protection, with all her heart.

But Gorvenal had been killed, and he could no longer protect Lila, nor Lumilin, its people, or any of the kingdoms of mankind.

Eldred and Jadira stood and shared another kiss.

"Time to go!" the king called out. "Xailyn!"

The huge black swooped low and landed beside them. It lifted Eldred onto its back. A slightly smaller dragon set down, picked up Jadira, and headed east.

A male elf ran out to the king from Lila's left and said something to him. Eldred nodded to him. Eldred took off after Jadira, and the elf ran up the beach to Lila's right— taking a route nearer to her than any of the elves had yet.

Concern filled his face—as perhaps it had filled the others', but Lila only noticed it on the one coming so close.

Lila couldn't let him see her. She also couldn't do anything but stay still and not breathe. The elf stopped. He had blue eyes—the bluest she had ever seen. The elf waved skyward and resumed running to her right until he had gone out of sight.

Lila exhaled. A dragon flew by carrying that elf and a set of huge sacks strapped to its back. Another flew after the others with a rider and similar cargo. Two more blacks passed with a rider each.

Black dragons, Dark Elves, huge sacks of cargo, all flying east from Yalus.

Lila had succeeded in not being seen. She stood straight. Six dragons and six elves flew away from her. More than ever, she was all alone.

38

Taulus

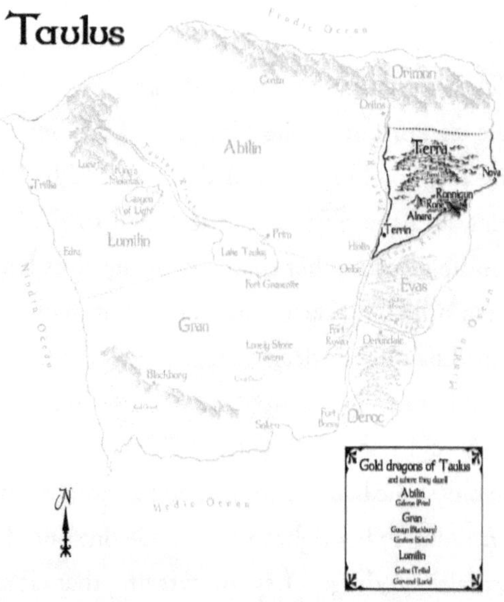

A dragon's cry sounded in the distant black of Ri's mind and then came again, a little louder.

It echoed softly in the blackness.

Ri cracked her eyes open to leaves above her.

A dragon screamed above them in the dim light of—Ri had no idea how long she had been out or whether it was morning or evening. She searched but couldn't find a shadow because of the thick treetop canopy. That also meant the dragon had no chance of seeing her. And it might be a very good thing if it could, but she wouldn't yell wildly for it.

She needed to get a look at the dragon to guess if it were friendly.

With all her weight on her right leg, Ri got herself upright. Her bow already rested across her. She threw her quiver over her shoulder and gently put her left leg down—it hurt as badly as before, but her balance had improved. She scanned for an opening in the leaves. She considered climbing, rotated her aching left arm, and when the throbbing in her leg intensified, decided she couldn't make it up a tree.

The dragon's call sounded farther away.

Ri made for the main path leading from Rone. She would risk exposing herself there. Her leg dragged on the first step, and she almost stopped. Her second step brought the same hesitation, but when her third came quicker, her fourth followed fast, so she trudged on.

She made more noise than she ever remembered making in the woods and added that embarrassment to her list of others.

She grew cold, despite her effort. Did that mean it was morning? A small clearing revealed a tiny speck of dim sky—which didn't answer her question.

Ri closed in on the road.

She stumbled then ran at a thin tree, reached out, and caught herself before falling. She grew dizzy, as she had the night before. She leaned on the trunk to keep herself upright.

The call of the dragon sounded faintly.

Ri pushed herself off the tree and continued to the road. She scolded herself for falling asleep. Why couldn't she *at least* have woken up sooner?

She spotted the edge of the woods and stumbled again but kept upright. Then the ground went out of balance. A little farther, she told herself. Just a little farther. She *had* to make it—she glanced at the mixture of wet and dried blood on her leg—and she had to make it *soon*.

She dragged herself on, step after step, cringe after cringe, stumble after stumble. Near the path, shadows stretched to the east—it was evening. Ri had been unconscious the whole day. She scolded herself again for wasting so much time until finally she reached two thin trunks at the tree line by the road. To the right, in the direction of the dragon cries, she found clear sky. The other way—to Rone—clear path.

Ri stepped out onto the dirt road. Definitely evening. She felt cold because of her loss of blood, not the air temperature, she reasoned. She leaned against a tree to shift her weight off her bad leg.

The call from the dragon sounded quiet… distant.

Ri waited. The path didn't wind near her, meaning she would have to walk a long way up it for a different view of the sky.

No new sound came. No savior flew by.

It would be such a long way to limp…

Red! High in the distance. Ri leaned forward as if the inches would matter. Long tail, a rider—maybe two. Maybe

Farlan. And she flew away from Ri.

"Hey!" Ri called but quieter than she had intended to. The dragon didn't react.

"Help!" It came out softly, weak as Ri had grown. The red didn't deviate from her flight. Rustling came from behind Ri. She didn't see anything. She turned back, and the red flew north.

"Help!"—even quieter.

The dragon definitely appeared to have two riders. West would have been to Terrin, so if it was Farlan, she could certainly have been out searching for Ri and her scout team. Why else would she make all that noise?

More rustling came from the woods behind Ri. The red would not hear her, she decided. But maybe she would see fire, or the smoke from one. Animals might also be drawn to the bright flames. Ri would have to keep watch for them.

Others might notice the fire—men, elves, or dwarves. And while they might not be friendly, they very well could be. She hadn't seen any of the little creatures since they ran from Rone and hadn't come across any Dark Elves since they had attacked her team.

Ri was thirsty. And hungry. And dizzy. She would have to take a chance at some point, and since she was unable to stop her leg from bleeding, sooner seemed better than later.

She was so cold. She would start a fire on the path.

39

Taulus

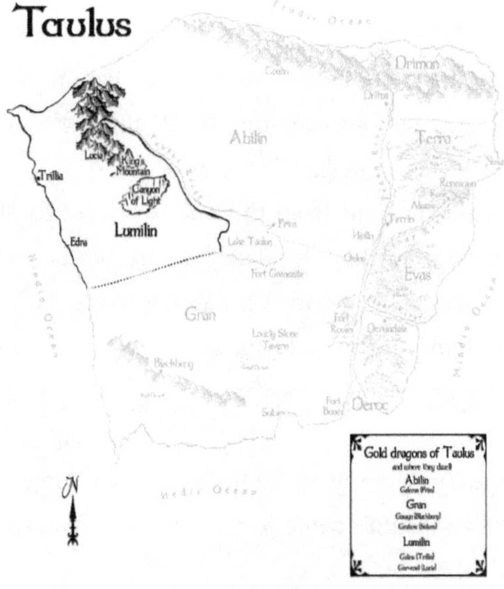

The sun hung low over the conclusion of the tournament outside the white walls of the south end of Trillia. Past the rows of tent merchants, colorful flags and banners whipped in the wind and boisterous fans filled the low bleachers at the jousting track.

"Let's watch some," Gall called to the twins riding in front of him.

"Let's find Mother first," Avery called back.

"She'll still be there in an hour."

Avery shrugged at Avril.

"We won't stay long." Gall rode ahead and veered off the main path. The twins followed.

The hoots and hollers of the spectators grew more distinct as they neared, then they mostly quieted. Gall led Avery and Avril toward a relatively thin section of the crowd. The sound of hooves hitting the ground quickened.

Bam! A knight's shiny helmet briefly came into view beyond the merchants, between spectators.

"Jousting," Gall called.

At a short post where a few tethered horses stood, Gall dismounted. The twins got off their horses, and they all tied up their animals.

"Come on." Gall led Avery and Avril between tents toward the crowd.

A man under a small canopy to the left yelled, "Ale! Get your ale here!"

Gall pivoted and headed that way.

"Ale?" The short man held out a cup.

Gall asked the twins, "You two?"

They shook their heads.

Gall handed the man a coin and took the cup and his change. He sipped the ale then tilted the cup back and gulped it. "Ah." He tossed the man the change he had just made and put out two fingers. "Was good."

The man handed Gall two fresh cups. "Glad to hear it."

White canopies lined the opposite side of the jousting

track, providing shade for families dressed in colorful fabrics and wearing bright, glistening jewels. Less gaudy accessories adorned those sitting in bleachers on the near side of the track. Gall led the way into a crowd of onlookers standing in the dirt and patches of trampled grass.

"'Scuse me." Gall slid between people, being careful not to spill either of his ales. "Pardon." He sipped at each cup to reduce the risk of a sudden slosh costing him any of the precious liquid. "'Scuse me," he repeated, nearing the front.

"Rude!" an old woman called from behind them.

"Hmm?" Gall found her angry glare.

"Shoving your way to the front," she said.

He motioned to the twins with his ales. "It's their first tournament."

The woman scrunched her face at him.

"And"—Gall made a face of his own—"it's my fault we're late?"

She stretched out a thin finger. "Shouldn't have wasted your time for those drinks."

"Yeaaah," Gall said. "We're gonna keep going."

She scowled while the twins followed Gall forward.

He found the tallest man in the front row and asked him, "Would you mind, sir? It's their first tournament, and"—he noticed the old woman glaring at him—"I don't want to block anyone's view."

"Not at all." The man stepped backward.

"Thank you." Gall moved in front of the extremely tall man and pulled Avery in front of him. Avril followed. Gall pointed with his ale at the box beyond the center of the far lane. "That's King Adrian."

The twins nodded and watched the workers raking the lanes.

"Isham," the tall man said, extending his hand for Gall to shake.

Gall held out his occupied hands. "Gall."

"Gall?" Isham brought his hand to his chin. "That short for something?"

Gall squinted. "Yes."

"Hmm…" Isham shrugged. "Well, you're just in time for the last run. Drefan and Grimm. After the first four, points are tied. A few broken lances is all so far."

Avery asked, "And the winner wins the whole tournament?"

"Yes, sir," Isham said.

Avery looked at the king's box. "Which one's Sir Beal?"

Isham pointed. "See the beautiful woman, sitting, in light blue?"

Avril pointed at a woman who held hands with the man beside her. "Her?"

"Yup," Isham said. "Her husband is Beal."

"Is he as good as everyone says?" Avery asked.

"Yes," Isham said. "He isn't fighting this time because he wins every tournament. No knight in Lumilin can match him."

"No knight in Taulus," a man near Avery chimed in. "Beal slew a dragon. In the north, when the big purple attacked his company."

"He could have waited for Galina or Gorvenal," another man added, "but he didn't."

"He went out alone," the first man said. "Dared the beast to confront him."

"And with his sword, Lucen, he slew him," the second said.

"He thrust his blade"—the first man shot his arm into the air—"up through the dragon's skull!"

Avery and Avril watched Beal, who laughed and nodded to the king.

"He is our champion," Isham said.

Gall finished an ale, dropped the empty cup on the ground, and burped.

King Adrian rose and called out, "What a tournament!" The crowd cheered until the king calmed them. "It is time to find which of these is our"—he looked at Beal—"second finest knight."

Beal stood, clasped his hands, and while everyone cheered, bowed slightly to the king then to the crowd—right, left, and center—before returning to his seat.

"He's humble too," Isham remarked.

Avril glanced at Gall.

"What?" He shrugged.

She rolled her eyes.

"Enjoy," the king said. "And please, enjoy the festivities tonight!"

The crowd cheered, and the king sat down.

A tall knight in silver, dirt-spattered armor rode a big horse out of the tent at the end of the lane.

"Drefan," Isham said as cheers rose and boos countered them.

The open visor on Drefan's helmet revealed focus.

A wider knight in dirty black armor and a matching helmet rode out as well. Isham identified him as Grimm.

The boos turned to cheers and the cheers to boos. Knights who had already fought lined the edge of their tent to watch. Most were out of their armor and covered in dirt, and many had a tall ale mug or wine goblet in hand.

"What's on their shoulders?" Avery asked as the combatants made their way to opposite ends of the track.

"The target for the other rider," Gall said. "A steel plate. You get points for breaking your lance on it and more points for hitting it and knocking the other rider off."

Squires walked out with wooden lances for each knight, handed them to the warriors, then ran from the lanes.

Grimm nodded to Drefan, who returned the gesture and lowered his visor. Grimm slid his closed.

They started toward each other, lances held vertical. The horses picked up their pace. The crowd quieted. The knights lowered their weapons toward horizontal as they neared. The horses ran harder. Each knight aimed his lance at his foe's shoulder. They made last adjustments.

BAM!—both hit.

Grimm's lance shattered, and Drefan rocked backward as his weapon pushed into his foe. Grimm flew from his steed. The crowd roared when Grimm hit the dirt. Drefan threw his lance down and pumped his fist in triumph.

The cheering rose, Avery contributing loudly.

Drefan circled and pumped his fist again. Grimm got to his feet, and Drefan jumped to the ground.

The crowd quieted.

As Grimm trudged away, Drefan caught up to him, grabbed his shoulder, and spun him around. Drefan put out his hand, and after a brief hesitation, Grimm took it and shook.

The crowd roared.

Grimm walked off. Drefan waved, and the cheers grew. He waved to the families in the boxes then spun to those in the bleachers, and they chanted, "Dre-fan, Dre-fan, Dre-fan!"

Avery and Gall exchanged smiles. After a moment, Avril added her own.

The victorious knight waved to the standing crowd.

"Drefan, Drefan, Drefan!"

"Beal!" someone called.

"Drefan."

"Beal!" The name could not be mistaken.

"Drefan."

"Beal!"

"Drefan."

"Beal, Beal, Beal!"

Drefan turned to the king's box.

"Beal, Beal, Beal! Challenge Beal!"

Beal rose, put out both hands, and shook his head.

"Beal! Fight him!"

Beal motioned for the crowd to quiet, and eventually, they did.

"Thank you!" Beal called, and the crowd roared until he urged them to calm again. "Sir Drefan is your winner today."

"Boo. Boo! Fight him!"

Beal looked at King Adrian.

"Boooooo!"

The king rose and quieted the crowd. "You would like to see Beal in action?"

"Yeah! Yes!"

Adrian turned to his queen.

She smiled and nodded.

"Yes! Whoo! Beal!"

The king put up his hands and waited for all to quiet. "All right."

The crowd roared. Beal smiled at his grinning son then shrugged to his wife. She smiled, and he kissed her cheek. Beal leapt over the wooden railing and down from the royal box to the dirt.

"One run!" the king called.

A boy who must have been Beal's squire squeezed between spectating knights at the tent at the lane's end and sprinted to his knight. After a short conversation and some pointing, the squire sprinted away. Beal waved to the crowd on both sides of the track as he walked after him.

Avril and Avery turned around.

"Whaddaya think?" Gall asked.

"It's great," Avery said.

Avril shrugged but smiled.

"Do you think he'll win?" Avery asked.

"Of course!" said the man who had begun the story of the dragon slaying.

"Beal *don't* lose," the second man added.

"Since he was young," the first man said. "From the first tournament he fought in, he ain't lost."

"I seen 'em all," the second man said.

"Me too," his friend added.

The pair went on describing Beal's spectacular feats of arms. Beal had almost lost on two occasions, years before—once in combat with swords, and once jousting—but fought back heroically both times to win. And though it was mostly tournament and sport, the men had a few stories about Beal easily tracking and capturing thieves and others who upset the peace in Lumilin. They told tales of his incredible records in training and retold the story of when he slew the purple dragon.

Gall enjoyed his ale. Avril paid close attention to the stories, but Gall took the most satisfaction in seeing Avery apparently eating up every word. When the boy spotted a half-elf in the crowd, Gall explained that while those of mixed-race could not be knights in Lumilin—as they also could not in Gran—and thus could not participate in the tournament, a small number lived in each kingdom.

"Beal!" the crowd screamed.

The champion of Lumilin emerged from the big tent to the right, atop his horse, in shiny silver armor.

Drefan rode to the left side of the track, and the crowd quieted. Beal's squire walked to his knight with his wooden lance. Beal took it, and Drefan received his lance from his squire.

"We'll still love you, Sir Drefan," someone yelled, and laughter rolled through the crowd.

Drefan raised his hand in thanks. Beal nodded to his opponent, and the knights lowered their visors. Beal sat tall. His horse stood firm. Drefan shifted in his saddle. His horse was chomping at the bit. Drefan adjusted his grip on his reins.

They trotted toward each other then sped to a gallop.

Faster, their horses ran. Faster. The knights lowered their lances. The animals pushed harder. Drefan aimed his lance. Beal waited… then aimed his.

BAM!-bam. Beal's hit hard, his foe's soft. Drefan shot from his saddle.

The crowd gasped as the tournament winner flew to the ground.

Drefan lay motionless.

Beal dropped his lance, wheeled his horse round, and jumped down. He ran to Drefan, who curled his leg inward. Beal slid in the dirt to him. Drefan moved his other leg then leaned on an elbow and lifted his visor.

The crowd breathed loud sighs of relief.

Beal grasped Drefan's shoulder, and the crowd was so quiet that everyone could hear him when Beal asked, "Are you all right?"

"I am," Drefan answered.

Beal put out his hand, and Drefan grabbed it. Beal pulled the defeated knight to his feet.

Gall tapped Avery's shoulder. "Let's go."

The twins turned to him.

"Beat the crowd," Gall said.

They followed him back through the cheering crowd, the way they had come.

When they neared the hitching post, Avery asked, "Think you could beat Beal?"

Gall untied his horse. "I've no need to fight him. He seems an honorable knight."

"But if you did," Avery said, "would you win?"

"Yes."

"Really?" Avery untied his horse and gestured back to the jousting track. "Did you see that?"

"I don't lose, I told you. Not tavern fights, not throwing rocks, not feats of arms with thieves. Not flipping quarters into cups. I don't lose *anything* to *anyone*." Gall stepped up to his saddle. "I sure as shit wouldn't lose with a lance or a sword in my hand."

Avery didn't press the question further as they rode into Trillia, ahead of most of the crowd, to find the twins' mother.

40

Taulus

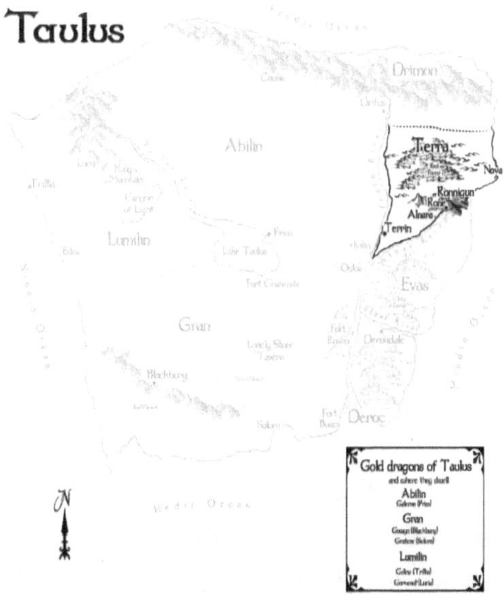

Ri lay on the side of the path at the tree line with her bow leaning on her quiver beside her. The fire warmed her and gave the only light with the thick clouds overhead. Her head rested on a large piece of wood she'd have to sacrifice to the crackling flames eventually. The red dragon and its hopeful call had long since gone.

A blanket of tranquility wrapped around Ri, holding her

gently but securely as her eyes slid shut.

She opened them. She couldn't sleep. She couldn't let herself. She shouldn't have been tired, which meant that the sleep tempting her, wave after heavier wave, might be one from which she wouldn't awake.

She glanced at her bow—the gift from Launfal she had obviously never deserved. She certainly didn't after costing her friend his life.

Soft rustling came from all around her. Ri lifted her head and scanned for little creatures in the woods with gray skin and yellow eyes. Raindrops hit her. She rested her head back on the log, and the rain continued, soft but steady.

Ri wondered where the creatures had run to—who they had attacked. *If* they had attacked. Perhaps they had been on the move, gathering for a larger operation.

Perhaps that wasn't it at all. She couldn't know.

And she might never know. Because she had been so stupid.

Ri wanted to tell her parents that she loved them. She wished she lay in her soft bed, safe under its covers, surrounded by the tall, thick, granenite walls of her home castle. She wished being princess of Abilin had been enough for her.

Ri remembered her much younger self playing with her brothers, running, hiding, arguing… she loved Kalen, Chance, and Gregory dearly.

She recalled the single time she had played the role of a captured princess meant to be rescued and how she'd hated it when her brothers refused to let her do *anything* except wait and fret about being imprisoned by an imagined evil king. She ran crying to her mother before the game was finished, and Ri didn't remember what she said over her sobs, but her mother held her before going to talk to her brothers. After that, they never asked her to play the helpless damsel again.

Her fire crackled. Ri wiped her face dry of rain with her bloodied sleeve. She rolled her head to the side, and it began getting wet again. Maybe she had been a fool back then too. And maybe her mother had been as well, for letting her get away with it. Not that she should blame anyone but herself.

Her harp—Ri rolled her weary eyes. She pictured her father yelling at her for skipping her lessons, being exasperated when she continued to argue, and eventually calming down, saying that he understood but insisting that she had a duty to play. And like her comfortable bed and all her fine dresses and jewelry, playing the harp under the instruction of one of the finest teachers in Abilin was a privilege. It should have felt like one.

Her thoughts shifted to God and paradise. To dwell with the Creator as Charles had as king and Catherine had as his queen—Ri had earned no place among them. Her end would not be paradise. Even if such a place truly existed, waiting for the deserving beyond their mortal life, after what Ri had done, after how she had lied, her death would lead to nothing. Her life would end on Taulus, and that would be all.

A dot—high against the clouds, out of the corner of Ri's eye. Blurry. Moving. Dragon. Green, she guessed, not the red from earlier. The lack of light in the sky made it hard to be certain, but if not green then perhaps darker… purple. Its flight remained steady.

Another dragon—lower, left. Ri sat up and swept rainwater from her face. No rider. Shorter tail than the one before. Not Farlan.

Gold—huge! Swooping low from behind her.

"Gowyn!" she called.

Corina. He spun and descended to her fast.

Ri tried but failed to get to her feet.

The dragon hit the road hard. Wet dirt and rocks flew at Ri. Gowyn swept his wing in front of him to blow the cloud away.

"I'm sorry!" she called.

Are you all right?

"My leg." She rolled to expose the wound. "And my arm."

Gowyn leaned close to inspect them.

"I've lost a lot of blood. There were these creatures… I've never seen them before."

We know, Gowyn said. *They've spread throughout the forest.*

"My team… they're dead." Fresh tears surfaced. "Naelon, Emlyn, Egan, Addis… and Launfal."

The creatures did that?

"No!" Ri yelled. "Dark Elves!"

Gowyn peered into the woods. *Hmm…*

"King Eldred. I saw him. He didn't kill my team, others did. But I saw King Eldred with Bardric in Rone."

We feared as much but did not know for certain. I must tell my father. Farlan, with Prince Erwyn and your brother Gregory, are looking for you. I will take you to them first. Erwyn can help you. Gowyn reached for Ri. *Grab your bow and arrows.*

Ri shook her head.

Gowyn took her in his paw. *We've no time to waste.*

"I don't want them." Ri grimaced as he moved her onto his back.

Can you hold on?

She wrapped her arms around Gowyn's wet neck as she had around the tree branch from which she had spied on the dwarven city. "I'll try." She laid her head on the dragon's golden scales.

He kicked dirt onto the low logs of her fire then jumped into the air.

Ri closed her eyes, and her grip loosened. She slipped backward.

Corina!

She grabbed him tighter. "Sorry."

I might not catch you this near to the ground. Hold on.

Ri sniffled. "I'll try." Into large drops of rain, they rose over the treetops, and for once the view of the expansive forest and the Green Mountain Range didn't excite Ri. Her leg throbbed. Her arm ached. Her eyes shut.

I'm so sorry, she thought. The realization that she would never get a chance to say it to anyone who mattered washed over her. A gust of wind and rain hit her face, and Gowyn's flapping wings pushed more mist onto her. She had waited too long to light the fire, to call for help. Her hands slid down Gowyn's slippery scales.

Ri could see Bardric shaking Eldred's hand. She heard the thump of Addis hitting the ground, and the second thump, of Launfal's limp body smacking dirt, sent shockwaves just as powerful through her. Her palm and fingers felt the bark of the tree she clutched.

Corina…

She gripped Gowyn tighter.

They had risen high above the forest, headed west. A dragon glided in the distance. Ri's eyes slid closed again.

Darkness. It became familiar. Her leg hurt less in the darkness, her arm not at all. Blessed darkness… the rain quieted. She did not feel drops hitting her.

Stay awake, Corina, Gowyn said.

"Mm." She pressed her head into his neck. He beat his wings, and she floated higher and lower through the darkness—the blackest black she had ever known.

She had let down her mother and father. She had before, and she remembered the worst times—when she had been so ashamed—but she'd always had a chance to tell them she knew it. They were right, she had been wrong. It often took a while, but eventually she understood. She could not complete that cycle this time. She could not promise to do better. This time, she would not get the chance to show them she had really learned.

Drowned in a sea of black, Ri floated alone, arms outstretched. Gowyn had left her. Her fingers did not feel his scales. She did not hold his strong body. She floated, free of him, free of everything. However long she would linger in that darkness—until it too had gone and nothing at all remained—she deserved it.

Talons clutched her.

"Corina!" Gregory yelled.

I've got you, Farlan said.

Ri's eyes opened to steady rain. The red dragon put Ri on her saddle in front of the Red Elf Prince Erwyn. He wrapped his arm around her stomach.

Heat! Ri inhaled sharply.

From where Erwyn held her, a hot burst poured into Ri.

She sat straighter. She grew hotter—out to her limbs, her fingertips, and toes, and up to her cheeks and the tip of her head. The throbbing in her wounded leg faded.

"Corina," Gregory repeated, "are you all right?"

Ri breathed in, and a more gentle warmth flowed from her core to every extremity. "Yes." She rotated her arm—no pain.

"You've lost a lot of blood," Erwyn said.

"Yeah," Ri said as the heat softened further.

The elven emote stuck his head forward to see her face. "You will be fine."

"Thank you." Ri stretched her neck and adjusted her leg. It didn't hurt at all, and when she felt for the stab wound, she found nothing but smooth skin.

"We were worried sick," Gregory called from the rear of the saddle, over the rustling of rain hitting the treetops.

"My father as well," Erwyn added, taking his hands from Ri, letting her hold Farlan herself.

Ri began to cool. "I'm sorry," she said loudly, for her brother, Erwyn, and Farlan to all hear. More quietly, she added, "Everyone's dead. Naelon, Launfal... All of them."

"Gowyn told us," Gregory said.

"I lied," Ri said. "I saw Bardric talking to King Doxton in Dritus, but I didn't hear anything of substance."

"We figured as much," Erwyn said.

Ri's shoulders slumped. "I just wanted a real mission."

"You got one," Erwyn said. "It was our mistake to play along."

"Well, lie or not," Gregory said, "all signs point to Rone being at the center of this. Most of its dwarves have gone missing."

Farlan said, *We are headed there now to see what the few dwarves remaining in the city have to say for themselves.*

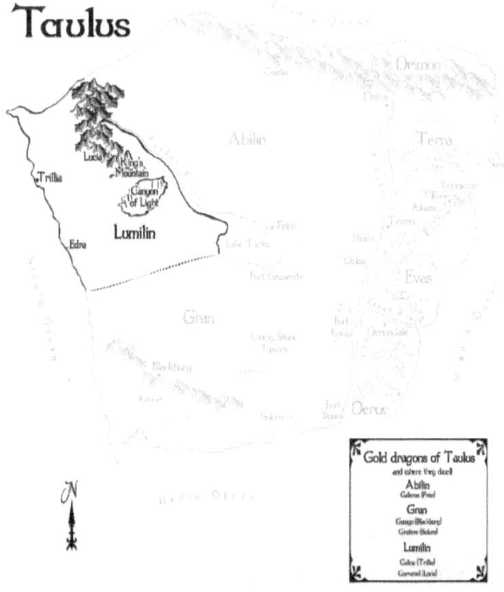

41

Gall enjoyed the salty air filling his nostrils as he, Avery, and Avril slowly rode to the open, arched entrance in the high white wall at the narrow south end of Trillia. Above the entrance, inset in the stone, a thin outer arch of sapphire glistened. Fires burned bright atop the walls, spaced evenly between the guards holding tall spears with shiny tips.

Shortly after sunset, the twins had resisted Gall's strong

suggestion to veer off the path out to the cliff's edge for a quick look at the ocean. But he couldn't blame them. They'd have their chance, Gall understood, after he went on to Conlin and they stayed behind with their mother.

Gleeful spectators from the tournament rushed past Gall's and the twins' horses on the wide, smooth road constructed of the white granenite that made up the entire city. The determined crowd aimed to beat the lines at the pubs, Gall reasoned, as that's precisely what he would have done had he been traveling alone.

Past the gate, Avery stopped, and his sister and Gall pulled up beside him. Blue and yellow banners hung from buildings lining the main road into the city. The occasional tall, precisely trimmed tree added an earthy tone to the scene. Gall called over passersby to a guard—a knight of Lumilin assigned to the city—beside the entrance, "We're looking for a… house. Pinnacle."

"The brothel," the guard said. "Fine ladies there… fine ladies." He motioned into the city. "Up to the first circle, then right. It's off the street."

"Thank you." Gall gestured for Avery to lead, and the boy did. Gall had discussed it with them. Since their mother had worked at a brothel before, that she might do so again seemed perfectly logical. Thankfully, the place had a good reputation.

Galloping hooves sounded behind them. People hurried to the roadside, so Gall and the twins followed suit. A pair of lordly looking men raced by, and then everyone spread across the path again and continued on their way.

Men and women ducked into pubs and houses or turned onto side streets. Some children followed their parents while others roamed free, many reenacting confrontations from the tournament they had just witnessed and naming the knights whose part they played. Fires burned on roofs, illuminating the road, the colorful banners, and the glittering gemstones adorning facades and columns in the dwindling daylight.

"It's beautiful," Avril called out.

"What is?" Gall asked.

"Trillia. Everything."

"The jewel of Lumilin," Gall said.

Avril looked back at him. "The jewel of *Taulus*, I thought people said."

"Depends on who's doing the saying."

"How big's the city?" Avery asked.

"Long," Gall said. "The castle is all the way up the road, at the end. But the city's narrow." Gall pointed toward his left. "Built to maximize its oceanfront land." He pointed right. "Away from the coast, there's a lot of what counts as Trillia outside the walls, because they ran out of space."

The road opened to a wide circular path, and at the middle stood a huge, three-tiered fountain with water running down into a crystal-clear pool.

Avery led the group to the right, around the southernmost of four evenly spaced circles running north up the middle of Trillia and leading to the White Castle at the end, where a fifth would have been. High towers, with smooth pyramidal spires, rose from each corner of the square castle.

The twins and Gall passed a pub boasting the widest variety of seafood in the city. A bakery claimed to have the freshest bread. An inn advertised last-minute vacancies for tournament spectators and their impressive rooftop view of the ocean. A quarter of the way around the circle, Avery turned right, onto a large side street.

"Now where?" he asked.

Gall pointed at a glowing alley. Avery headed for it.

Torches lined the walls of the alley. Two horses could barely walk abreast, so Gall followed the twins. The entrance at the end of the alley had been draped in red silk. Its wooden door opened.

Two slender women emerged—one blond, one brunette—wearing long, pink skirts and black tops that left their midriffs exposed.

"Please." The blonde reached for the reins of Avery's horse.

Avery looked at Gall.

"When a beautiful woman says please"—Gall smiled—"I find it's very hard to say no."

She pleasantly nodded to Gall then held Avril's horse.

Avery and Avril dismounted, and the brunette flashed Gall a smile.

He got out of his saddle. "Even at the slightest glance…"

The women led the horses to the right of the entrance and paused to motion to the door before heading around the building. The door opened again, held by another blonde.

Avril stepped past her brother and went in first. He and Gall followed. They stood in a dim foyer lit by a small cauldron of flame with a curtain hanging on each side of it.

The woman brought her hands behind her. "Welcome to Pinnacle. How may we be of service?"

"We're here to see Isabel," Avril said.

"Oh," the woman said. "I'm sorry. She is unavailable."

"Why?" Avery asked.

"She's working upstairs at the moment."

Avril's eyes glazed. "But, but—"

"I am sorry."

"When will she be available?" Gall asked.

"In the morning. It's going to be a busy night."

"Let's go." Gall motioned to the twins. "We'll come back in the morning."

With sunken shoulders, Avril followed Avery to the door.

Gall went to the woman and whispered, "If you see her before then, tell her that her children are here in Trillia and will return in the morning."

"Oh!" The woman brought her hands to her face. "Of course! Avery, Avril?"

"Yes," the twins said.

"She's upstairs!" The woman headed to the right. "She's doing paperwork. Accounting, I think." She pulled open the curtain. "Come."

Grinning, the twins headed into a long, dark hallway of closed doors.

After Gall entered, the woman joined them at the first door. "Here." She unfastened a silver bangle on one wrist, revealing a key at its end. "Your mother doesn't *work* here. She's with Mr. Calvert, the owner." The woman opened the door to a stone staircase and called up, "Isabel?"

"Yes, dear?" came a warm voice.

"People to—"

Avril ran up the stairs, with Avery right behind.

"See you." The woman motioned for Gall to follow the twins.

He did, slowly. He heard the sounds of their reunion as he made his way up the stairs.

"Oh, Avril! Avery!"

Avril laughed. More than one of them was crying.

"My babies," their mother said.

Gall reached the top step into a spacious room with windows opened wide to east Trillia. Sitting at her dark wooden desk, Isabel held her children tight while tears streamed down both her and Avril's faces. Avery grinned as wide as they did.

"Mom!" Avril leaned away. "That's Gall."

Isabel stood from her chair, still resting a hand on each of her children. "Thank you for seeing them here safely."

"It was my pleasure," Gall said.

"What can I offer you to show my gratitude?"

"Oh." Gall put out his hands. "There's no need."

"He's a knight," Avril said.

Isabel asked, "Will you be in Trillia long?"

"Just tonight."

"Then a room downstairs? Our finest, for the night."

"Thank you, but that's not necessary." Gall figured he might end up in a place just like Pinnacle, but that seemed more appropriate than accepting such a reward when he had done no more than honor his end of his bargain with the twins. "I'm going for a drink, and then we'll see where I end up."

"Breakfast then. Please."

"Well…" Gall rubbed his chin. "We've been on the road a while. Didn't necessarily plan on being up and out for breakfast."

"An early lunch," Isabel said. "I insist."

"Please?" Avril asked.

"Please." Avery matched her pleading expression.

"All right," Gall said. "An early lunch. I'll be back tomorrow." The twins smiled.

"Thank you," Isabel said. Then she hugged her children tight.

As he headed downstairs, Gall heard Isabel say, "You're taller, Avery."

"No, I'm not," Avery said.

Gall reached the last step.

"And your hair's a mess," that warm voice said.

"Mommm…"

Gall smiled.

———

Gall picked The Blue Crown, a nice pub known for employing one of the prettiest staffs in the city. After the beauties at Pinnacle, he had found the prospect of settling for less unacceptably unappealing.

Inside was brighter than the tavern in Blackburg. Smiles, laughter, and warm, noticeably clean faces filled The Blue Crown. Blackburg's patrons had been drinking after an exhausting day of work or training. Trillia celebrated an end to consecutive days of celebration, which in Gall's experience was not an uncommon occurrence, though the nature of the occasion tended to vary widely between festivals, ceremonies, and lavish parties.

Gall made his way to one of the two open tables in the whole place—small, in the back corner, with a good view of the long bar and the other tables and booths. If he could have picked one table in the whole pub, that would have been his choice.

There, Gall thought, that's all the reward necessary for getting Avery and Avril here. A good bit of luck. A nice spot to drink at. And actually, he needed to remember to thank them again for getting him out of jail in the first place. In truth, their relationship had been mutually beneficial. A plan hatched by clever youths that had gone well.

Gall leaned back in his seat. He had been right in his expectations of their mother, he decided, chief among them that Isabel had been very warm and quite pretty.

A dark-haired waitress with a cute little face and a cute little skirt came to the table and put her hands on her hips. "You fight in the tournament?"

"Nope," Gall said.

"Oh. What can I bring ya then?"

"Whisky."

She spun, and her skirt swooshed with her hips.

Gall tilted his head, watching. "Bring a bottle."

She spun all the way around and smiled before heading for the bar.

"Trillia," Gall said quietly, watching her thin legs go. "Well worth the trip."

"Hey." A less thin woman with broad shoulders grabbed the chair opposite Gall. "This taken?"

Pretty. Dirty blond hair. Fit. Nice breasts.

"It is now," Gall said.

She slung her bag onto the chair back and plopped down in the seat.

Light blue eyes. Dirt smudged on her chin. Worn slacks and shirt.

"You fight out there?" Gall asked.

"Uh huh." She glanced behind her.

"How'd you do?"

"Shoulda done better." The woman faced Gall and relaxed into her chair like she really needed to. "What's your deal? Didn't see you out there, but looks like you ought to have been."

"I'm passing through. Just here for the night."

She clicked her tongue. "Got it."

The waitress returned with a full bottle and a short glass. She set them on the table. "Another glass?"

The newly arrived knight asked, "Whisky?"

"Whisky," Gall confirmed.

The knight looked at the waitress. "Yeah."

Gall watched her leaving to fetch it.

"What's her name?" the woman across from him asked.

"Dunno. I would've asked, but you're here now."

She cocked her head. "How chivalrous—the very definition."

Gall put out his hands. "I am nothing if not that."

She glanced at the waitress bringing her glass. "She your type?"

Gall looked her up and down. "She's most men's type."

The waitress set the glass on the table. "Anything else?"

The female knight shook her head.

"No, my sweet." Gall smiled. "But thank you."

Her skirt swooshed again as she spun away.

The knight poured herself a glass. "What's your name?"

"Gall."

She began filling his glass. "Skyrah."

"Skyrah?"

She lifted the bottle to stop its flow. "Got a problem with it?"

"No, that's a *fantastic* name."

"Thank you." She tilted the bottle, finished pouring, and set the whisky on the table. "I have often heard that sentiment more eloquently put but rarely so enthusiastically."

Gall nodded. "You from Trillia?"

"Lucia." She leaned back and sipped her drink.

Gall took a sip himself. "And how *did* you do in the tournament?"

"Middle of the pack." She sighed. "About the same as last time."

"Keep practicing," Gall suggested.

"I practice enough."

"Practice less, then. Think less. Just show up and fight."

She gave him a surprised look. "Yeah…"

He drank and shrugged.

She drank and laughed.

"There he is!" a voice called.

Gall spotted the tall man who had stood aside for them at the tournament.

"Beal!" the crowd yelled as Isham led their champion through.

"Thank you." Beal smiled, nodding to those left and right as he passed. "Thank you."

"Well fought, Sir Beal."

"Thank you, thank you."

Isham pointed. "There, in the corner." He let Beal step in front of him.

Skyrah raised an eyebrow at Gall, who shrugged again.

Beal made his way between and past his adoring fans.

"Ale?" someone asked him.

"No," Beal said. "Thank you."

Another patted him on the shoulder. "What'll you have?"

Beal shook the man's other, outstretched hand. "Nothing, but thank you." He proceeded to Gall's table.

"Whisky?" Gall took hold of his bottle.

The crowd quieted and listened.

"Perhaps some wine later, at home with the wife. I am Sir Beal of Trillia."

"I'm Gall, this is Skyrah. It's a pleasure to meet you." Gall motioned out toward the bar with both hands. "A great pleasure, apparently."

"Yes," Beal said. "The people of Trillia are most kind to me." He pointed at Gall. "And if I'm not mistaken, the people of Blackburg were once most kind to you."

Skyrah looked at her tablemate.

Murmurs rolled through the crowd. "*Gall?* Who is he?"

"Not for a while," Gall said.

"But you are Sir Gallchobhar?" Beal asked.

Gall sipped his drink. "I am."

The murmurs grew louder. "Knight of Gran. Blackburg. Sir Gallchobhar."

Beal nodded. "It is *my* great pleasure to meet *you*."

"Why?" Skyrah asked.

"This is a renowned knight. The finest in Gran."

"Not finer than you, Beal!" a man near the bar called.

"Thank you!" Beal responded then pointed at Gall. "But *this* knight, his skill with a lance is legendary. His talent with a knife… his raw strength was unheard of. Against the best in his kingdom, he once won the ten-mile race in the morning and the hundred yards the same afternoon."

"You're stronger," a woman yelled.

Beal turned round. "His broadsword shattered shield, armor, and stone alike, they say."

"He's never fought you!" another woman called.

"No," Beal agreed. "He has not."

Gall filled his glass.

"But he won every tournament he ever fought in," Beal said.

"Did he slay a dragon?" a man asked loudly.

Beal looked at Gall.

"No dragon," Gall announced to the pub.

The crowd liked the answer and made knowing noises and remarks.

Gall stuck out his lower lip in fake disappointment.

"Fight him!" the bartender called.

"Yeah!" the crowd agreed. "Show him, Beal!"

Smiling, Beal raised both hands to quiet them.

"Gran's nothing," a man yelled. "Garbage!"

"Yeah!"

"Please!" Beal called to them. "Please." The crowd settled. "I am not here to challenge Sir Gallchobhar. He is not my enemy." Beal turned to Gall. "I do not wish to fight you."

Gall raised his glass. "Nor I you, Sir Beal."

"Boo!" the crowd called. "Boooo."

"Please!" Beal quieted them again. "This is an evening of celebration. Enjoy your drinks, and let me talk with this good knight."

The crowd's murmuring grew slowly.

"Max," Beal said to the bartender. "A round for all on me."

The crowd cheered and returned some of its focus to their drinks and their company.

Beal demonstratively widened his eyes to Gall and Skyrah.

"The price of fame," Gall said.

"Indeed." Beal glanced at Skyrah. "And well aware of that price, I would not keep you long."

"What can I do for you, Sir Beal?"

"Just Beal, please. Be my guest tomorrow, for dinner. Both of you, of course."

"I'll be gone by then, unfortunately."

"Then lunch," Beal said. "I should like my son to meet you. He is a young knight of the city."

"Got plans for lunch. Bring your boy by here."

"I would, but I would like my wife to meet you as well, and I would rather not bring *her* here."

"Mhm." Gall rolled his whisky around his glass.

Beal nodded backward. "I could tell this crowd that you've challenged me to combat tomorrow evening. Once word spread—and it would spread—it would be very hard for you to leave the city before seeing the contest through." He paused. "But I'd rather not. Not at all. I'd rather spend that time with good wine, good stories, and exciting company at my home. We'll have a fire on the balcony overlooking the ocean."

Gall sipped his drink, thought of the warm salty breeze, and then… of the twins with their mother. "Fine." He pointed at Beal. "But I'm expecting *good* wine."

"And we shall have it," Beal said. "Thank you."

"Thank *you*."

"Skyrah," Beal said. "Gall."

They both nodded, and Beal walked away.

"Scared?" Skyrah asked.

"What's that?"

"Assumed you'd want to fight him." Skyrah refilled her glass. "Figured you for the cocky type." She sipped her whisky. "Guess I figured wrong."

"I'd win," Gall said.

"Oh? At what?"

"Anything. I don't lose."

"Hmm…"

"You heard him," Gall said. "Those stories are true. Basically."

"Uh huh." Skyrah put down her glass. "Let's play a game I don't think you will win."

"What game?"

Skyrah leaned forward and motioned for Gall to do the same. Inches from him, she grinned. "Who can drink faster."

"Ha." Gall leaned back. "You won't beat me at that."

She took his glass from him, filled both of theirs a third of the way, then set the bottle on the table. "We'll see." She held the glasses close together to verify they contained an equal level of liquid. She put Gall's down. "We'll see…" She raced her glass to her mouth and chugged.

Gall grabbed his and beat her—barely. "Cheater."

She wiped her mouth with her hand. "Fill 'em up."

Gall did, hers first, to the same level as before. As soon as he filled his, she grabbed it and chugged.

He took hers, gulped it down, and set the glass on the table the instant before she did.

She wiped her mouth with her arm, swallowed the last of the liquor, and smiled.

"What'll ya try next?" Gall asked.

"Not sure! Fill 'em."

Gall did, watching her closely.

She reached her hand out and covered his on the table. "Don't worry. Calm down. I need a minute."

Skyrah waited her minute then lost again. She waited longer after that before her next attempt and Gall's next victory. In between, they chatted a bit about who they were and where they had come from and discussed at length technique with a sword, shield, and lance. Gall found her an eager listener.

Skyrah prodded him about Beal and how he could be so sure he'd win. Gall told stories—in detail, as they had time to kill in between rounds of whisky—of different games, competitions, and fights he had won and how he simply did not lose.

"Never?" she asked, leaning on her arm for support, looking into Gall's big brown eyes.

"Nope," Gall said.

"*Never?*"

"No."

"Then challenge Beal."

"Why?"

"Show me how good you are." Her arm slipped off the table.

Gall laughed.

"Come *on*," she urged. "Lancing, sparring, something… anything."

Gall liked the blue in Skyrah's eyes.

"Please." She leaned forward.

Gall leaned close. Her lips looked so soft.

"*Please.*"

Gall kissed her. "All right."

"Good." She leaned away. "One more round."

Gall poured the drinks. "And then?"

Skyrah grabbed her glass. "And then you take me to the

nearest bed in the nearest inn."

Gall swigged his drink. "Trillia." He set his glass down first. "Well worth the trip."

42

Taulus

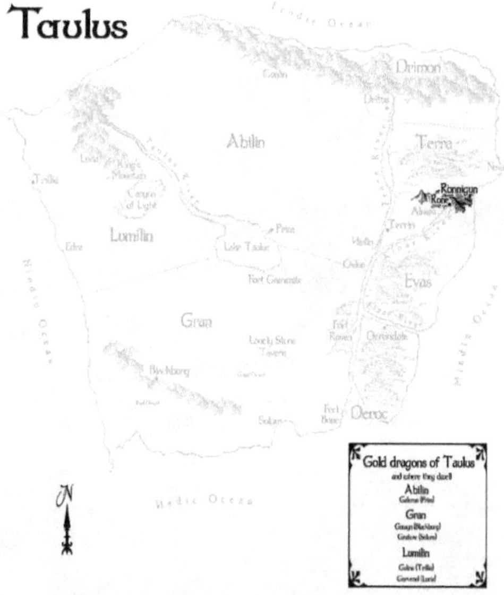

On Farlan's back, getting soaked in steady rain, Ri and her rescuers flew toward Rone. Ri had changed from her bloodied scouting attire to a long green dress more befitting a princess—but hardly the circumstances. Flashes of lightning let her spot the long cave mouth where she had seen King Eldred and Governor Bardric. A Red Elf emerged and jogged up the mountain path.

Thunder rumbled. Lightning lit the clouds.

"Wow." Ri saw dragons of every natural color filling the mountain city's central square, along with golden Grafere.

"They've been all over the sky," Gregory said.

"And the forest, hunting orcs," Erwyn added. "Let's hope those dwarves are more forthcoming with information."

The only ten dwarves Ri noticed in the city stood dripping wet in the rain surrounded by the dragons; armed, angry-looking Red Elves; and a smaller number of knights from Gran and Abilin.

"What about the rest of Ronnigun?" Ri asked.

"We sent scouts to every town," Erwyn said. "The dwarves in all of them claimed to know nothing of what happened here in Rone or in the forest."

Farlan landed beside a huge blue. Ri recognized him as one from far-off Lumilin. Ri and the others slid off Farlan.

A Red Elf followed a dwarf down the hill. "Found one more." He shoved the short dwarf splashing through a puddle into the pack with the other ten.

Matthias, a Red Elf general, made his way over to Ri and whispered to her, "Where are the rest?"

"Dead," Ri whispered back.

Matthias brought a hand to his heart. "Naelon? Launfal?"

"All of them." Ri choked up once more.

Matthias's heavy face grew angry. "These dwarves…"

"No," Erwyn said loudly. "Dark Elves."

Dragons, men, elves—everyone within earshot turned to him.

"Our scouts were attacked without warning," Erwyn

called to them. He left Ri out of his explanation. "One escaped, badly wounded, and we just found him to hear his report. They saw Eldred and Bardric shaking hands outside that cave." He pointed up the mountain.

"Eldred." Matthias clenched his fists. "So it is confirmed."

Gregory asked, "What have you found here?"

"Tunnels," Matthias said. "Very long, some very deep, running out into the forest from a big chamber in that mountain. The orcs must have been there, but the dwarves"—he motioned toward the eleven dwarves, all of them smiling smugly—"aren't talking."

A dragon's voice suddenly echoed in Ri's mind. *We'll see.* Everyone turned to watch as Galeron and Gowyn landed fast. The crowd parted, making way for the golds. Ri expected a nod from Galeron, the protector of Abilin, or Gowyn, who had just saved her, but neither of them acknowledged her.

Thunder boomed. Both dragons marched straight for the dwarves.

Galeron called to them, for all to hear, *Why did Eldred come to Rone?* He halted before the line of the city's inhabitants and craned his neck low to them for their answer. *Where did the rest of the dwarves go?*

The dwarves smiled up at the golds.

Galeron grabbed the dwarf on the end and slammed him headfirst into the muddy ground. Blood and dirt splattered the nearest onlookers. Galeron released the dead body, sucked in air, and shot flame just over top of the dwarves. He grabbed the next in line and screamed. *Tell me!*

The dwarves' faces focused. Low thunder rumbled.

Galeron's chest heaved. He slammed the dwarf's head into the ground.

Gowyn scanned the crowd of anxious humans and elves. *Have they told you anything useful? What the orcs are, or where they came from?*

"No," General Merton of Abilin said.

The rain poured down hard and loud.

Galeron looked at the mountain. *The tunnels led under there?*

"Yes," the general answered.

That wide entrance leads into the big chamber?

"It does."

Galeron grabbed another dwarf and crushed him between his claws. He let the limp body fall to the ground. *I will return for the rest of you.* Galeron jumped and, with Gowyn following, flew up to the entrance where Ri had seen Eldred. The big blue Ri recognized trailed them.

"Let's get up there," Gregory said.

Farlan brought her head low to him.

"Don't think Galeron would mind," Gregory added.

Ri shrugged and wiped her wet hair out of her face.

Gregory motioned for Farlan to lean all the way down and concluded, "Nah, he won't."

The princes of Abilin and Terra and Abilin's princess got on Farlan and flew to the cave mouth to join the other three dragons.

Galeron and Gowyn stretched their long necks into the entrance.

Farlan landed. *What brings you all the way from King's Mountain, Eilig?*

Galina sent me, the blue answered. *Word reached her of strange little creatures in Abilin, in Hinlin. She sent me to find Galeron and see what he made of them. I came for that then stayed when the trouble began in the forest.*

Surprised she didn't send Gorvenal, Farlan said.

She would have, Eilig said. *But he was not in Lucia, and she could not find him anywhere.*

Galeron and Gowyn pulled their heads back out of the mountain.

It's massive, Gowyn remarked.

Galeron inspected the edge of the cave mouth. *And significantly older than this entrance. That cavern has been there a while.*

There could have been an army of orcs packed in there, Gowyn said. *Orders of magnitude beyond what we've found thus far.*

The sound of running footsteps drifted out of the cave. Ri stiffened, ready for anything, but the dragons simply watched the entrance. A Red Elf skidded to a halt as he exited the cave, huffing for air.

"Selvyn," Erwyn said, "what is it?"

The elf composed himself. "At the far end of the cavern, there's a cliff—deep and wide. The cave doesn't end."

"Did you go down?" the prince asked.

"I will, but I need rope to be sure I can get back up."

Erwyn nodded, and Selvyn jogged for the city center.

Farlan, Galeron said to the red dragon. *You're small, get in there.*

I'm not that *small,* she said.

You're smaller than me. Go.

Farlan leaned low so her passengers could dismount. Once they had, she walked to the entrance and got even lower. Her head and neck presented no problem on the way in, but her wet back squeezed against the rock as she tried to pass.

Ow. She advanced slowly, squeezed on… then stopped. *I don't think I can make it.*

Galeron drove his shoulder into Farlan's hide, and the red roared as she shot through the entrance. Farlan stuck her head out into the rain and glared at Galeron before retreating into the cave.

Ri, her brother, and Erwyn ran inside. The flickering glow from the torch on the wall at the entrance lit the overlook but barely penetrated the cavernous void, which made Farlan's long, flapping wings and slender body seem puny. Ri had seen her share of dwarven halls, chambers, and deep mines under mountains, but none were as empty or dismal. She looked at the ceiling—she had never seen one so tall. Farlan shrunk as she flew into the distance.

"Wow." Gregory's loud sentiment echoed softly.

"A great many orcs would have fit in here," Erwyn said.

"Where did they come from?" Ri asked.

"Where did they go?" Gregory added.

The group followed Erwyn's lead to the end of the overlook. Farlan faded from Ri's view into the darkness completely.

Erwyn knelt and gazed at the ground below. "I cannot say."

Gregory grabbed the torch from the entrance and returned. He crouched. "Footprints." He waved the torch low to the scattered, three-toed impressions in a thin layer of dirt. "But not everywhere."

"One would expect there to be more," Erwyn said. "That if legions of orcs covered this ground, their prints would be so numerous that we could not clearly distinguish so many of them."

Gregory nodded.

"Farlan's been gone a while," Ri said.

"Oh," Erwyn said, "not so long yet."

Farlan had *to come back*, Ri pleaded to herself. If she didn't, Ri would blame herself. It might not make sense, but she would anyway. Another life lost to her terrible lie.

Gregory went to the wall and held the torch high. "How long do you think this cavern has been here?"

Erwyn walked over and gently placed his fingertips and palm to the wall. He inspected it closely. "Many hundreds of years."

"How many hundreds?"

Erwyn turned to him. "Many."

"Where would all the orcs go?" Ri asked. "If that tunnel keeps going, where would they attack?"

Flapping wings made them all turn to Farlan's approach.

Erwyn said, "Perhaps we will learn that now."

The tunnel is huge. Farlan landed and squeezed her way outside.

Ri and the others ran out into heavy rain.

Farlan stretched out, stood tall, and said, *At the end of the cavern, the floor drops off a cliff—a big drop—and there's a tunnel. I flew down it for a while.*

Galeron tilted his head. *Flew?*

It was no trouble, Farlan said. *We could have fit two abreast, no problem. Bones and droppings of cattle, mostly, littered the floor. Fresh water flowed into a vast pool in a large room off the tunnel.*

Where did the tunnel go? Gowyn asked.

Farlan shrugged. *Perfectly straight.* She glanced at the mountain. *East.*

"The mountains run to the coast," Erwyn said. "If the tunnel lets out there, Eldred could attack Nova to the north then head up the coast to the dwarven lands of Drimon."

But he hasn't, Gowyn said. *Not yet. One of us would have seen something.*

Eilig asked, *Could they still be in the tunnel? Waiting?*

I heard nothing, Farlan said. *I smelled nothing alive. But the ocean is a long way off.*

Galeron said, *Eldred didn't leave Deroc to wait. He's been waiting his whole life.* He leapt into the air. *Eldred is long gone.* He darted down to the crowd at the city center.

Gowyn and Eilig followed, and after Ri, Erwyn, and Gregory got onto Farlan's back, the red trailed.

Galeron landed fast, skidding on the wet ground before the dwarves, and Eilig landed behind him. As Farlan touched down, Ri heard Galeron say, *Eldred is headed for Trillia.*

The drenched knights of Gran and Abilin gasped.

"How could he?" General Merton asked.

The dwarves smirked. Lightning flashed. The hard rain fell harder.

"He heads east," Prince Erwyn said. "On a dragon, he could fly around the globe."

Thunder boomed. Ri, Gregory, and the prince jumped off Farlan.

What? Eilig asked. *How, with all his elves with him?*

He's found a way, Galeron said.

A dwarf stuck his head forward. "Eldred asked me to tell you, *mighty* Galeron, that when he burns that opulent *jewel* of a city to the ground, when he watches its finely dressed, finely perfumed elite screaming in the flames alongside the common folk, that a certain regret will nag at him."

Galeron slid his head down the line to the dwarf, who went on, "He regrets that after all his long years in Deroc, plotting and scheming in his swamp, that his best plan, the one he selected from among all those he devised, did not begin with the destruction of Prim."

Lightning forked across the clouds.

Galeron calmly asked, *How does Eldred intend to burn a city made of granenite?*

The dwarf grinned. Water dripped off his smug face. "No stone in Taulus is trouble for the queen of the black dragons."

Galeron leapt into the air, letting out a fearsome roar.

Thunder burst and crackled.

"The daughter of Xodon!" the dwarf yelled.

Galeron flapped his wings hard, rose, and headed west, with Gowyn, Grafere, and Eilig behind him.

"Her name's Xailyn!" the dwarf screamed.

Thunder rumbled.

Gregory stepped forward and called to the dwarves, "Black dragons?"

"You were all so certain you had wiped out every last one of them. So pleased. So disgustingly *proud* of your genocide."

"Why do this?" Gregory asked. "Why help Eldred?"

"Oh…" The dwarf's smile faded. "He has his reasons, we have ours."

"Well? Yours?"

"Ronnigun is nice." The dwarf shrugged. "Not too hot, not too cold. It's near the ocean. But in the north, cold air fills the days and nights in the mountains of Drimon. Every day. Every night. *Always*, a chill blows through that air."

"You want more land?" Gregory asked.

"We do." The dwarf's countrymen grunted in agreement. He called out to the crowd of men, women, and elves, "You all have far more land than us and far better land. And your history tells of how you took that land, and how you held it, and how you fought for it with might and magic. We came to Taulus last. There have never been dwarven emotes. Our history tells of how we graciously appreciated your kindness for giving us your scraps, the land you did not want. And our history is full of the castles and caverns and monuments we built for you. And that is all. So yes, young Prince Gregory, we want more land—a lot more—and we want to take it by force."

The first of many shouts and curses came from the crowd. "Bastards! Damn dwarves!"

Lightning lit the sky.

Someone said, "They must have gone under the cover of darkness."

A knight of Gran called out, "How can there be black dragons?"

"Take them away," Erwyn ordered a group of his elves. "See what else we can find here. Question all the dwarves in Ronnigun regarding what we have learned. I will return with this news to Terrin."

Ri watched the three golds ahead of Eilig racing west in the violent sky. It was a bad dream, she told herself as the big dragons flapped their wings. Soon she would wake up in Dritus, perfectly dry, warmed by a roaring fire and a cup of sweet hot cocoalan, and savor the majesty of the mountains out her window on a crisp, clear day.

Gregory came over and pointed at a green dragon. "Branor will take us to Prim."

The entire crowd scrambled to set their own travel plans.

"Will they make it in time?" Ri asked her brother.

Gregory watched the golds and the blue flying away, shrinking into the distance. "If Eldred began his trip when the fires and everything started in the woods, then no, I don't think they will."

Ri grimaced.

"But perhaps Galeron flies faster than I think," Gregory said.

Ri crossed her arms and observed the hectic city center. "So many dragons are here—were here. Galeron, Gowyn, Grafere... So many dragons."

Branor walked over.

Gregory put his hand on his sister's shoulder. "Eldred's set a good plan in motion. I don't know what's going to happen in Trillia, but we need to get back to Prim."

43

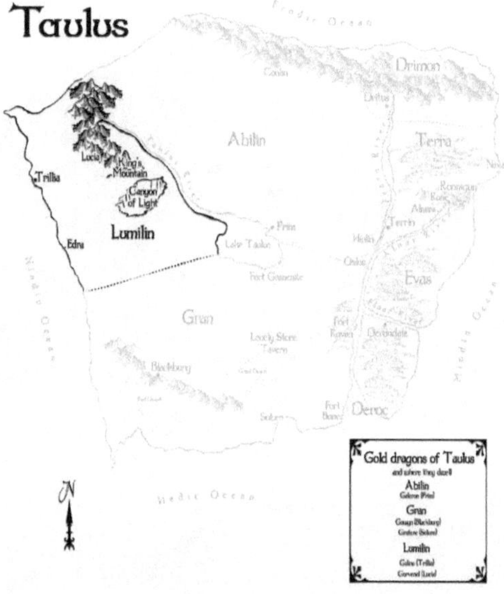

In their third-floor room in the nearest inn to The Blue Crown pub, Gall awoke with Skyrah's hand on his bare chest and her head smushed against his arm. He admired the shades of brown mixed in her messy blond hair. He noted the ends of the strands that hit the smooth skin of her back and pictured the bare rest of her hidden beneath the white sheets. *Gorgeous woman*, he thought. And fun! Fun at the pub, really fun in bed. Details of the end of the night came to him hazily, but they found their way. He pieced them together, and… God, she had been fun!

Her eyes cracked open.

"Good morning," he said.

She lifted her head and squinted in the pale light coming through the window beyond the foot of the bed. She shut her eyes again and rested her head back on Gall. "Why are you awake?"

"I just am." Gall kissed the side of her head.

"Mm."

He kissed her cheek.

She smiled. "It's *too* early."

"I know," he said. "Those twins and their mother asked me to breakfast. I made it lunch."

"Why aren't you hungover?"

"Just not." He looked her over. "You know, you didn't need that drinking game to get me here with you."

"I know." She buried her head into the nook of Gall's neck. "Game was for me."

"Oh?"

"Less sober, I'm more fun."

"Oh. I like it."

"Yes, you did." She pulled herself closer to him. "Now be quiet and sleep with me some more."

44

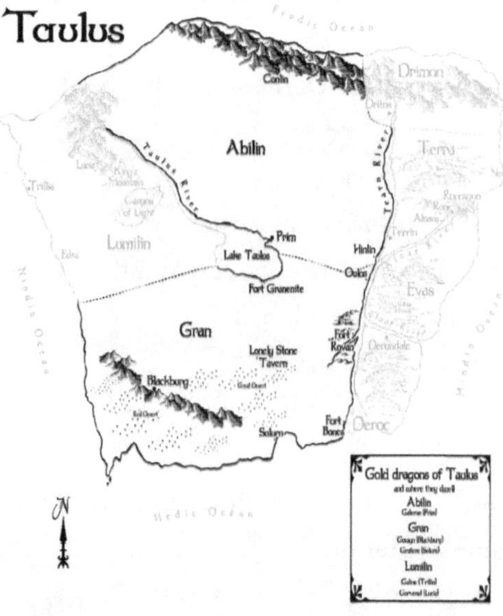

With the rain and clouds behind them, the sun had risen
over the central plains of Abilin. Galeron raced westward
with Gowyn and Grafere close behind and Eilig trailing
considerably. Galeron had known Eilig long enough to
know that the big blue was giving it his all to get to Trillia.
He had no doubt that Eilig would do anything he could to
warn Galina of the evil headed her way, and if he made it

too late for that, to fight alongside his dear friend in defense of her city, whatever the cost.

But the golds simply flew faster. Their lungs filled with more air and their muscles pumped their wings harder. More than half the journey to Trillia remained before the four dragons.

Father, Gowyn said.

Galeron stared ahead and kept flying. He estimated that a third of Lumilin's army lived in Trillia—a third of a much smaller total force of late. Gran and Abilin hadn't seen as steep a decline, but as the years of peace wore on, interest in soldiering had waned in the kingdom that had hardly even fought in the Dark Wars and had fought so little in the centuries since.

Father! Gowyn called.

Galeron glanced back but didn't slow.

Gowyn stopped. *What if it's a trick? And Eldred means to return to the east and not strike Trillia?*

Galeron spun and hovered. His chest heaved. *He will attack Trillia. He, those with him, and that black dragon. And if she is truly queen, surely she is queen of others.*

Gowyn flew toward his father. *But—*

You are right. Galeron lowered his head. *If his force is large enough, while we race west, Eldred may also return to the east, and with us in the middle, he could bring his attack to both shores.*

Grafere said, *And that might explain where the dwarves and elves from Rone are. They've stayed to the east, probably underground.*

Eldred splitting his forces reduces his risk, Gowyn said. *He could be defeated at Trillia and still have his eastern assault to lead. What do we do?*

Galeron looked west then at the others. *Gowyn, return east. Warn King Ervain of this possibility on your way, though surely he is already preparing his defenses in Terra. Gather what dragons you can and head for the coast.* Galeron pointed at him. *But do not fight if you cannot win decisively. I would rather Eldred or Bardric make a little headway in the east than we suffer a catastrophic loss there while we are still unraveling their plan.*

I understand, Gowyn said.

Galeron turned west and flapped his wings—but he hesitated. *Unless they drive all the way to Prim.*

Gowyn tilted his head. *Hm?*

Do not let them take Prim, my son. Fight for that first city and its good people. If the battle comes to Prim, find a way.

Gowyn nodded. *Prim will not fall.*

Galeron sucked in a deep breath and, with Grafere, resumed his race to the west. Gowyn headed east, the way he had come.

———

From the dragon Branor's back above the castle in Prim, Ri watched men, women, and children below loading carts full of belongings they would bring inside. Others beyond the circular Middle Wall of the city moved inward, stopping at the busy markets to buy or barter for whatever food and supplies they could. No one remained beyond the outer

Great Wall. Knights everywhere scrambled to move weapons into defensive positions. Branor landed outside the king's hall in the castle grounds.

Gregory jumped off. Ri stayed put.

"Coming?" Gregory asked her.

The dragon gave her an inquisitive look, and Ri imagined Branor taking her somewhere far from Abilin, somewhere she could be alone.

"Yeah." Ri slid off but made no move to go with her brother.

A guard with a tall spear pushed open the big door as Gregory approached.

"Gregory!" the queen called from inside. "Where is Corina?"

"Trillia is under attack?" the king asked.

Gregory motioned his sister forward. "She's here," he called to their mother. "She's fine. Yes, Galeron believes Eldred flies for Trillia."

They didn't know, Ri reminded herself. Her parents thought she had been in Terrin the whole time, which clearly worried them anyway with all that had happened in the forest. But the lie that had doomed Launfal and the others was her secret, at least in Abilin. And she hadn't really been wrong at all.

Yet her friends were dead, and *that* remained her fault.

She headed for the hall. She would see her parents quickly and then shut herself in her room. War in Taulus seemed imminent and unavoidable. Ri felt so powerless in the face of such awful certainty. The battles she had longed for would soon begin, but Ri would not be a part of the fight. She had been childish, hoping for war long before she concocted her story for King Ervain. Then she had lied, and her friends had died for it.

Her soft bed would not change what she had wished for or what she had done, but it would not judge her either. It would not laugh at her. It would not scold her. Ri would have taken those condemnations more readily than ever, because they felt more deserved than any she could ever imagine. That also made them utterly pointless, unlike any others, ever.

She would rush to her room, lock the door, cover herself with her bed's thick blankets, and shut her eyes. Perhaps she would find a few moments of peace in a dream.

———

Taylan walked south slowly. The River Tearn ran loudly to his left. Faint hints of red still stained its water. Taylan didn't know why it had turned that color. He had no idea why all the dragons beyond the river had cleared the skies over the forest, landing somewhere for a time only to take flight again and race in all directions. He didn't care.

Taylan's ankle hurt with each step. Somehow when he had been healed after Oulos, the emote had missed that injury. Or maybe Taylan had reinjured it. He couldn't remember. His lower back stung and throbbed, but the hurt that caused that lay beyond any emote's reach.

Taylan didn't know if he wished he had saved Valencia. The orcs in his head, the ones he had burned and jolted to death, kept asking, but he could not answer them. Taylan hurt because he had let her die, but had he saved her, he would have hurt differently, because of how she had hurt him.

Taylan had thanked God for Valencia after all the terrible things God had done to him. But the days of those thoughts seemed an eternity ago, a distant memory, an emotion utterly lost. While he could no longer experience an ounce of the joy he had felt then, he found fleeting moments of spiteful pleasure in the notion that he had struck back at that same damnable God when he had let Valencia die.

Yet his heart ached for her.

Heading west across Valencia's lands had no appeal, nor did going north, in a retreat to the homeland he knew so well. Beyond the Tearn, the Red Forest had never been his home, despite it being his father's, and the White Forest, with its thick outer line of trees, appeared as unwelcoming as ever. So while he picked apart each of his last conversations with Valencia and wrestled with explanations for what about himself had so soured her to his affections, Taylan took one painful step after another to the south.

45

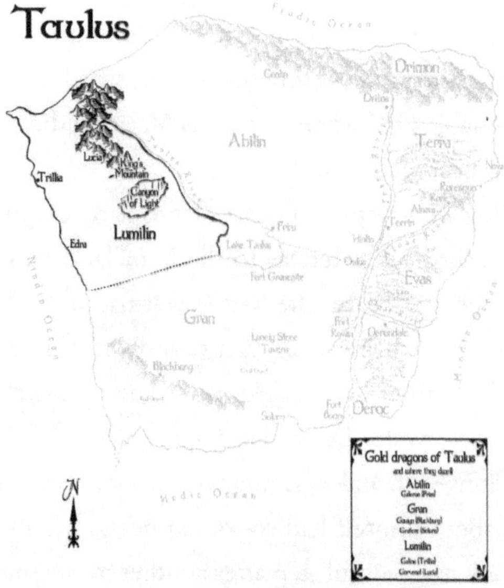

On the large balcony on the top floor of the brothel Pinnacle,
Gall and Skyrah sat opposite Isabel and the twins at a long table
laden with the remains of an excellent meal. Miles Calvert, the
brothel's owner, who had been introduced to them as Isabel's
friend, sat at the head of the table.

"Thank you for lunch," Gall said to Miles. He considered
calling the meal breakfast since he and Skyrah had stayed in

bed so long and their walk over revealed that all of Trillia had gotten a similar late start after the post-tournament celebration.

Miles nodded. "You are welcome."

"And thank *you*, again," Isabel said, "for seeing my children safely to me."

Gall shrugged. "They did it. They set me up. They got me out of jail. They're smart kids."

Isabel pulled them to her. "Yes, they are." Avril accepted the hug with a smile. "My little angels." Avery rolled his eyes and gently pushed off his mother's arm.

Miles finished his glass of red wine. "So it's dinner tonight with Sir Beal, then you're off for Conlin in the morning?"

"Yes."

Miles refilled Gall's wine, then Skyrah's, and asked her, "And will you be going with him?"

"Miles…" Isabel gave him a look.

"What? It's a simple question. She doesn't have to answer."

"I'll head back to Lucia." Skyrah placed her hand on Gall's leg under the table. "But tonight should be fun."

"Beal was incredible," Avery said to his mother. "You should have seen him joust."

"Paperwork wasn't going to do itself," Isabel said. "But I'm glad you saw him. And I'm glad you'll see him around the city. Compared to most knights, he's a breath of fresh air. He's the best in Lumilin, but he's not arrogant or cocky. He's a good man."

"Some people like arrogant." Gall covered Skyrah's hand with his. "Or so I've been told."

Miles and Isabel chuckled.

Skyrah shrugged. "We'll see if you can back it up at Beal's."

Miles turned to Gall. "Oh?"

Skyrah finished sipping her wine and pointed at Gall. "He said he'd challenge Beal."

"Did he?" Isabel looked at him.

Gall waved his hand. "I'll think of a simple game."

"We'll see," Skyrah said.

"I have no wish to fight the man," Gall said.

"He's won every tournament and competition for a decade," Miles said. "I can't remember the last he didn't, actually."

"I think you'd win," Avery said.

Gall nodded to him. "Thank you." He looked around the table. "But I doubt it will come to physical combat. I don't think he's interested in that, either."

"We'll see," Skyrah said.

Avery's face fell.

Gall noticed it, along with Avril's more subtle reaction. He asked the boy, "Want to come?"

Avery lit up. "Yeah!"

"Avery," his mother said, "let Sir Gall—"

"It's fine. And who knows"—Gall glanced at Skyrah—"maybe she'll convince me to challenge Beal to something interesting." He turned to Avril, who sat quite close to her mother. "How 'bout you? His son's going to be there. Beal's handsome, I'd have to imagine—"

"Yes," Avril said. "But I was already going to say yes."

Gall folded his arms. "Uh huh… It'll be fun. Maybe I'll get you two to drink again."

Her mother raised an eyebrow. "Again?"

"Yes, *again*," Gall said. "Avery finally let his guard down a little, and Avril's very funny when she's drunk." Gall stood. "And with that, we shall say another thank you and be on our way." He finished his glass of wine and wiped his mouth with his sleeve. "We'll come by before dinner, and we can all go to Beal's together."

Skyrah got up. "Where to now?"

Gall burped. "A walk?" He patted his stomach. "I could use it."

Vincent's horse nudged his face. The dozing guard of Trillia brushed the animal away. Soft ocean waves would lull him into a deeper sleep, despite the bright sun overhead. He packed the sand serving as his pillow tighter and turned on the beach to lay facing the water.

Vincent's head ached less than it had earlier. Last night had been fun, despite not knowing how he had ended up so far north of the city. Recalling how much he had drunk every night of the tournament, he figured he could have felt worse. Actually, he *should* have felt worse. But a little more sleep was all he needed.

A wet tongue licked Vincent's cheek.

Vincent opened his eyes. He wiped his face with his sandy hand and wondered if his horse somehow knew that he should have been on duty, on watch in Trillia. Vincent squinted at the White Castle far in the distance. Someone would cover for him. Or they wouldn't, and it wouldn't matter.

His horse lost interest in him and walked away. Vincent gazed out at the ocean.

Dots on the horizon?

Ships or… well, ships. What else would be in formation so far out?

Vincent widened his eyes.

Dark dots.

Beyond the rolling waves, six dark dots lined the horizon, and they were growing.

Ships from where? And why so far out at sea?

To the south, Trillia remained quiet. No alarm had sounded. The ships must not have been any concern.

Unless Trillia hadn't seen them yet.

Vincent sat up and looked at his horse—no supplies, so no telescope.

The trade routes did not run that way. Ships from Edra would not approach from so far off shore.

Vincent stood and brushed sand from his pants and shirt.

Movement from the northernmost dot. Sails flapping in the wind.

He ran his fingers through his sandy hair.

Actually… not sails.

Wings flapping. Vincent could see the same flapping down the line of dots.

Black, he realized. *Black* dots, not merely dark.

Trillia remained quiet. It would not be a quick ride back.

Vincent headed for his horse. It didn't make sense… but surely someone in the city would see the dots soon.

Vincent got on his saddle and looked out at the ocean—definitely flapping, definitely black.

By the time Vincent got to Trillia, it might be too late to flee.

He rode off the beach, to the east. Lucia was far, but anywhere seemed better than the coast.

Vincent picked up into a gallop, glanced at Trillia shrinking to the south behind him, and assured himself that someone in the city would notice the danger headed their way. Someone had to.

Gall strolled with Skyrah on the path atop the oceanfront wall of the city. He was glad Avery and Avril were coming with them to Beal's that evening. Gall usually felt some sense of accomplishment after any of his jobs for hire, but he was especially satisfied to have completed his latest task—to have gotten the twins to their mother, to the next chapter in their life.

Gall and Skyrah passed a sleeping guard who sat facing the battlements with his back against the wall.

"Recovering from last night, I'm sure," Gall remarked.

"Maybe," Skyrah said. "They sleep up here all the time." She pointed at a long, single-story, solid stone house a few blocks away atop the hill that rose above the wall. "That's Beal's there."

"Nice view." Gall scanned the series of hills running north. They formed small valleys at the city's main circles while rising in between them, where they were dotted with large houses. "Lots of nice views."

"Expensive views," Skyrah said. "But that's no problem for the elite of Trillia. And Beal's was a gift from the king—to him *and* his wife."

"Why her? *Because* she's his wife?"

"She's an emote—a strong one. A star in their ranks. Since long before she married him."

Gall went to the ledge and gazed out at the water. Skyrah joined him. A gust of wind blew her long hair. While she moved it out of her face, Gall said to her, "Two beautiful views."

She put her arms around him, and he held her while they kissed.

She leaned back. "You're off to Conlin tomorrow?"

"And you to Lucia?"

Dong! A bell to the north rang. *Dong!*

"What is it?" Gall scanned the city below.

Skyrah backed out of their embrace and did the same. "No idea. That bell's on the wall." Skyrah pointed at the guard tower.

Dong—Dong!

They both looked at the ocean.

Dong—Dong!

Gall squinted at the horizon beneath high, sparse patches of white clouds. "You see those dots?"

"Way out there?"

"Yeah," Gall said.

Dong—Dong!

"Ships? Dragons?" Skyrah asked.

Gall shrugged.

"They've gotta have a scope in the watchtower with the bell," Skyrah said.

"Let's go."

Dong—Dong!

They jogged toward the tower, watching the evenly spaced dots out over the water and occasionally looking down at the city, where reaction to the bell consisted of people exiting their homes but finding no answers from their neighbors, and guards running into other guards with an equal lack of information.

Dong—Dong!

The dark dots grew.

"How many you see?" Gall asked.

"Six. How far you think?"

"Not sure. Far."

Galina streaked over Gall and Skyrah, who stopped to watch the huge gold dragon head out to the ocean.

Dong—Dong!

Galina flapped her wings and hovered in place, gazing at the dots in the western sky.

Dong—Dong!

She turned and flew north, fast—toward the castle.

"Come on." Gall ran hard for the semi-circular tower rising from the outside of the wall, making sure Skyrah could keep up until he got close and sprinted ahead.

A guard whipped the long bell rope to and fro. *Dong—Dong!*

"Hey!" Gall bounded up the steps to the young guard, his bell above him, and a standing telescope. "What is it?"

"Dragons." The guard appeared pale. "I… I…"

"Yes?" Gall urged. "You? You?"

Skyrah reached the tower.

"Eight miles. I think…" The guard put out his hands. "I think they're *black* dragons."

Gall grabbed the telescope and peered through.

"I… I just started this week," the guard said. "Got stuck working the day after the tournament. But it's a blue sky, and… and those ain't blues."

"No, they are not." Gall slid the telescope to the right. "Ring the bell."

The guard pulled on the rope.

Dong—Dong!

"And they ain't purples," the guard added.

"Not purples." Gall backed away from the scope. "Ring it."

Dong—Dong!

The guard gulped. "So I rang my bell like they said, if I see anything."

A more senior guard of Trillia ran up into the crowded tower. "What is it?"

"Black dragons," Gall said. "Keep ringing the bell."

Dong—Dong!

"What?" The second guard looked out to sea.

"Six of them, with riders," Gall said.

The older guard raised his arm to block the sun. "Where'd they come from?"

"Dunno," Gall said. "Doesn't matter. They're bad news."

"I must tell the king," the older guard said.

"Galina went," Skyrah said. "I think."

"What if she didn't?"

"Go," Gall said.

The older guard nodded and ran down the stairs. Skyrah and Gall followed.

"What should I do?" the tower guard called.

"Ring your bell!" Gall called back.

Dong—Dong!

Skyrah stepped off the staircase. "And us?"

Gall gazed at the dragons. "Weapons. Armor. We've got… half an hour before they reach this wall."

Skyrah squinted out at the horizon. "You sure?"

"Maybe less," Gall said. "See if Beal's at home on our way to the twins'?"

"Sounds good." She followed him while he ran slow enough for her to keep up.

Dong—Dong! The bell rang.

Dong—Dong! Another bell joined it farther north on the wall.

Galina landed in the courtyard of the castle.

Bells along the entire oceanfront wall rang. *Dong—Dong!*

Knights ran out to Galina while others, the captain of the

king's guard among them, watched bleary-eyed from the wall.

"Are those *black* dragons?" the captain, who had likely celebrated along with the rest the night before, called.

Yes, Galina said. *King Eldred and a small number of Dark Elves are with them.*

"But how?" the captain asked. "There *are* no more black dragons."

"And the Treaty of Solurn!" a knight shouted.

The treaty is broken, Galina said to the skeptical, hungover knights. *I have fought such dragons before. I fought the first of them. I assure you, six black dragons bear down upon this city.*

"What do we do?" another knight asked Galina then looked at his captain.

King Adrian rushed out of the keep. "Dragons approach this city?"

Attack this city, Galina corrected the king.

He took a step back from the big gold. "Are you sure?"

Quite sure, King Adrian.

"Why?" His face contorted. "How could they?"

"Black dragons, m'lord," the captain called from above on the wall.

"But they are all dead," the king said.

Galina leapt into the air, got above the wall to look at the ocean, then let herself fall and land hard in the courtyard. *Eldred rides the largest, and if my old eyes aren't mistaken, the dragon is Xodon's kin.*

The knights gasped.

"Xodon," the king said. "But that was so long ago."

We did not know he had a child. She must have been hidden her entire life.

"Where?" Adrian asked. "Why?"

I do not know where. It does not matter now. King Eldred and his queen are riding black dragons for this city. I do not know what comes next in their plan, for surely this is not its end, but at hand is an attack. Trillia is in grave danger.

"Can you fight them?" the king asked.

There are six.

"Will Gorvenal come?"

I've dispatched a message to Lucia, calling for his assistance, but I have been unable to find my son for days.

"Eilig?"

He is in eastern Abilin.

"Galeron then?"

I sent messages to Prim and to Blackburg and Solurn.

"Gran," the king scoffed. "They would never come."

Gowyn would. And Grafere.

"But not in time," the king said.

No.

Adrian met the looks of his knights and guards in the courtyard and up on the wall. His face grew stern. He raised his fist. "Ready the defenses!"

Approving yells challenged the ringing of the city's bells.

"Defend Trillia!" the king called, motioning for Galina to lean low toward him. Softer than the roused knights' growing cheers, he said to her, "Fly me to Lucia."

I will do no such thing.

"This city will burn." He watched his hustling subjects. "Our walls will melt in those dragons' fire. Were it not *black* dragons…"

But it is *those evil dragons, and your people need you here.*

"These people will die," the king said. "Soon. But I can lead a more organized defense from Lucia. *They* are my people too. You *must* take me and my wife there."

Galina did no more than blink.

"Kiara is with child," the king went on. "*Finally,* I am to be a father. And I am told a son is likely."

Galina sat upright. *You have commanders in Lucia who can lead that defense, or whatever strategy is deemed appropriate. Trillia's people would be wise to flee to there, and I advise you to order their evacuation immediately while you prepare to fight here to give them time to go. I leave to seek help from those nearby and pray I can return with enough to matter—to kill Eldred or at least give the people of this city some chance to reach safety.*

Galina leapt into the air and flapped her long wings to hover before him. *You are King of Lumilin, and this is your capital. Rally your knights in their fight for your people! Lead them against Eldred. Whatever his ultimate plan, his death could halt it on your shores.*

"But—"

Lumilin's knights, tucked away in the corner of Taulus farthest from Deroc, have never known a battle like this. Galina beat her wings. *Victory would mean glory for them—for your kingdom—for all time.*

"But my child," Adrian said softly.

Send Kiara to Lucia or, better, on to Abilin, farther from this harm's way, and if she survives and you do not, let her raise your unborn child.

Galina rose into the air, and a quick glance before she raced off cemented her confidence that the largest attacker of her city, a massive monstrosity of a dragon, was Xodon's daughter.

Dong—Dong!

Gall and Skyrah ran past a man outside his home pointing at the bell in a watchtower on the oceanfront wall. "What's going on?" he called to a guard running by.

The guard threw up his hands. "I don't—"

"Black dragons!" Gall yelled.

Dong—Dong!

The commotion in the streets became a frenzy. Gall and Skyrah ran another block.

"There," Skyrah called. She followed Gall up the hill to Beal's home.

"Galina flees!" A woman at the bottom of the hill pointed skyward. "She's abandoned us!"

Gall and Skyrah stopped to watch Galina race east, over the wall of Trillia.

"She'll be back," Skyrah said to Gall. "Let's go."

They ran the rest of the way up the hill, and Gall pounded on Beal's heavy wooden door.

No answer came.

Gall hit it again and waited.

"Not surprising," Skyrah remarked.

"'Spose not. To the twins'."

Heavy hooves sounded behind them, and Beal raced up the hill. "Sir Gall, Lady Skyrah."

"Sir Beal," Gall said.

Beal got off his horse. "Come." He pushed in the door, and a gust of ocean wind rushed out at them. The granenite walls of his home deadened Trillia's ringing bells. Beal led Gall and Skyrah past a kitchen smelling of marinating meat and seasoning and out to his balcony. "Lorelei?" he called.

Lorelei stood at the balcony's walled edge gazing out at the incoming dragons over the ocean.

The slender woman turned. A tear slid down her face. "Elven riders, I think."

"Yes." Beal went to wipe her cheek.

She beat him to it.

Beal motioned behind him. "Sir Gall and Lady Skyrah."

Lorelei gave a strained smile and nodded. Gall and Skyrah returned the nod.

"They are Dark Elves," Beal said. "Twenty-five minutes out. We believe King Eldred rides the largest."

"And you will fight them," Lorelei said.

"Yes."

"Then why did you come?"

"To see you, in case…"

"And you." Lorelei looked past her husband at Gall and Skyrah. "Why are you here?"

"Got another stop to make," Gall said. "You're on our way. Figured if Beal was here, a minute to hear his plan could only help."

Lorelei glanced at the six dragons closing in. "His plan is to fight and to die."

Beal grasped her arm. "Lorelei—"

"By order of the king!" a knight outside yelled. "This city is to be evacuated."

Gall, Skyrah, and Beal ran from the balcony and out the front door. The bells rang loudly, and the frenzy intensified as men, women, and children rushed in and out of homes and to the city gates.

"Leave your things!" the knight at the bottom of the hill called. "Take only what you need. Head for Lucia!"

Lorelei appeared in front of Gall and Skyrah. "You will stay and fight?"

"Aye," Gall said.

"Yes," Skyrah said.

"As *you* must," Beal said to Lorelei. "All will not be evacuated in time. You can help Trillia's people escape with their lives."

She took her husband's hand. "Leave with me."

Outside, someone shouted, "The king has left! He flees with Drefan!"

"Beal." Lorelei moved close to him. "Come with me. *Live* with me."

"What about them?" He motioned to the city.

"They flee," she said. "So they might survive this."

"And we can give them time. We can give them a chance. It is my duty. It is yours."

"My duty is to you," Lorelei said. "Since we married, since I met you…" She sniffled, and tears rolled onto her cheeks. "Since before I met you… all I've wanted was *you*."

"My love…" Beal wiped two of her tears away. "My Lorelei…" He took her other hand. "I am a knight of Lumilin—of Trillia. You are an emote of the city. We cannot change that now. Not at this urgent hour."

She stepped back from him. "What about our son?"

"Braden will do his duty as a knight of the city."

Lorelei shook her head and walked through the house back out to the balcony.

"We might kill Eldred," Beal said, following her with the others. "We must try."

Gall said to Skyrah, "We need to be going."

Lorelei stared out at the growing dragons. "You two, why don't you run with our wise king?"

"I don't run from battle," Gall said.

"Even when it is hopeless?"

"It is *not* hopeless," Gall said. "Not with me here."

"We're lucky you are," Beal said.

Gall nodded. "It will be a hard fight, but there are *only* six dragons and *only* six elves. And there's me and Beal and the knights and emotes of the city. This battle may cost many lives. But not mine. We *will* win. I *always* win."

Lorelei huffed.

"Knights don't run," Skyrah said. "Not those of any worth. And honestly… I like my chances with these two in battle better than fleeing without them."

"This is not the end." Beal walked to his wife. "If enough brave men and women fight, and fight hard, we can win this day." He gently turned her to face him. "And we can save so many lives while we do."

"I'll see you on the wall?" Gall asked Beal.

"Seems best to me," he said.

"Come on." Gall headed out the front door for the twins' place, with Skyrah following.

Galina watched the black dragons' ceaseless advance on her noisy, frantic city. Before her, Lumilin's king fled with a large mounted guard. Men and women from the city ran and rode after him in disarray. Smart parents had been quick to leave with their children. Galina didn't blame those citizens for leaving. She wished they streamed out of the city faster, and she would have helped them flee if she had time.

But she blamed King Adrian. His cowardice was robbing Trillia of many of its finest knights, including Drefan, who had won the tournament. And because of those games, more than half the kingdom's knights were at risk, either preparing to defend the city or fleeing from that responsibility. Galina flapped her wings and let out a cry for help to any dragons who would hear. She raced on to the east.

Where had Gorvenal been the last few days? Might he be on his way from Lucia after receiving the message his mother had dispatched the day before, questioning his absence from the tournament? Doubt filled Galina's heart. Gorvenal was farther than Lucia—she did not know where, but her son felt so far away.

She cursed herself for having sent Eilig to the east in his stead then realized that cunning King Eldred might have killed everyone in Hinlin to draw attention to that side of Taulus on purpose.

From the north, Cador flew toward her.

Galina headed to the young green, thinking that the blacks would tear him apart in battle and wondering if older dragons who had witnessed—and some fought—vicious blacks before would answer her call.

Galina, the green said.

Cador. She met him in the sky.

He peered past her. *Where do those black dragons come from?*

I do not know. Galina turned to watch them with Cador. *Perhaps from a remote island in the middle of the vast ocean, or perhaps they stayed hidden, under a tall mountain of the mainland.*

Cador stared at the dragons. *Any chance this isn't an attack?*

No, Galina said. *Eldred's father created his dragons for one reason—conquest. Eldred and the six with him fly no banner of peace. I've no doubt what they mean to do to Trillia.*

Will you try to stop them?

Yes. No matter what happens to me, if I can kill Eldred, and maybe the descendent of Xodon that he rides, his advance may never reach deep into Taulus.

And if you cannot? Cador asked.

Then I will have done all I can to give those fleeing the city a chance.

What if the dragons follow them from Trillia?

Then I hope my son, or Eilig, or Galeron, or Gowyn has

arrived to protect them. I hope others will come as well.

Cador finally broke his gaze from the black dragons. *What can I do?*

Find others, Galina said. *Bring them to fight for Trillia.*

What if none will come?

Convince them, Galina said. *I wish those dragons who covet the beauty of Taulus's mountains, rivers, trees, and plains could see the beauty in the people of Trillia. They are not perfect, and many of the most well known are the farthest from it, but that city is more than those few. Convince them of all the precious lives that are at stake.*

I will try, Cador said. *And I will be back, no matter what.* He turned to go.

Galina stopped him. *Cador, black dragons are powerful and savage. Xodon's kin is huge and doubtless strong. Do not underestimate them in battle.*

Cador nodded and headed east.

Galina raced south, in search of any others who might come to her city's aid.

Dong—Dong! The city's bells rang. *Dong—Dong!*

Outside the door to Pinnacle, Skyrah put her hands on her knees and breathed heavily from their run. "Kinda wish I hadn't had that wine at lunch."

Gall sensed adrenaline coursing through his veins, not the effects of a little wine. "How could we have known?" He pushed open the door.

"Take only what you need, ladies," Miles called down the

hall. The sound of drawers opening and closing filled the house. "We leave in five minutes." He turned to Gall and Skyrah. "They're upstairs. The kids don't want to go."

"How long is it to Lucia?" a woman called.

"Four days," Miles answered.

Gall and Skyrah ran up the stairs. He heard the twins before he reached their half-open door.

"We can help," Avril said.

"Please let us stay," Avery begged.

It heartened Gall to hear they wanted to—especially Avery. Gall burst through the doorway.

"Gall!" the twins called.

"She won't let us stay," Avery said.

Avril crossed her arms. She looked angrier than he had ever seen her.

"Your mother's right," Gall said.

Avery protested, "But—"

"It's too dangerous." Gall put out his hand to stop him then let it fall. "I'm glad you want to stay—both of you. I'm proud of you for it. But you're too young."

Avril said, "But—"

"Too inexperienced," Gall said, "is more accurate. You won't survive long out there."

"*We* may not," Skyrah added.

"I'll see you after," Gall said. "In Lucia, or when I return from Conlin."

Avery looked down.

Gall went on, "I'll tell you all about Galeron's sword and Gaiva's shield and the Thorns I take them from."

Avril's gaze went to the floor.

"I'll see you then," Gall said. "All right?"

"Yes," Isabel said with urgency in her voice.

"All right?" Gall repeated.

Avery looked up at him. "Fine."

"Yeah," Avril said.

Gall turned to their mother. "Leave now. Those dragons'll be here in fifteen minutes." He pointed at her. "Don't wait."

"All right," she said. "Good luck to you both."

"You too," Gall said.

"Good luck," Skyrah added.

"Be brave out there, Avril," Gall said. "Avery. You two *are* old enough for that." He started to go, but with his hand on the door, he turned to the twins. "You two are *ready* for that."

Gall and Skyrah ran downstairs and outside—*Dong—Dong!*—to Trillia's ringing bells. They hurried to the inn to don their armor and retrieve their swords and knives.

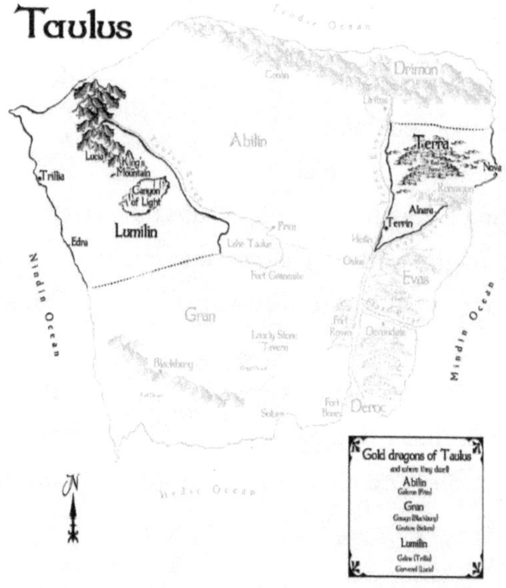

46

Galeron spotted King's Mountain in the distance. The snow-covered highest peak in Taulus presided over the land as ever, despite the changing winds whirling around it.

Past the mountain, Galeron would reach Lucia, but he would not make it to Trillia for hours more. He expected the Canyon of Light would be emptied of its dragons, its inhabitants either watching the battle at Lumilin's capital or, having seen or gotten word of it, fleeing to the east. He came up with a few who might join the fight.

Galeron's muscles ached with each flap of his wings. His lungs burned with each breath and not with the fire he could spew from his belly—a ferocious fire that would be of no use to Trillia by the time he and Grafere arrived.

They would be too late to save the city from his failure to see Eldred's plan coming—or to suspect Eldred of any plan at all. Where Galeron had regarded himself as vigilant, his long flight gave him hours to consider how lazy and blind he had been.

Yet he would not slow. He drove his wings down faster. Maybe, somehow, he would make it in time…

But to what end? To his death before the black dragon queen and her minions? Eldred would not have set his plan in motion with her alone. There had to be others, and from Galeron's injuries sustained in wars past—the piercing stabs, vicious bites, scorching burns, and snapped and shattered bones—he knew well the strength and rage those black dragons would bring to battle. He recalled the wounds that could not be healed before they took the lives of those so dear to him—one, his mate Gaiva, most dear of all.

How many could Galeron fight on his own?

Yet he wasn't alone. He had Grafere beside him and Eilig racing after. What if others came? What if Galina—mighty Galina—still lived, furiously, nobly battling the blacks when Galeron got there? Surely Gorvenal would fight with his mother. If Sir Beal and the knights of Trillia mounted a heroic defense of their city and took a couple of Eldred's dragons with them before they burned in their terrible fire, maybe they had a chance. Just maybe…

————————

Over the Red Forest, Gowyn neared the Mindin Ocean off the east coast of Taulus with Farlan, two greens, and a blue, and two hopes. First, that one or two additional dragons would join them before long, and second, and most importantly, that their time and effort would be wasted because no attack was coming to that shore. Could Eldred *really* have been so patient that he had bred enough blacks in secret—and let them mature enough under the mountain in Rone to be ready for war—to launch simultaneous attacks?

There. Farlan gazed out at the water.

Six black dragons, one of the greens said.

Headed for Nova, the other added, nodding to Taulus's easternmost city at the beachfront edge of the forest.

It is too many to fight, Farlan said.

Yes. Gowyn slowed along with the others. *Two or three, maybe. But six is too great a risk. Nova will fall. The light of the next dawn will shine in Taulus first upon the city's ashes.*

The blue asked, *Do we search for the dwarves from Rone and the elves you say may yet be in hiding?*

No, Gowyn said. *Leave that to the others already searching. Let us get a little closer to learn what we can from this attack. The elves have never faced one like it, and we may need to protect any who flee Nova.*

————————

Jadira had donned lightweight leather armor. Her short swords and bow were secured to the saddle of the dragon she sat upon. She patted his black scales. "Soon."

Rayne shot fire from his snout into the air, pressed on, and said to Jadira, *That wall will not be so abhorrently white for long.*

"No." Jadira watched knights scurry atop Trillia's seaside barrier. "It does not deserve the pure color." Across the shrinking stretch of calm ocean separating her from the city, she saw bells rocking to and fro in the watchtowers. She heard their faint, repeating clamor of warning.

Pointless warning, Jadira thought. Eldred rode Xailyn to Jadira's left, and to the Dark Elf queen's right, to the south, the line of four more blacks ended with the other female dragon, Nykara. Trillia didn't stand a chance.

Magnificent Trillia… Jadira could not deny the grandeur of the city they approached. Imprisoned in Deroc her whole life, she had been told the tales but had never seen its brilliant walls, the blue cliffs they had been built above, the castle at the north end, or atop the rolling hills, the palatial homes built for a view of the ocean. And as the city that had never been destroyed in battle—had never even been assaulted by a force of any consequence—stared down its doom, those fine houses would offer a spectacular view of their impending destruction.

As they neared the homes with each flap of Rayne's wings, Jadira made out decorative accents in their stone, pieces of ornate furniture on their balconies, then the patterns on shade-providing umbrellas and thick cushions covering chairs.

Do you see Sir Beal out there? Rayne asked.

"Not yet. But he's there somewhere."

The knight's reputation, all reports that had made their way to Deroc agreed, was warranted, but it would not matter. That his wife was a strong emote would not either. She would die with all the emotes who stayed to fight, and Beal would follow her to the grave once she could no longer help him.

Beal does not worry me.

"Nor me," Jadira agreed. "One brave knight will not save Trillia from six black dragons."

Galina would not save the city either. Eldred—Jadira's love, her delightfully cunning king, the soon-to-be king of all of Taulus—Jadira adored him and trusted his grand plan, but he was wrong to presume the powerful gold would be defeated without killing any of his precious blacks. One would fall—not her strong Rayne or his massive Xailyn— but one of their other dragons. Perhaps two.

But Galina would die. Eldred was correct in that assessment. And the city would fall fast. No man or woman of Taulus had ever been tested as they were about to be, and they would fail their test. Eldred's surprise attack would succeed. Galeron was nowhere in sight. He would not arrive in time, nor would his son or Grafere.

Xailyn flapped her huge wings and let out a cry from between her long, pointed teeth.

Rayne followed suit then flexed his fingers, displaying his sharp talons.

Bursts of fire shot from down the line of dragons.

Jadira watched the frantic knights atop Trillia's wall pause, their terror-stricken faces becoming clearer every moment. She exchanged smiles with Eldred… how she *loved* his smile.

Most must have fled the city, Jadira reasoned, including cowardly King Adrian and his daft young wife. But they would all be dealt with soon enough. The black dragons would sweep ashore as a tidal wave of irresistible fire.

As the wave—and its twin in the east—crashed down upon and crushed Taulus from both sides, the entire world would fall. Too few golds could oppose them, and no more waited in hiding for the war about to begin. All would be conquered, and Jadira, free of her swamp cage forever, would be crowned queen of Taulus.

On Eldred's throne, she would make love to the king of everything and everyone—Jadira had seen it, and dreamed it, and dreamt it again as Rayne flapped his wings to drive their journey to its end, and its beginning, in Trillia.

Jadira would conceive a son and daughter with her king, and they would be prince and princess of Taulus. She had dreamt that often. And when Jadira had led her people to freedom from Deroc and for the first time in centuries her kin had children of their own, they would all be born lords of Taulus.

The bells stopped swinging, and their ringing stopped.

Good, Rayne said. *That dreadful racket was not going to save them.*

"Nothing will," Jadira said. "So many must have fled that the capital of the kingdom of Lumilin can no longer even man its alarms."

Trillia would fall first. Its hastily organized defense stood no chance. After waiting so long, Jadira savored the sight of their line of black beauties to the south closing in on the coast with each beat of their wings.

Beal would fight heroically, Jadira had no doubt. He would be a testament to humanity. But one superlative knight would not be enough to save the city.

47

Taulus

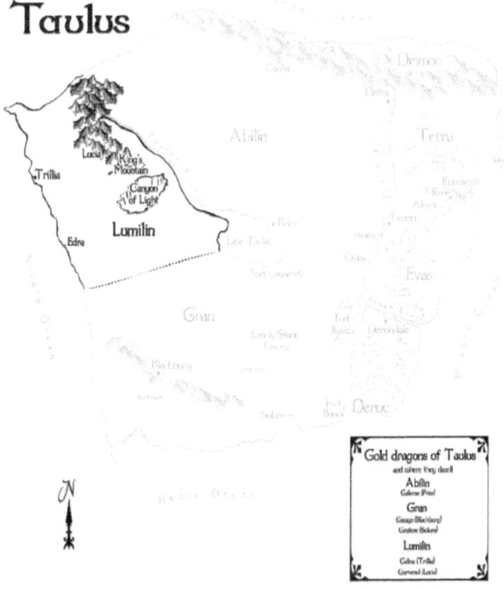

Gall, atop the southern end of the wall in Trillia with Skyrah, recognized King Eldred out over the ocean, riding the largest dragon and headed for the castle at the north end of the city. It would not be long. Queen Jadira rode the foul beast next to him, a big male. The other four—three male, one female—and their riders completed the widely spaced line of darkness that stretched toward Gall. The afternoon sun and high, puffy clouds gave the blacks no cover, nor did they offer those scattered along the wall a single moment of peaceful sky free of the impending attackers.

Two minutes, Gall reckoned.

A seagull squawked and raced south, like all the birds Gall had seen while waiting and watching. There wasn't much else left for Gall to do.

The dragons would arrive and lay waste to Trillia, Gall accepted that. They beat their black wings in the rapidly shrinking distance. They focused their pale red eyes. So many in Trillia would perish. No matter the outcome of the battle, no matter what the concentrated defensive forces at the castle, those spread atop the wall, and the ones in the city streets accomplished, the city would burn. Trillia's buildings were made of granenite, but everything within them was not. Trillia would be devastated.

One of the beasts in the middle of the line called out. The blacks next to him screamed in answer. Fire shot from the first. The dragons beat their wings harder.

The two in the middle carried huge, stuffed sacks on their backs along with their riders. The nearest dragon on the end headed for Gall and Skyrah's position. The knights had each donned mail armor that would provide little defense from direct blasts of fire, though Skyrah's steel shield might block indirect flames.

A hundred seconds until the assault began.

Gall looked into Trillia behind him, up the rolling hills of the finest homes, and back down. While the bells had stopped, the ringing still sounded in Gall's head. From the height of the wall and with the ocean waves drowning out shouts, calls, and frantic hurrying, the men, women, and children running for the city gates seemed to do so in eerie silence. Only a baby's wail rose above the din, but it too faded when a loud wave crashed into the rocks below. Gall watched the people run for Lucia. A small minority exited to the south, perhaps for more distant Edra. He guessed that Trillia had more than half emptied.

The blacks screamed and screeched out over the water, their cries spanning the line that bore down on Trillia. Streams of fire followed, and Gall could make out clearer details of the nearer flame.

A clattering of hooves came from the south end of the wall. "Be strong, knights of Lumilin!" Beal rode past and called to them, "Ignore their screams and bright show. Those dragons bleed the same as the rest in Taulus, I assure you." When he reached Gall and Skyrah, Beal stopped and glanced at the city. "For their sake, let's hope you're as good as all those stories, Sir Gall."

"Likewise, Sir Beal. Are the heavy launchers ready?"

"A few," Beal said. "And some nets, but little else. They've hardly ever been used..." He gripped his reins tighter. "There just wasn't time..."

"'S'all right," Gall said.

"Not a lot of people left to *use* those weapons, either," Skyrah remarked.

"Many have fled," Beal said. "But the bravest remain."

"Any advice for fighting a dragon?" Gall asked.

"We'll outnumber them." Beal looked at the incoming

line. "And we'll need to. They're big and strong… and *fast*. Unbelievably fast when they want to be." He turned back to Gall and Skyrah. "But we will outnumber them, and the chaos of that kind of fight may present opportunities."

"It will," Gall said. "Six opportunities head our way. Next time, people won't be able to say that Beal has slain a dragon while Gall has not."

Beal loosened his grip on his reins. "I will give the toast when we share an ale to celebrate it."

They shook hands firmly. Beal and Skyrah did the same.

"Fight well," Beal said to her.

"You too."

Beal nodded, rode north up the wall, and called to the knights, "We've trained for this!"

The nearest black dragon roared and shot fire into the sky.

A hint of heat reached Gall as he studied the scales of the rapidly approaching creature. "She's on the young side."

"That's something," Skyrah said. "She's coming right for us. You sure this is the place to be? Most of the rest of the knights are in the city. Their fire will melt these walls to the ground."

"They'll do it for show, eventually," Gall said. "But those beasts are not here for this granenite. There are only six elves out there. They didn't come to lay low the walls for an accompanying army. They came to burn everything behind the walls to the ground."

The closest, angry black cried out and belched fresh flame. Her elven rider held a silver bow in his lap and carried a curved sword on his hip.

Skyrah raised her hand to block incoming heat. "What's your plan?"

"When she flies by, she'll be breathing fire," Gall said. "Maybe reaching for us with her talons, but definitely fire. I'm gonna roll to the left and crouch against this wall, which will block the flames. They'll burn granenite, but they have to be real close for their fire to be hot enough to do it."

Skyrah nodded.

"Then…" Gall drew his sword. "When she's lower after swooping to grab us—and this is why we're on the wall— I'm going to jump onto her back and stab down like this." He brought his arms above his head with his sword pointed out and made a two-handed downward cut.

The dragon cried again—louder, closer.

"She can see you," Skyrah said.

Gall tapped the flat end of his blade against the wall. "Well, I'm doing it anyway."

"And then?" Skyrah asked.

"And then I'll kill the rider and find another dragon to fight."

Skyrah drew her sword as the black closed in. "The elf might be an emote, ready to heal the dragon during the battle."

"Good point. I may have to kill him first then."

"Right," Skyrah said.

"I'm glad we had this little talk," Gall said.

She smiled.

"What's *your* plan?" Gall could hear the reptile's labored breaths.

"What you're doing, but I'll be round two. If you kill the rider and the one he rides before I jump down at them, even better."

The dragon roared as it approached, and its rider nocked an arrow on his bow string.

Gall and Skyrah got to the ready with their swords. The other knights on the wall prepared their blades, spears, and arrows.

"You know…" Gall noticed the silver eyes of the elven rider. "I'm really going to miss those twins."

"Your confidence falters now?" Skyrah continued to focus on the incoming dragons.

"No." Gall met the beast's stare above her ugly jagged snout. "When I go to Conlin tomorrow." He looked at Skyrah. "You should come with me."

Stone-faced, she turned to him. "Tomorrow, we will go to Conlin."

The dragon screamed and shot out a straight line of fire that ended in an exploding ball. The black burst through the flames and belched another stream.

Avoiding the worst of the scorching blast, Gall and Skyrah rolled left. They ducked low against the wall as the dragon's talons reached for them. The elf's arrow flew. Gall pushed Skyrah down, and it hit the wall above her, dropping harmlessly on her shield as the black swooped low into Trillia.

Gall rose, took two steps to the battlement on the city side, and pushing off on his third, dove out at the beast torching the thin, scattered crowd below. The elven rider fired at Gall, who parried the arrow with his vambrace before landing and plunging his sword into the scales of the dragon's back.

The wyrm shrieked and writhed.

"Nykara!" the rider cried, clutching his dragon.

"Whoa!" Gall's legs flew into the air as the beast tried to shake him off, but he kept from falling by holding fast to his sword, which was lodged firmly in Nykara's back.

Arrows from knights atop the wall near Skyrah rained down, deflecting off the black's scales but forcing its rider to stay low. Nykara whipped round and shot fire at the archers, torching some and scattering the others. She flapped her wings to propel herself to them and raked her claws across the top of the wall. Broken knights fell to the street.

The elf rider readied an arrow and aimed at Gall. Skyrah leapt from the wall and drove her shoulder into the rider. He dropped his bow as they grappled and fell into the city.

"Skyrah!" Gall called.

The dragon swooped low, Gall still clinging to her back, and caught the pair in her paw. Nykara landed on the road past the southernmost of the circles running through the city and rolled them out of her grip. Skyrah drew her sword, but the dragon smacked her into the stone wall of the house across the street.

Gall withdrew his sword from the beast, releasing a stream of bright blood, and stabbed a fresh spot on her back.

Nykara screamed and bucked. *Get off!* she called into Gall's mind.

He held firm.

Off! Nykara spun and grabbed for Gall but missed. With

her other paw, she hit her mark, sending Gall, sword in hand, flying from her.

Gall hit the street rolling. Skyrah got to her feet and wiped blood from her nose. Another black flew overhead, belching fire onto the buildings to the north and the screaming, fleeing people of Trillia. A huge steel bolt shot at the dragon from the wall, but he swerved out of the way and went to destroy the weapon.

The pained dragon Gall fought crouched low to the elf, who held her neck. The elf, who Gall did not make for a young one, rested his cheek on Nykara's black scales. Her breathing calmed. The elf whispered to her. The flow of her blood slowed, and the animal's wounds closed. The Dark Elf gave a sly smile to the healed dragon and drew his curved sword.

The savage creature stretched her neck high and let out a triumphant screech.

Ten mounted knights raced to join the battle but paused when Nykara leaned low and spewed fire at the white stone of the inn beside them. The granenite grayed, then blackened, then the relentless flames softened the roof's sharp edge. The ceiling caved in, the wall melted low, and the furniture inside erupted in flame. Her fire ended.

The knights resumed their charge. Gall did the same. The beast reached for its rider but leapt into the air instead to dodge a massive bolt shot from the wall. Gall went for the elf, and Skyrah followed him, launching into her attack the moment after Gall. The elf parried strikes from each of them.

Puny maggots, Nykara said. She breathed fire at the knights, who mostly avoided it, many falling from their saddles to do so. They shot crossbows up at the creature and either missed or saw their bolts glance off her hard scales. The knights—on horse and on foot—drew swords and prepared to dodge her next attack.

The elf swung his blade. Gall blocked it with his own, and noticed a gold dragon with a rider to the north, entering the city over its eastern wall.

———

Galina's golden wings flapped in the blue sky, propelling her and Layden, the emote she carried in a saddle on her back, toward the male dragon and rider wreaking havoc on the knights along Trillia's oceanfront wall. Layden's hand rested gently on Galina, warming her hard scales, her pumping muscles, and all that lay beneath. He carried a bow and a quiver of fine arrows, but Galina had instructed him not to shoot the targets they approached.

Galina glanced to the north, beyond the fires raging in the middle of the city to the bashed and burning castle at the far end. Beal and his knights defended the king's fortress from the blacks encircling it, and they could defend it a little longer. Galina would get to Eldred, Jadira, and their dragons after taking care of the younger one nearby.

Galina had flown over the stream of people fleeing the city behind their king as fast as their legs, horses, carriages, and carts could carry them. That emotes fled among them Galina judged to be a good thing, but the knights' presence gave her mixed emotions. They should have been defending their city, not running from it. But the city's people needed defending even outside its walls.

Already the bloodied, charred, and still-burning bodies of knights, emotes, and too many ordinary citizens who hadn't evacuated in time littered the hills and streets of Trillia, evoking memories of dark wars past. Yet the images in her city struck her as acutely fresh, for Galina had never seen such fire, destruction, and death in Trillia, or anywhere in Lumilin. What wasn't granenite burned, and the hard stone melted under the awful fire from the six blacks. Cador had not returned. None had come, but Galina could stand idly by no longer.

She had the young dragon at the wall in her sights. Having cleared his prey from the walkway, or left their dead bodies strewn atop it, the black turned to face the city and perched there with his rider focused completely on the stone beneath him. The dragon brought his snout low, close to the granenite, inhaled, and spewed fire down hard. A small gulf of melting stone formed in the wall around the flame and expanded outward. Galina drew nearer.

She had survived two great wars—had helped *win* them—and seeing her enemy wholly preoccupied with his act of needless destruction, Galina set her mind on winning the battle at hand by taking care of the dragon she bore down on and then fighting Xodon's daughter—and all the rest— until they lay dead in the streets of her precious city. Let that weak king flee. Let his knights follow him. Galina would win this day without them. She flapped her wings hard.

The crevasse in the wall grew beneath the dark dragon. Heat from his fire warmed Galina. A tattered, heavy net with weights on its ends burned beside him, clearly having never ensnared its target. The elven rider stared at the melting stone below him. Galina prayed they would keep their attention fixed there a few moments more. She picked the spot on the black's neck to chomp. She'd tear his neck so wide open that even if that elf were an emote, his magic would not save the dragon before Galina grabbed the healer and crushed him in her talons.

The net had failed, but Galina would not.

She opened her mouth wide and recalled the taste of tough black scales and the juicy meat beneath.

The elf noticed her and smacked the side of his dragon. The beast jumped off the wall. Galina drove her shoulder into the dragon.

He roared as Galina held him.

The black chomped at her neck, but she smashed her head into his to drive it away. Galina grabbed the rider and squeezed until his bones crumbled. She threw him onto the ocean rocks outside the city.

The dragon punched Galina's chin, breaking her grip on him. He shot fire at her, but she rose over it, whipped her tail across his face, and sank her hind talons into his shoulders. She drove the roaring reptile down and slammed him into the top of the wall.

He flailed up at her as she chomped her sharp teeth into the jagged scales near his shoulders. She ripped her mouth away, and blood poured from the feebly punching dragon.

She chomped higher, and the beast quit punching. His arms fell outstretched, and his heaving chest slowed to a stop. Galina let his lifeless body fall over the wall, out of her city, into the water.

"Five left," Layden said.

Galina surveyed burning Trillia. As usual, she found herself of the same mind as the emote. Five black monsters left to kill. Four to the north, one to the south, occupied by a group of bloodied but bravely fighting knights—she launched herself off the wall to the north, toward the castle.

Five left, Galina said, echoing Layden.

The fires beneath her raged and the city's people fled, but in between the battles at the far north and south, no fighting went on. The Dark Elves had no army. Their assault depended solely on their dragons. Galina gazed to the east. If only Gorvenal would come… or Galeron, Gowyn, or Grafere.

Black dragon flame softened the base of the castle's southeastern tower until it crumbled in a cloud of dust and stone. The beast that had done it noticed Galina approaching and let out a cry. The other three turned to the gold.

As all four blacks came at Galina, she rose higher into the sky to provide a respite for those fighting on the streets below. She sized up Xodon's massive daughter, who King Eldred rode, and the next largest black, who carried Jadira— they would be a challenge. Two younger dragons with riders and stuffed bags on their backs seemed easier pickings.

Galina rose above Trillia, and Eldred led his dragons up to meet her and pointed east. One of the young blacks broke off that way, toward the fleeing citizens beyond the wall.

Galina flapped her wings and pushed higher and closer to her enemies. She couldn't save those people yet. She'd go straight for Eldred. While it might not end the war immediately, his death would doubtless hasten that end's arrival.

Galina began to level off.

Eldred or Jadira, Galina told Layden. *Do not waste your arrows elsewhere.*

Eldred's dragon took the lead. To his left, Jadira's flew steady while the young black to Eldred's right roared like a child.

Galina could save so many lives… if only Eldred had come with fewer.

Daughter of Xodon, Galina called out as they neared.

Xailyn, said the dragon Jadira rode. *Queen Xailyn. And I am Rayne. We are going to kill you now.*

Eldred smiled.

Xailyn and Rayne darted at Galina, who dodged. An arrow from the third's rider sailed harmlessly past. Xailyn grabbed for Galina, who dove low, beneath them all.

Galina's tail whipped at Eldred, but Xailyn twisted to get him out of the way. Layden snapped an arrow at Jadira, who tilted her head to avoid it.

Galina punched the youngest dragon back from her then took a blow from Rayne in the shoulder before grabbing that paw and throwing him away. Xailyn scraped her talons across Galina's chest.

Galina cried out and rose over a ball of fire, blood dripping off her.

Layden's hand on her scales brought the gold dragon calm and closed her wounds.

The young black punched Galina's chest, but Galina landed the stronger blow to his chin. She whirled round, found Eldred, and shot fire his way. His dragon's thick scales blocked the brunt of it. Xailyn smashed Galina across the face, and Rayne bit Galina's back. She roared and knocked him away.

Layden's touch calmed Galina. The gash in her back closed.

The young black lunged at her. Galina dodged and caught him. She chomped his throat. He whimpered, and Galina chomped again.

Xailyn dug two talons deep into Galina's back. The gold let the young black out of her grip. His head dangled from his gashed neck. Weak flaps of his wings slowed his descent but did not keep him from falling. His rider looked up at Rayne as the dragon's eyes rolled back.

Two down, Galina thought as she whipped round fast and Xailyn's talons withdrew from her.

Thunk—an arrow sank into the left side of Layden's chest. Galina turned to see Jadira securing her bow to her saddle then standing on her dragon's back.

Layden! Blood ran from where the arrow had plunged into him. The holes in Galina from Xailyn's talons were healing extremely slowly.

Layden dropped his bow.

Layden…

"I'm sorry." His eyes shut, he slumped to the side, and

his warm touch on Galina cooled then faded to cold.

Arms outstretched, Jadira dove headfirst into the air toward the falling black dragon.

Rayne came at Galina. He punched, and she swerved to avoid it. Rayne smacked Layden, sending him plummeting to the city below.

Xailyn bit at Galina and missed, but Rayne didn't. His teeth sank into Galina's shoulder.

Diving Jadira grabbed the falling dragon's neck and swung herself onto him in front of his rider.

Galina punched at Rayne but hit weakly. Rayne bit back into her shoulder.

Xailyn got behind Galina and wrapped her arms around her and her wings. *Your son died quickly,* Xailyn said. *We expected more fight out of him.*

Galina roared and struggled between Rayne and Xailyn.

Xailyn bit in deep, and only the black queen's flapping wings kept Galina in the air.

You won't win, Galina said, her eyes growing heavy even as she spotted the fleeing citizens of Trillia beyond the wall being scattered and torched by the black Eldred had sent after them.

Galina thrashed and drove Rayne away.

But Xailyn still held on tight to her back. *Who will stop us, if this is the best you can manage?*

Rayne returned and drove his talon into Galina's heart.

The healed young black flew into sight with Jadira sitting calmly upon him.

Galeron, Galina said as Rayne shifted his talon inside her.

Galina watched as flames enveloped those running from her city, young and old. Both noble and common wore the same blood and burns of the attack. So did knights who had begun the battle as fighters and then fled when the fighting got too tough.

Xailyn chomped on Galina's throat.

The gold's eyes closed. *Galeron...* Her effort ended.

––––––––––

Gall spotted the mighty gold high in the sky to the north, limp, falling beneath three black dragons. He rolled out of the way of Nykara's tail, which he had just slashed while Skyrah was keeping the elf occupied so he couldn't heal the beast again. Three other knights remained, focused on the dragon.

A loud thumping crash to the north must have been Galina's body hitting the ground.

Fire shot at Gall from his foe's black snout. Gall dove out of the way. Skyrah crouched, and her shield blocked the flame from the spinning dragon, whose open palm smacked Gall along the ground. Her tail knocked two other knights away.

Gall glimpsed two white horses galloping from the south with riders in blue. One continued north on the road separating high rising blazes, while the other—Lorelei—stopped beside a fallen knight, whose broken chainmail was covered in red. She reached down to him, and the grimacing man grasped her fingertips.

"It's not safe here!" Gall called to Lorelei, getting to his feet and wiping sweat from his brow.

Lorelei smiled warmly at the healing knight. He stood and nodded to her.

Nykara belched a fireball at the pair. The knight dove, and quick horsemanship got Lorelei out of the way of the burst.

"Get out of here, Lorelei!" Gall yelled.

The healed knight sprinted to the south, away from the battle.

Lorelei glared at the fleeing knight then made eye contact with Gall. She shook her head as she looked away. After a long breath, Lorelei gave a "Hya!" and launched herself into a hard ride north toward the castle.

Gall stared after her, only vaguely aware that a braver knight had stabbed Nykara's paw and that the dragon had grabbed her attacker and flung him high into the air.

Gall came back to himself at a call from Skyrah, who was still fighting the elf. The elf punched her, and she ducked under his sword swing. Gall ran that way. The elf swung into Skyrah's shield. She swung her blade, and the elf sidestepped her thrust and slashed across her leg. Gall closed in. Skyrah dropped to a knee and blocked the elf's strike. His boot to her arm sent her shield out wide. He hit her sword aside and swung down at her neck.

Gall blocked it. He lifted his blade and cut. Both hands on his sword, Gall drove the elf backward, cut after cut.

Nykara came at them. *Die!*

Skyrah got to her feet, covered in dirt and blood, and joined Gall against the elf. He parried their blows, but Gall hit hard. The elf's balance faltered, and his blocks barely came in time.

You first. Nykara reached for Gall but missed. *Then the woman.*

The elf blocked Skyrah's strike. Gall prepared to swing at the elf, but when the dragon lunged at Gall with her mouth open, he leapt, spun, and chopped down with all his might.

Blood poured from the base of Nykara's slashed neck.

The wide-eyed elf rushed toward the wounded beast.

"No." Gall ran into the elf's way, and when the elf leapt higher than any man could, Gall jumped higher than he ever had before, swinging his outstretched sword. Gall nicked the elf's foot, and the stunned emote crashed to the ground.

Gall landed, and when the elf tried to rise, Gall slashed across his shoulder and stomach. The elf's head turned aside, and he lay lifeless in a growing pool of his own blood.

The wounded dragon took flight to the north, following the granenite road between raging fires. Blood ran from Nykara's tail and paw but ran fastest from her gashed neck. Her mouth opened like she might roar, but blood came out instead.

Gall located Skyrah. "You all right?"

She wiped her face of dirt and blood. "Yeah." She lifted her sliced leg and grimaced. "You?"

"Fine." Gall looked at the fleeing dragon. "Gotta go after her."

A knight of Trillia who lay wounded on the ground whistled loudly.

A big horse galloped to him. Gall and Skyrah ran over.

The knight on the ground pointed at the animal. "Like your chances better than mine at this point."

Gall mounted the horse. "I'll send an emote for you."

"Appreciate it," the knight said.

Skyrah got on behind Gall, who snapped the reins. "Hya!" He kicked the animal's side, and they raced after the wounded black.

The hurt knight called to them, "Kill the bitch!"

Gall and Skyrah rode between fires lining the granenite road and consuming everything in their paths—homes, shops, taverns, inns—up the city's hills and down. The solid stone, spared from destruction, was turning black in the heat. Trillia had pools of water to douse such blazes, pumps to pull more water from the sea, and unsurprisingly, no one to handle those operations during the battle.

But the fire could be dealt with later. The dragons had to be defeated first, and Nykara was close to being next among them. Gall could not let her be healed or else their battle would have been largely for naught.

With the bleeding dragon distancing herself from her pursuers, their horse breathed heavily, block after block, laboring under the weight of two riders and their armaments. But the animal's effort never waned. Gall and Skyrah followed the trail of blood around the second city circle. Far ahead at the castle, three other blacks swarmed, swooped low, and belched flame. Fires rose high. The largest dragon dropped a flailing knight from her talons into the flame.

To the east, beyond the city wall, two greens and a purple halted their approach and hovered before heading south, where a black breathed fire down from the sky, presumably onto fleeing citizens. No more Galina, but Gall hoped the natural dragons would help him inside the city when they finished with the dragon out there.

Nearing the third large circle, amidst increasing numbers of fallen knights and bloodied and burned unmoving men and women of Trillia, the dragon they chased slowed and shrieked. Nykara dipped in flight. Her head drooped to the side where blood poured from her neck.

Jadira, on her dragon, raced toward the injured black.

"No." Gall kicked his horse's side and closed in on the bleeding dragon.

Nykara dropped lower, farther to the right. Two other blacks—a huge one carrying Eldred, and one smaller— followed Jadira, fast.

"Hya!" Gall urged his steed on, sword in hand, certain that one more good slash through that beast's neck would do it. "Hya!"

He spotted a small group of knights charging down the road from the north. He recognized Beal and Grimm, the tournament runner-up—and Lorelei trailing them. They rode after Eldred and the three evil blacks, who neared the circle where wounded Nykara dropped lower in the sky.

Jadira, too, closed in on the dragon.

So did Gall.

The youngest of the three blacks flying with Eldred darted backward and down over top of Beal, knocking three knights and Lorelei from their horses. The dragon shot fire at the emote.

Beal spun his horse. "Lorelei!"

She screamed as she burned. She fell to her knees and turned to her husband.

Another, closer shot of dragon fire consumed her. Her charred body disintegrated to ash as the flames ended.

Nykara crashed to the street. Gall let out a cry of pure rage. He stood in his saddle and, pushing with all the strength in his legs, launched himself at the dragon, raising his sword high in both hands. Above the bleeding beast, Jadira slipped off her dragon.

Eldred's dragon swooped low, punched Gall out of the air, and landed. She grabbed him, pinning his arms. The black giant squeezed.

"Gall!" Skyrah shouted and rode to him.

Gall pushed against the crushing grip. He couldn't swing his sword. He heard his ribs crunch and felt his pelvis crumble. He screamed as his arms snapped.

Little man. Eldred's dragon threw Gall, his sword clattering to the street, into the rubble of a fire-blackened home on the roadside.

He saw Skyrah attack Eldred's dragon. The spinning wyrm's tail knocked stones, large and small, onto Gall's back. Pinned to the ground, Gall couldn't feel his legs. A fireball exploded in Skyrah's face as she got her shield up. A second belch of flame from the black engulfed the steel, Skyrah's body, and their horse before reducing them to a lump of ash topped by a melted sword and shield. The dragon Gall had nearly slain—should have slain—got to her feet, with Jadira riding and no visible slice in its neck. She joined the assault on Beal and the two other charging knights.

Gall coughed blood. The youngest dragon pounded a knight into the street. The second largest bit a knight in half. Nykara's tail knocked Beal's horse to the ground. Beal rolled out of the way of Eldred's dragon's fire burst and got to his feet with both hands on his sword. He stood alone against the four foul beasts as towering fire ravaged the city behind him.

Gall coughed, and more red dripped from his mouth. Large chunks of granenite wall covered him from the middle of his back to his feet. He didn't know what all was broken— half his body felt crushed, the other half was numb—but his arms, legs, and hips for sure. He could not rush to Beal's aid; he could hardly breathe.

So hard to breathe… Gall closed his eyes.

But Beal fought on—Gall distinctly heard Lumilin's champion's grunts of effort as he thrust and swung his sword at the dragons and dodged their attacks.

Gall opened his eyes to the dragons surrounding Beal.

Gall forced his broken arms to push off the ground. He cried out and hardly budged.

Eldred's dragon avoided Beal's thrust and took a slice to her arm when she reached for him. The second largest dragon poked his talon into Beal's back and out his gut. The knight's head fell backward. The dragon withdrew his talon, and with blood pouring from his stomach, Beal slumped to his knees then fell to his side on the ground.

Gall labored for air. He tensed his broken arms. He

couldn't move. He closed his eyes again.

A mountain of darkness crashed down on him. Gall fought for final thoughts before the end—before he flickered away to nothing.

Gall missed Skyrah.

He had lost.

48

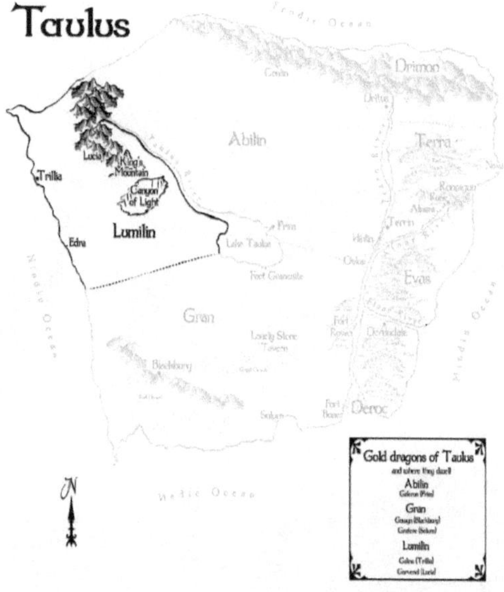

Galeron identified the line of people the moment he spotted them. He had known before he had seen them, yet still his heart managed to sink deeper. The men and women rushing away from Trillia pointed and shouted for him as he raced high overhead with Grafere close behind and Eilig a blue dot behind them in the sky. Lumilin's king and queen led the exodus with the royal guard, which neither surprised nor pleased Galeron.

While the first men and women rushing to Lucia appeared to be in reasonable health, before long, the line grew ragged, with slower-moving, badly wounded individuals and entire families bringing up the rear. The broken and dazed rode carts and wagons, many of them damaged as well. Blood-covered faces, torn clothes, arms hanging in makeshift slings—most people were injured and many limped or sagged with each step. Emotes tending to the wounded were extremely scarce, and every one appeared utterly exhausted.

The burnt grass and, to Galeron's great dismay, burnt flesh confirmed for him what he had feared. The dwarves in Rone had not been lying. Eldred and his dragons had attacked Trillia.

Two dragons—a green and a purple—flew toward Galeron over a long line of charred, unmoving bodies on the ground. Hazy smoke blurred the sky near the coast, far behind them.

Galeron, Cador called. *Grafere.*

Cador, Galeron responded as the golds rapidly approached. *Tiane.*

Cador and Tiane slowed.

Galeron did not. *What of Trillia?* He raced past the natural dragons.

Cador flapped his wings to follow Galeron. *Devastated. The battle's over. Some knights and emotes stayed to fight, but I didn't see any prisoners. Just... death.*

Eldred? Grafere asked.

Yes, Cador said. *With Jadira and a few others—and five blacks.*

Xodon's kin? Galeron asked.

His daughter. She's enormous, Tiane said. *There were six blacks at the start. Galina killed one.*

Galeron spun. *Where is Galina?*

Tiane caught up to the golds. *Killed.*

We watched it from afar, Cador said. *We couldn't get to her in time. Galina took on three blacks at once, Xodon's daughter among them.*

Galeron tilted his head up then back to Cador, who said, *One of the other blacks went for the people leaving the city.* He glanced down at the refugees of Trillia, many of whom had stopped to watch the dragons' conference in the sky. *We fought him off, eventually.*

He killed Loren, Tiane said. *He killed a lot of people. He was so strong… so savage.*

The blacks are powerful, Galeron said. *It is a sad loss but a noble one. Loren's efforts doubtless saved many lives. Where are Eldred's dragons now?*

The castle, last we saw, Cador said.

What of Sir Beal? Grafere asked.

The fighting's done, Cador said. *If Sir Beal remained in Trillia, he surely fell.*

Galeron looked at the people below, who had noticed Eilig closing in and were pointing. *Cador and Tiane, help the worst off to Lucia.*

Do nothing for the king, Grafere said. *Unless he comes under new attack. He seems to have escaped the destruction of his city in fine health.*

Eilig called to the group, *Trillia?*

Defeated, Galeron said.

Once Eilig reached them, Galeron and Grafere headed west, fast but slower than before so the blue could keep pace. Cador and Tiane descended to a mixture of cheers and pleas from the wounded below.

Where is Galina? Eilig asked.

Dead, Galeron said.

From battle with Xodon's daughter, Eldred, and their dragons, Grafere added.

Flame flickered in the distant, fallen capital of Lumilin. Sections of its outer wall had been melted. Five blacks perched atop the smashed and melted towers and walls at the north end of the city. Like King Eldred, Queen Jadira, and the other Dark Elves standing with them, the dragons directed their focus down into the castle ruins.

As Galeron and the others approached, the patches of scorched ground surrounding the trampled exit route became frequent. The smell of smoke prevailed. Bloody corpses, strewn body parts, and piles of ash marked the road from Trillia. The carcass of the fallen green dragon, Loren, lay ahead.

Two dragons at the castle were larger than the others—the female the largest. She turned toward the incoming dragons.

Xailyn, Galeron said to Grafere and Eilig, pressing westward over the increasingly crowded field of the dead.

Xailyn jumped off the wall and headed toward them, while the Dark Elves turned to watch.

The daughter of my enemy, Galeron said. *Who I failed to vanquish as I thought I had.*

The other black dragons followed her from the castle. Grafere looked at Galeron. Xailyn let out a shrill yell, and Eilig turned to the mightiest golden dragon in Taulus.

They would be tired from their flight and battle. Galeron slowed. *But so am I. So are we.*

The second largest of the blacks screeched.

Galeron hovered in place. Grafere and Eilig followed suit, and the dark dragons halted their advance.

If we could stop them now, here, Galeron said, *we would save so many lives.*

A young black shot flame skyward.

All the children…

A black shrieked.

I would risk battle with you two at my side. Galeron glanced at Grafere and then Eilig. *Against long odds, against ferocious enemies… I would cherish that fight.*

The blacks flapped their menacing wings while Trillia burned behind them.

But Jadira is an emote, Galeron said. *A talented one. And they may have others. We have none, and if we failed, it might spell doom for all of Taulus.*

A dragon next to Xailyn screamed.

The age of peace we have enjoyed has ended. The fight to come will decide the character of the age to follow. Galeron steeled his gaze. *And we will fight. Do not doubt it. Do not harbor hope that it can be escaped.* Galeron's face softened. *But not today. We cannot win this day. Trillia is lost. If an attack comes quickly to Lucia, it may suffer the same fate. The city's defenses are not impressive, but there are more dragons nearby who might oppose this darkness.*

A young black roared.

I cannot guarantee who will fight, Galeron said. *But there is no better choice for these people. We will assist Cador and Tiane in getting them to Lucia, see if my son has found black dragons on the other end of Taulus, and ensure that the kingdoms of men, elves, and dwarves know what has happened here and what may be headed their way.*

Galeron, Grafere, and Eilig turned to the east as Xailyn led her dragons back to the ruined castle.

49

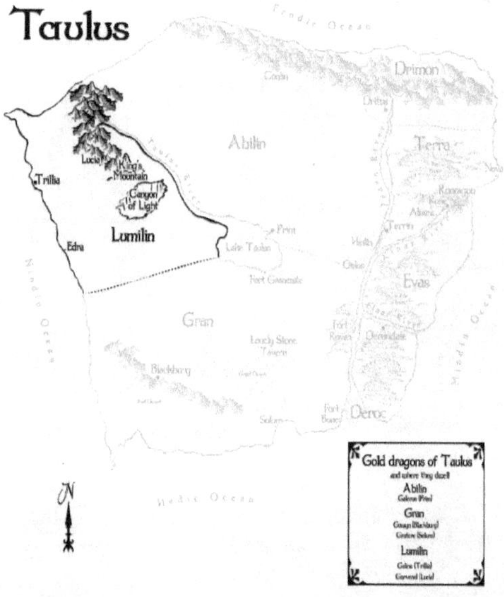

Gall's eyes cracked open. Past the smashed fountain in the middle of the circle, the sun shone above a gulf in the melted western wall of central Trillia. Smoke rose from the smashed, battered, and burnt buildings before him.

At the left side of his field of view, fire flickered. A ringing in Gall's ears drowned out all sound. He pictured the melted, crumbling castle in the jeweled city's north and tried to turn his head that way for a glimpse between buildings. But strain as he might, he couldn't move at all. He shut his eyes. The ringing continued in his head.

A girl. Young. Thin. Amidst the wreckage, Gall had seen her from the corner of his eye. The depths of his mind had held onto her, and her image finally made it into his consciousness. Fire burned behind the girl, but far away, near the wall. Not a danger to her.

Gall's eyes slid open. The ringing in his ears eased. There she was, at the edge of his vision, just as before. He turned his head to see her better.

A young knight stood with the girl. Gall had never seen him before, but…

The girl knelt and took hold of a fallen knight's shoulder. Gall had witnessed a sharp talon drive through that man when he could do nothing but watch. The girl moved her long brown hair aside and rested her pale cheek on the broad chest of the champion knight of Lumilin.

Avril… the ringing noise had given way to quiet and the soft crackling of fires all around. Gall had to be dreaming. Or dead. He might as well have been. The battle lost. Him, a loser. He could have slain that dragon if he had been a little faster. He could have beaten Jadira to her. Then he would have picked his next target and lured it away so he only engaged a single black beast instead of the whole group. It could have worked. He *would have* found a way. Skyrah would still have been alive.

Skyrah…

Gall had not beaten Jadira to the dragon. Gall had failed.

Poor Skyrah…

Beal raised his head off the ground. Avril lifted her head from his chest. The knight raised his arm.

The weight and shape of a hand touched Gall's shoulder, but he couldn't turn enough to see.

"I'm here," a young man's familiar voice said. "It's Avery."

A warm hug held Gall's wide back, and then he *could* turn to see crumbled stone covering his lower half and the boy holding him above it. "Am I dead?"

"No." Avery lifted his head and smiled then focused and returned his cheek to Gall's back. "You'll be fine."

Gall could feel his legs again. He tried to move them, and he moaned. His legs felt broken.

"Easy," Avery said. "Wait."

Gall surveyed the destruction and death—trees uprooted and torched; buildings melted, burnt out, or reduced to rubble; and the bodies of broken knights, emotes, and men and women who had failed to flee. Small fires flickered everywhere.

Gall watched as Beal got to his feet, retrieved his sword, and sheathed it. With the other knight and Beal, somber-looking Avril headed Gall's way.

Avery asked, "Do you think you can pull yourself out from under this rock?"

Gall lurched forward. "Ow."

"Slowly," Avery said.

With strength returning to his arms, hands, and fingers, Gall gripped the ground, pulled himself forward, and grunted. His legs inched out from under the stone. Gall pulled harder, and he slid faster. He groaned as his feet came free, then he rolled over and rested on his back.

With Avery's hand on his shoulder, Gall caught his breath and watched his legs and feet mend. "Where is your mother?"

"Gone," Avery said.

Gall stopped feeling better.

"We couldn't save her." A tear slid down the young emote's cheek. "The black dragon attacked outside the city. Mom and Miles tried to run with us, but... they couldn't avoid the flame. They were too slow. They turned to ash." Avery sniffled. "By then, we couldn't help them."

"I'm sorry," Gall said.

Avery wiped tears from his cheeks, keeping one hand on Gall. "So we ran... past so many dying and dead... we ran as fast as we could back here to help you. We found Braden looking for his father."

Gall began feeling better again. "You and your sister healed your mother when your father beat her?"

"Yes," Avery said.

"You healed the other women he brought home and hurt after she left?"

"Yes."

Gall got to his feet and called to the fallen city's champion. "Sir Beal."

"Sir Gall," Beal called back, blank faced, as he neared.

Gall looked at Avery then Avril. "I'm sorry about your mother."

Avril broke into tears and fell into Gall's open arms.

"Where is Skyrah?" Avery asked.

Gall held Avril tightly. She cried softly while he looked over her head to where the ash that had been Skyrah lay. He recalled their lunch, their laughter, their red wine, and his hand holding hers on his leg. "Gone."

Avril backed up from Gall and wiped her face with both hands.

"I'm Braden," the young knight beside Beal said.

"My son," Beal added quietly.

"I saw Lorelei," Gall said. "I am sorry."

Beal took a long breath. "As am I."

"We need to go," Braden said.

"The king?" Gall asked.

Avril sniffled. "Don't know."

"He was far ahead of us," Avery said. "The black dragon flew out there. People were screaming, there was fire everywhere… I don't know."

"Where are the dragons now?" Gall asked. "And the Dark Elves?"

"On the castle walls," Braden said. "Staring into what's left of it."

Gall moved so he had a view between buildings and spotted one of the black-winged creature's backs. "Staring at what?"

"Don't know," Braden said. "But before they see us, we need to get out of here."

"South gate?" Gall asked. "East?"

Beal shook his head.

"They'll spot us running outside the city," Braden said.

He pointed at the western wall. "There are tunnels and stairs down to the base of the cliffs. We should hide there until nightfall and leave by the ocean."

The twins looked at Gall.

"Sounds good to me." He motioned to the wall. "Lead the way."

Braden did, jogging south down the road with Beal behind him and the twins and Gall last. Gall picked up his broadsword on the way, spun it in his hand, and took a few practice cuts before noticing Grimm's lifeless body, sheathing the weapon, and resuming his jog behind the others toward the oceanfront wall.

Among the smoldering buildings and the city's fallen defenders, Gall spotted too many children who had failed to make it to safety. Some lay beside or in the arms of equally lifeless mothers or fathers, while others had died alone.

Between buildings, Gall caught a glimpse of the five dragons atop the castle. He stopped. Eldred and Jadira stood with them, holding hands, staring down from the wall. The two blacks who had arrived with stuffed bags on their backs no longer carried their cargo.

Gall flicked his nail against the pommel of his sword hilt.

He had lost. He hated it. The most meaningful battle of his life, the truest test he had ever faced, and he had failed. He clenched his teeth and wrapped his hand around his sword's grip.

"Gall!" Avery called in a soft voice.

Gall let go of his sword. He made for the tunnel that led into the Azure Cliffs.

He had failed Skyrah… beautiful, fun Skyrah, who he would never see again.

But that Eldred's plan seemed to be still unfolding meant that while Gall had lost a friend and a battle, he could yet win the war.

He *would* win the war, he told himself. He *had* to win.

THE END OF BOOK I

Connect Online

Thanks for reading. If you enjoyed the story, please leave a review at your favorite online retailer.

Get the latest updates about S.M. Perlow's works by signing up for his newsletter:

smperlow.com/newsletter

Find him online at:

smperlow.com

twitter.com/smperlow

facebook.com/smperlow

Works by S.M. Perlow

Vampires and the Life of Erin Rose

Novels
Choosing a Master
Alone
Lion
Hope
War

Short Stories
Alice Stood Up

—

The Grand Crucible

Novels
Golden Dragons, Gilded Age

—

Other Works

Novels
Stealing the Holy Grail

Short Stories
The Girl Who Was Always Single